D1144129

Also by Chloe Neill from Gollancz

A ChicagoLand Vampires Novel

TWICE BITTEN

CHLOE NEILL

The right of Chloe Neill to be identified as the author of this work
has been asserted by her in accordance with the
Copyright, Designs and Patents Act 1988.

First published in Great Britain in 2010 by
Gollancz
An imprint of the Orion Publishing Group
Orion House, 5 Upper St Martin's Lane, London WC2H 9EA
An Hachette UK Company

1 3 5 7 9 10 8 6 4 2

A CIP catalogue record for this book is available
from the British Library

ISBN 978 0 575 09937 1

Printed in Great Britain by
Clays Ltd, plc

www.chloeneill.com

www.orionbooks.co.uk

The Orion Publishing Group's policy is to use papers that are
natural, renewable and recyclable products and made from wood
grown in sustainable forests. The logging and manufacturing
processes are expected to conform to the environmental regulations
of the country of origin.

'Diplomacy is the art of saying "nice doggie"
until you can find a rock'

Will Rogers

Chapter One

join the club

Early June
Chicago, Illinois

It was the beginning of Route 66, the spot where "America's Main Street" began to traverse the United States. Buckingham Fountain, the heart of Grant Park, was named for the brother of the woman who donated the fountain to the city of Chicago. By day, the fountain's main jet shot one hundred fifty feet into the air, a tower of water between the expanse of Lake Michigan and the expanse of downtown Chicago.

But it was late now, and the jets had been turned off for the night. The park was officially closed, but that didn't stop a handful of stragglers from walking around the fountain or perching on the steps that led down to Lake Shore Drive to take in the view of the dark and gleaming waters of Lake Michigan.

I checked my watch. It was eight minutes after midnight. I was here because someone had been leaving me anonymous notes. The first ones mentioned invitations. The last one had invited me to the fountain at midnight, which meant the mysterious someone was eight minutes late.

I had no clue who had invited me or why, but I was curious enough to make the drive downtown from my home in Hyde Park. I was also cautious enough to show up with a weapon—a short pearl-handled dagger that was strapped beneath my suit jacket on my left side. The dagger had been a gift from Master vampire Ethan Sullivan to me, the Sentinel of his House of vampires.

I probably didn't look the part of the stereotypical vampire, as the Cadogan House uniform—a slim-fit, well-tailored black pantsuit—wasn't exactly the stuff of horror movies. My long, straight, dark hair was pulled into its usual high ponytail, dark bangs across my forehead. I'd donned a pair of black Mary Jane–style heels which, my preference for Pumas notwithstanding, looked pretty good with the suit. My beeper was clipped to my waist in case of House emergencies.

As House Sentinel, I usually carried a katana, thirty-odd inches of honed steel. But for this meeting, I'd left my katana at home, thinking the sight of a bloodred scabbard strapped to my side might inspire a bit too much attention from human eyes. I was, after all, in the park after hours. The members of the Chicago Police Department were going to be curious enough about that; a three-foot-long samurai sword wasn't going to instill much confidence that I was here only for introductions and conversation.

And speaking of introductions . . .

"I wasn't sure you'd come," a voice suddenly said from behind me.

I turned, my eyes widening at the vampire who'd addressed me. "Noah?"

More specifically, it was Noah Beck, leader of Chicago's Rogue vampires—the ones not tied to a particular House.

Noah was bulky—broad shoulders topping a muscular frame. His brown hair stood up in spiky whorls. His eyes were blue, and tonight his jaw bore a trace of stubble. Noah wasn't cover-model handsome, but with the build, strong jaw, and slightly crooked nose, he could fill the leading role in an action movie with no problems. He was dressed, as he usually was, in unrelieved black: black cargo pants, black boots, and a snug, ribbed black T-shirt to replace the long-sleeved version he'd worn in cooler weather.

"You asked to meet me?"

"I did," he said.

When a few seconds passed without elaboration, I tilted my head at him. "Why not just call me and ask for a meeting?" Or better yet, I thought, why not call Ethan? He was usually more than willing to send me into the arms of needy vampires.

Noah crossed his arms over his chest, his expression so serious that his down-thrust chin nearly touched his shirt. "Because you belong to Sullivan, and this meeting isn't about him. It's about you. If I'd signed those notes, I figured you would've felt obligated to tell him about the meet."

"I belong to *Cadogan House*," I clarified, making it known that I didn't, contrary to popular opinion, belong to Ethan. Not that I hadn't considered it. "That means I can't guarantee I won't spill whatever you tell me," I added, letting a small smile curl my lips. "But that depends on *what* you tell me."

Noah uncrossed his arms, slipped a hand into one of his pants pockets, and pulled out a thin red card. Holding the card between two fingers, he extended it toward me.

I knew what it would say before I took it from him. It would bear the initials "RG" and the white stamp of a flowerlike fleur-de-lis. An identical card had been left in my room in Cadogan House, but I still didn't know what it meant.

"What's 'RG'?" I asked him, returning the card.

Noah took it, slipping it back into his pocket. Then he looked around, crooked a finger at me, and began walking toward the Lake. Eyebrows raised, I followed him. That was when the history lesson began.

"The French Revolution was a crucial time for European vampires," he said as we walked down the steps that led from the park to the street below. "When the Reign of Terror struck, vampires got caught up in the hysteria—not unlike humans. But when the vampires began to turn over their fellow Novitiates and Masters to the military, when they were guillotined in the street, the members of the Conseil Rouge, the counsel that governed vampires before the Greenwich Presidium took power, began to panic."

"That was the Second Clearing, right?" I asked. "French vampires squealed about their friends to ensure their own safety. Unfortunately, the vamps they turned over to the mobs were executed."

Noah nodded. "Exactly. Conseil vampires were old, well established. They enjoyed their immortality, and they weren't eager to become mob victims. So they organized a group of vampires to protect them. Vampires willing to take aspen for them."

"A vampire Secret Service?"

"That's not a bad analogy," he agreed. "The vampires who were asked to serve named themselves the Red Guard."

Hence the RG. "And since you gave me the card, I'm guessing you're one yourself?"

"A card-carrying member, quite literally."

We crossed the street to the lawn in front of the Lake, then walked across grass to the concrete shoreline. When we stopped, I glanced over at Noah, wondering why I was getting the history lesson and the details on his secret life. "Okay, interesting history lesson, but what does all this have to do with me?"

"Impatient, are you?"

I cocked an eyebrow. "I agreed to a secret midnight meeting you didn't want my Master to know about. You're actually getting profound restraint."

Noah smiled back slowly, wolfishly, his lips gradually spreading to reveal straight white teeth—and needle-sharp fangs.

"Why, Merit, I'm surprised you haven't guessed yet. I'm here to recruit you."

It was a full minute before he spoke again. In the meantime, we stood in silence, the two of us staring out at the Lake and the bobbing lights of sailboats near the shore. I'm not sure what he was thinking about, but I was contemplating his offer.

"Things have changed since the RG was founded," Noah finally said, his voice booming in the darkness. "We make sure the Presidium doesn't overstep its authority, like a check and balance on the power of the GP. We also ensure the balance of power between Masters and Novitiates stays relatively stable. Sometimes we investigate. On rare occasions, we clean up."

So, to summarize, Noah wanted me to join an organization whose main goal was keeping Master vampires and GP members from having too much power, or from using that power indiscriminately; an organization whose members spied on their Masters.

I blew out a slow breath, something tightening in my stomach.

I didn't know Ethan's position on the Red Guard, but I had no doubt he would see my joining them as the betrayal of all betrayals. Serving as a Red Guard would pit me directly against Ethan, charging me, a Novitiate vampire, with watching and judging him. Ethan and I didn't have an easy relationship; our interactions were an uncomfortable tug-of-war between our being confidants and colleagues. But this went far beyond our usual brand of mutual irritation.

In fact, it was *exactly* the kind of thing Ethan already feared I'd do—spy on the House. He may not have known about the RG invite, but he knew my grandfather, Chuck Merit, served as a supernatural liaison to the city of Chicago, and he knew my family—the Merits (yes, Merit is my *last* name)—was connected to Seth Tate, mayor of Chicago. Those ties were close enough to concern him. Involvement in something like this would be the icing on the conniption-fit cake.

And that begged an interesting question. "Why me?" I asked Noah. "I'm only two months old, and I'm not exactly warrior material."

"You fit our profile," he said. "You were made a vampire without consent; maybe because of that, you seem to have a different kind of relationship with your Master. You're a child of wealth, but you've seen its abuses. As Sentinel, you're becoming a soldier, but you've been a scholar. You've sworn your oaths to Ethan, but you're skeptical enough not to blindly follow directions."

It was a list of traits that probably made Ethan nervous on

a daily basis. But Noah seemed convinced they were just the kind of things he was looking for.

"And what is it, exactly, that I'd be doing?"

"At this point, we'd like a latent player. You'd remain in Cadogan House, stand Sentinel, and stay in communication with your partner."

I lifted my eyebrows. "My partner?"

"We work in pairs," Noah said, then bobbed his head at something behind me. "Right on cue."

I glanced back, just as the vampire reached us at the shoreline. He was well suited to spying; even with my improved hearing, I hadn't heard him approach. This vamp was tall and lean, with longish auburn hair that just reached his shoulders, blue eyes set beneath long brows, and a chiseled chin. He wore a short-sleeved shirt with a collar, the bottom tucked into his jeans. Tattoos ringed each bicep—a flying angel on one arm, a slinking devil on the other.

I wondered what he was conflicted about.

The newcomer nodded curtly at me, then looked at Noah.

"Merit, Sentinel, Cadogan House," Noah said to him, then glanced at me. "Jonah, Guard Captain, Grey House."

"Guard Captain?" I asked aloud, shocked to the core that the Captain of Scott Grey's own House guards was also a member of the Red Guard. A vampire in a position of trust, whose purpose in the House was to guard the Master, to keep him safe, moonlighting for an organization with an inherent distrust of Masterdom? I guessed it wasn't the kind of thing Scott Grey would be thrilled to learn.

And seriously—was I channeling Ethan Sullivan or what?

"If you accept our offer," Noah said, "Jonah will be your partner."

I looked over at Jonah and found his gaze already on me, his brow furrowed. There was curiosity—but also disdain—in his eyes. He apparently wasn't too impressed with what he'd seen so far of the Cadogan Sentinel.

But since I wasn't interested in going to war with Ethan and thus had no plans to become Jonah's partner, I managed not to care.

I shook my head at Noah. "It's too much to ask."

"I understand your reticence," he said. "I know what it means to take the oaths to your House. I've taken them, too. But for better or worse, Celina's been released. I'd lay short odds on our futures being decidedly more violent than our recent past."

"Not great odds," I solemnly agreed. We'd put an end to the killing spree of Celina Desaulniers, former Navarre House Master. We'd promised the city of Chicago that she was tucked away in a European dungeon, serving time for arranging those murders, but the GP had put Celina back into circulation. She no longer had control of Navarre House, and she blamed me for that inconvenience. She'd come back to Chicago annoyed about her incarceration and eager for a fight.

Noah smiled sadly, as if he understood the direction of my thoughts. "The sorcerers have already predicted that war will come," he said. "We're afraid that's inevitable. Too many vampires have too much pent-up animosity toward humans to keep peace forever—and vice versa—and Celina has done a bang-up job of rousing them. She plays an unfortunately good martyr."

"And that doesn't even touch the shifter issue," Jonah pointed out. "Shape-shifters and vampires have a long, bloody history, but that's not stopping the Packs from heading to Chicago." He glanced at me. "Word is, they're meeting this week. That fit with what you've heard?"

I debated whether I should answer, thus giving away a precious bit of Cadogan House–gleaned information, but I opted to tell him. It's not like the info would be kept under wraps for long. "Yes. We've heard they'll be here within the week."

"Reps of all four Packs in Chicago," Noah muttered, eyes on the ground. "That's like the Hatfields moving in with the McCoys. A centuries-old feud, and the warring parties camping out in the same city. It reeks of trouble." He sighed. "Look, "I'm just asking you to consider it. The only thing we'd ask of you now is a commitment to remain in Cadogan House on standby until . . ."

Until, he'd said, as if he believed a coming conflict was inevitable.

"You'd remain latent until we can't keep the peace any longer. At that point, you'd have to be prepared to join us full-time. You'd have to be prepared to leave the House."

I'm sure there was shock in my expression. "You'd want me to leave Cadogan House without a Sentinel in the middle of a war?"

"Think a little more broadly," Jonah put in. "You'd be offering your services, your skills, to all vampires, irrespective of their House affiliation. The RG would offer you a chance to stand for all vampires, not just Masters."

Not for just Ethan, he meant. I'd no longer be Ethan's Sentinel, his vampire. Instead, I'd be a vampire who stood apart from the Houses, from the Masters, from the Presidium, in order to keep the universe of vampires safe . . . and keep Celina and her rabble-rousers at bay.

I wasn't sure what I thought about the request or the RG. "I need time to process this," I told them.

Noah nodded. "This is a serious decision, and it deserves serious consideration. It's about your willingness to step outside your House to ensure all vampires are well protected."

"How can I reach you?" I asked, and wondered whether that question alone meant I'd crossed a line I wouldn't be able to step back from.

"I'm in the phone book, listed as a security consultant. In the meantime, we haven't spoken, and you've never met Jonah. Tell no one—friends, relatives, colleagues. But consider this, Merit: Who needs a Sentinel more? The vampires of Cadogan House, who have a corps of trained guards and a powerful Master at the helm . . . or the rest of us?"

With that, he and Jonah turned and walked away, fading into the darkness of the night.

CHAPTER TWO

FIRE IN THE BLOOD

One Week Later

The intent, I think, was perfectly innocent. We'd been called together, the vampires of Cadogan House, for a demonstration of self-defense techniques. It wasn't unusual that we were training—vampires were expected to be able to fend for themselves. After all, thousands of years of living beneath the human radar tended to make them a little paranoid. And Ethan and I were enjoying our own (also perfectly innocent) training sessions as I learned to wield my vampire strength.

But Ethan decided that circumstances (i.e., Celina) necessitated *more* training. I hadn't been equipped to take on Celina when she'd shown up at the House a week ago to attack me. And if I, the vampire Ethan was convinced was stronger than most, couldn't do it, he was understandably nervous about the safety of the rest of Cadogan's three hundred nineteen vampires.

So I'd made the trek from my second-floor room to the Sparring Room in the basement of Cadogan House. Lindsey, a fellow House guard and my bestest vampire friend, had joined me so we could learn how to better protect ourselves from Chicago's special brand of vampire crazy.

We hadn't expected to get a peep show in the bargain.

"Dear God," Lindsey said breathlessly as we stepped into the Sparring Room. We stopped at the edge of the tatami mats that covered the floor, lips parted and eyes wide as we surveyed the sight before us.

Two vampires in the prime of their immortal lives moved across the floor, muscles flexing as they grappled, bare-handed, in attempts to throw the other down. They were sparring without weapons, no swords or steel, using hands and feet, elbows and knees, and the extra physical bite of being vampire.

And they were half naked. Both were sparring barefoot and shirtless, wearing martial arts–style white *gi* pants, the gleaming gold disks of their Cadogan House medals around their necks.

Lindsey's gaze was locked on Luc, Captain of the Cadogan House guards. Luc was a former cowboy turned vampire soldier, complete with broad shoulders, fuzzy chest, and curly, sun-streaked hair that he suddenly stopped to push out of his face, muscles tensing as he moved.

Across from Luc was his opponent: Ethan Sullivan, Master of Cadogan House and the three-hundred-ninety-four-year-old vampire who'd brought me into the world of the fanged— without my consent, but admittedly because my other option had been a speedy death. He stood a little more than six feet tall, and the top half of that six feet—the long, lean line of flat stomach and high pecs, along with the trail of blond hair that dipped down from his navel and disappeared into the waistband of his pants—glistened as he swiveled for a roundhouse kick.

Luc, I think, was supposed to be playing the attacker, but Ethan was doing a fine job of holding him off. For all the Armani suits and supermodel-good looks, Ethan was a skilled warrior—something I'd been forced to remember when I'd swung my katana at his throat a few nights ago.

As I watched him fight, goose bumps pebbled my arms. I assumed my blue irises were shifting to silver as heat began to rise through my body, the fire fanned by the sight of Ethan in motion, dipping and weaving and spinning as he faced down his opponent. I wet my lips, suddenly bloodthirsty even though I'd had convenience blood, bagged by our supplier, Blood4You, less than twenty-four hours ago. And, more important, I'd taken blood directly from a vampire only a week ago.

I'd taken blood directly from him.

He'd fed me during the final chapter of my transition to vampire, when I'd awoken with a thirst so strong for blood I would have killed to get it. But I hadn't needed violence. Ethan had offered his wrist willingly, and I'd taken full advantage, watching his eyes silver as I took the nutrition that somehow sealed my transformation to predator, to vampire.

I smoldered as I watched him, his muscles shifting and flexing as he moved with the slinking grace of a panther. I could have justified the warmth in my belly, called my reaction a consequence of my now fully functioning vampire biology, the result of watching a predator in his prime, or a Novitiate's attraction to the Master who made her.

But that didn't do Ethan Sullivan justice—not even close.

He was almost too handsome to be real, with blond hair framing a gorgeous face, cheekbones that New York models would pay for, eyes that shone like chips of emerald. Six feet of golden skin stretched taut over muscle, and I could attest

that all six feet were equally perfect. I'd caught an acciden-
tal glimpse of Ethan as he was satisfying his former mistress,
who'd betrayed him to join Celina's band of merry evildoers.

It wasn't hard to imagine that he was the top of whatever
food chain we belonged to—not when you watched his long,
lean lines moving across the room.

Not when you watched the tiny bead of sweat that was
slowly—ever so slowly—tracing its way down the middle
of Ethan's flat abdomen, one brick of muscle at a time, just
threatening to slip into the waistband of his pants.

To be sure, Ethan felt the attraction as well. He'd offered
to make me his mistress even before Amber decamped to join
Team Desaulniers. We'd shared a couple of kisses, but I'd
managed to resist taking him up on the rest of his offers. Ethan
wanted me, without doubt. And I wasn't stupid enough to argue his attractiveness, which was undeniable.

But Ethan was also completely infuriating—slow to trust,
easy to accuse—and still not entirely sure how he felt about
me. Not to mention his baggage: his smug sense of superiority
and his willingness to use those around him, including me, to
meet political goals. There was also the fact that our last kiss
had occurred less than twenty-four hours before I'd broken off
my fledgling relationship with Morgan Greer, the vampire who
replaced Celina as Master of Navarre House. I'd walked away
from that kiss with fire in my blood and guilt in my heart.

Surely I could find a relationship with a better concoction
of emotions. Once I had that thought in mind, my rationality
returning, my blood began to cool.

"It should be illegal for smug vampires to look that good,"
Lindsey said, clucking her tongue.

"That is so true," I agreed, thinking a little less hotness

would make my relationship with Ethan a lot simpler. I lifted my gaze away from the fighting vampires to scan the rest of the room. The balcony that ringed the Sparring Room was filled with vampires, men and women. The women, and a few of the men, stared at the action below them, eyes hooded, cheeks flushed, all of them enjoying the sights below.

"On the other hand, they're the ones creating this pec-tacle."

I slid her a glance, arching an eyebrow. "Pec-tacle?"

"You know, like spectacle"—she paused to point at her breasts—"but with more dude nipples. Do you disagree?"

I returned my gaze to the Master vampire who was currently leaning over to pick up a *bokken*, a wooden practice weapon, from the mat. Muscles clenched and tensed as he moved, nipples pert on his chest.

"Far be it from me to disagree," I said. "They have created quite a pec-tacle. And when they put it out there like that, they can hardly expect us not to look."

Lindsey gave me a nod of approval. "I don't know where the bravado comes from, but I like it."

"I'm trying it on," I whispered back, which was true. The transition to vampire hadn't been easy—psychologically or physically—but I was beginning to get the hang of it. I'd essentially gone through the physical change twice, since the first time around hadn't quite taken. (Ethan, in a fit of guilt, had drugged me through the first transition, which apparently forestalled the complete change.) That was on top of my move out of the Wicker Park brownstone I'd shared with my former roommate—and former best friend and nascent sorceress—Mallory, and into Cadogan House. I'd managed to hold my own when dealing with my parents and their fusty friends, a step I'd taken at Ethan's request when we were trying to keep vampire raves out of the press. And, not counting the two times I'd faux-battled Ethan, I'd managed to subdue Celina approximately fifty percent of the times she'd come looking for a fight, which wasn't awful, as batting averages went.

With that excitement under my belt, here I was, a new vampire in the historic position of Sentinel, guarding the House against creatures both living and dead. I'd gone from graduate student to vampire fighter nearly overnight. And now Noah Beck wanted to be the one to capitalize on that.

"Merit. *Merit.*"

Although Lindsey said my name at least a couple of times, it was the jostling that finally did it, breaking me from the memory of my meeting with Noah and bringing me back to the Cadogan House Training Room, to Lindsey, who'd nudged me with her shoulder to get my attention, and to Ethan, who stood before me, hands on his hips, shoulder-length blond hair tied back, one eyebrow arched condescendingly. Luc was nowhere in sight . . . and all eyes were on me.

"Um, yes?" I asked.

The vampires snickered.

"If you're finished with your daydreams," Ethan said into the silence of the room, "perhaps you might consider joining me?"

"Sorry, Liege," I muttered, and stepped out of flip-flops and onto the mats, sheathed katana in hand. I was already in my training ensemble—a black sports-bra-type top and yoga pants.

I followed Ethan to the middle of the floor, very aware that dozens of vampires were following our movements. He stopped, turned to face me, and bowed. I did the same.

"It is important," he began, loud enough for all to hear, "that you be prepared, should the need arise, to fight. And to master that fight, you must first master the steps. As you also know, our Sentinel hasn't yet mastered the art of sparring. . . ."

He paused just long enough to give me a pointed look. So sparring wasn't my thing. I was good at the Katas—the building blocks of vampire sword fighting. I'd been a ballet dancer, and there was something very dancerly about the moves. They were positions, forms, steps that I could memorize and practice and, by repetition, perfect.

Sparring was different. Having grown up with my nose in a book, I had no experience at fighting beyond a couple of experimental kickboxing classes and a few run-ins with Celina and her assorted minions. I knew my weakness. I spent too much time trying to think *through* the fight—trying to find an attacker's weaknesses, to exploit them—while at the same time trying to keep from *overthinking* the fight. That had become even harder in the last week, as I'd worked with Luc to keep the cacophony of smells and sounds that threatened, post-change, to overwhelm me, down to a dull roar.

"But her work with the Katas is unparalleled." He arched an eyebrow at me—half challenge, half insult—and took a step backward. "Sentinel," he said, his voice lower now, the order just for me, "Katas, if you please."

"Liege," I said. I lifted my sword with both hands, my right hand on the handle, left hand on the sheath, and moved my hands apart, unsheathing it with a quick whistle of sound, light glinting from the polished steel. I walked to the edge of the mat and placed the lacquered sheath on the floor beside it.

Then, with all the confidence and bravado I could muster—easier now that I'd been asked to join a secret corps of vampire warriors—I returned to him, faced him, and gripped the katana in both hands.

"Begin," he ordered, and took steps backward, giving me room. There were seven two-handed Katas and three more single-handed moves. Those were new to me. But I'd been practicing the traditional Katas since I'd become a vampire, and, frankly, I wanted to show off a little. In the week that we'd been working together, Ethan had seen me practice the Katas only in traditional fashion—one Kata at a time, my movements timed and precise. But that wasn't all I could do. . . .

I bladed my body, katana poised before me. "Fast or slow?"

He frowned. "Fast or slow?"

I smiled cannily beneath my fringe of bangs. "Pick your speed."

"Vampires?" he asked aloud, but his gaze on me. "Fast or slow?"

There were "slow" stragglers, but the majority requested "fast."

"Fast, it seems," he said.

I nodded, centered my weight, and moved. The first kata brought the sword arcing across my body, then returning to the center position. The second was a downward strike. The third and fourth were combinations. The fifth, sixth, and seventh were combinations with spins and parries.

In traditional form, when the focus was on precision and control, each Kata took ten or fifteen seconds.

But done fast, I could work through the entire set in twenty seconds. I'd learned speed from my former trainer, Catcher, a sorcerer with a penchant for katanas and sword fighting. (He was also, not coincidentally, Mallory's boyfriend and my grandfather's employee.) Catcher demanded I practice the moves over and over, thinking repetition would force the muscle memory. It had—and it had allowed me to use my increased vampire strength, speed, and agility to push the forms into a single dance of movement so quick my body blurred with the speed of it.

After I'd challenged Ethan in our second duel, he decided he needed to supplant Catcher as my trainer. But he didn't know how much Catcher had taught me. . . .

I finished the seventh form, spun to a stop, sword between my hands, perpendicular before my body. The lights above us caught the gentle curve of the steel, the entire room suddenly silent.

Ethan stared.

"Do it again," he said, his words barely audible, a glint in his eyes. I didn't mistake the glint for lust. Although the chemistry between us was keen, Ethan was unambiguously, ubiquitously political—always maneuvering.

I was a weapon.

I was *his* weapon.

That glint? Avarice, pure and simple.

"*Liege*," I said, tilting my head in acknowledgment and returning to the beginning position.

I completed the moves again, sword arcing perpendicular to the floor, slicing downward, an across-and-up combination, then the arc-and-spin combinations, the backward thrust, the overhead strike. I ended in the final position.

"Again," he ordered a third time, and I obliged.

By the time I'd run through the Katas in sequence again, and then done seven or eight repetitions of one or two favorite Katas at his request, my chest was heaving with the effort, my hands slippery around the rayskin-wrapped handle of my sword. I glanced up and saw that the vampires in the wooden balcony that ringed the Training Room were leaning forward, arms on the railing, curiosity in their expressions. They tended to look at me that way—either, because of my strength, as a curiosity or, because of my unfortunate habit of challenging Ethan to duels, as a freak.

For what it's worth, I was really planning on breaking that habit.

"Well done," Ethan said quietly, then addressed the balcony. "I believe that answers more than a few questions about our Sentinel. And while she's onstage"—he tilted his head toward me—"anything our new social chair would like to add about upcoming Cadogan events? Picnics? Mixers?"

A blush spread to the roots of my hair. Ethan had named me House social chair as punishment for challenging him. As punishments went, it was pretty light. But it was also mortifying, and it took me a moment to get myself together.

"I'm thinking about something for summer solstice. A barbecue, probably. I thought we'd invite vampires from the other Houses."

The room went silent as Ethan considered the idea—and his audience waited for the verdict.

"Good," he finally said with an authoritarian nod, then looked back at the crowd. His expression changed to something much more serious.

"We thought at one time," he began, "that our superiors believed assimilation with humans was best. That staying under the radar was the best way to ensure our survival and to keep peace with the supernaturals around us.

"To some extent, Celina has made that impossible. With all

due respect to our friends in Navarre House, she has sought, at every opportunity, to increase our profile, to alienate us from humans, and to alienate us from ourselves." In a rare moment of humanity, Ethan looked down at the ground, worry furrowing a line between his eyes.

"We are on the brink," he said. "The brink of what, exactly, remains to be seen. As it stands, we've been gifted with a time of peace and relative tranquility, a time in which the Houses have blossomed financially. But our coming out, by hook or by crook, for better or worse, has put us back in the public eye—a public that hasn't always been kind toward us. Whether our pseudocelebrity will last—who knows?

"And now, as you may have heard, the shifters are preparing to meet this week in Chicago. We've been informed that during this convocation, they will decide, for one and all, whether to stay in their respective territories or to return to their ancestral home in Alaska. If they go, and the tide turns against us— Well, I don't need to remind you about our shared historical experiences with shifters."

There was mumbling in the crowd, a spike of discomforted magic in the air. Shifters had retreated before when vamps had been in trouble. Vamps blamed shifters for the resulting deaths, and vampires now feared that if the human tide turned against us, shifters would do it again, leaving us here holding the supernatural baggage.

"As you know, we don't have formal allies within the Packs. They have avoided such ties. But my hope remains that should we face animosity or anger or fear, they will agree to help us."

A male vampire stood up. "They've never helped before!" he shouted down.

Ethan regarded him thoughtfully. "They haven't. But suggesting that they 'owe us' hasn't worked. We will do what we can to form new connections between us. And in the meantime . . ."

He paused, and the room was silent as the vampires waited for his next words. My issues with Ethan notwithstanding, he knew how to work a crowd.

"In the meantime," he continued, "I ask you, not as your Master, but as your brother, your colleague, your friend. Be careful. Mind the company you keep. Be aware of your surroundings. And most of all, don't be afraid to come to me. Any of you. Anytime."

Ethan cleared his throat, and when he spoke again, his voice was crisp, clear, and Master-like again. "Dismissed," he said, and the vampires in the balcony began to file out of the Sparring Room.

Ethan walked toward us. "My apartments," he told Luc, then glanced at me. "You, too."

"Your apartments?" I asked, but Ethan had already turned away, smiling politely at a vampire who'd trekked down from the balcony. I didn't know her, but her goal was obvious enough in the cant of her hip, the subtle play of her fingers as she pushed her long dark hair behind her ears. She leaned toward him and asked something. He laughed and chuckled politely, then began explaining—with visual aids—how to correctly position her hands on the handle of her sword.

My lip curled involuntarily, but before I could get out a snarky comment, I felt a tug on my ponytail. I glanced back.

"Let's go," Luc said.

"What did he mean by 'his apartments'?"

"We have a meeting."

The last time we'd had a meeting, Ethan had told me about

raves, mass feedings in which humans became unwilling vampire snacks. "About the raves?"

"Not today," Luc said. "We haven't heard anything else about raves since the attempt to blackmail us went bad. Malik's working up a long-term strategy. Today we're talking shifters. Let's go—unless you want to keep watching?"

I stuck out my tongue at him, but I followed when he headed for the door.

The basement of Cadogan House was all business, most of it violent—Training Room, Sparring Room, Ops Room, arsenal. The first floor, like the second and third, was about decor. Soft lighting, French antiques, hardwoods, expensive furniture. "Five-star hotel" had been my first impression. The rest of the rooms were equally fancy, from Ethan's masculine office to his luxe apartments.

We took the central staircase to the third floor. When we reached Ethan's apartments, Luc grasped the handles of the double doors in both hands, then pushed them open.

I'd been in Ethan's rooms before, but only briefly. As far as I could tell, Ethan's chunk of the third floor had three rooms—the main living room, a bedroom, and presumably a bathroom somewhere in the back. It was as elegantly appointed as the rest of the House—from the hardwood floors to the warmly painted walls; from the onyx fireplace to the expensive, tailored furniture. It looked more like a suite in a fine hotel than the home of a vampire in the prime of his (immortal) life.

This trip, I gave the room a careful look, scanning for hints into the psyche of the Master of the House. And there were plenty of details to peruse—the detritus of his four hundred years of life dotted the room. A bow and arrow hung on one wall. A campaign chair and desk that looked like it would fold for travel, maybe remnants of Ethan's time as a soldier, sat in one corner. A low buffet-style chest was centered on another wall, a spread of objects on top of it. I ambled over, hands behind my back, and surveyed the goods. There were two silver trophies styled like giant cups, a picture of men in early-nineteenth-century garb (but no Ethan amongst them), and a flat stone with symbols carved into the top.

After I'd given them a once-over, I glanced up and checked out the rest of the room. That was when I spied it in a corner—in one corner, inside a tall glass case, sat a gleaming Fabergé egg.

"Oh, wow," I said, walking toward it to get a better look. A pendant light shone above it, illuminating the lustrous, spring green enamel and the snarling, golden dragon that wound around it.

"It was Peter's," Luc said.

I glanced back at him. "Peter's?"

"Peter Cadogan." Luc walked toward me, arms crossed, then gestured toward the glass case. "The Master vampire who founded Cadogan House. It was a gift from a member of the Russian royalty." He tapped a finger on the glass. "Peter was from Wales, and it's a representation of the Welsh dragon. See the eye?"

I nodded at where he pointed. A round red gem was placed at the dragon's eye. Six white lines radiated from its middle.

"It's a star ruby," he said. "Incredibly rare."

"And incredibly expensive," added a voice behind us. We both stood straight again and glanced around. Ethan walked in, still in his *gi* pants, around his neck a navy towel bearing a silver monogrammed "C."

"Shower," he said. "Make yourselves at home." Ethan walked toward the doors that led to his bedroom. He opened one, slipped inside, and closed it behind him again.

"I could have used a shower," I pointed out.

"I know. I can smell you from here."

I was halfway to discreetly sniffing my armpit before I realized he was just trying to rile me up. "You're funny."

"You're easy."

"You were telling me about the egg?"

"Oh," Luc said, then scratched absently at his temple. "So Peter met this Russian duchess, and they bonded. Completely Platonic, from what I understand, but he did her a favor of some kind. She wanted to repay him, so she commissioned the egg and threw in the ruby for good measure."

"I suppose it pays to have friends," I concluded, then dropped my tone to something a little more serious. "Speaking of Peters, any developments on a replacement for our former colleague?" Peter Spencer had been excommunicated from the House for betraying us to Celina, for assisting in her blackmail plans and her ploy to create more anti-shifter fervor amongst vamps, and anti-Cadogan fervor amongst humans.

Luc busied himself by picking at a bit of dust on the egg's glass case. "Not really ready to talk about that, Sentinel."

I nodded, not entirely surprised by Luc's reaction. He'd punched a divot into the Ops Room conference table when he'd discovered Peter's treachery. The hole had been repaired, but the table hadn't yet been refinished. It was like a stain marking Peter's betrayal. And it wasn't surprising Luc wasn't eager to invest in someone else.

I wanted to say something—to offer my condolences or

even a simple "I'm sorry"—but a knock on the hallway doors stopped me short.

"Preparations for our guest," Luc said as the doors were opened by a man in a white chef's jacket. He smiled politely at Luc and me, then moved aside so that a second chef, this time a woman in white, could wheel a cart into the room.

The cart was piled with trays, and the trays were topped by silver domes.

It was *room service*.

"What guest?" I asked as, with hotel-like efficiency, the woman began removing the domes and stacking them one atop the other.

She revealed a spread of food: crackers; cheeses; a rainbow of fruit, from lush berries to slices of buttercup yellow mango to spring green coins of kiwi; and tiny sausages speared by toothpicks. I had a pang—Mallory loved those things. But we were still on the outs, and thinking about her still hurt. So for now, I focused my attention back on the movable feast . . . and the tray of small pastries arranged around a poppy-seed-dotted pink dip.

"The guest is Gabriel Keene," Luc said. "He's dropping by to talk to your liege and mine."

I gave a soft snort. "I assume that means you're involving me in shifter shenanigans this week?"

"I'm surprised at you, Sentinel."

Ethan walked back into the sitting room. He was in black suit pants and a white button-up, no tie. The top button was unbuttoned, and he'd skipped the suit coat. Luc and I were still in workout gear, so it was practically business casual in here today.

"We so rarely involve you in shenanigans," Ethan said,

then nodded at the woman who'd wheeled in the cart. "Thank you, Alicia. My compliments to the chef."

Alicia smiled, then collected her stack of steel covers. She turned and left the room, and the man who'd held open the doors gave us a final smile before he walked out again, closing the doors behind him.

"You involve me in shenanigans at every opportunity."

"She has a point, Liege."

Ethan clucked his tongue. "Captain of my Guards and he carries the standard of my Sentinel. Oh, how quickly they turn."

"You're first in my heart, Liege."

This time, Ethan snorted. "We'll see. Well, at any rate, we'll see where Gabriel's allegiances lie."

He looked over the trays before nabbing a bottle of water, twisting off the top, and taking a drink.

"Nice spread," I told him.

He nodded. "I thought it polite to offer Gabriel something to eat, and I assumed I'd have a greater chance of keeping your attention if I fed you first."

I'd have to give him that one. I loved to eat, and the non-stop vampire metabolism hadn't done much to dampen my appetite—quite the opposite. "Let's just remember, Sullivan, that I want you for your smoked meats and your smoked meats only."

He barked out a laugh. "Touché, Sentinel."

I grinned at him, then plucked a piece of cheese from the tray and popped it in my mouth. It was rich and earthy, but it had that weird aftertaste that fancy cheese always seemed to have. "So," I began, after I'd nabbed a couple more chunks for good measure, "why's Gabriel coming to the House?"

"You'll recall he wanted to speak about security arrangements for the convocation?"

I nodded. Gabriel had mentioned it when he'd dropped by a week ago.

"As it turns out, you were the security arrangement."

I blanched. "*I'm* the security arrangement? What does that mean?"

Ethan took another drink before recapping the bottle. "It means, Sentinel, that we're throwing you to the wolves."

CHAPTER THREE

HİDE-AND-SEEK

"I've loaned you to Gabriel," he added by way of explanation.

I could only blink. "I'm sorry; it sounded like you said you've loaned me to Gabriel?"

"Well, well," said a voice at the threshold. "Aren't I lucky, getting a loaner Sentinel?" Without so much as a sound, Gabriel Keene, Apex of the North American Central Pack of shape-shifters, had made his way into Ethan's apartments. He stood in the doorway, hands still on the knobs, light from the hallway spilling around him into the room.

Gabe walked inside, then shut the doors behind him. "Your second in command ushered me up. I told him no introductions were necessary."

"Gabriel," Ethan said, extending a hand and walking toward him. Gabriel shook it, his heavy black boots clunking on the hardwood floors as he moved.

They were an interesting contrast: Ethan—blond, rangy, and dressed in a crisp shirt and suit pants; Gabriel—tousled brown hair, broad shouldered, and dressed in jeans and a black T-shirt. Ethan was no slouch, but Gabriel was just so *masculine*, and all that shifter energy practically sucked the air from the room. I considered his very pregnant wife, Tonya, a very lucky girl.

When he and Ethan had finished their manly handshaking, Gabriel looked over at me. "What's the going rate for a loaner Sentinel these days?"

"*Patience*," said Luc and Ethan at the same time.

A hint of a smile crossed Gabriel's face. I rolled my eyes.

"You remember Luc, Captain of my Guards?" Ethan said, gesturing toward Luc. "And Merit, of course?"

Gabriel nodded at each of us in turn.

"Help yourself to the food," Ethan said, extending an arm toward the cart.

Gabriel shook his head, then gestured toward one of Ethan's tailored sofas. "Can I sit?"

Ethan nodded graciously, then joined Gabriel at the seating area. Luc followed. I grabbed a cracker and did the same, but sat cross-legged on the floor.

"Just finished training," I told Gabriel with an apologetic smile, then pointed at the empty Louis XIV chair beside Luc's. "I'd prefer not getting a lecture about ruining the antiques."

"My Sentinel is currently high on a mix of cheese and carbohydrates," Ethan chummily told Gabriel. "Respectfully, I'd ignore her if I were you."

"I'll leave that job to you. Perhaps we should get to the point?"

"Feel free."

Gabriel frowned, then crossed his right ankle over his left knee. "It might be best if I started at the beginning. Shifters are an independent bunch. I don't mean that we live a solitary existence—quite the opposite. We are organized into Packs, after all. But we tend to live in the margins of human society. Vamps tend to think of us as a tent and Jeep crew, a hog and Harley crew, a rock 'n' roll and straight Jack Daniel's crew."

Although I'd heard that description, the only shifters I knew other than Gabe—Jeff Christopher, a shifter/computer genius and one of my grandfather's employees, and Chicago's Breckenridge family, who were as rich and well-heeled as they came—were exactly the opposite. On the other hand, the Brecks had tried to blackmail us. . . .

Gabriel shrugged, and his voice softened a bit. "That description isn't entirely untrue. And that means that from a temperament standpoint, Pack members are generally uninterested in humans, in other sups. They aren't interested in strategy."

"What are they interested in?" Luc asked.

"Family," Gabriel said. "Their families, their children, the unity of the Packs. They're loyal, and to a one, they'll follow as the Pack decides. But that attitude can make them, let's say, insular."

Ethan wet his lips, as if preparing to broach an uncomfortable subject. "There have been rumblings about the Pack's returning home to Aurora."

Aurora was the ancestral home Ethan had mentioned earlier, a remote town in the wilds of northern Alaska. From what I understood, it was where shifters congregated when they needed to get away from human machinations. It was also a place to hide out—to disappear to when things got rowdy . . . or when vampires got into trouble. It was their collective retreat when supernatural life got too sticky.

I'd been a vampire for less than three months. The drama was occasionally overwhelming, so I understood the urge to retreat. But I wasn't thrilled about the idea of being left behind.

To his credit, Gabriel managed not to squirm under Ethan's scrutinizing stare. But a low wash of magic filled the room, like a silent growl, unpleasantly acerbic. I fought the urge to roll my shoulders against the uncomfortable tingle. I also opened the telepathic connection between Ethan and me to offer up a silent warning.

He's getting angry, I told him. *Tread carefully*.

I'm willing to test the waters, Ethan answered back. That answer was surprising—Ethan was generally strategically conservative.

I also used to think only he could trigger the connection between us. Apparently, he'd just been ignoring me.

"My intent is to have the Packs convene; the ultimate decision on that will be made by the Pack leaders. But assuming that conversation goes well, we'll convene, and we'll decide whether to remain among humans, or return to the woods. And if the Pack decides that we go," Gabriel weightily added, "then we go."

"Why now?" Ethan asked.

"We know the sorcerers are beginning to see things, that prophecies are beginning to bubble up. Prophecies of war. Of coming battles."

Ethan nodded. We'd heard Catcher offer up just such a prophecy.

"Have you heard talk about underground groups?"

Ethan leaned forward. "What underground groups?"

Gabriel donned the expression of a man about to impart bad news. "Anti-fang groups. Humans who think vampires

showing themselves is the first sign of some coming apoca-
lypse . . . or the second American Civil War."

Ethan went quiet.

"We hadn't heard," Luc put in. "No rumbles, no chatter."

"Like I said, the movement is still underground. We've
heard about meetings in eastern Tennessee, but it sounds like
they're still rural, publicized by word of mouth, handwritten
flyers, that kind of thing. But sooner or later, they'll go elec-
tronic. We'd prefer not to be here when that happens."

Ethan sat back in his chair, but not before sharing a meaningful glance with Luc. I assumed they were talking silently
about some strategy for getting information on the anti-fang
groups.

"You'll understand my concern," Ethan said, "about your
leaving. If you take your numbers, your skills, your power, if
you merge back into the wild, then you leave us here."

"Alone" was the word Ethan didn't say—alone against a
tide of human opinion that was, if Gabriel was right about the
underground rumblings, already beginning to shift against us.

Gabriel shook his head. "If we stay, what's to become of us?
I understand your fear—"

Ethan held up a hand, stopping him. "With all due respect,
Gabriel, you *don't* understand our fear."

That caused another spike of adrenaline, this time emanating from Ethan's direction. Tensions were rising, the collective
burden of years of animosity between these two men and the
people they sought to protect.

Gabriel stood, then paced to one end of the room. He
leaned back against the far wall, putting space between himself and the rest of us, then raised his gaze to us again.

"You're lucky, in a sense, that humans think they understand vampires. They may have believed you were myth, but they also believed they understood your biology. Humans have alternately sought to join you, or to exterminate you. But us? We'd be seen as animals. Research subjects."

Although Catcher had once told me that Jeff could handle himself, I had the suddenly ferocious urge to find and embrace him, to ensure that he was safe from anyone who'd try to do him harm.

"If we stay," Gabriel said, his gaze on the floor, "then outing ourselves, or being outed, is inevitable. And nothing pleasant would follow."

The weight of his words hung in the ensuing silence.

"Then perhaps," Ethan said after a moment, "it's time that we come to understand each other as we are, without unrealistic expectations between us."

"I'm not sure we can clear the slate," Gabriel said. "Too much history."

I saw the quick flare of disappointment in Ethan's eyes, and my heart clenched. I also saw my opportunity, so I took it. I stood up, then glanced between them, and used a little of that speechifying technique Ethan was so very good at.

"We have a window of opportunity," I told them, then looked at Ethan. "The majority of humans, at least for today, think vampires are cool. The animosity may be building again, but for today, *we're safe*."

Then I turned to Gabriel. "If this convocation happens, it will be to talk, right? To decide what to do?" At his nod, I continued. "Then you have time to make a decision. You have the luxury to chart a course, instead of just reacting to a crisis, when stepping away to protect your people feels like the only real option."

I paused for a moment, blinking as I figured out what to say next. When nothing flowery came to mind, I just told the truth. "I don't envy either of you the decision of what to do next. And I haven't been a vampire long enough to have the same sense of history that you do. But maybe it's time to try something different?" I looked at Gabriel. "Convene. Talk to your people about Aurora. But think about asking something more of them. Something more than what they've given before."

I looked at Ethan, whose head was tilted thoughtfully—appreciatively—as he gazed back at me. "Vampires are well connected," I reminded him. "If shifters stay and they're forced out of the closet, what can we do about it? How can we help? If they sacrifice for us, how can we make sure they aren't going it alone?"

I opened my mouth to continue but, realizing I'd said everything that needed to be said, snapped it closed again. The next steps would have to be their own.

There was another long moment of silence, broken when Gabriel finally nodded. "Maybe I will grab something to eat," he said, then walked toward the cart.

With that simple gesture, the tension evaporated.

I couldn't help but share with Ethan the victorious grin that lifted one corner of my mouth. He rolled his eyes but rose from his chair and walked toward me.

"Impressive," he whispered when he reached me.

"All in a night's work."

He bobbed his head toward the Apex currently perusing the spread of cheese and meats and crackers. "He's a man after your own heart."

"He's not the only one who appreciates my love of food. I mean, you might consider how well I've trained you."

He arched a dubious eyebrow, and his voice could hardly have been more sarcastic. "Excuse me?"

Luc chuckled from his chair, chin on his hand, as he watched us with obvious amusement. "Oh, I got this one, Sentinel. Liege, respectfully, you had this meeting *catered*."

Ethan's expression went a little wan.

I considered that a victory, too.

By the time we'd reconvened, Gabriel and I had eaten our fill of Cadogan snacks. We were gathered in the sitting area once again. I sat cross-legged on the floor; Ethan, Luc, and Gabriel sat on the chairs and couches.

"Now that we've discussed the philosophy," Ethan began, "how can we assist with your projects?"

Gabriel popped a wedge of summer sausage into his mouth. "First off, we're meeting tomorrow night—the leaders of the American Packs." He glanced over at me, amusement in his eyes. "Bonus points, Kitten, if you can name the other Pack leaders."

"You should know this from the *Canon*," Ethan put in. I rolled my eyes, but played the part of the dutiful pupil . . . and thanked God I'd actually read the reference guide's chapter on supernatural populations (Chapter 7: "Sup's On!").

"Oh, uh, Jason Maguire, Consolidated Atlantic. Robin Swift, Western." I squeezed my eyes closed, trying to mentally flip back through the pages of the *Canon* to find the final name. "Great Northwestern . . . Um."

"Here's a hint," Luc said. "His name is half cartoon tiger, half football player."

The lightbulb went on. "Tony Marino, Great Northwestern."

Gabe nodded. "Well done. Anyway, the point of this meeting will be to make sure the alphas are on board. The Packs will take their cues from their alphas. I don't need Robin and Jason and Tony to make a decision on staying, but I need them to agree that taking the question to the Packs is the right course of action." He sat forward, elbows on his knees, hands clasped before him. "I need them to accept the possibility that the status quo will undergo a profound change by the end of the week, one way or another."

"Do you expect them to refuse the convocation?" Luc asked.

Gabriel frowned, his gaze on the small plate in his hand as he picked over its contents. "I'm not expecting a lot of drama from Jason or Robin," he said, "but Tony's another story. The Great Northwestern is headquartered in Aurora, and he's quick to hit the panic button. He likes playing king of the castle. And if he thinks there's any argument that we should go home, he'll try to send us there, and without a convocation first." He shrugged. "Alphas don't issue dictates from on high, nor do we simply follow our own agenda. We make the best decision for the Pack; we embody the collective voice, in a manner of speaking. Well, we'll find out when we find out. I'll get you the address of the meet. When you get there, find Berna. You can hardly miss her."

Ethan nodded in understanding. "And after the meet?"

"Assuming all goes well, we'll convene on Friday."

Today was Tuesday. "Are three days enough time," I wondered aloud, "to get all the Pack members into Chicago?"

"It won't be all the Pack members, just the activists. Some are here already; some are waiting for directions. You know the Breckenridges—the kind of lifestyle they lead. They're very tied down to the land. Most of us are more mobile."

"Where will you meet?" Ethan asked.

"We've nailed down a spot in Ukrainian Village—some of our members have connections to the neighborhood from the Old Country." He shrugged. "It's lower profile than renting out a ballroom at the Hyatt."

Ethan nodded. "And where do we come in? You said you wanted to speak about security arrangements. Was that in reference to the convocation or to the meeting, or both?"

Gabe gestured with a cracker. "Both. And I actually had both you and Merit in mind. You're both skilled, capable. You bring something extra to the table."

Something fanged, I silently wondered, or something involving samurai-quality steel?

"You remind them why we're meeting," Gabriel said, as if in answer to my silent question. "You remind them what's at stake, and why I've asked them to travel from Aurora or Charleston or the Bronx to Chicago. You remind them of the consequences of deciding to resettle, of leaving human and vampire affairs behind. And besides," he added, looking at me with humor in his gaze, "you have the attentions of one of my favorite Pack members. I understand you and Jeff Christopher are friends?"

My cheeks heated with a warming blush. Jeff was a friend; he also had a magnificent crush on me. More important, he'd done vampires some pretty serious favors, helping us figure out that Peter had been the saboteur assisting Celina from within the halls of Cadogan House.

"Jeff is a fabulous friend," I agreed.

"He was an integral part of our resolution of the Breckenridge threat," Ethan added.

Gabriel nodded. "Jeff's good people, and your grandfather,

Merit, has done right by him. Jeff's in a good situation, and he's not into playing the politics of a vampire-shifter conflict. But I'm not sure he's in the majority. I'll be honest, Ethan. I think the odds they'll decide to head home are pretty good—sixty, seventy percent maybe. And if that's what they decide, I'll abide by that decision. My responsibility is to give voice to the debate, to let them reach the best decision for the Packs, however that might be defined."

"I understand," Ethan said quietly. "I appreciate your candor, and that you're taking the question to the Packs at all." But it was easy to tell that was not what he wanted to say, and that he had more choice words for the possibility that the shifters wouldn't, for once, make the right call.

Gabriel looked at Ethan. "I know you have a security staff, and that they're probably capable of doing this on their own. But I'd consider it a personal favor if you could be there. Having a Master in attendance shows the Packs that vampires are prepared to listen, not just judge. That's important."

Ethan let the weight of those words hang in the air for a moment. "At this point, do you anticipate violence?"

I assumed he asked because shifters, like sorcerers, seemed to have some kind of tap into the future.

"I'll be honest—it wouldn't surprise me. We're talking about folks with a lot of pent-up emotion and some very specific ideas about whether they should head out for a long vacation or suffer through a summer in Chicago because vamps aren't playing nice. I'm paraphrasing there, of course." Gabe's tone couldn't have been drier.

"I don't have an objection to participating," he said. "But since we're effectively asking her to risk herself for the sake of those who may, ultimately, forsake her, I think it best that

Merit be allowed to decide for herself whether she'll assist."
He glanced at me, probably saw the shock on my face, and
lifted his brows in question. "Merit?"

It took me a moment to gather myself, not because of the
question—I was oath- and honor-bound to help protect Cadogan House, and this surely counted amongst those duties—
but that he trusted me enough to ask the question.

"Of course," I said, sliding my gaze to Gabriel and nodding
to let him know the deal was done.

He blew out a slow breath, then leaned forward and put
his snack plate on the tray-topped ottoman that sat between
him and Ethan. "One more thing," he said. "In terms of the
rules of engagement, I need to request that you not take action unless you're acted upon. I think the benefits of your
being there outweigh the risks, but you make an unsolicited
move on a shifter in front of four Packs, and we won't be hy-
pothesizing about a war. We'll be in the goddamned middle
of one."

"Point taken," Ethan said after a moment.

With that, Gabriel stood up, then glanced between Ethan
and me. "I know this isn't the kind of thing you normally sign
up for. I appreciate your help, even if you are playing the to-
ken vampires." He glanced at Luc. "I assume you'll want advance materials?"

Luc nodded, blond curls bobbing around his face. "That'd
be appreciated."

"Done. Once we're sure this thing's a go, I'll send directions to the location, some interior maps in case you want to
think about protocols, exits, whatever. And do me a favor—no
Armani. It won't work for this crowd."

"No Armani," Ethan agreed.

"Then I'll send you the pre-meet address in a bit, and I'll see you tomorrow night." He slid his hazel-eyed gaze my way. "Leather, maybe, Kitten?"

"I'm sure she'll find something appropriate," Ethan darkly interjected, holding out a hand. "You have my contact information. We'll await the details."

They walked toward the door, the leader of vampires and the leader of shifters, the fate of thousands in their hands. They shook, and when Ethan opened the doors, Helen—the House's den mother—was waiting there, presumably to take Gabriel back downstairs. Ethan must have used his telepathic mojo to give her instructions.

When he'd closed the doors again, Ethan headed straight for the cart and popped open a box of Blood4You.

"And they say vampires are dramatic," Luc intoned.

Ethan finished the box of blood in a single gulp, then crumpled the container in his hand. When he looked at us again, his normally green eyes swirled with remnants of quicksilver. He'd gone a little vampy, and I wasn't sure if that was because of the blood, or because the blood was bringing him back down from full-vamp mode.

Luc plucked his own box of blood from the cart and popped in the attached, disposable straw. "Nice little speech you gave there, Sentinel."

I shrugged. "I'm a Merit. We can give good talk when the need arises."

"It was well done," Ethan agreed.

I crossed my arms and tilted my head at Ethan. "If they leave, is it really such a loss? I mean, we've survived, and they've never taken our side before, so why does it matter? Even if worse comes to worst—if Celina manages to start some kind of internal war amongst vampires or if humans turn against us, what would it matter if they're gone?"

"Vampires are predators," Ethan said. "Humans walk the line between predator and prey. But shifters are kith and kin of the earth itself. They have powers that would put even Catcher's abilities to shame. We leak magic. Sorcerers can use that magic, funnel it, mold it to their wills. But shifters *are* magic. They are part of all that is around them. If they retreat, we lose that connection to the world, to the earth, to Chicago, and we'll all be less for it. We lose their strength. We also lose their numbers. We lose potential allies who could help stand up for us—and as you pointed out, who could rely upon us to stand up for them."

"If they forsake us again," Luc quietly said, "the stakes could be much worse—we won't just be fighting an army of French peasants with muskets and the occasional bayonet."

"Well, let's not continue to beat the poor dead horse," Ethan said after a moment. "The pre-meeting is tomorrow night. We'll show up, wield our steel, and probably learn a good deal more about shifters. That's all we can do for now." He looked at me. "I'm a bit concerned about your sparring should the need arise for it. You still haven't managed to beat me one-on-one."

"But she works the Katas like a master," Luc said, taking his drink box back to the couch. "At least she's half skilled."

"I'd prefer to be good at both," I said, in between bites of sausage. It was good stuff—meaty and savory, with just the right amount of kick.

"It will come," Ethan said, his tone all quiet confidence. "Given the piecemeal nature of your change, let's be patient. Well, at least until we train tomorrow evening."

"Maybe tomorrow will be the big day," I said, hoping we wouldn't have much longer to wait. And speaking of issues that awaited resolution . . .

"Since we're here, what can you tell me about the Red Guard?"

Both Ethan's and Luc's heads jerked up so quickly, and with such alarm in their expressions, you'd have thought I'd suggested vampiricide.

Ethan sat down on the sofa, then rolled his shoulders as if the tension there had suddenly become unbearable. "Where did you learn about the Red Guard?"

I pulled a corner from a square of cheddar and popped it into my mouth, aiming for nonchalance. "There were some references in a couple of vampire history books I found in the library."

When Ethan arched an eyebrow at Luc, he stuttered out an answer.

"Oh, well, you're on a need-to-know basis, Sentinel," Luc said, then raised his eyebrows at Ethan, as if getting the okay to continue. "And right now you don't need to know."

I took the axiom, assuming Luc was quoting some movie I hadn't heard of, and glanced over at Ethan. He was staring back at me, his expression flat. I guessed he wasn't eager to discuss the RG. I knew he'd be conflicted about the organization and its purpose, but I'd expected vitriol, not silence. Maybe I'd actually managed to render him speechless. Given his vast love of speechifying, that was quite an accomplishment.

"Okay," I said, standing up. "In that case, if we're done for the day, I'm heading out." I glanced at Ethan. "I'll meet you first thing in the Sparring Room."

Ethan nodded. "Dismissed."

"I'll walk you to the stairs," Luc said, hopping off the couch. He glanced back at Ethan. "I need to see a girl . . . about a girl."

"And speaking of things I don't need to know," Ethan said lightly, then waved him off with a hand. "Go see her."

Luc staked a toothpick of sausage and cheese before accompanying me to the door. When we were out in the hallway, the doors closed behind us, Luc began to spill.

"RG is the vampire version of a law enforcement internal affairs department," he said. "But with a regulator bent. They were created to guard the original French council members, but they stuck around. Now they're more of a watchdog organization. That makes them controversial."

We headed for the stairs, then trotted down to the second floor. "And that's why Ethan doesn't like to talk about them?"

"Sentinel, does Ethan Sullivan strike you as the type who appreciates challenges to his authority?"

"Not really his bag," I agreed. That was exactly why I'd held off giving Noah an answer. It wasn't that I thought keeping an eye on the Masters was a bad idea—case in point Celina—but I could appreciate Ethan's sensitivity.

We stopped in front of the door to my favorite room in Cadogan House—the library.

Luc eyed the door, then me. "You looking for more inappropriate information?"

"If I didn't keep you two on your toes, Luc, what fun would you have?"

He shook his head in amusement, but then turned around and headed right toward the stairs . . . and toward Lindsey's room. "Gotta see a girl about a girl?" I called after him.

He answered with a gesture. That's what I got, I supposed, for baiting a vampire.

Grief was a miserable emotion. A friend once told me the hurt that came with the end of a relationship was painful because it was the death of a dream—the future you'd imagined with a lover, a loved one, a child, or a friend. That loss was its own painful, nearly tangible thing. You had to reimagine your future, perhaps in a different place, with different people, doing different things than you might have first imagined.

In my case, it was imagining a future without my best friend—without Mallory.

We'd said hurtful things, things that put an obstacle between us. We'd talked since then, but that breach was still there, a barrier that seemed impassable, at least for now.

It was perhaps the most frustrating kind of breakup—when the person you loved lived down the street, in the same building, or across town but they were still inaccessible to you.

I couldn't bring myself to call her. It didn't seem right—like a call would have violated a silence we'd agreed upon.

That's what put me in my car two hours before sunrise—two hours before the sun would send me deep into unconsciousness (and worse, if I wasn't careful)—heading north from Hyde Park to Wicker Park, Mallory's neighborhood.

I swore to myself that I wouldn't drive past the brownstone we had shared; that seemed a little too stalkerish even for me. Besides—seeing the lights on, the glare from the television, the shadow of people in front of the picture window—would only make me that much more miserable. Her life wasn't just supposed to go on. I know it sounded petty, but this was supposed to be hard for her, too. She should have been grieving, as well.

Instead, I stayed on Lake Shore Drive. I drove past her exit, the Lake on my right, then turned off the radio and rolled down the window. I drove until I'd run out of street. And then I pulled over.

I parked and got out of the car, then leaned back against it and stared out at the water. With much-needed space between me and Wicker Park and Cadogan House, I let down the defenses I'd erected, and let the sounds and smells of three million people, not to mention vampires and shifters and fairies and nymphs, take me over.

And in that noise and ocean of sensation, I lost myself for a little while, finding the blankness, the anonymity I needed.

I stayed there, my gaze on the water, until I was ready to go home again.

The House was still lit when I returned, the vampires inside not yet settled in against the rising of the sun. The mercenary fairies who guarded the gate stood quiet and still outside it. One of them nodded when I walked past. After I made it through the gate and onto the House's blocks-wide grounds, I stopped and glanced up at the sky. It was still an inky indigo black. It was a little while yet until dawn.

My soul was quieter than it had been when I left, but I wasn't quite ready to go back inside. Instead, I stepped onto the lawn and headed across it, then around the House. Cadogan's backyard was like a playground for night-bound vampires—barbecue, pool, and fountain inside a neatly trimmed garden. It was empty now, the vampires—even if not asleep—already indoors.

I walked to the kidney-shaped pool, then knelt beside it and trickled my fingers across the surface of the water.

I didn't look up when I heard soft footsteps.

"It's a nice evening," he said.

"Yes, it is." I flicked the water from my fingers, then stood up again. Ethan stood on the other side of the water in his suit pants and shirt, hands in his pants pockets, hair tucked behind his ears, gold Cadogan medal peeking from the triangle of skin at the hollow of his neck.

"You left?"

I nodded. "For a little while. Just to clear my head."

He cocked his head at me. "Shifters?"

I assumed he was asking if they were the reason I needed space. "Sorcerers," I corrected.

"Ah," he said, then lowered his gaze to the water. "Mallory?"

"Yeah. Mallory." He knew we'd fought. I didn't think he knew that he'd been what we'd fought over—part of it, anyway.

Ethan crossed his arms over his chest. "The transition can be a challenge for friends. For loved ones."

"Yes, it most definitely can," I agreed, then opted to change the subject. "What are you doing out here? Shifters?"

"Yeah," he mimicked, a hint of a smile on his face. "Shifters."

"Maybe the shifters have it right," I said. "I mean, heading off into the woods, keeping to themselves."

"Your theory being that if you don't have contact with anyone, you can't be hurt by them?"

That was a very astute conclusion for a four-hundred-year-old vampire who usually seemed clueless about human emotion. "That would be the idea, yes."

This time, when he looked at me, there was sadness in his eyes. "I don't want to see you become cold, Merit."

"Not wanting to be hurt isn't the same as becoming cold."

"Not at first," he said. He walked to a low brick wall that surrounded the pool and leaned back upon it, ankles crossed in front of him, arms still crossed. And then he looked at me, the pool lights making his eyes glow like a cat's.

"Now that you've finally completed the change, beware the creep of insensitivity. Humans accept the concept of death; they may not wish for it, but they recognize that the decay of the human body is inevitable. Vampires, on the other hand, have the possibility of immortality. They implore strategy to protect it, and they often forget about the details of life between the change and the aspen stake."

He shook his head. "You are a wonder of vampiric strength, yet you treasure your humanity and care greatly about those who were in your life before your change. Stay that way," he said. "Stay just the way you are."

"Quit flirting with me, Sullivan," I said dryly, but I wasn't kidding. Ethan was seductive enough when he was being snarky; I wasn't prepared for complimentary Ethan.

"I'm being completely honest," Ethan said, lifting a hand and holding up two fingers. "Scout's honor."

I made a doubtful noise, then glanced up at the sky. As the earth turned on its axis, the indigo of evening was beginning to shift and lighten.

"We should get inside," I suggested. "Unless you want to test your sunlight allergy defenses?"

"I'll pass," Ethan said, standing and holding out a hand. I walked past him, across the backyard and to the brick patio that spanned the back of the House, then to the back door.

When we reached the door, he reached to grasp the handle, but then paused.

I glanced over at him.

"I'm not your father, you know."

It took me a moment to find words. "Excuse me?"

"I'm capable of giving you a compliment and being completely sincere about it."

I opened my mouth to snipe back, but I realized he had a pretty good point. Offering a compliment to goad someone into doing something was just the kind of thing my father would do. I gave Ethan credit for recognizing the difference.

"Then thank you," I told him, a hint of a smile at my lips.

He nodded graciously. "You're welcome. I'll see you in the evening."

"Good night, Sullivan."

"Good night, Sentinel."

CHAPTER FOUR

WHAT HAPPENS IN CHICAGO . . .
STAYS IN CHICAGO

I woke suddenly, jolting upright in my bed in my room in Cadogan House amidst a pile of books about American shifters. I pushed my long bangs from my face, realizing I'd fallen asleep again in the midst of studying. That was the tricky thing about living by the fall and rise of the sun—it was a deep, dizzying descent into unconsciousness when the sun began to rise, and a gunshot ascent when twilight fell again.

"Welcome to the life of vampires," I muttered aloud, a greeting a former friend—a former boyfriend—had once passed along. I organized the books into piles on my bed, then stood up and stretched. I'd at least thought to change into pajamas before I sank into unconsciousness, my LICENSE TO ILL tank top rising up as I lifted my arms over my head and stretched. The orange tank didn't exactly match the blue Cubs boxers I'd paired it with, but who was going to see it? As far as I was concerned, sleeping in ugly, comfy duds was one of the major advantages of being single.

And I was very definitely single.

I'd actually been single for a while, if you didn't count the few weeks I spent nearly dating Morgan. He'd "won" the right to date me by challenging Ethan in front of half of Cadogan House, Noah, and Scott Grey. We'd had a handful of half-hearted dates afterward. Unfortunately, while the "half" part was from my end, Morgan seemed to be all-in from the get-go. I didn't feel the same, and he was convinced my reticence had something to do with my relationship, physical and otherwise, with Ethan. I could admit Ethan was on my mind more than made me comfortable, but calling our prickly interactions a "relationship" was like calling an office softball team the Cubs. Bats were swung either way, but it just wasn't the same.

Having stretched out, I glanced back at the alarm clock. It was mid-June, so the days were still getting longer, my hours of awareness shrinking a little each day until the summer solstice would click the clock back in the other direction. Figuring I could delay my inevitable training session with Ethan for only so long, I put the stacks of books on the floor, then followed with my feet.

I didn't bother with a shower since I was training with Ethan, but I did change into my sports bra and yoga pants, then threw on a fitted Cadogan T-shirt. I was hungry and headed for a pre-training breakfast, and I didn't want to show up in my minimal workout gear.

When I was dressed and shoed and had my katana in hand, I took the stairs up to Lindsey's third-floor room. She'd become my meal buddy. Her room was also my after-work hangout. The value of bad television after a night of supernatural drama really should not be underestimated. "Mind-numbing" had its role in the life of a vampire.

Lindsey stood in her open doorway, cell phone in hand,

when I arrived. Since she was the guard corps's resident psychic, I assumed she'd guessed I was headed her way. Unlike me, she was dressed in her Cadogan black suit, her long blond hair pulled into a sleek, low ponytail at the base of her neck. She crooked a finger at me, then walked back inside.

"Babe, I have to go. My breakfast date is here. I'll talk to you later. And don't forget about those pants I love. No—the latex ones. 'Kay. Hugs. Bye." She snapped her phone closed, then looked back at me, grinning at what I'm sure was a look of horror on my face.

I really couldn't fathom a single thing to say. But I'd apparently moved out of the Carmichael-Bell love shack and right into the House of Latex.

I mean, I knew Lindsey had been flirting with Connor. He was, like me, a newbie Cadogan vamp. But "latex" was not a word I needed to hear this early in the evening.

"I can't believe you aren't being supportive," she said, rolling her eyes. She toed into sensible black heels as she slid her phone into the pocket of her jacket.

"I'm—I'm supportive. Yay, Lindsey." My tone was flat, but I gave her a halfhearted fist wave.

Once she was shoed, she put her hands on her hips, one blond eyebrow arched. "I've found the love of my very long, very immortal life, and all I get is 'Yay, Lindsey'? Some friend you are."

"Love of your life? Connor? Are you sure?" That time, my voice actually squeaked.

She nibbled the edge of her lip like a love-struck teenager, then put her hand over her heart. "I'm wicked sure."

We stood there in silence for a minute. "Yay, Lindsey," I said again, when words failed me.

She sighed and rolled her eyes. "Fine, fine. I'm not having a lusty, sordid affair with a hot, nubile Novitiate. That was my dry cleaner on the phone."

I resisted the urge to ask how she was going to explain "latex" the next time she talked to her dry cleaner. . . . On the other hand, that actually kinda worked.

"Thank God," I said. "I was having Mallory and Catcher flashbacks."

She pushed me back out the door, then closed it behind us. We began the trek to the first floor and the Cadogan buffet. "Was it really that bad? I mean, Bell is *hot*. H-A-W-T hot."

"So hot you lost your appreciation for spelling?"

"Yeppers. Surface-of-the-sun hot."

"You know who else is hot?" I asked her.

"Don't say 'Luc.'"

"Oh. My. *God*," I said, putting my hand against my chest in mock surprise. "You *are* psychic."

She grumbled, as she was wont to do every time I brought up the name of the boy she should have been chasing. Not that I was nosy . . . but they'd be so good together.

And then she brought out the big guns.

"I'll be ready to discuss Luc with you," she said as we trotted down two flights of stairs to the main floor, "when you're ready to talk about your plan to ensnare the second-prettiest blond vampire in the House."

"Is Luc first in that calculation?"

Lindsey snorted, then tugged at her own blond ponytail. "Hello?"

"Well, however you calculate it, I have no plans to ensnare anyone." We took the long, main hallway to the back of the House, where the old-school cafeteria was located. Wooden tables and ladder-back chairs were placed in front of a stainless-steel buffet where vampires could help themselves. There was not a slice of processed cheese or a cellophane-wrapped snack cake in sight.

"Uh-huh," Lindsey said, leading the way to the buffet. She got in line behind a dozen or so Cadogan vampires—all dressed in the requisite black. The room was filled with them, vamps preparing for an evening of work in the House or a night out in the Windy City. Cadogan House was akin to a company town, so some of the vamps were employed by the House—like the guards—while others worked in the Chicago metro area and contributed a portion of their income back to the House. (Cadogan House vamps got a stipend for being House members, so the work wasn't technically necessary, but vamps liked to be productive.)

Of the House's three hundred eighteen vampires (having lost Peter and Amber), only about one-third actually lived in the House. The rest lived elsewhere but retained their affiliation, having sworn their oaths to Ethan and his fanged fraternity.

Lindsey and I moved slowly through the line, pushing our plastic trays along the steel rack and nabbing food and drink as we passed. Since I'd fought yesterday, and would be fighting again in a few minutes, I didn't want to overdo it, but there were a few essentials I needed: a pint of Type O; a mess of protein (satisfied today by sausage links and patties); and a solid dose of carbs. I plucked a couple of biscuits from a warming pan and arranged them on my tray before grabbing a napkin and silverware and following Lindsey to a table.

She picked a seat beside Katherine and Margot, two vamps I'd first met in Lindsey's room during a night of pizza and reality television. They smiled as we approached, then adjusted their trays to make sure we had room to sit down.

"Sentinel," Margot said, pushing a lock of gleaming, short dark hair behind her ear. She was absolutely gorgeous, with a bob of dark brown hair that curved to a point across her forehead, and long, whiskey-warm eyes that would have been equally well suited on a seductive tiger. "Training tonight?"

"Indeed," I said, sliding into a chair and popping a chunk of biscuit into my mouth. "After all, what would a day in Cadogan House be if Sullivan couldn't humiliate me?"

Lindsey nodded. "Lately, that would be very unusual."

"Sad but true," I agreed.

"Were you serious about the barbecue?" Katherine asked, her long brown hair falling around her shoulders, a lock at the top pulled back with a small barrette. Kat was pretty in an old-fashioned way—with the big eyes and fresh face of a girl from a different time. She'd been born in Kansas City when the town was thick with stockyards and cattle. Her brother, Thomas, was also a member of the House.

"Aspen-stake serious. Folks have been asking for a mixer," I said, nudging Lindsey with an elbow. She snorted, then sipped orange juice from her glass.

"I'm not sure if you're aware," she said, "but I'm not up for a mixer."

We all stopped and looked at her. Margot tilted her head. "Is that because you've dumped Connor, or because you're an official item?"

"Please say 'dumped,'" I murmured. "Please say 'dumped.'"

This time, she elbowed me. "We are no longer an item. He's just so . . ."

"Young?" the three of us asked simultaneously.

"Sometimes," she said, "I wonder what life as a vampire would be like without all these other vampires around."

Margot stuck out her tongue at Lindsey.

"You'd miss us terribly," I reminded her. "And you'd miss Luc."

She got quiet.

"I'm not responding to that," she finally said.

Margot, Katherine, and I grinned at one another, figuring that was answer enough.

Ethan was already in the Sparring Room, already in his *gi* pants and a white jacket belted with a purple sash. He was barefoot in the middle of the tatami, unsheathed katana in hand, sparring with an invisible opponent. He thrust the sword behind him, then turned and pulled it back, wrenched it upward, and swung it around his head. When the sword was down again, he executed a butterfly kick, legs flying parallel to the ground, the tip of the sword following, a deadly punctuation to the move. He was fast enough that speed blurred his movements, making him a haze of white and gleaming steel amidst the antique weapons and wood of the room.

He was a thing to behold, was Ethan Sullivan.

He fought alone for two or three more minutes, then came to a stop on his knees, katana raised before him.

I pulled off my Cadogan T-shirt, then stood at the edge of the mat.

He lifted his verdant gaze to me, and we stood there for a moment just watching each other.

Ethan shook his head. He rose to his feet, then moved toward me. "You have an audience, Sentinel," he said by way of warning, as if there'd been a risk of my taking him right here on the Sparring Room floor. I humphed. I'd said no to him before. I could do it again.

But that didn't mean I was thrilled to be on display again. I lifted my gaze to the balcony. It wasn't as bad as an "audience"— only a dozen or so vampires in the seats—but that was a dozen more than I needed. "Awesome," I muttered. I began to slip the katana from its scabbard, but he shook his head.

"No need to unsheath it. You won't need your sword."

I slid it home again, then looked at him in confusion. We were supposed to be picking up where Catcher and I left off. Since I clearly needed to work on my sparring technique, I had assumed that was where we'd pick up. Now I was just confused.

Ethan resheathed his own sword and placed it on the mat, then outstretched his hand. When I handed him my scabbard, he did the same to it. Then he stood again and tilted his head, gesturing to someone behind me. "Luc, if you please."

I hadn't realized Luc was in the room, so I turned around to say hello. But before I could find him, the lights went out— literally. The room was suddenly pitch-black.

"Ethan?"

"We're working on a different skill today," he said, his voice moving away.

I squeezed my eyes closed, hoping that would help me adjust to the darkness, then opened them again when I heard his footsteps move closer. Because I was a predator, my vision was better than it might have ordinarily been in the dark, but I still couldn't see much.

That was how he caught me with a low kick that sent me sprawling across the mats.

"Sullivan! What the hell?" From my new spot on the floor,

I blew the ponytail from my face and pushed up on my hands. I stood up, keeping my body bladed, my hands before me, my knees soft, in case he pounced again.

"You must learn, Sentinel, to anticipate."

I rolled my eyes. The first time I'd fought him, he'd used all the *Matrix* moves. Now he was working *Star Wars* for techniques. He really did not have an original training thought in his head.

"And how do I anticipate?" I asked him.

"We've discussed your senses having improved after you completed the change."

I didn't answer. I didn't know how good his vision was, but I wasn't going to give away my position and give him another easy shot. Still, I could hear him moving around me, slinking around in a circle like a big cat preparing to attack.

"You've been working over the last week to tune out the ambient noise. To manage the increased sensitivity in your hearing, your sight, your smell. Certainly, that much awareness can be a distraction. But you are vampire. You must learn to utilize all your senses, to use that noise, that information, to your advantage."

I heard the whip of his pants as he kicked. I ducked down just as the cotton whistled over my head.

Then I heard the pat of his feet when he touched down again.

"Good," he said. "But don't just defend. Fight back."

I heard him pace away. I rose again and assumed the basic defensive position again. If I became a member of the Red Guard, was this how Ethan and I would find ourselves? Battling each other under cover of darkness? Not quite enemies, but not quite friends? I'd been putting off my decision about the Red Guard. It was probably time to give that some thought. . . .

But not before I took this opportunity to kick his ass.

I heard him walk around me, circling again, waiting for his moment to strike. Could he hear as well as I could? Were the lights on for him, metaphorically, because he could detect my movements?

Well, either he could or he couldn't. It didn't matter; it was my turn to move. He circled counterclockwise, two or three feet behind me. I waited until he was at six o'clock, then shifted my weight, raised my left knee, and stuck out with a fierce back kick.

I might have hit him had he not completely anticipated the move and dropped down beneath my kick. By the time I'd made it around and brought down my kicking foot again, he was up and spinning out with a low roundhouse. I had no time to react, and just as he'd done the first time I challenged him, he knocked my feet right from under me.

I hit the mat again.

"Again," he said into the darkness.

I silently mouthed a curse, but I got up again. This time, I didn't wait for him to prepare. When I could hear him in front of me, I turned my hips and aimed a roundhouse kick at his head. I missed, but I heard him stumble backward, feet tripping across the mat as he dodged the move.

"So close," I murmured.

"Too close," he said back. "But that's better. You're listening for movement, which is good. But that's not all you can do. Luc," he said again, and my heart tripped a little, wondering what else he had in store. Binding my hands together? Flooding the room with water?

Luc answered back a second later, this time with sound. A cacophony of noise—barking, talking, screaming, honking, clanking, chirping—began to pour into the room. It was completely deafening, the bass loud enough that I felt the vibration in my bones, in my echoing heartbeat.

Ethan didn't even give me a moment to adjust. He punched, but he'd misestimated my location, and his fist glanced off my shoulder. Of course, he was still a Master vampire, and the strike still hurt. Had I been closer to him, he'd have broken bone. I wondered if the sound was distracting to him, too.

A second later, he was in my head.

You cannot rely only on sound, he said. *You must quiet the noise, be able to feel an enemy beside you, be able to fight even in utter darkness.*

How am I supposed to learn that? I asked back, shifting my weight from front to back as I waited for him to strike again.

You are a nocturnal predator, he said. *You don't need to learn* how. *You just need to learn to trust yourself.*

I was on my way there, I hoped.

I took a moment and closed my eyes. Technically, that was pointless, given the depth of the darkness in the room, but it helped psychologically, like I was actively working to shut out the din. My eyes closed, I focused on the noise and worked to build up my mental blockade.

But I didn't have time to get it done. He was on me again. This time, he punched forward not to injure me, but to taunt. His fist hit my left shoulder, but before I could throw him off, he was gone. Then his heel hit my back—not with enough force to knock me down, but with enough force to push me. I stumbled forward, arms waving as I tried not to trip over my own feet.

Thank God the lights were off. The Master vampire taunting the Novitiate would have been a pretty comical sight.

You're not concentrating, he silently said, his voice ringing over the clamor of honking trucks.

My skin was beginning to itch with irritation. It was loud, and it was dark, and I was being pushed and prodded by a Master vampire who relied on action flicks to teach me how to fight.

I'm doing the best I can, I assured him.

He kicked again, the back of his foot hitting my side. I parried my forearm against his leg, but he was gone and away without effective contact. I'd forgotten about his speed . . . the fact that he could move with supernatural efficiency. I was fast at the Katas, of course, but those were practiced moves. As we obviously knew, sparring was an altogether different kind of animal.

I've seen you do better, he answered.

A tingle of magic lifted in the air, maybe related to the teasing cant of his words. I felt that tingle—like a breeze in the air—across my face.

He was standing in front of me.

It took me a second to realize what I'd done—that I'd determined where he was standing with neither hearing nor sight . . . but with magic. Might as well take advantage.

I punched out, but he blocked me with his forearm. Before I could protest, he turned, and his back was to mine and his hand was on my arm and he was using his leverage to throw me to the ground.

And there I was, flat on my back again.

The fall hadn't been especially hard, but it was hard enough to take the wind out of me. When I could breathe again, I barked out a curse.

You're hardly trying, was his response. This time, there was venom in his voice.

I picked myself up off the ground. *I don't know what you want me to do.*

Then he was in front of me again. I struck out, but he grabbed my arm again and yanked me closer. *Fight, goddamnit.*

Too pissed off to consider the possibility that he'd baited me, I did just that. I rotated my wrists to grab his hand, then pushed his arm up at the elbow. I twisted, and then used my body weight to push him off balance and throw him down. I finished the move on his side on one knee.

Better, he said, flat on the ground, but there wasn't much time for celebration. Before I had a chance to react, he was up again, and he'd pulled me around and down on my back.

And then he was back in his favorite position—spread-eagle on top of me, his hands pinning my wrists to the floor.

I rolled my eyes in the darkness.

Ready to tap out? he asked.

I ignored the perk of physical interest and answered with action, lifting my left leg in a scissor kick and using inertia to reverse our positions. I managed to get on top of him, but I didn't stay there for long. He rolled me over again, and then I rolled him over again, and there we were, two vampires, rolling around on the floor like children. I was again glad the lights were out and we were out of view of the rest of the House. (Or so I assumed. Were they better than I at seeing in the dark? If not, they were getting a pretty crappy show.)

I finally managed to throw him off, then scrambled to my feet and felt the slight vibration in the mats as he bounced back onto his. We circled each other for a moment, but when I raised a hand to block a shot I was sure was headed toward my face, he grabbed my wrist, then yanked me toward him until my body was snug against the long line of his.

My heart tripped.

We stood there in darkness, my mind absorbed by the feel of one of his hands around my wrist, the other pressed to the small of my back.

Ethan was tall enough that the top of my head just reached his chin. I kept my gaze level with his collarbone—afraid that if I looked up, he'd use the move as an excuse to look down. Our lips would align, and that would be the end of me.

Slowly—treacherously slowly—he lowered his head, his lips against my hair. Goose bumps rose on my arms; my eyes drifted closed; my skin tingled with an intoxicating combination of lust and power. We were leaking magic again, the sharp, bright prickle of it filling the space Ethan and I occupied.

That was when my eyes flashed open, as I realized what he'd been trying to teach me.

He let me loose my hands, and I pressed one palm against his chest to push him back a few steps. He moved willingly and gave me space to learn.

I couldn't see in the dark, and I certainly couldn't hear with the din of noise around us . . . but just as I'd done a moment ago, I could sense the magic in the air. That punch hadn't been a fluke. Detecting magic was a different kind of sight, but it was a kind of sight just the same.

There, in the dark, a few steps in front of him, I lifted a hand and trailed my fingers over the electric currents around us, feeling the bumps and ridges of magic as it leaked from our bodies. I could sense the knotted mix of our magic in the space between us, and the slow fade of sensation the farther I drew my fingers away.

I let my fingers rise and fall as the pressure shifted, not unlike sticking a hand outside a moving car's window.

Most important, the current shifted as he moved, creating a breezy tingle beneath my fingers. I felt him move to my right, body straight as he faced me and then aimed a roundhouse kick at my face.

It was his favorite move, and he'd signaled it perfectly.

I dropped low, and as he came around I offered up my own roundhouse, a low kick that brought his other leg out from beneath him.

He hit the ground.

As if by his silent command, the music went off, and the lights came on. I blinked into the sudden vacuum of noise and the brightness of the overhead lights.

The room, the audience, was completely silent, probably absorbed by the sight of the Sentinel on her feet—and their Master on the ground.

I wouldn't call it a victory. After all, I only really tripped him.

But that was something. It wasn't everything, but it was a step forward.

Ethan put his hands behind him, then lifted his legs, rolled his body weight, and flipped onto his feet. He slid me a glance.

I swallowed, not entirely comfortable that I'd put my Master on the floor again, even if I had eventually come to learn the lesson he'd been trying to teach.

Then his expression softened.

"Better," he said.

I bowed respectfully, the student thanking the teacher for a lesson well taught. That lesson done, it was time to move on to the next crisis. "When do we leave for the pre-meeting?"

"In an hour. Get changed and meet me in the basement."

I nodded, then walked back to the edge of the mat and grabbed my T-shirt, shoes, and, most crucial, my katana. I assumed I was going to need it.

CHAPTER FIVE

BOYS' NIGHT OUT

"What do you wear if you're playing security for alpha shape-shifters?"

I stood in front of my open closet in a robe, but glanced back at Lindsey, who sat cross-legged on my bed, a bag of strawberry licorice sticks in her lap.

"Nothing at all?" she said with a grin.

"I'm wearing clothes."

"Spoilsport. But if you're going to play prude, might as well play sexy prude. Didn't you say Gabriel mentioned leather?"

The snark aside, she had a point. After all, I did own a set of buttery black leather that had been a gift from Mallory and Catcher for my twenty-eighth birthday—snug pants, bandeau-type corset, and trim, motorcycle-style jacket. It was a fabulous outfit, but it was so urban-fantasy book cover.

"Vampires in leather are so cliché," I said.

"I'm not disagreeing with you, but the shifters would appreciate it. They're all over leather."

"Yeah, I got that sense." But that much leather—and that

little torso coverage—wasn't my ideal fighting ensemble, so I flipped through some tank tops, looking for something that might replace the bandeau bra. On the other hand, leather pants and a tank top seemed a little too Linda Hamilton.

"Maybe a compromise," I murmured, pulling the leather jacket from its wooden hanger. I laid it on the bed along with my Cadogan suit pants and a simple black tank, then stepped back to take a look.

The jacket added a definite element of kick-assery to the slim-fit pants and tank. The outfit was still all business, but the kind of business that promised repercussions if the deal didn't go through. With a bloodred katana at my waist, and a gold Cadogan medal around my neck, I might be able to pull it off.

"Well," Lindsey said, "that's a Merit I can get behind. Try it on."

When I was dressed, I grabbed a black elastic from the top of my bureau and pulled my hair into a ponytail. Since I'd be with Ethan, I skipped clipping on my Cadogan pager, but I slid my cell phone into one pocket of my jacket and picked up my katana.

Outfit assembled, I spun around so Lindsey could get a look. She nodded and stood up. "Only one question—can you work that outfit? Can you *own* it?"

I glanced back at the mirror, took in the leather and sword, and smiled. "Why, yes. I believe I can."

I met Ethan in the basement beside the door that led to the underground parking garage. I had actually sashayed down the stairs, ready to stun Mr. Compliment into silence.

As luck would have it, I was the one surprised, because I hadn't been the only one to rethink my ensemble: Ethan apparently took Gabriel's "no Armani" instruction to heart. He came downstairs in *jeans*. Perfectly shaped jeans that fit his hips, then fell to cover dark boots. He'd paired them with a snug gray T-shirt that was practically molded to his chest. His golden hair was loose, framing cut cheekbones and killer green eyes.

I'm strong enough to admit it—I stared.

Ethan gave me a slow, eyebrow-arched perusal, masculine appreciation in his eyes. When he finally nodded, I assumed I'd passed the test.

"You're wearing *jeans*."

He glanced over at me with amusement, then typed numbers into the keypad beside the garage door. Ethan's sleek, black Mercedes convertible and a few other vehicles owned by higher-ranking vampires (i.e., not newbies like me) were parked inside.

"I am capable of dressing as the occasion requires."

"Apparently," I muttered, irritation in my voice. That was a childish emotion, sure, but the man wasn't supposed to look better than me. He was supposed to be awed by my new, sleek style.

Not that I cared what he thought, I lied to myself.

Ethan beeped his security system, then opened the passenger side door for me.

"So very gracious," I said as I climbed inside, arranging my katana inside the tiny coupe.

"I have my moments," he replied, his gaze on the garage around him, then shut the door behind me.

When he was equally ensconced, we drove up the ramp to

the security door, which lifted upon our approach, then headed out into the dark, summer night, zooming past the handful of paparazzi who stood at one corner of the lot, cameras at the ready. Since we were a captive group—nearly one-third of the vampires in the House returning to the roost before each sunrise—they hadn't yet bothered tracking us around when we left Hyde Park.

"Where exactly are we going?"

"A bar called Little Red," Ethan said. "Somewhere in the midst of Ukrainian Village." He nodded toward the GPS panel in the dashboard. It was already plotting our way toward the neighborhood, which was in a chunk of Chicago known as West Town.

"Little Red," I repeated. "What does that mean?"

"It's a reference to Little Red Riding Hood, I assume."

"So the shifters are wolves? Jeff said their shape had something to do with their power."

"They aren't all wolves. Each shifter transforms into one animal, and the animal runs in the family."

"So if one of the Brecks was a badger, all the Brecks would be badgers?"

Ethan snickered. "And given our experiences with Nick Breckenridge so far, I'd be happy to learn he was a badger."

Nick had been an unwilling participant in Peter's blackmail scheme. And in the process, he'd transformed from a former boyfriend of yours truly to a growly pain in the ass. "Badger" seemed entirely apropos. "Agreed."

"Unfortunately," Ethan said, "the families don't generally publicize their particular animals. So other than being on very, very good terms with a shifter, the only way for an outsider to know the animal is to see the shift. That said, one would presume the more powerful members of the Pack—Apex and the like—are predators. Bigger, badder, fiercer than the rest."

"So, wolves or grizzlies or something, rather than least weasels."

"Least weasels?"

"They're real," I confirmed. "I saw one in a nature center once. Tiny little guys. So Gabriel—what do we know about him?"

"The Keene family—Gabriel's father, great-uncle, grandfather, and so forth—have led the North American Central Pack for centuries. We've had independent confirmation they're wolves."

"Independent? Did that come from your secret vampire source?" My grandfather had representatives of three supernatural groups in his employ—Catcher for the sorcerers, Jeff for the shifters, and a third, secret vampire source who kept his profile low in order to keep from pissing off his Master. That anonymity notwithstanding, my grandfather sometimes shared the info he received with Ethan.

It had occurred to me that Malik, Ethan's second in command, might be the anonymous vampire. Malik knew everything that went on in the House, but usually kept to himself. He was intense, but seemed to be on the side of truth and justice. Providing secret, but crucial, information to the Ombud's office, information ultimately used to keep supernatural peace in Chicago, seemed right up his alley.

"Independent," Ethan said, "as in it didn't come from a vampire. I suppose we are throwing you to the wolves," he added after a moment, "although you're not exactly the type to go traipsing through the woods, basket in hand, to grandmother's house."

"No," I agreed, "I'm not. But I am the type to take the Volvo to my grandfather's office, bucket of chicken in hand."

"Sounds like a good trip."

"It was. You know I love food. And my grandfather. But not necessarily in that order."

Traffic wasn't bad as we moved north, but it still took twenty minutes to reach West Town. Ethan made himself comfy for the ride—one arm perched on the door, one on the steering wheel at three o'clock.

Eventually, we pulled off I-95 and into a neighborhood, then made a few more turns onto a commercial street of brick buildings that probably had its heyday in the 1960s. Now they sat largely empty but for a few industrial dry cleaners and international bakeries. At this time of night the street was empty of pedestrians . . . but plenty full of bikes.

The bikes, I guessed, were a marker for the Packs. In this case, it was a row of retro-looking cruisers—low, curvy motorcycles with lots of chrome and red leather—parked one beside the other, a dozen or so in all. They were lined up in front of a brick building that sat at the corner. A round, glowing white sign—like a full moon in the midst of Wicker Park—bore the words LITTLE RED across it in simple red letters.

"That must be it," I said as Ethan maneuvered the Mercedes into a parallel parking spot up the block. We emerged from the car and into the thump of rock 'n' roll music, which spilled onto the street when the door opened. A leather-clad man with a short beard and dark blond ponytail mounted one of the bikes, started the engine, and rode away.

"One fewer shifter we'll be able to get to know," I whispered to Ethan, who humphed in response.

We belted on our katanas, then walked down the block toward the door into the bar.

The bikes weren't the only indication that something different was going on in Ukrainian Village. When we reached the corner where the front door sat kitty-corner to the street, I spied a trio of gouges in the brick wall. I stopped and peered more closely, then lifted my fingertips to the brick. They were clean marks, long, evenly spaced, and deep into brick and mortar.

These weren't gouges, I realized. They were *clawmarks*.

"Ethan," I said, then gestured toward the scratches.

"It's a sign," he explained. "That this is a Pack place."

And here we were, vampires walking into their den.

But since we were here, and there was nothing to do but do it, I took the lead and pushed open the door.

The bar was one narrow room—a handful of tables in front of a large picture window, a long wooden bar along the other side. The hard-driving music was loud enough to bruise my eardrums, and I winced at the throb of it. The sound burst from a jukebox in a corner, that machine the only decoration that didn't involve advertisements for beer, whiskey, or Malört, Chicago's wickedly strong version of absinthe.

Men in leather jackets with NAC in giant, embroidered letters across the back sipped at the tables, somehow managing to chat over the roar of the jukebox. I assumed NAC stood for the North American Central Pack.

The hair on the back of my neck lifted. There was something unnerving about the place, about the tingle of magic that filled the room, as though the air itself was electrified.

The shifters looked up as we entered, their expressions not exactly welcoming. Apparently none too thrilled about the vampires in their midst, they stood and pushed back chairs. My heart raced, my hand moving to the handle of my katana, but the shifters headed for the front door. Within a matter of seconds, they were gone, leaving us in the middle of the bar, rock 'n' roll still pouring out around us.

Ethan and I exchanged a glance.

"Maybe the food's bad?" I wondered loudly, but that couldn't be the case. The bad vibe notwithstanding, the smells in the bar were fabulous. Under the top note of cigar smoke was something delicious—cabbage and braising meat, as if cabbage rolls were steaming in the back room. My stomach growled.

"Help you?"

We turned to face the bar. Behind it stood a heavyset woman, wearing a T-shirt with LITTLE RED and a cartoon girl in a red petticoat and hood emblazoned across the front. The woman's short, bottle-blond hair was teased above her head, and there was suspicion in her eyes.

This must have been Berna.

"Gabriel," Ethan, stepping beside me, said over the music, "asked us to meet him here."

One hand on the bar, one on her hip, the woman indicated a red leather door near the end of the bar. "Back," she half yelled, then arched an eyebrow as she looked me over. "Too thin. You need eats."

I'd only had a chance to open my mouth to respond—which, given the meat-and-veg smell of the place, would have involved a resounding "yes"—when Ethan smiled politely back at her.

"No, thank you," he called out.

She sniffed at Ethan's answer, but turned back to her well-shellacked bar and began to wipe it down with a wet rag.

Ethan headed for the red door.

So much for the cabbage rolls, I thought, but followed him.

Before he opened it, his hand on the tufted leather, he initiated the telepathic connection between us. *Sentinel?* he silently asked, checking in before we made the final plunge. I shook off the sudden, but refreshingly brief, vertigo. Maybe I was getting used to the sensation.

I'm ready, I told him, and in we went.

I was thankful the room was quieter than the rest of the bar, but the air was thick with old magic. I'm not sure I would have normally been able to separate new from old, but this felt different from the magic I'd felt around vampires or sorcerers. It was the difference between sun and moon. This was ancient magic; earthy magic; the magic of damp soil and sharp lightning, of grassy, windswept plains on cloudy days; the magic of dust and fur and musky dens and damp leaves. It wasn't unpleasant, but the sheer difference between this prickle and the magic I was used to unnerved me. It was also exponentially more powerful than the tingle I'd felt around the few shifters I knew.

Four men—four *shifters*—sat around an old-fashioned, vinyl-topped, aluminum-legged table. Four heads lifted when we walked in the door, including Gabriel Keene's. He gave me a once-over, then offered up a slow grin that lifted the corners of his mouth.

I guessed he liked the leather.

After looking me over, Gabe shifted his gaze to Ethan; his expression became businesslike.

I tried to keep my eyes on Gabriel in order to give the rest of the alphas time to check out the vampires who'd stepped onto their turf. But my occasional glimpses gave me basic details—all three had dark hair and the stiff shoulders of folks not thrilled to be in the back room of a bar in Ukrainian Village, vampires in their midst.

Finally, Gabriel nodded and gestured toward a wall that was empty but for a couple of small, cheaply framed movie posters. I followed Ethan over there and stood beside him. I wasn't expecting immediate trouble, but I gripped the handle of my katana with my left hand, rubbing my fingers across the leather cording, the friction somehow comforting.

I didn't have to wait long for action.

"The name of the game," Gabriel said, pulling a deck of cards from the middle of the table, "is five-card draw." He shuffled through the cards twice, then put the deck back on the table. The alpha to his right, who had short dark hair and a square jaw, the rest of his face hidden by aviator shades, leaned forward and knocked his knuckles against the deck.

With movements so smooth you'd have thought he was a professional, Gabriel began flicking cards to the others.

"We're here," he said, "because, barring objections, we're convening in two days. We're here to discuss ConPack."

The alpha at Gabriel's left, who slouched in his seat, had a few days of stubble on his face, narrowed brown eyes, and shoulder-length dark hair that was tucked behind his ears. He cast a suspicious gaze our way.

"In front of these two?" he asked. He gave Ethan a couple of seconds of derisive staring, then gave me a leering, up-and-down appraisal. A couple of months ago, I would have blushed a little, maybe looked away uncomfortably. Given that he was a shifter and, by the looks of him, a bully, I probably should have.

But even if my skills at fighting needed work, I was still a vampire, and bluffing was one of the first lessons Catcher had taught me. I knew how to give back the arrogance other sups threw at me.

Slowly, serenely, I arched a dark eyebrow back at him and raised the corners of my mouth into a not-quite smile. The look, I hoped, was equal parts vampire moxie and feminine wile. Whether he was intimidated, I didn't know, but he finally looked away. That was good enough for me.

Gabriel, his expression all nonchalance, picked up his pile of cards and fanned them in his hand. "You agreed to these arrangements, Tony, if you'll recall."

So the bully was Tony, head of the Great Northwestern Pack and the man who ruled the shifter retreat in Aurora.

"Bullshit," Tony coughed out in reply. He would have been handsome, but the chip on his shoulder tightened his features unflatteringly.

"My lieutenant," Tony continued, "agreed to the arrangements because that was the only way we could get a word in edgewise. You called the convocation, Keene. Not me, not Robin, not Jason. *You*. Speaking for myself, we don't want it." He shrugged. "The Bering Sea was pretty and blue when I left it. Things are fine in Aurora, and we're happy to keep them that way."

"It's your *job* to keep them that way," said the third man.

This is Jason, Ethan silently told me.

Jason was brutally handsome—green eyes, dark hair with just a little wave to it, killer cheekbones, curvy lips, the tiniest bit of a southern drawl in that honeyed voice. Altogether, it was a dangerous combination. "You're the protector of the keep."

"And that's exactly my point," Tony muttered, tossing a

couple of cards on the table with a flick of his wrist. "I am the protector of the keep. And when the time has come to retire to that keep, we do it. We don't convene to 'talk it over.' That is political, strategic bullshit." He glanced over at Ethan. "Vampire bullshit. All due respect, vampire."

"Ditto," Ethan said, a surprising amount of venom in his voice. I bit back a proud smile; he seemed to be adopting a little of my snark.

"Things in Chicago—," Gabriel began, but he was interrupted by Tony, who put out a hand.

"Things in Chicago don't concern us," Tony said. "There aren't any Packs in Chicago, and there's a damned good reason for that. Chicago isn't a shifter city."

Tony's animosity charged the air in the room, that prickle of magic now strong enough to lift the hair on my arms. I shifted uncomfortably, my lungs tight as the pressure in the room shifted, a magical side effect of the buildup of shifter tension.

"Chicago is a city of power," Gabriel said quietly, throwing a card onto the table, plucking a new card from the remainder pile, and adding that one to the fan of cards in his hand.

At least, that was all I saw him do, but those simple motions cut through the magic in the air. I sucked in a breath, the weight lifting from my chest. Apex, indeed.

"And that we don't have an official presence here," Gabe continued, "doesn't mean we won't be affected. Vamps are out. They're in the public eye, for better or worse, and we can't expect that humans will be satisfied with the notion that bleeders are the only supernaturals in the world."

"So that's your position?" asked Jason. "You're bringing us here to, what, get us to agree to announce ourselves?" He shook his head. "I won't do that. The vamps came out of the closet, and they got riots and Congressional hearings. We come out, and what do we get?"

"We get experimented on," said the fourth and final shifter, who must have been Robin, head of the Western Pack. He was the one with the dark sunglasses. "We get incarcerated in military facilities, shipped to God knows where so stratcom officers can figure out how to use us as weapons." He lifted a hand and flipped up his shades; I nearly flinched at the sight of his eyes—milky blue, staring blankly in our direction. Was he sightless?

"No, thank you," he quietly said, then lowered his sunglasses again. "Count me out, and count out the rest of the Western Pack. We aren't interested."

"I appreciate the fact that you've guessed my agenda and you're ready to vote," Gabriel said dryly. "But this isn't the convocation, and I haven't offered a resolution, so let's keep our fortune-telling to ourselves, shall we?"

There were humphs from the table, but no outright objections.

"What I want," Gabriel continued, "is to state the question and ask the Packs. That's my agenda. Do we stay and face the coming tide?" He glanced up and raised his gaze to Ethan. The two of them stared at each other, fear and power and anger combined in Gabriel's expression, the "coming tide" apparently vampire related. "Or do we leave now?"

"Which of those decisions is safer?" Tony asked.

"And which," Jason put in, "is more irresponsible?"

"Instability," said Robin. "Death. Warfare. And not among shifters. Not among the Packs. Vampire business is not our business. It never has been."

And there's the rub, Ethan silently told me. *Their unwillingness to step forward.*

No, their unwillingness to sacrifice themselves, their families, on our behalf, I corrected, but kept the thought to myself. It was a decision they'd made before, during the Second Clearing. And while I sympathized with the vampires who'd been lost, I understood the shifters' urge to protect themselves from the chaos. I'd leave it to the philosophers to decide whether what they'd done had been morally repugnant.

"The viability of this world is our business," Gabriel said. "The Packs are large. Social networks. Businesses. Financial interests weren't an issue two hundred years ago. But they arc now."

Tony put a card on the table with a decisive snap, then plucked a new one from the stack. "And how much of your friendly new attitude has to do with our sword-wearing buddies over there?" He looked at me, lip curled, hatred and a creepy kind of lust in his eyes. "Particularly the chick?"

Gabriel offered a low growl that made the hair at my neck stand on end. I gripped my katana tighter and glared back with menace I didn't have to feign.

"Because you are a guest in this city," Gabriel said, "I'm going to offer you an opportunity to apologize to Merit, to me, and to Tonya."

"Apologies," Tony threw out.

Gabriel rolled his eyes but, maybe in deference to Tony's status, let it pass. He glanced over at Robin. "Childishness aside, I hear your point, brother. I only bring the issue to the Packs. They'll decide as they will."

The room went silent. After a time, Robin nodded. Jason followed suit.

It was a long, quiet time before Tony spoke again. "When we convened in Tucson," he said, "we pledged to adhere to the rule of the Packs. To let the majority decide the fate of the others." He looked down at the table, shaking his head ruefully. "Damned if we thought the possibility of sending our sons and daughters into war was going to be the result of that decision."

When he looked up again, his eyes swirled with something deep and unfathomable. It was the same mystical revelation I'd seen in Gabriel's eyes when we'd first met, right before he made a cryptic remark about our intertwined futures. It was a visual expression, somehow, of a connection to the things he'd seen, the places he'd been, the lives he'd known . . . and lost.

I didn't know what he'd seen, or why his reaction was so strong. I knew what we were asking of shifters—Gabriel had explained it well enough the night before. And Gabriel had mentioned the rumblings of humans unhappy about the fanged among them. But there was a pretty big gap between complaints and violence, and we weren't there yet.

Regardless of the depth of his emotion, or how unwarranted his fear seemed today, he also seemed to understand the numbers were against him. Finally, he relented with a nod.

"We convene two nights hence," Gabriel concluded. "We'll offer a resolution to stay or return, and we'll let the cards fall where they may."

ConPack was a go, and so the game began again.

They played cards for nearly two hours, two nearly silent hours, in which their decisions to call or fold or raise were the only words spoken. Ethan and I stood behind them, one Master vampire and one newbie guard, watching four shape-shifters gamble in the seedy back room of a cabbagey bar.

"As we have agreed to the convocation," Gabriel said, his gaze on his cards as he interrupted the silence, "if the decision is made to stay in Chicago, it may be time to consider allying with one of the Houses."

I felt the sharp spike of magic around the room, and not all of it shifter. When I looked over at Ethan, his eyes were wide, lips parted. There was hope in his expression.

"There's never been an alliance between Pack and House," Jason said.

"Not formally," Gabriel agreed. "But as a colleague recently pointed out, the Houses didn't have the kinds of political and economic power they do now."

I stood a little straighter, realizing I'd been the colleague he was referring to.

Jason tilted his head to the side. "You're suggesting an alliance would actually benefit us, as opposed to just benefiting vamps?"

"I'm suggesting that if we stay, friends will be invaluable. I imagine the Houses would be willing to entertain that kind of notion." Gabriel glanced over at Ethan, who was trying very hard, I could tell, not to look overeager.

"No, you're suggesting we make some kind of permanent arrangement with *vampires*." Tony all but spit out the words, the magic around him turning peppery, vinegary, as if his fury changed its flavor.

"The world is changing," Gabriel countered. "If we don't keep up, we risk ending up like the pixies—creatures of dreams and fantasy and fairy tales. No one thought they'd come to that kind of end, did they? And in the end, running back to the forest didn't save them."

"We are not *fucking* pixies," Tony muttered. Apparently fed up with poker and vampire politics, he threw his cards down on the table, then stood up.

I tightened my grip on my katana, but Ethan nodded me back.

"Convocation is one thing," he said, punching a finger into the tabletop for emphasis. Anger swirled in his eyes like a freshly stoked fire. "But I'm not playing nice with vampires—I won't lose family—because you feel guilty about something that happened two hundred years ago, something none of us was involved in. Fuck that."

Tony clapped his hands together and threw them up like a dealer leaving his table. Then he disappeared out the red leather door, leaving it swinging angrily behind him.

CHAPTER SIX

THE ENEMY OF MY ENEMY IS MY . . . FRENEMY?

Tony might have walked out, but he left a wake of thick tension behind him. We all looked at Gabriel, waiting for direction.

"Let him go," he said, then began piling up the cards that Jason and Robin pitched onto the table. "He'll calm down."

"He usually does," Jason muttered, and I assumed this wasn't the first time Tony had thrown a temper tantrum. His concerns were understandable, the risks real. But dramatics weren't exactly helping.

"I don't know," Robin said, his shaded gaze on the door, "but this feels different."

The door opened again, and a man who had Gabriel's same sun-streaked hair and golden eyes looked in, one eyebrow arched in amusement. He wore a snug black T-shirt and jeans, his body long and lean. His shoulder-length hair was a shade blonder than Gabe's, but his week's worth of facial hair was a shade darker.

That difference aside, there was no mistaking the relationship. They both had deep-set eyes and brutally handsome faces, and he exuded the same aura of power and unadulterated maleness. This was a younger Keene, I guessed.

"Commotion, bro?" he asked.

"Drama," Gabriel replied, then glanced over at us. "Ethan, Merit, this is Adam. Adam, Ethan and Merit. Adam is the youngest of the Keene brothers."

"Youngest and by far the smoothest," Adam said, checking out Ethan and me in turn. When he got to me, I saw a flicker of interest in his eyes, the appreciation of trim leather and scabbarded steel. His gaze lifted, met mine, and I felt the same punch of power and history I'd gotten when I'd met Gabriel. But Adam's punch, maybe because he was younger, had a greener, rawer feel.

Regardless, it took me a moment to drag my gaze away from Adam Keene and those hypnotic golden eyes, and I got a look of chastisement in green ones when I finally managed it.

Well, chastisement or jealousy.

I arched an eyebrow back at Ethan, then turned to Gabriel. "Brothers?"

"I'm the oldest. Mom wanted a big family, and she thought it would be funny if we were named alphabetically. She made it all the way to baby Adam, here, before she learned better."

"Hello, baby Adam," I said.

He smiled, a deep dimple perking up at the left corner of his mouth. My stomach wobbled a little.

Oh, yeah. This one was dangerous.

"Down, boy," Gabe said. "If she's going to be taken in by a Keene, it's not going to be you." He glanced back at me and winked. If I hadn't seen him with his wife and would-be son and hadn't known he was happily married, I'd have thought he was flirting with me. As it was, I figured he was showing off for baby brother.

Without warning, Gabriel pushed back his chair and stood up, then walked to the red leather door. His expression was severe.

Confused, I looked at Ethan. *What's happening?* I silently asked him. He looked at the door for a moment and, for the first time since I'd known him, seemed unsure of the protocol.

But when the other shifters followed Gabriel back into the bar, Ethan followed. I stepped in line behind him.

We found the alphas and the baby brother at the bar's front window, their broad-shouldered backs to us, their gazes on the dark street outside. The bar was silent—the music now off— and their body language was tense, the magic in the air prickly and bated as if they were waiting for something to happen.

"Robin?" Gabriel asked, without turning to face him.

Robin shook his head. "I don't feel him. I don't feel anybody."

"I don't like this," Gabriel said. "Something's off. And it's too quiet out there."

"Sentinel," Ethan said, "do you sense anything?"

"What kind of anything?" I asked.

"The shifter who left," Gabriel said. "Do you sense him . . . waiting?"

I closed my eyes, and with some trepidation dropped my guard against the sounds and smells of the world. I immersed myself in a thick, warm blanket of sensation, of latent magic, of the heat and smell of nearby bodies.

But there was nothing unusual. Nothing out of the ordinary—assuming a bar full of very intense, magically leaking shifters was *in* the ordinary.

"Nothing," I said, opening my eyes again. "There's nothing unusual out there."

I spoke too soon. That was when I heard it—the rumble of exhaust pipes. The hair at the back of my neck stood on end, something in the air outside suddenly tripping my vampiric instincts, something that vibrated the air in a way that wasn't explained by the roar of the hog. A tang filled the air— the sharp, astringent burn of exhaust and something else . . . gunpowder?

Maybe because of that last dose of training, my mouth and body were moving before my brain had a chance to catch up.

"*Get down!*" I ordered, taking the necessary steps forward, my hands at their shoulders, pressing them down, and when they didn't budge, I yelled it again.

They hit the ground just as the hammer clicked outside, milliseconds before bullets shattered the glass in the picture window.

Adam had dropped on top of Gabriel, his arms a protective cocoon over Gabriel's head. Ethan had done the same thing to me. His body was over mine, his arms over my head, his lips at my ear. The contact made me shudder with desire, even as chaos broke out around us. And I wasn't thrilled about the role reversal; I was *his* guard, after all. I was supposed to protect him. But my rank as Sentinel didn't stop him from surrounding me with his body and from yelling, "*Be still!*" even as I struggled beneath him, trying to reverse our positions to keep him out of harm's way.

Be still, he silently repeated, as I huddled on the floor, enveloped by the feel and warmth and smell of him.

"What the fuck is this?" Gabe yelled out, his voice thick with fury, magic peppering the smoke-and-glass-filled air.

"Everyone behind the bar!" Jason said, glancing up, equal menace in his eyes. I'd only ever seen two shifters angry—Nick Breckenridge and his father, Michael. At the time, they'd been pissed at me and Ethan, thinking we'd leveled a threat against them. They'd been protecting family, a shifter instinct. Now I saw the same ferocity in Jason's eyes—the anger at being threatened, the need to protect family.

I nodded at Jason, pulled one of Ethan's hands into mine, and gave his body an instructional shove. "*Bar*," I yelled at him as bullets continued raining around us, a hailstorm of steel. The vicinity of it prickled my instincts further, making me want to fight and give chase—and not just because my Master, the one who'd made me, was in the line of fire.

No—I wanted to fight because I was a predator, two months past the first time I'd felt the tug of flight-or-fight. I'd tempered my steel with my own blood . . . and I was ready to feed that steel with someone else's.

Ethan maneuvered his body off mine, then let me tug him to his feet. We did a half run, half crawl to the bar, then dropped behind it, moving to the end to give the shifters room to join us. They crawled in behind, then turned to put their backs to the bar, whipping out weapons to respond to the cavalcade of bullets.

"Put the guns away!" Gabriel said over the din. "This is going to be enough of a police clusterfuck. We don't need our bullets being analyzed, too."

Guns were dutifully lowered, but cell phones quickly replaced them; calls were made, I assumed, to the alphas' respective Packs.

I turned back to Ethan, giving his body a once-over. *You're all right?* I silently asked him, then raised my gaze to his eyes.

They'd gone silver.

My stomach sank, my first thought that one of the shifters had been shot and Ethan was vamping out. There could hardly have been a worse time for biting.

But then he lifted a hand to my cheek, his silvered pupils tracking across my face, as if assuring himself that I was okay. *I'm fine*, I told him.

That was when Gabriel, on my other side, let out a string of curses. I immediately looked to the left and offered my own swear—Berna had just emerged from a door on the other side of the bar, shock in her expression.

"What in the sam—"

Someone called out, "Berna—get down! Go back!"

She looked toward us, but she was too surprised to process the order, even as bullets flew through the air.

Someone had to get to her.

Someone with *speed*.

I was up and moving before Ethan could stop me, vaulting over alphas on my way to her side. Bullets still rushed around us—the perpetrator well armed and apparently prepped for a prolonged assault—but I ignored them.

After all, I was immortal.

She was not.

I felt the tear of bullets as I ran toward her, knife-hot pain ripping through skin and muscle. There was panic in her eyes when I reached her, a cloud of astringent fear marking her spot in the bar. I'm sure my eyes had silvered—not from hunger, but from adrenaline—and the sight of it must have frightened her. But we needed to move, and I didn't have time for comforting.

I also had less than a second to make the decision whether

to move her back into the room she'd come from, or take her away to the bar.

I had no clue what—or whom else—that door led to. The kitchen? The back exit? If so, a secondary assault on the building?

No, thanks. I opted for the bar and the devils I already knew. I put myself between Berna's body and the window, then used the speed and strength I'd been gifted with to half run, half tow her back to the bar.

When we were tucked behind the barricade, I situated her in the corner, which I thought offered the most protection from still-flying bullets.

She looked up at me, her face pale, but her expression just this side of pissed off. Blood blossomed across her shoulder. "Shots!" she said, jerking her chin toward her wound. "At me!"

I ignored the internal prick of interest, the sudden pang of hunger that tightened my stomach. This wasn't just blood—it was shifter blood. Like the difference between tomato juice and a Bloody Mary, the smell carried an extra tang of something—something animal.

Something intoxicating.

I shook my head to clear the thought. Now was definitely not the time. . . .

Focusing on the task at hand, I pulled the T-shirt away from her shoulder and found a gouge at the edge of her collarbone. She was bleeding and the skin was torn, but it didn't look like the bullet had actually penetrated.

"I think it just grazed your shoulder," I told her.

"*Meh*," she said. "Flesh wound."

I looked around the shelves beneath the bar, then grabbed

a stack of folded white towels. I pulled off one towel from the wad, lifted her arm (and got a *hiss* of pain for my effort) and pressed the rest of the stack to the gash. I used the loose towel to hold the make-do bandage around her arm, pulling it tight enough to keep pressure on her wound, but not so tight that I cut off her circulation. She was a waitress, after all; she was probably going to need that arm.

"I've seen worse," she petulantly said, but sat still while I knotted the ends.

"I don't care," I told her, then pointed a finger in her face when she opened her mouth to retort. "You're bleeding, and I have fangs. Don't push me."

She snapped her mouth closed with an audible *click*.

I sat down again, the sting of the shots I'd taken now beginning to echo through my body as the world began to slow again.

Before I could blink, Ethan was in front of me, checking my body for wounds. I heard the *plink* of metal on the floor beside me and looked down. A bullet rolled across the floor, its end flattened. There was a corresponding hole in the thigh of my pants, the skin beneath it bloodstained, but healthy and pink. Score one for quick-speed vampire healing.

I looked up again and found Ethan's eyes on me, another bullet in his open palm. From the sting in my shoulder blade, I assumed that was where I'd taken a second hit.

You could have been killed.

Doubtful. But she could have.

He looked at me for a moment, concern in his eyes. And then, finally, his expression shifted. Instead of fear, there was pride. My move to help Berna might have scared him, but he was proud I'd made it.

Of course, he'd played the hero, too. *Thanks for covering me at the window*, I told him.

He nodded, a blush creeping across his perfectly sculpted cheekbones. I gnawed the edge of my lip, the protectiveness in his eyes curling something deep in my abdomen. He didn't speak, but he nodded, as if admitting the emotion in his eyes.

And I had no clue what to do with it.

Heavy seconds passed before I turned back to the shifters. Adam and Robin still had weapons in hand, but they'd obeyed Gabriel's order not to fire back. Jason, on hands and knees, was crawling toward the far door, maybe to find out if it offered us an exit.

Adrenaline giving way to fear, that idea was suddenly very appealing. Sure, the shooter was outside and we were tucked behind a solid oak bar. But what was to stop him from deciding he wanted a little one-on-one contact, and rushing the bar? Yes, I'd proven I could play the strong Sentinel when necessary, but the thought of being rescued sure seemed attractive right now.

I thought about Noah's offer and the fact that I'd have a partner in Jonah if I consented to joining the Red Guard. Having backup certainly would have come in handy, although I doubted the shifters would appreciate an underground vampire army's being called in to deal with their problems.

Luckily, I was saved the necessity of giving Noah's offer more thought—the shooting suddenly stopped, and the low growl of a bike let us know the shooter was retreating.

Silence fell . . . at least until the cursing began.

Adam popped up first, his gaze scanning the bar front and street outside. "Clear," he said, and the rest of us followed. I helped Berna to her feet, preparing her for a trip in the ambulance that was beginning to whine its way down the street, undoubtedly called by someone in the neighborhood who'd heard the barrage of shots.

I was almost embarrassed to look at Ethan, the thing that had passed between us in the midst of the attack too personal to acknowledge in front of strangers. Despite our positions, he'd thrown his body over mine with no hesitation, inserting himself between me and danger. And then there was the look in his eyes. It seemed unlikely I was the target of the drive-by, but that didn't make his effort any less meaningful than the last time he'd come to my rescue—the night I'd been attacked and made a vampire.

His bravery notwithstanding, now things just seemed awkward, like we were teenagers who'd suddenly become aware of their attraction to each other.

Ethan finally glanced back at me, his gaze emotionless, his expression flat. He'd turned off the emotion, so I adopted the same Master vampire look and nodded back at him, a quick, efficient gesture that said nothing of the thing that had passed between us. Denial seemed the easiest response.

"I'm assuming," Ethan said aloud, turning back to the shifters, "that one of you was the target of that hit?"

"All signs point to Gabriel," Jason said, arms over his chest as he looked across the destruction in the bar. "This ConPack was his idea."

I understood the ruefulness in his voice. The bar was in shambles. There was nothing left of the picture window but the few jagged scraps of glass that remained in the frame; the rest of it was in piles on the checked tile, scattered amidst the remains of the bar's neon signs and shredded beer posters. A breeze swept through the gaping hole in the front of the bar, carrying the scents of hot metal and gunpowder and the sounds of sirens as they hurried toward us.

"There are three Pack leaders in here," Adam pointed out, "not just the leader of the North American Central. The target could have been any one of you."

"Valid point," Gabriel said.

Adam leaned toward me. "By the way, you did good. I'm not sure Sullivan gives you enough credit."

I appreciated the compliment. I'd have appreciated it more if it had been accompanied by a pan of cabbage rolls, but a girl took what a girl could get. I grinned at him beneath my fan of bangs. "I know. I'm kind of a big deal."

He snorted with amusement.

"One Pack leader is noticeably absent from the group," Ethan said. "And the manner of the hit—that we heard a bike before and after—suggests it was a shifter."

"Tony was riled up when he arrived," Robin put in.

There was silence at that suggestion.

Jason finally shook his head. "Tony isn't that stupid. Not to attempt a hit right after storming out of the room. Besides," he added, as three police cars pulled to a stop outside the bar, "this only creates more drama. Draws more attention to the Packs." Car doors slammed as police burst from the vehicles, hands on their holsters.

More attention, I thought. Just the thing the shifters wanted to avoid. And maybe that attention was the shooter's motivation? "Would more drama and attention make the Packs more interested in leaving for Aurora? To stay out of the public eye, I mean?"

Heads turned my way.

"That's not a bad thought," Gabriel said. "It would be a

ridiculous plan, if that's what the shooter had in mind, but a good thought." He dropped his voice to a low whisper. "Since we're all about to be interviewed, let's keep the supernatural drama and the complicated lies to a minimum, shall we? Skip the biological details but spill the rest. We were playing poker and planning a family reunion. We wrap up the game and our meeting, and the next thing you know . . ."

The next thing you know, Chicago's finest walk in the door.

They took statements from all of us, four uniforms and a couple of plainclothes detectives, walking us through the details of the drive-by as a forensic team plucked through glass and kindling for bullets or other evidence that might lead them to the shooter. I kept to the basics Gabriel had laid out—telling the tale exactly as it had progressed, but leaving out the bit about why the shifters really planned to meet.

The cops generally seemed to buy it. They were probably curious about why two vamps were in Ukrainian Village, katanas belted to their sides, at a meeting of folks who were planning a family reunion. But they knew who I was—whether because I was Chuck Merit's granddaughter or Joshua Merit's daughter, I wasn't sure—so they kept the intrusive questions to a minimum. I played innocent (which, of course, I actually was), and they seemed satisfied enough by my answers.

After we were interviewed, Ethan and I stood outside on the sidewalk, loath to walk away and leave the shifters alone, but not interested in being charged with interfering in a police investigation. We were still outside when a familiar Oldsmobile pulled up.

"We've got company," I said, nodding toward the car, a smile blossoming on my face.

My grandfather emerged from the driver's side; his right-hand man, Catcher Bell, stayed in the front seat, a cell phone pressed to his ear. Catcher was twenty-nine and a little rough around the edges, but that gruffness actually enhanced his appeal. His head was shaved, his eyes pale green, his body a slab of tight muscle and the occasional tattoo—including a circle cut into quadrants across his abdomen.

Jeff emerged from the backseat. He was dressed in his usual emsemble—a long-sleeved button-up shirt with the sleeves rolled up midforearm and a pair of khaki pants. Jeff was twenty-one and, to the unfamiliar, would have seemed to have the sweet bashfulness of a boy with a very big heart . . . but not a lot of worldly experience.

That assumption would be wildly incorrect. Jeff was a shifter who had a way with the ladies and was rumored, at least by Catcher, to be more than capable of taking care of himself. I took Catcher's word for it.

Jeff ambled over. He smiled at me, then nudged me with a shoulder. "How's my favorite vampire?"

"She likes being someone's favorite, especially on days she gets shot."

"You got shot? How? Where? Are you okay?" He put his hands on my arms and began looking me over. His eyes widened at the hole in my jacket where the bullet had penetrated. "You have to be more careful."

I happened to glance up and catch the smile on Ethan's face; he was clearly enjoying this. I gave him an arch look, but removed Jeff's hands, then pressed a light kiss to his cheek. "I'm fine. Let's worry about your people today. What the hell happened here? I thought the Packs were supposed to be big happy families?"

His expression went unusually serious. "That's exactly what I'm about to find out." Without another word, he turned on his heel and walked toward the bar's front door. The two shifters who stood outside keeping watch moved aside to let him in, both nodding their heads respectfully as he passed.

The kid was definitely a wonder.

"Fancy meeting you here," my grandfather said, offering me a smile before offering a hand to Ethan, who took it, then shook.

"Mr. Merit," Ethan said.

"Chuck, please, Ethan," my grandfather said. "Mr. Merit was my father." He looked at me again, and his expression turned to worry.

"You got shot?"

"A couple of times, as it turns out. They aren't lying about the immortality thing."

He blew out a breath of relief, then leaned forward and pressed his lips to my forehead. "I worry about you."

"I know. I take care." *At least as much as possible*, I silently added. I cast a sly glance at Ethan. And even when I didn't take as much care as I might, I had a vampire in the wings, ready to take a shot on my behalf.

I wasn't sure if that thought was comforting or not.

"You'd better," my grandfather said, then pulled back.

"Everybody is fine except for the bartender," Ethan explained. "She took a shot in the shoulder, but it looks like it was a through-and-through. Merit played EMT. She did good."

My grandfather huffed out a breath. "Of course she did

good. She's my granddaughter." He took a step forward and lowered his voice. "It appears you've gotten yourselves involved in another shifter controversy. Word is, you're doing a favor for Gabriel?"

Ethan nodded. "He asked that we be a presence at this meeting and the convocation."

My grandfather's caterpillar eyebrows lifted in surprise. "So they are convening, then?"

"They managed to reach an agreement," Ethan said. "At least before the chaos set in."

"Not that the chaos is to anyone's surprise," said a voice behind us. I turned and found Catcher frowning at the bar and slipping a cell phone into his pocket. I guessed he'd finished up his call. In addition to his snarky personality, Catcher was a connoisseur of snarky T-shirts. True to his style, today he wore jeans and a black tee that read IT'S NOT ME; IT'S YOU.

"Ethan. Merit," he said, without looking at us. "Attempted hit?"

"That's how it plays for now," Ethan said, then tilted his head at my grandfather. "Given that the city isn't aware of Gabriel's biology or the Pack's, I assume you're here because we're here?"

"The administration knows about shifters," my grandfather explained, "but there's no need to stretch the publicity further than they're comfortable with. Vampires were involved. That means I'm involved. We'll do what we need to do to ensure the CPD has the information they need, without revealing information Mayor Tate doesn't think they need to know." Although Tate knew we existed—vampires and shifters alike—he was standoffish when it came to actually dealing with the Houses.

"He's keeping the biology hush-hush?" I asked.

My grandfather nodded philosophically. "He's keeping the men and women of this city safely at home, and not out on the streets rioting because they've discovered more strangers in their midst." Since Celina's announcement of the vampires' existence had initially led to riots and chaos, I understood his point.

Catcher bobbed his head toward the bar. "Why the hit?"

"Political rivalry," Ethan offered. "There seems to be some strain between the American leaders about whether to stay in Chicago—"

"Or bail," I finished for him.

"The alphas don't seem thrilled about the prospect of staying, of not heading back to Alaska. I know you aren't investigators," Ethan added, "but there's a possibility Tony Marino, head of the Great Northwestern, was the source of the violence. He left in a fit, and the shots were fired by someone on a bike minutes later. Not strong evidence, but maybe it's something to look into."

My grandfather nodded. "We'll get on it. I'm not sure what we'll find in the ether, but we'll see."

I wondered if Noah or the RG had information that my grandfather didn't have access to. Would it pay to join the RG, to increase my access to information about the Houses on a national scale?

"Did Keene give you any details about the security work he wanted to talk to you about?" Catcher asked.

"Merit and I *are* the security arrangement, as it turns out. He wanted us here tonight, obviously, and he wants us at the convocation on Friday." Ethan frowned. "But if shifters are willing to take shots at him under cover of darkness, I'm not sure there's a lot we can do beyond minimizing the collateral damage."

"I assume the bartender was some of that collateral damage?" my grandfather asked.

"I think it's a safe assumption the bullets weren't intended for her," Ethan confirmed.

The debriefing accomplished, my grandfather headed for the bar. I shifted my gaze to Catcher. He and I had things to discuss, so before he walked away, I touched his arm. He glanced back, his eyebrows raised in question.

"How's Mal doing?" I asked him, but my silent questions were much different: *Has she said anything about me? Mentioned me? Does she miss me?*

"Why don't you call her and ask her yourself?"

I gave him a flat stare. "The phone works both ways," I pointed out. Besides, she's the one who'd pushed me about Ethan, and who'd thrown my "Daddy issues" into my face. It might have been immature to avoid making the call, but she had as much to answer for as I did.

Catcher rolled his eyes haggardly. "She misses you, okay? My life will be much, much simpler when you two make up."

God bless him for being confident that would happen.

"How's her training proceeding?" Ethan asked.

Despite Catcher's unpleasant relationship with the Order, the governing body for sorcerers and sorceresses and Mallory's new bosses, his face blossomed into a proud grin. "Excellent. She's kicking ass."

"Of course she is," I said, and when my grandfather glanced back from the door of the bar, gave Catcher's arm a little shove. "Go play with Chuck."

"Going," he said. "And remember what I said. Do the right thing, Merit. Call her, even if it's awkward."

I had no doubt it needed to be done. Unfortunately, I also had no doubt it would be awkward. I was never great on the phone, and as much as I missed my girl and didn't want my fangs and her magic to come between us, it still wasn't a call I was ready to make.

Some days it didn't pay to be a grown-up.

It was thirty more minutes before the extra police cruisers began to pull away from the curb, and ten more before Jeff, Catcher, and my grandfather emerged from the bar, leaving the shifters behind them.

"What's the good word?" I asked when they approached.

My grandfather shook his head. "Gabriel doesn't think Tony is capable of this."

"Is he being objective?" Ethan asked.

Catcher shrugged. "Hard to say, but he does know Tony better than the rest of us."

"It doesn't read like an assassination on Gabriel," Jeff said, his delicate features pulled into serious concentration. "The shots were at the bar, not any particular shifter. The shooter could have attempted to push his way inside, used a rifle, tried a sniperlike approach." He frowned. "This reads more like a message—an attack against the Packs or the meeting, not Gabriel specifically."

"The forensics folks will process the bullets," my grandfather said. "Maybe they'll find some trace, figure out the target and the perpetrator."

"I, for one, would feel a lot better knowing the crazy shifter shooter was off the streets," Jeff said, stuffing his hands into his pockets. But then he looked at me, a glint in his eyes. "Unless someone was willing to offer up some one-on-one protection?"

"Keep dreaming," I said, but patted his shoulder cordially.

"Come on, Casanova," Catcher said, steering him toward the car. "Let's go use that hard drive you reformed."

"Reformatted."

"Whatever."

We made our goodbyes, and my grandfather followed Catcher and a sheepish Jeff back to the Olds and their South Side office.

The remaining shifters—Gabriel, Adam, Jason, Robin, and a handful of blondish men I assumed to be more alphabetically named Keene siblings—walked outside and congregated near the door. A delivery truck pulled up to the curb, and two more men hopped out, then began lifting flats of particle board to place over the broken window. While the other brothers began to order and direct the repairmen, Gabriel, Adam, and the other Pack leaders walked over to where we stood.

"We appreciate your discretion tonight," Gabriel said.

"It is the better part of valor," I pointed out.

Ethan rolled his eyes. "Vampires no longer have the luxury of discretion, but I understand the need. Will you be able to keep the convocation under wraps after this?"

"I'm not worried about it. We'll get in, we'll meet, we'll get out, and we'll disperse back to our respective territories."

"And whose territory is Chicago?" Ethan asked, his head tilted to the side. "You said Chicago was a city of power. Whose power?"

Gabriel shook his head. "You don't want to know the answer to that one, vampire. While we're waiting for the conference, we'll focus on the investigation here."

"And until then?" Ethan asked, then glanced around between the men. "Do you all have security you're comfortable with?"

Gabriel nodded. "I'm not worried about the day-to-day; it's the en masse meeting of Pack members that has me concerned. Are you still up for working the convocation, given the drama?"

Ethan considered the idea. "What are the odds that I'm putting myself and my Sentinel right into the line of fire?"

Gabriel barked out a laugh. "Given what we've seen so far, I'd guess one hundred percent." He leaned in toward me. "Pack whatever steel you can find, Kitten. You'll probably need the arsenal."

"Do you have a final location?" Ethan asked.

"Same neighborhood, but we're finalizing the details." His voice flattened as he glanced back at what was left of the bar. He checked his watch. "It's two thirty now. Let me clean up things here, and I'll give you a call before dawn."

Ethan nodded, then extended a hand to Gabriel. "We'll wait for your call, and we'll be prepared for the worst on Friday."

Gabe barked out a laugh as they shook on it. "You are ever the vampire, Sullivan. Ever the vampire."

"What else would I be?" Ethan mused aloud.

The deal struck, we turned to get into Ethan's car.

"By the way," Ethan said when the car's motor was humming, "I like the jacket."

The awkwardness that had seemed to exist between us earlier faded in the close confines of the car. Maybe because he liked the jacket, maybe because I had to miss out on Berna's cabbage rolls, he let me call Saul's, my favorite Wicker Park pizza stop, to order up a Chicago-style to go. He pulled up to the curb, and I came out fifteen minutes later with an extra-large "Saul's Best"—three inches of crust, cheese, meat, and sauce (in that order). Ethan, surely, would scoff at the grease, but it was perfect to satisfy a vampire's late-night, post-drive-by hunger. Or so I figured, this being my first drive-by.

When I returned to the car, Ethan was on his phone. The phone was on speaker mode, so I listened as he filled in Luc and Malik about the night's events, the upcoming phone call with Gabe, and our new Friday night plans.

I got an arched eyebrow when I slid in, pizza box on my lap, probably at the size of the behemoth. It steamed the knees of my suit pants, no doubt leaving a disk of grease in the process. Good thing I had a couple of backup pairs. I didn't think Ethan would approve of a grease-stained Sentinel.

When his call was done, and my stomach was rumbling loud enough to fill the car with sound, we began the trek back to Hyde Park.

"It's been a long night," he said. "Assuming you're willing to set aside a piece or two of that for me, we'll camp in my rooms and wait for Gabriel to call."

Since I'd been in his apartments the day before—and since I had seven or eight pounds of Saul's Best on my lap—I didn't give that invitation the kind of clearheaded thought it deserved. And it did make sense to think that we would relax over pizza in Ethan's quarters while waiting for Gabriel's follow-up call, mulling the night's events and considering strategy for the convocation and pre-meeting.

Well.

I was half right.

CHAPTER SEVEN

LOVE THE ONE YOU'RE WITH

"Pit stop," Ethan said when we'd arrived back at the House and made our way to the main floor. We walked back through the hall toward the cafeteria, but stopped at a door on the right-hand wall. Ethan pushed through it, and I followed him into a gleaming stainless-steel kitchen. A handful of vampires in tidy white jackets and those ballooning chef's pants chopped and mixed at various stations.

"Now, this is the kind of kitchen a Novitiate vampire deserves," I approvingly said, taking in the sights and sounds and smells.

"Margot?" Ethan asked aloud. One of the chefs smiled back at him, said something in French, and pointed farther into the kitchen. Ethan bobbed his head at her, took the pizza box from my hand, and started down the aisle between the chefs' stations. He said hello to the men and women along the way; since I didn't know any of them, I offered polite smiles as I passed.

I also didn't know Ethan spoke French.

But I did, of course, know Margot. She sat on a stool beside a giant slab of marble, watching as a young man with dark hair rolled out dough on the floured marble.

"Watch your pressure," she said before lifting her gaze and smiling at Ethan.

"Liege," she said, hopping off her stool. "What brings you and"—she slid her gaze my way, measuring whom Ethan had brought into her lair, then offered me a sly smile—"Merit to my neck of the mansion?"

Ethan placed the pizza box on a clean spot of counter. "Merit and I will be waiting on a call in my rooms. Could you arrange this and deliver it upstairs with some plates and silverware?"

She arched a curious eyebrow, then lifted the pizza box, her lips twisting into a smile. "Saul's Best," she said fondly, one hand over her heart. "He got me through culinary school. And given our culinary history to date, I'm assuming, Liege, that our Sentinel had some input on this choice?"

"It's not my usual fare," he agreed.

Margot winked at me. "In that case, excellent choice, Merit."

I smiled back.

Margot closed the box again, then clapped her hands together. "Well, let's get this going. Something to drink, Liege? You still haven't opened the bottle of Château Mouton Rothschild you picked up in Paris."

Being a Merit, and having been raised by my father to appreciate the difference between Cabernet and Riesling, I knew she was talking about high-dollar wine . . . and pairing it with junk food. "You want to drink a Mouton Rothschild with pizza?"

Ethan looked amused. "I'm surprised at you, Sentinel. Given your diet, I'd have thought you'd appreciate the combination. And we are in Chicago, after all. What better to drink with Chicago's finest than something nice from France?"

A girl couldn't argue with logic like that.

"The Rothschild is fine," Ethan said, putting his hand at my back to turn me toward the door again. "Mcrit is hungry, so all due haste would be appreciated."

Since he was right, I spared him a sarcastic retort, but I couldn't stop myself from glancing back to check Margot's expression. It didn't look good: arched eyebrow, crossed arms, and much-too-curious stare.

I was *so* going to hear about this later.

The lights were already on in his apartments, soft music playing, and, despite the season, a golden glow emanating from the fireplace in the corner. It looked like his room had been prepared by staff members for his return. Apparently Master vampires got sunrise turndown service.

I sat my scabbard carefully on a side table.

"Make yourself at home," Ethan said, "such as it is." He slipped off his jacket, flipped it around like a matador's cape, and placed it carefully on the back of a desk chair.

When he plucked his PDA off the desktop and began to thumb through it, I took the opportunity to give the room another perusal. It was, after all, a record of Ethan's four-hundred-year existence. If the *stuff* didn't give some clue to the puzzle that was Ethan Sullivan, I wasn't sure what would.

Hands behind my back, I walked to the wall opposite the Fabergé egg, where an embroidered heraldic crest was mounted in a cherrywood frame. The crest bore an oak tree with red acorns, a symbol I'd seen before.

I pointed to it, then glanced back at him. Ethan stood with one hand on the back of the chair, his BlackBerry in the other.

"This is the same crest that's on the shield in the Sparring Room?"

He glanced up, nodded, and turned back to his PDA. "It's my family crest. From Sweden."

"What was your name?" I asked. Morgan had once told me that vampires switched identities every sixty or so years in order to keep from arousing too much human suspicion when they failed to age like their friends and families. "Ethan Sullivan" was his current name, but I assumed he hadn't been born to that name—not in Sweden nearly four hundred years ago.

"My family name was Andresen," he said, thumbs clicking at the keys. "I was born Jakob Andresen."

"Siblings?"

He smiled wistfully. "Three sisters—Elisa, Annika, and Berit—although I was often away from them. I was in the army—a man-at-arms before our lieutenant asked me to run an errand. When I came back, information about our opponents' positions in hand, he promoted me."

Apparently done with his messages, Ethan placed the PDA on the desktop, slid his hands into his pockets, and glanced up at me. "I was an artillery captain when my time came."

Ethan wasn't usually this talkative about his past, so I crossed my arms over my chest and gave him my full attention. "When you were killed?"

"When I was *changed*," he corrected. He gestured toward a spot at the crux of his left shoulder and neck. "An arrow at dusk. Night fell, and the vampires emerged, stripping the battlefield of blood, including my own. It was easy to come by on a battlefield, of course, not that they were particular. Vampires were different then, closer to animal than human. They were roaming bands of scavengers, taking what blood they could find. Within that band, that first band, there was a leader. Balthasar. He'd been watching the camps, knew my position, decided I'd know enough about war, about strategy, to be an asset to the rest of them."

So in a way our changes had been similar. Ethan, changed in the midst of war, the victim of an attack. The change, although giving him life after a certain death, undertaken without his consent. Pulled into a corps of vampires to be a warrior, to offer his strategic services. Me, changed in the midst of Celina's battle for notoriety, the victim of her staged attack. Changed by Ethan to save my life, without my consent. Brought into Cadogan House to be a warrior, a soldier protecting the House.

When I began the genetic change from human to vampire, he'd drugged me. He said he didn't want me to have to experience the pain of the transition since it wasn't a transition I'd asked for.

Maybe I now knew why.

Ethan paused, his gaze on the floor, his eyes tracking as he recalled some ancient memory. "When I arose after the change, I imagined myself a monster, something unholy. I couldn't go home, couldn't bring that home to my family. Not like I was. Not like that. So I joined Balthasar and his band, and we traveled together for a decade."

"What happened after that?"

"An enterprising young vampire—a vampire Balthasar had made—decided that the band would be better under his authority. And that was the end of my relationship with those particular vampires. After that, I traveled. Wars were common in those years, and I had knowledge about strategy, skills. I joined a battalion here and there, traveled south until I found a peaceful bit of earth to call my own. I lived off the land. Learned to read and write. Tried to build a new life and not attract too much human attention."

My voice soft, I asked, "Did you ever marry?"

"No," he said, shaking his head. "No. As a soldier, I didn't feel I had the luxury of keeping a family at home." He smiled wistfully. "My sisters were children enough for me. I was a coward, I suppose, that I didn't go back to them, didn't give them a chance to accept what I'd become. But that was a much different time, and I'd have been returning home a demon. A true monster. I couldn't bring myself to do it."

"When did you join the House?"

"Many, many years after I left Sweden, I met Peter. He founded Cadogan House, and I joined him in Wales. And when he was gone, I became Master. I moved the House here to Chicago"—he spread his arms, gesturing to the mansion around him—"and here we are."

"And here we are," I agreed. I knew that wasn't all of his history. But I knew enough about some of the more scandalous recent parts—his affair with Amber; his relationship with Lacey Sheridan, a former Cadogan guard turned Sheridan House Master—not to ask more than I'd probably want to know.

"A suggestion, Sentinel," he said. "Write down the things you wish to remember, and keep those records close. Secured. It's surprising how much you forget as the years go on." With that advice, he pushed off the desk and walked toward me. He stopped just in front of me, our toes close enough to touch, and just . . . stood there. My heart began to pound as I waited for action—a touch or kiss—some end to the anticipation that lifted goose bumps on my arms.

I opted to end the tension myself. "You shouldn't have shielded me when the shots were fired."

He offered me an imperious look.

"Ethan, it's my job. I'm supposed to protect you, not the other way around. Luc would have put my head on a pike if you'd taken a hit."

"How do you know I didn't?"

I opened my mouth, then closed it again. "Did you?"

His eyes went to sultry slits. "Do you want to look and see?"

"Not especially." Liar, liar, pants on fire.

Ethan arched an eyebrow and began to lean in. . . . Then he reached around to pluck something from the table behind me. When he pulled back, folder in hand, I rolled my eyes at my reaction. The man just *unbalanced* me.

He opened the file and began to peruse it, pacing across the floor as he considered its contents. I blew out a breath, relaxing incrementally at the realization that however he might flirt, we really were here on business. Whatever the attraction between us, he was first and foremost a leader of vampires.

A knock sounded at the door.

"Come in," Ethan said without glancing up.

The doors opened, but with considerably less fanfare than the last time food had been delivered. After giving me a devilish look, Margot wheeled in a cart sans steel covers. The pizza had been mounted on a footed platter, an army's worth of supplies around it: red chili flakes; grated parmesan cheese; small glass bottles of water; napkins; silverware; wineglasses; and, of course, the wine.

Ethan looked it over. "You did a respectable job of finding dinner this time, Sentinel."

I put my hands on my hips and looked over the tray and the plateau of pizza. "Well," I said, "even a born-and-bred Chicagoan needs a break from red hots and double cheeseburgers now and again."

"More's the pity," Margot snickered, and I smiled. I had a pretty good sense that I was going to like that girl. And then I was distracted by chocolate.

I pointed at two three-leveled stacks of it in varying shades of brown. "Chocolate cakes?"

"Chocolate mousse cakes," Margot corrected. "A chocolate genoise bottom, topped by layers of milk chocolate mousse and ganache. We're training a new pastry chef, and he wanted to practice his mousse-making skills." She glanced at Ethan expectantly. "Anything else I can do for you, Liege?"

"I believe you've made our Sentinel happy enough for the both of us."

"Very well. *Bon appétit*," she said, then bowed a little before turning for the doors.

"Thank you, Margot," Ethan said, and she disappeared into the hallway, the doors closing behind her, but the bounty left behind.

We had our fill of pizza and ridiculously fabulous wine. Ethan had been right—expensive or not, it paired incredibly well with the saucy, cheesy pizza.

By the time Gabriel called, we'd moved to the sitting area, a landline conference phone and our wineglasses on the ottoman between us. I sat cross-legged on the floor, my boots kicked to the side. Ethan sat on the sofa, one leg crossed over the other.

Gabriel hit it out of the park on his first at-bat. "Kitten," he asked, "did Sullivan give you a raise?"

I crossed my hands on the table and leaned toward the phone. "Sadly, Gabriel, he did not. I believe my skills are sorely underappreciated."

"I have trouble believing that's true, Kitten. But vampires are vampires."

I had a feeling shifters used that phrase quite often, and not flatteringly. But when I glanced up at Ethan, he wore a look of amusement. He had one bent elbow on the chair back, his chin between his thumb and forefinger. His head was tilted, his smile crooked and kind of drowsy, as if he were actually . . . relaxed.

"Any developments in the investigation?" he asked.

"Nothing I wanted to know about. Tony's bike was found about a half mile from the bar. The forensic team has it now. The Ombud is serving as liaison. He let us know the CPD's testing it for gunpowder residue, that kind of thing."

Ethan frowned. "I'm sorry to hear that."

"You and me both," Gabe said. "This meeting is supposed to be about plotting out a new course for shifters, not tired, old attitudes." He sighed audibly. "Ah, well. Shit is what it is, right?"

"That's what we hear," Ethan said. "So I assume that means Tony has been bumped up to the top of the suspect list?"

"That would appear to be the case. It complicates things, of course. Endangering alphas isn't looked highly upon, as you might imagine. I don't want to bring the Packs together with that kind of sword above our heads, but we may not have a choice."

"Have you settled on a location for the convocation?"

"We have. We'll be at St. Bridget's Cathedral. It's here in the neighborhood."

I couldn't stop the words from popping out of my mouth. "St. Bridget's? You're meeting at a *church*?"

"We are indeed, Sentinel. Did you think shape-shifters were on the outs with all things holy?"

A blush warmed my cheeks at the chastisement. "Of course not. It's just . . . Well, it's a church. It's not the first place that comes to mind." Especially as the location for a meeting of, as Gabriel had put it, hog-loving and Jack-drinking bikers.

"Fewer prying eyes and less collateral damage," Gabriel said. "Sullivan, I don't know what you'd like to see beforehand; I can have my people send Luc the building specs, that kind of thing."

"Fine by me," Ethan agreed. "I assume that's all you need from us tonight?"

"Actually, it isn't." Gabriel paused for a moment, long enough for Ethan to offer me a look of curiosity. I shrugged.

"I appreciate what you did tonight—both of you. You volunteered to jump into a conflict that isn't yours, and I can't thank Merit enough for what she did with Berna. She took a risk—took a chance—to protect her. You did good, Kitten. You did real good."

I smiled earnestly back at the phone. "Thank you, sir."

"Anywho, we've got a Pack social gathering tomorrow night. Jeff suggested you two might be interested in joining us—meeting a few more of the Keenes, getting a sense of who we are as a group. Partly, it's a thank-you. And I don't think we'll have the same kind of security issues to worry about."

I glanced up from the phone to Ethan to gauge his reaction.

His eyes were wide with surprise, his lips curled into a very self-satisfied grin. "We'd be honored, Gabriel. Thank you for the invitation."

"Well, good. One small issue—we'll be at the Brecks'. They have a large house, as you know, so there's room to hold us all."

There was an awkward pause. "And how are things between you and the Brecks?" I asked.

That prompted an even longer pause. "They've offered to host the potluck to help mend the fence," he said. "Beyond that, it's between the Brecks and the Pack. Is the location going to cause any discomfort for you?"

At my reassuring nod, Ethan offered, "We'll be fine."

"Good to hear it. Ten p.m. tomorrow. I'm out."

With that, he hung up.

Ethan reached forward and tapped a button on the phone, then looked at me. "Back into the den, I suppose?"

"It looks that way. I wonder if this will be *our* chance to mend fences with the Brecks—"

"Or if we'll irritate them further by crashing a shifter party?"

"That had occurred to me," I agreed. "Either way, there's only one thing to do about it now." I unkinked my legs and stood up again.

Ethan smiled lightly. "Two or three centuries of peace?"

"Well, that, sure. But I was thinking chocolate mousse."

I'd somehow become Ethan's culinary guide to Chicago. I'd gotten him to eat deep-dish pizza, to try Chicago-style hot dogs, and to dive into a double bacon cheeseburger. I wasn't sure I could take credit for the chocolate since Margot put the tray together, but I figured my sheer enthusiasm counted for something.

While Ethan called Luc to advise him that Gabriel would be forwarding convocation materials, I plated up the chocolate cakes. When the columns of chocolate—from the cake layer to the pillowy mousse to the deep chocolate top—stood in the middle of crisp, white dessert plates, I grabbed two silver forks. I turned to carry the plates back to the sitting area, but he was already standing behind me. I offered up a plate and fork, and pricked the tip of it into the top of the dessert, piercing through the layers.

I happened to glance up at him as I prepared to take a bite, and found his gaze on me, his head tilted, a softness in his eyes.

"What?" I asked.

A corner of his mouth tipped up. "You probably don't want to know."

"*Ha,*" I said, assuming his thoughts were lascivious, then lifted the tiers of velvet brown to my lips. I closed my eyes as I reveled in it. It truly was chocolate heaven, and Margot was a goddess.

"Good?" he asked, his voice so low and slow, I wasn't sure he was asking about the dessert. I told myself to focus on the dense taste of chocolate, and not on the question in his tone.

When I opened my eyes again, he was still looking at me, his eyes crystal pools of green.

"What?" I asked.

He arched up a sardonic eyebrow.

I shook my head. "Chocolate or no chocolate, we're not doing that."

Ethan humphed, then stepped forward. "You missed a little," he said, raising his hand to my face. His fingers at my jaw, he swept his thumb across my lips.

And while we stood there, staring at each other, he lifted his thumb to his own beautiful mouth and sucked away the chocolate.

My lips parted. Although my very skin was on fire and my lips felt swollen from his touch, I managed to whisper, "You aren't playing fair."

"I'm not playing, Sentinel."

For a moment, we stood silently, neither of us responding to the obvious invitation. Ethan took the plate and fork from my hands and placed them on the cart. Then he took my hand and pressed it to his chest, to the crisp cotton of his shirt. His heart thudded beneath my palm, his blood racing beneath my fingertips.

I had a sudden memory of the blood we'd shared—me on my old bed in Mallory's house, Ethan on his knees before me, his wrist offered to sustain me through the rest of the change. But even half crazed from the bloodlust, I'd rejected it. I couldn't drink; I wasn't ready to take that step, especially not with him. Sharing blood had seemed too intimate a thing to do with someone I was already conflicted about. But then he'd carefully bitten his own wrist and offered it again. And while his control was usually momentous, he had surrendered and allowed me to see the silvering of his eyes. He had allowed me to see his want, his desire. That was enough for me. I'd gripped his arm and brought his wrist to my lips. I drank—for the first time really, *truly* drank—and while I fed my fevered need we stayed there together beneath an arc of hunger and desire and lust strong enough to electrify the air.

The memory hit me like a freight train, and I yanked back my hand, shocked by its intensity.

As I looked at him now, I saw the knowledge in his eyes. He knew what I'd remembered, but also that the memory wasn't going to change my mind. "You are so stubborn."

I gave him a pointed look. "You've always known that. You've known who I am from the very beginning."

"I know you aren't the same as the rest of them."

"I wasn't made like the rest of them," I pointed out. "I didn't ask to become one of your vampires. I became a vampire because you chose to make me one."

"And what, Sentinel, did I make you?"

The room was silent for a moment, until I lifted my eyes to his. I wondered what he saw in mine as he stared back. Did he see the same, strong desire, tempered by my own hesitation?

"Did I make you strong?" he asked. "Did I make you capable?"

A corner of my lip lifted. "I am who I am. You just made me vampire."

While I still had the strength to do it, I took a few steps backward. "We aren't far to dawn. I should probably head to my room. Did you need me for anything else?"

"I need you for many things."

Oh, but it was so easy to be flattered by the thought that a man so intensely handsome wanted me so fiercely. Of course, that was exactly the problem. "You *want* me for physical satisfaction."

When I got no response, I glanced up at him again, thinking my flippancy had angered him. But there was no anger in his eyes, just liquid, rich quicksilver—the color of hunger.

My spine tingled, not just with arousal, but with something

baser—a kind of vampiric appreciation, an interest in whatever game we were beginning to play.

The question was, was I prepared to lose?

He moved forward and took my hand, then joined our fingers together, raising our linked hands between us. "You would be worth any cost."

"Whether I'm worth it isn't the question." My voice was lush and low, and surprised me with its depth. Apparently the bravado I'd been faking with Lindsey hadn't been all a show— as a vampire, I had plenty of confidence in my feminine wiles. And, more important, I would be the one to decide whether he was worthy of my attentions.

"Why do you doubt me?"

"Because we've had this conversation before. At Mallory's. In the library."

"I am beginning to remember—" He stopped, shook his head, then started again. "I am beginning to remember what it means to need things. Laughter. Companionship. Love." He leaned forward and pressed his forehead to mine. "And I need you, Merit."

I swallowed. Those were words I hadn't expected to hear, hadn't been prepared to hear. *I want you*, sure. *I desire you*, maybe. But not *need*—not the admission of it, of the weakness he connoted with it. That simple, four-letter word laid me bare, stripping away the defenses I'd so carefully constructed.

"Ethan." My voice was barely a whisper, barely enough to push through the thick silence, but there was still warning in my tone.

A warning he ignored.

That was when he moved—when he reached up, cupped my face in his hands, and pressed his lips to mine. He stayed there, his mouth on mine, for a long time, before he finally drew away. But he kept his hands on my cheeks and kept his shining eyes on my face.

"You undo me, Merit. Wholly and completely. You don't take me at my word. You challenge me at every opportunity. And that means when I'm with you, I am less than the head of this House . . . and I am more than the head of this House. I am a man." He stroked my cheeks with his thumbs. "In my very, very long life, I need you more than I have ever needed anything."

This time, I didn't wait for him to move.

CHAPTER EIGHT

HUNGRY EYES

I kissed him. I slid my hands around his waist as he slid his hands around my neck, tangled his fingers in my hair, and pulled me closer. He kissed me hungrily, greedily, as if he'd been starved for me.

My body ignited, every cell on fire, and I kissed him back as if I couldn't get close enough. I nipped at his lips and tangled my tongue with his, magic beginning to spill through the room as passion flared between us.

"Shirt off," I said, and he pulled back, his eyes widening at my boldness.

I smiled secretively. I guess working on my bravado had been worth it.

Ethan stepped back and licked his lips. "I have waited a long time for you."

My fingers, which shook with nerves and anticipation, tugged at the bottom of his gray T-shirt, and ever so slowly pulled it up to reveal an ever-larger band of perfect skin above his waist.

"I don't want to rush you," he quietly said, "but I have things planned yet before the sun rises."

"Patience is a virtue," I told him. I slid my hands up the flat plane of his stomach, raising the shirt one brick of muscle at a time. When I'd gone as far as I could go, he lifted his arms and pulled it over his head.

"I will only entertain teasing for so long," he said, but closed his eyes and sighed, his muscles tensing beneath my hands as I traced a finger down the center of his stomach. I felt the sharp intake of breath and saw the pained pleasure on his face as I tugged the belt at his waist. Fingers nimbled by sword practice, I unfastened the buckle and pulled it through the loops, then dropped it to the floor.

His eyes flashed open—and flashed silver. "Merit," he growled.

I glanced up at him through my bangs, slipped off my leather jacket, and pulled the elastic from my hair, letting it fall loose around my shoulders.

Ethan stepped forward, sliding his hands into my hair and pressing his mouth to mine.

After a long, hungry kiss, Ethan finally pulled back, chest heaving, lips parted. He stared at me, his pupils fully silver, and let his fangs descend.

My heart pounded, the human nervous with anticipation, the vampire eager for action.

"Merit," he said, then dipped his head toward my neck, letting his fangs graze the skin above the blood pulsing in my arteries. "You know what it would be like," he whispered, his breath hot at my neck, enticing me to another memory of the blood we'd shared together. "You know how it would feel. For you to take what I offer."

I shuddered from the memory, from the wine-warm taste of his blood on my lips, a flavor that had bloomed with heat and life and magic. It had been like drinking fine wine infused with pure electricity.

And now he offered it again . . . to be twice bitten.

I opened my mouth to answer—still not sure what words would spill from my mouth—but he pulled back.

"First things first," he said, then took my hand and led me toward the double doors to his bedroom.

I paused at the threshold, our arms stretched between us, hesitation suddenly overtaking me. He'd done this before with a woman who'd betrayed him, a woman assigned to provide him pleasure.

Was I just the second round?

Ethan glanced back, and I looked up at him, reluctance in my eyes. He smiled softly, then tugged me forward. When our bodies were aligned again, he lowered his lips to my ear. "More than I have ever wanted anything," he repeated, then stepped back again, eyebrow raised. "And you are vastly overdressed."

I almost played coy, but I was past the need. The desire in Ethan's eyes made bashfulness unnecessary. I stepped inside the room and closed the doors behind us. Then I pulled the tank over my head and unzipped the suit trousers, letting them fall to the floor.

That left me in the middle of Ethan Sullivan's apartments, wearing nothing but the length of my dark hair and a couple of scraps of black silk.

And then I slipped away the silk.

I could hardly have planned a better seduction.

He let out a haggard breath, silvered gaze dropping to my bared breasts. Ethan wet his bottom lip, then glanced up, staring at me beneath mile-long lashes and half-closed lids. It was a look of such hunger and desire that my own fangs descended.

With vampire speed, he stripped himself of jeans and boxer briefs. And then he stood naked before me, this man who'd seen the crumbling of empires and had a store of knowledge humans would never be able to match. The sight of this naked man—this vampire who had been my greatest enemy, my fiercest desire—pushed every rational thought from my head. The first seconds after I'd become a vampire, the world had shifted on its axis, becoming louder, brighter, *more*.

But the entirety of that new world was nothing compared to the view before me, his sizable erection demonstrating the ferocity of his desire, his hungry eyes on me. Every muscle was defined, from his long, lean legs, to the lines of muscle at his hips, to the cording in his arms.

Without waiting, like the predator he was, he stalked one foot at a time toward me. Instinctively, regardless of my own needs, I backed away from him, prey escaping from predator.

That only enticed him more.

I backed away until I hit the door . . . until there was nowhere else to run.

Golden hair falling around his face, he half smiled at me, victory in his expression. He caught my wrists in his hands, raised them above my head, and pressed them to the wood behind us.

"You are caught, Sentinel." His voice was rough.

I looked up at him through my own half-hooded eyes. "I wasn't trying to escape, Sullivan."

Even in lust, we were challengers, our bodies the scorecards in our personal battle against each other.

He kissed me, lips playing at mine, heat and friction and

bare skin between us. And then he moved forward another inch and pressed his body against me, one thigh between mine, his marked arousal between us.

He loosed my hands, and I wrapped my arms around him, curling my fingers into the skin at his back. His hands moved to my face, fingers at my jaw as he weakened me with kisses, with the teasing nips of his teeth, with his fangs and the possibilities they presented.

Without warning, Ethan dropped to his knees, his hands sliding as he moved, and then his long fingers were around my breasts. My eyes fell shut, my body arcing forward into his hands.

"Beautiful," he whispered, and then his mouth at my stomach, pressing kisses to my navel, his hands at my breasts, his fingers busy building a fierce and furious need.

I groaned at the sensation—lovely and inciting and completely unsatisfying all at the same time. I took a haggard breath and felt as if my skin were on fire.

Ethan chuckled. "You seem to be enjoying yourself, Sentinel."

Slowly, I opened my eyes. "No 'Sentinel.' No 'Sullivan.' Ethan and—"

I paused, not sure if I was willing to take that step, to offer up my first name, to give him that right.

He smiled softly. "And *Merit*," he decided for me, that crisp tone gone. He sounded not like a Master among vampires, but a god among men. He pressed his cheek to my stomach.

"I am undone," he said softly.

I melted, my heart stuttering its rhythm. My hands found his hair, and I stroked the golden silk locks until he pulled one hand away and pressed his lips to the palm of my hand.

And then he was on his feet again. "Bed," he murmured harshly and, with a hand around my wrist, guided me toward it. When we reached it, he switched our positions and lowered me down. I watched, eyes wide, as he moved above me, crawling along the length of my body. And then the weight of his rangy form was on mine and his lips and teeth were at my mouth, and his kiss turned frantic, lips and tongues and teeth and hands pushing, pulling, biting, nipping, trying furiously to get closer.

He braced an elbow against the bed and used his other hand to torture me, fingertips slipping across my ribs, the teasing nearly bringing me off the mattress, and then across the flat of my stomach and the tops of my thighs.

And then his fingers reached the core of my body, and I arched upward, even the slightest touch like licking flames across my skin.

"*Ethan.*"

He chuckled earthily. "I've only just begun, Merit," he warned, and then he began in earnest.

Some minutes or hours or days later, when I lay boneless and well satisfied, Ethan raised his gaze to mine again. His eyes were silver, his fangs descended.

"There is no going back," he said. "Not after this."

But I'd already made the decision to go forward. I had no interest in going back.

"I want you," I told him, leaning up to press a kiss to his jawline.

That was proof enough for him. He moved forward again, and when our bodies were aligned, he pressed forward . . . and pushed the air from my lungs.

I arched my back, my hand reaching out for the headboard behind me, savoring the fire in my belly, the warmth of his body, the scent of his cologne, stronger now that we were together.

In every possible way.

My lashes fell again.

One arm on the bed to support his weight, he cupped his other hand at my face.

"Merit," he breathed across my lips. He'd said there was no going back, but he was asking me again without words: Was I sure? Was I ready? For the act, the deed, and everything else that would follow it? The changes that would result?

I answered in the same way he asked—with my body. I arched my hips upward, pressed my nails into his skin, pulling him tighter against me. *"Ethan."*

He growled, then dropped his forehead to mine and began to move his hips, filling my body, bucking his own against mine. He moved perilously slowly at first, his lips at mine, the movement a taunt, a tease, a promise of what could be.

A promise of things to come.

"Ethan," I said, nipping back at his lips.

"Yes, Merit?" There was amusement in his voice.

"I will only entertain teasing for so long."

He chuckled throatily. "Someone told me once that patience is a virtue."

I wrapped my legs around his waist. "Someone wasn't in a hurry at the time."

He moved forward with such force that I actually gasped, my eyes flashing open, as if my body were shocked by the primal feel of it. "Someone should learn not to rush," he said, lips at my ear, then nipped at my neck.

"Ethan," I said, my lids already fluttering. He took that as an order, and began to move fiercely, his lips peppering mine with kisses as he worked his hips against mine. My body burned from the inside, smoldered as he fanned the flames higher.

"I want your teeth on me," he hoarsely whispered. *"Now."*

The parts of my body that hadn't already been on fire instantaneously ignited.

Hips still bucking, he lowered his head, putting his neck within fangs' reach. I slid my hands into his hair and pressed a kiss to the skin above his jugular, feeling his pulse beneath my lips.

My fangs elongated again.

"Now," he said, and without a second thought, I leaned up, and I bit. I tasted fire and wine and *Ethan*, his life's essence, his life's force. The drink of all drinks. The hunger of all vampires.

His blood.

My throat moved in time with his ferocious thrusting. Above me, he groaned, the sound thick and guttural, as if he was giving voice to ecstasy.

Goose bumps lifted on my arms, magic seeping into the air as we took our pleasure.

And then his body arched, and he put a hand at my jaw so he could look into my eyes. So he could watch the expression on my face. *"Merit,"* he said.

The look in his eyes—possessive and primal—pushed me over. I sucked in a breath and called his name, fire spilling across my body, my eyes closing with the force of it, every muscle tensing, contracting, and, as the flame and power arced between us . . . *releasing.*

Seconds or minutes or hours later, I clutched at his back, his lips at my ear, his breath in gasps, even as tremors shook my body, my breathing ragged.

After a moment, Ethan pushed himself onto his elbows, kissed me roughly, and pressed his lips to my forehead. Then he dropped back to the bed, positioned himself on his side, and pulled my body against his. I nestled in front of him, his arm beneath my head, the warmth of his body cocooning mine once again.

We lay there together quietly, even as the sun fought the horizon behind the shutters in his room, two lovers savoring the fleeting cover of darkness.

"What's your favorite thing?" he whispered, his lips at my ear.

"My favorite thing?" I traced a fingertip across his long fingers, across the veins in his hands.

"Tell me something you haven't told another vampire."

The question was as sad as it was sweet. He wanted to know something dear to me . . . as long as it was a secret I'd held dear from others. Something I hadn't yet brought across to the supernatural world into which he'd brought me.

"You know I'm a Cubs fan?"

"Yes, although why remains a mystery."

I glanced back at him. "You're not a White Sox fan, are you?"

"Of course not," he huffed out. "I hardly follow baseball."

"But if you did?"

There was silence for a moment. "If I had to, I'd root for the Yankees."

I let out a groan. "I can't believe I just did what I did with a

Yankees fan. You really should have given me a little warning. Included a disclaimer. Something."

"It's just baseball."

"Spoken like a Yankees fan. Anyway, you asked me what my favorite thing was. So, one year, I made this pledge to get a baseball signed by every Cub. I was going to donate it to this charity thing my mom was involved in. I was ten, and I spent a lot of time that summer at Wrigley, at practice, trying to get the guys to sign it. It took me four full months to get all the guys to sign it—there was a holdout."

"For a Merit? Say it isn't so."

"I know, right? Joe Mitchell was pitching back then, and he kept holding out on me. He knew what I was trying to do, but he also knew who I was. I managed to corner him once, but he wouldn't sign it until I got every other player's signature on my own. It was a test, I think. A character-building exercise—let's see if this Merit kid can do something on her own, not rely on her father."

"So did he sign?"

"He did. Gave me a 'Good job, kid,' and everything, just like in the commercial. But by that time, it was nearly September, and I'd been following these guys around for months. I'd done what I set out to do, but that ball was hard to part with."

"You didn't keep it, did you?"

"Oh, no. I gave it up, but it killed me. That baseball was like a touchstone. Not because it was collectible—although they did have a great season that year—"

"Go Cubbies."

I grinned. "That's my boy. It was more like the baseball was a scrapbook—an album of how I'd spent the summer. A reminder of the games, the players, the heat, the hot dogs, the entire experience." I was silent for a moment. "I wish I still had it. To remember the summer days, the sunlight. The heat."

"It helps to have those touchstones," he said. "Tangible memories of the people and places and things you wish to remember when they're gone."

"Is that why you have so many collectibles?"

"Well, part of the reason is merely the passage of time. I've lived the lifetimes of many men. I've seen things, and I've brought forward my own touchstones, as you said. But, yes, you're right. Those things remind us who we were. Being immortal doesn't make that any less important."

"That makes sense," I said, but it took time for me to answer him, to force the words from my lips. The sun had risen, and it was pushing me asleep.

"*Sleep*," Ethan said, and as if he'd issued a command I couldn't disobey, I did.

Sometime during the day, as I lay groggy and barely awake, I became conscious of his hands on my abdomen. I made a questioning sound.

He pressed a kiss to my shoulder. "I need you."

My body slow and sluggish as if moving through water, I turned my head and squinted at the clock on his nightstand. "It's two o'clock in the afternoon," I grumbled, and curled away from him, hitching up my knees and curving my hands into my chest. "Go back to sleep. You can have me at dusk."

There was a rumbly laugh behind me before his fingers splayed and dipped between my thighs. He kissed my neck, then flicked his tongue against the tip of my ear. "Please, Merit?"

My eyes still closed, I smiled a grin of feminine pleasure.

I'm pretty sure that was the first time Ethan had ever said please to me. How was I supposed to say no to that?

But then his voice turned more urgent. "*Now*," he growled, his erection against my back.

In answer, I slid my hand behind me and around to the small of his back, pressing his body closer.

"If we keep this up," I said quietly, "we're going to kill each other."

He shifted to raise his body over mine, silver eyes staring down at me. "We're immortal. That would be quite a battle."

I pushed a lock of hair from his eyes. "An historic battle."

"A battle for the ages. You could write about it."

I credited the hour, the fact that the sun was high above us, but that seemed the funniest thing I'd ever heard. I chuckled and soothed my hands down the sculpted muscle of his back. "Far be it from me to turn down a research project."

Some hours and two more interruptions later, the sun set again. I awoke, my stomach twinging nervously. We'd finally crossed the boundary between us.

Now what?

I yawned and stretched, still buried in piles of cool cotton blankets, then opened my eyes. Ethan stood beside his bureau, already showered and dressed in unbuttoned black trousers. He had just begun to button the button-down shirt that lay open across his torso. He glanced back, smiled politely, and finished fastening his shirt. "Good evening."

"Good evening?" I didn't mean to make it a question, not intentionally, but even I could hear the uptick at the end of the sentence.

Ethan chuckled, then moved to the bed, leaned over me, and pressed a kiss to my forehead. He must have seen the surprise in my eyes. "I told you I wasn't your father."

"I clearly wasn't giving you enough credit."

"I'm sure that's not the first time." He sat down on the edge of the bed, pulled on socks, then slipped into chunky black designer shoes.

I sat up, pulling the comforter around me. "Nor will it probably be the last."

Ethan snorted and, when he was shoed, went back to the bureau and slid trinkets and change into his pockets. "It's eight thirty. We'll need to leave for the Breck estate shortly, so if you'd like to pretty up before we leave, now would be a good time to do it."

I glanced down at the comforter. "Probably the blanket would be a little too casual."

"Probably," he agreed.

"It goes against everything I believe in to ask you this question, but what would you have me wear?"

He perched one elbow on the bureau, then linked his fingers together. "They want us to see them in their natural habitat, so to speak. I assume they'd ask the same of us."

"Armani for you?"

He gestured at his suit pants and button-up. "And jeans, I assume, for you?"

"But of course. Opportunities to wear denim to the office don't come along very often in Cadogan House."

Ethan chuckled, then pushed off the bureau and pulled a black suit coat from a valet stand. "I hear the Master can be such a pain in the ass."

He definitely had his moments.

CHAPTER NINE

WILLINGLY INTO THE DEN

I was on my way back down to the foyer—cleaned and re-dressed in jeans and a black short-sleeved button-up top with a chic Mandarin collar, my ensemble complete with katana and Cadogan medal—when my cell phone beeped. I immediately pulled it out, hoping it might be a text message from Mallory.

It was a message, but not from an old friend—from a would-be new one. Noah had sent a simple question: "STILL DECIDING?"

Since I very definitely was, I erased the message—and the evidence.

"Good evening, sunshine."

I glanced behind me at the main staircase as I slid my phone back into my pocket. Lindsey was bounding downstairs, her blond ponytail bouncing as she moved. She was on duty today and clearly prepped for a day in the House's Operations Room, clad in Cadogan black, her katana belted at her side.

She reached the foyer, then walked toward me and propped

her hands on her hips. "You don't look nearly as tired as I expected. Maybe he *was* the cure for what ails you."

I stared at her. "Excuse me?"

She rolled her eyes. "Oh, come on, Mer. We all heard you two at it last night, and some of today, actually. But thank Christ, I say. About time you two did the deed."

Her approval notwithstanding, a blush powered by profound mortification crept up my face. "You *heard* us?"

She grinned. "You shook the foundations. You threw a lot of magic in the air."

I was too stunned to speak. It had occurred to me that word might slip out, from Margot or otherwise, that I'd been in Ethan's apartments. It hadn't occurred to me that people could have heard us, or felt the magic we'd spilled.

"Dear God," I murmured.

Lindsey patted my arm. "Don't be embarrassed. It's about time you two made the beast with two backs."

I had to work to form words. "There are so many things wrong with that statement, I don't know where to start."

"Start with the details, Sister Sledge. How was it? How was *he*? Was he as phenomenal as we've all imagined him to be? Seriously. Spare no details, anatomical or otherwise."

"I'm not giving you any details. Anatomical or otherwise," I added, before she could amend her request.

There was disgust in her expression. "I can't believe you. You make it with the Master and you're being tight-lipped?" She clucked her tongue. "That is weak. At least give me the goods on the evening-after talk. Are you two official now? Dating? Relationshipping? What?"

"Well, we didn't really get into the details, but he was still there when I woke up this evening. No evening-after regrets, as far as I know. And he knows I'm not interested in a fling. I've made that abundantly clear." I grinned a little.

She grinned back. "That's my girl. Way to show him who's boss."

"Are we actually debating who's boss of this House?"

We glanced over simultaneously. Ethan stood at the bottom of the stairs, golden hair around his face, hands in his pockets, newspaper under his arm.

"Good evening, Liege o' mine. How was your day?"

Ethan arched an imperious eyebrow at Lindsey, then glanced at me. "Nice shirt. We need to make a brief detour before we take on the shifters."

"*Oh*," Lindsey knowingly intoned. "You're going to Navarre House?"

"We're going to Navarre House," Ethan confirmed.

I blinked. When he'd said "detour," I'd immediately imagined grabbing a hostess gift; a trip to Navarre House wasn't on the list. I'd never been there before, and the idea of going now didn't thrill me. And why not, you ask? Brief review: I'd be facing down an ex-boyfriend for the first time since our official breakup, while on the arm of the boy he'd thought I'd been cheating with, and only hours after I'd actually had sex with him.

Fabulous.

"Does she know?" Lindsey asked, bobbing her head toward me.

"Standing right here. Do I know what?"

"I'm going to tell her," Ethan said. "But we're short on time. I forgot to call Luc—please tell him I want to talk before dawn to review plans for the convocation."

"Aye, aye, Liege," she said, but leaned in to me before she walked away. "Seriously, well done. And I mean that."

I grinned after her and raised a quizzical gaze to Ethan. "What do I need to know? And why are we going to Navarre?"

He gestured for me to follow him, then headed toward the basement stairs. When I fell in line beside him, he pulled the paper out from under his arm. It was a copy of the day's *Chicago Sun-Times*. He flipped it open, then turned it my way.

"Oh, my God," I murmured, pulling the paper from his hands.

The headline on the front page—the *front page*—read, PO-NYTAILED AVENGER SAVES PATRONS IN SHOOT-OUT. A picture of me helping Berna into the ambulance was set below the headline. And there was one more surprise—the byline. Nick Brecken-ridge was listed as the author of the article.

As I carefully took the basement stairs behind him, I read through the first part of the story, which discussed the shoot-ing and my emergency work. So far, so good. But I had no idea why Nick Breckenridge, of all people, had written it. It wasn't that writing a front-page story wasn't his thing; he was an in-vestigative journalist with an impeccable reputation. He just didn't like me very much.

"How—why?"

"Perhaps you turned the Breckenridge tide—from animos-ity to a cover story."

We stopped beside the basement door. "This can't be hero worship. You know how Nick feels about me."

"You heard Gabriel's hesitation when he mentioned the Breckenridge House. Maybe, like, Nick and Gabriel are still on the outs. Gabriel did apologize, after all. He wasn't exactly thrilled about Nick's pissing off vampires."

"Okay, but convincing a Pulitzer Prize–winning reporter to write a story glorifying a vampire—a vampire he isn't particularly happy with—would take a lot of pushing. I'm not sure Gabe would want to waste political capital on me. Besides, I can't imagine he'd put pressure on Nick to put us on the front page of the *Sun-Times*. Gabe doesn't want that kind of attention. It would raise too many questions about why armed vampires were in the bar, or risk the paparazzi's thinking it was some kind of new vampire hot spot. He definitely doesn't want that. There has to be another reason."

And that mysterious reason made me wonder what price I'd have to pay with Nick. I wasn't sure whether it was better or worse if he wrote the story because he got an unsubtle nudge from his boss. "Probably about the same way I'd feel if I got a nudge from a Master," I muttered.

"What was that?"

"Nothing. What does this have to do with going to Navarre House?"

"The story gets considerably nastier as it goes along."

"What kind of nasty?"

"It reminds the reader that the vampires of Navarre House weren't nearly as, shall we say, philanthropic as Cadogan vampires."

"It talks about the park murders?" Those were the results of Celina's murderous escapade through Chicago's parks . . . and the U of C campus. I was supposed to have been victim number two, at least before Ethan found me.

He nodded. "That's why Morgan wants to see us. Since you're featured in the story and were friends with Nick, he probably assumes we had something to do with its creation."

Calling us friends gave my relationship with Nicholas Breckenridge a lot more credit than it deserved.

Ethan punched in his code, then opened the basement door.

"And how are you feeling about said article?" I asked, following him into the garage.

"Well, evidently I'm dating the Ponytailed Avenger, so I feel pretty good about that."

I stopped to offer him a snarky look. When he walked past me to the car, smug grin on his face, I rolled my eyes. But I hardly meant it. He had said "dating," after all.

We were on the road a few minutes later, silence reigning in the Mercedes as I finished reading the story. The article read like a primer on Cadogan and Navarre, from the Houses' leadership positions to their histories. It also mentioned that a woman named Nadia was Morgan's new Second. I hadn't known he'd promoted someone. On the other hand, I hadn't really thought to ask him about it.

That omission probably said a lot about our lack of potential as a couple.

"Where'd the information come from?" I asked, glancing up to realize that we'd moved from Hyde Park to Lake Shore Drive. Navarre was located in Chicago's Gold Coast, an area of chichi townhouses, condos, and mansions near the Lake and north of downtown Chicago.

"That was my second question," Ethan answered darkly, "right behind wondering what impolitic acts our young Master of Navarre might take upon seeing it." He glanced over at me. "Have you talked to him recently?"

"Not since the fight."

There was a moment of silence in the car, the tension evident by the faint *hum* of magic. "I see," he said.

There was disapproval in his voice. I tensed, anticipating an argument. "Is there something you'd like to say about that?"

When he looked over, his expression was mild. I couldn't tell if it was forced or not.

"Not at all," he said. "But it might add to his irritation at having seen the story."

I thought back to the things Morgan had said in our last two conversations, the accusations he'd thrown, the condescension in his tone. "Yeah, he's probably not going to be in the greatest of moods."

"Any suggestions?"

"Barring a complete attitude adjustment, did you happen to bring along any of those chocolate mousse cake thingies?"

Cadogan House was an historic Hyde Park mansion turned vampire dorm—a restored beauty.

Navarre House, on the other hand, was big and garishly white and took up the corner of one of the city's most expensive chunks of real estate. It was four stories tall and was marked by a giant turret at the corner, the entire facade wrapped in the same white marble.

"I think their turret is bigger than our turret," I said as Ethan pulled up to the curb.

"Celina always had a flair for the dramatic," he agreed.

I put a hand on his arm as we walked to the front door, which was all but hidden from the street by massive, leafy trees. He stopped and glanced down at my hand, then up at me.

"One of our disagreements—Morgan and me . . ." I picked over my words, trying to figure out a way to explain without being too, to use Lindsey's word, anatomical.

"Morgan thought you and I were involved. Previously, I mean." I stopped there, hoping Ethan got the point so that I wouldn't have to spell out exactly what Morgan had accused me of doing with Ethan.

"Ah," he said. "I see."

"We weren't, of course, but he wouldn't be convinced. So, in addition to the other reasons he won't be happy to see me, he may not be thrilled to see me with you."

Ethan gave a half snort, then walked up the stairs. Without so much as knocking, he opened the front door and beckoned me inside.

"What's funny?" I asked when I reached him.

"The irony. By accusing you of such wanton acts, he accomplished the very thing he sought to avoid."

"I'm not sure I'd say 'wanton.'"

Ethan leaned in, his lips at my ear. "I, Merit, would definitely say 'wanton.'"

I couldn't stop the grin that lifted a corner of my mouth, or the blush that warmed my cheeks.

"Besides," Ethan whispered, following me into the House, "I've decided that if the *Sun-Times* story doesn't top his list of things to accuse us of today, there is less hope for his skills as a Master than I might have imagined."

There'd been no security outside the door of Navarre House, no ten-foot-high gate, no mercenary fairies keeping a watchful eye on the premises. Navarre vamps saved that fun for the foyer . . . but the guards weren't the beefy types I expected.

Three women sat behind a semicircular reception desk made of glass and steel that was perched just inside the entrance. Each woman was posed in front of a sleek computer monitor. They all had dark hair and big brown eyes, and they all wore fitted white suit jackets. Each wore her hair up but in a different style—from left to right, funky bouffant, ponytail, and tidy bun.

They glanced up as we entered, then began to whisper and click keys on their respective keyboards.

I assume these are the gatekeepers? I silently asked.

Might as well be the Greek Fates, he replied.

"Name," said the one in the middle, looking up from the monitor to gaze suspiciously at us.

"Ethan Sullivan, Master, Cadogan House," Ethan said. "Merit, Sentinel, Cadogan House."

The other two women stopped typing and looked at me. Their expressions showed a range of emotions—disgust, curiosity, sheer feminine appraisal. All emotions, I assumed, motivated by the run-ins I'd had with their former Master, Celina, and their current one, Morgan. I was zero for two in terms of Navarre Masters.

"Identification," said the woman closest to Ethan. He reached inside his suit jacket and pulled a card from the interior pocket, then with two fingers handed it to the woman. She glanced at it, then began typing in earnest.

Thinking we were going to be here awhile, I took the opportunity to scope out the digs . . . and was surprised.

The open front room was huge, two staircases meeting at a second-floor balcony. The entire atrium was open to the roof, the room topped by a greenhouselike cage of Victorian skylights. Although those things seemed pretty European to me, the decor looked as if it had been taken from a modern-art museum. There wasn't much in the way of furniture or knick-knacks, and the few pieces there were had a sculptural quality. There was a white tufted leather sofa, a coffee table that consisted of a giant, curvaceous core of lacquered wood, and recessed lights shining onto giant canvases of black-and-white photography and pop art. All of it was set amongst gleaming, white marble floors and equally white walls.

"This is—," I began, my gaze on a painting that looked to

represent those rubbery grips that fit on number two pencils, but I found no words to describe it.

"Yes," Ethan said. "It most definitely is." He shifted beside me, probably not accustomed to waiting for service, then glanced down at the girls again. "We are expected."

Without looking up, the girl in the middle pointed a long-nailed finger behind us. We both turned. A bench sat in an alcove beside the front door, three bored-looking, supernaturally attractive vampires filling it—two women and a man in between them. They all wore suits and had briefcases across their laps. They were all perfectly polished, but there was a weariness in their eyes and in the slump of their shoulders. They looked as if they'd been here a while.

"Fabulous," I muttered.

Ethan blew out a breath, but his smile was back when he turned to face the Fates again. "At your convenience," he grandly said.

As it turned out, their convenience was seven minutes later. "Merit," the girl on the right finally said. I looked down at her extended hand, which held a translucent plastic badge the size of a credit card. It had VISITOR stamped across one side, and bore a hologram of a wide-winged bee—a symbol of the House's French roots, I thought, but rendered in twenty-first-century technology.

"Fancy," I said, then clipped the badge onto the bottom hem of my shirt.

"We have visitors' passes, as well," Ethan muttered, as if offended by the possibility that Navarre House was more organized—or more exclusive—than we were. He accepted a clip and added it to his suit, then looked at the women expectantly.

Silence.

He gestured toward the staircase. "Should we just—"

"Nadia will be down to retrieve you," said the one in the middle.

"We appreciate your assistance," Ethan said, then moved into the room's main space.

"We need a four-story atrium," I told him.

"Cadogan House is perfect as it is. We're not changing it to fit the fancies of an architecturally jealous Sentinel. Ah," he added brightly, "here she is."

I glanced up.

A woman was trotting down the stairway, one delicate hand on the marble banister as she glided toward us.

No—not just a woman. A *supermodel*. She was all effortless beauty. Her eyes were wide and green, her nose thin and straight, her cheekbones high. Her body was long and lean, and she wore leggings, knee-high boots, and a long, belted knit top. It was the kind of outfit I might have worn while traipsing through the streets of Manhattan during my college days. Her hair was long and medium brown, and it spilled across her shoulders like silk.

I leaned toward Ethan. "You might have filled me in on the fact that Morgan's new Second was practically a cover girl."

"Jealous again?"

"Not even slightly," I crisply answered, then elbowed him in the ribs. "But you're panting, Sullivan."

He offered a fake *oof* at the elbowing, then, hand outstretched, walked toward Nadia.

"Ethan," Nadia said with a beatific smile, taking his hand. They exchanged cheek-to-check kisses and whispers that made something turn in my belly.

That would be the jealousy kicking in, I silently thought.

"Nadia, this is Merit, my Sentinel," he said, gesturing at me. Nadia beamed at me, then held out both hands.

"Merit," she intoned, leaning in to kiss my cheek, as well. "It is lovely to meet you." Her voice carried the faintest French accent, and her perfume was exotic. Equally complex and old-fashioned, like something you'd pick up in a boutique in a forgotten Parisian *arrondissement*. It sang of flowers and lemon and rich spice and sunlight, all bottled together.

"My liege is in his office, if you'll follow me?"

Ethan nodded and fell in line behind Nadia, who trotted back up the stairs, her hair bouncing on her shoulders as she moved. Really—it was like watching a shampoo commercial. At the top of the staircase, we turned to the left, then took a wide marble hallway another twenty or thirty feet. The door was open. I blew out a breath and readied myself for drama.

CHAPTER TEN

MY (EX-)BOYFRIEND'S BACK

Morgan's office was a wide rectangular room that over-
looked Navarre House's back courtyard, a small but
well-tended space that must have been wedged
into the notch between the buildings on the block. The entire
back wall was a sheet of glass, the garden below well lit to
provide the Master a view of the space—and to provide any
Navarre vampires in the space a view of their Master. It was
definitely Celina's kind of architecture, her office a stage for
the audience of vampires in the garden below.

Tall panels of crimson silk hung at each end of the window, probably to be drawn forward during the daylight hours.
The rest of the office was sleek and modern and much less
feminine. At one end of the room sat a glass desk, upon which
perched a white computer and an array of white desk acces-
sories. Two ultramodern black and steel chairs sat in front of
it, and a seating area of modern furniture my parents would
probably have liked—good lines, but not very comfortable
looking—sat at the other end of the room. The office was vir-

tually empty of knickknacks, books, and collectibles. I wasn't sure if that was in deference to the modern design, or simply because Morgan, who was only about seventy years old, hadn't had time to collect much.

The Master vampire himself stood with his back to the door, facing the glass. Nadia said softly, respectfully, "Liege. The entourage from Cadogan House." He glanced back over his shoulder.

His dark hair seemed to have grown inches since I'd last seen him, even though that had been only a week ago. It waved around his deep-set, dark blue eyes and the long, dark brows that topped them. There were plenty of handsome men in the world, and plenty of men with lovely eyes. But Morgan's were different. Bedroomy, I'd called them, because his gaze seemed to sink into you, inviting you, tempting you, with its depth.

That gaze skimmed Nadia, then darkened when he saw Ethan and clouded completely when he saw me. Morgan had a dramatic personality, but he shuttered the expressions in his face—anger, betrayal, sadness—fast enough. Maybe he was taking to Masterdom after all.

He turned around. "Thank you, Nadia," he said, and Nadia nodded and left the room. From her deferential reactions, I was getting the sense that Navarre's Master occupied a different kind of position than Cadogan's Master. Or maybe the deference was just part of being second to a Master vampire— being acquiescent until the crown was handed to you. Malik, after all, generally seemed to defer to Ethan.

And speaking of, Ethan, crown firmly in hand, offered his opening gambit. "Merit has had no contact with Nicholas Breckenridge regarding the story. No contact at all, in fact, since the incident."

Morgan looked at me. "True?"

I nodded.

He walked toward his desk, then took a seat. Ethan gestured toward the bank of windows. "May I?"

"Be my guest," Morgan said crisply. They switched places, which still left me standing between them. Poetic, I thought.

"You know that Gabriel visited us after the blackmail was cleared up?" Ethan asked, his gaze on the courtyard below.

"I do now. I also know, thanks to the *Sun-Times*, that you and Merit apparently paid a visit to a bar in Ukrainian Village. Would you care to enlighten me?"

Ethan turned around, arms crossed over his chest. I guessed he hadn't been keeping Morgan up-to-date on our shifter interactions. Not that that was a surprise; he tended to keep details to himself.

"Gabriel asked that we be present at a pre-meeting of the alphas. We obliged."

Morgan sat back in his chair and crossed his hands behind his head. "Why did he want you there?"

"Security, most fundamentally. He also wanted vampires to be present, individuals who could remind the shifters of the purpose of the convocation."

"Mmm-hmm," Morgan said, then lifted up a folded copy of the *Sun-Times*. "It appears you didn't make the best security."

Ethan's jaw clenched. "The attack was external. One of the Pack leaders walked out. Shots were fired at the bar a few minutes later. It's possible those two things are connected, but Gabriel seems to have doubts. They're investigating." Ethan paused and looked down, as if contemplating how much to tell Morgan. Ethan, I knew, had his doubts about Morgan's temperament, about his ability to stay calm and make the kind of difficult political decisions that needed to be made.

I glanced over at Morgan and found his furrowed stare on me, his head tilted to the side. He could have spoken with me silently; although only a Novitiate and the Master who made her were supposed to have the ability to speak telepathically, Morgan and I had made that connection when he'd challenged Ethan for an imagined slight against Celina. Maybe he didn't want to speak. . . . He just had his own puzzles to ferret out.

Morgan's gaze suddenly snapped back to Ethan. "So the wolves invited the sheep into their den." He waved the paper in the air. "I'll skip the lecture about the need to keep all of Chicago's Masters informed, Ethan, since I doubt it would make much difference."

Score one for the newbie Master, I thought, even if he was right—and therefore out of luck. A lecture from Morgan wasn't going to stop Ethan from holding back information about his strategy.

"If we help them," Ethan said, exhaustion in his voice—probably since he wasn't used to having his decisions questioned by those of equal rank—"which we will, we show our willingness to act as a unified supernatural community. We do a favor, and we, perhaps, get a favor in return."

"If they actually needed you for security," Morgan said, "you might have a point. But shifters can take care of their own. Two vamps with swords won't change that, even if they dress her up in slutty leather."

I had to work to keep the anger off my face. Ethan could certainly be cold, but Morgan could be downright obnoxious.

"Your opinion is noted," Ethan said flatly. "And we will act as we deem in the best interest of our House."

"Oh, we're well aware of that," Morgan replied, then flung the paper across the room. Aided by Morgan's vampire strength, it zipped through the air like a Frisbee, finally coming to rest at Ethan's feet. Ethan glanced down at it, then raised his gaze to the Navarre Master again.

"Nothing in the article was our doing," he said. "We had no idea it was being written, and we have had no communication with the author."

He took a menacing step forward, his eyes cold and bright.

"But, more important," he said, his voice an octave lower, "none of the information in that article was untruthful. You may wish to hide behind your position as a Master, but recall the House from which you arose. Celina is responsible for the deaths of humans, deaths unrelated to her need for blood. Deaths she apparently undertook because the humans were convenient pawns in her quest for power. You may find denial convenient, but she was Master of this House, and this House will bear the burden of the decisions she's made, however horrible those decisions, however onerous those burdens. If you want to change the public's perception of the House, then change the *House*. Make it *your* House, a House of honor, a House that reaches out to other communities, a House that defends all vampires instead of taking up arms for one who has done us all a disservice by her deeds. A *profound* disservice," he added.

Morgan sat in his chair for a moment, then swallowed. The room was silent, at least until Ethan's cell phone buzzed. He patted the pockets of his suit jacket until he found it, then pulled it out and glanced at the screen. He glanced up at Morgan. "May I step outside to take this?"

Morgan was quiet for a moment. The office door opened and Nadia stepped inside.

"Liege?" she asked. He must have called her telepathically.

"Ethan needs to take a call. Will you take him to your office?"

"Certainly," she said. She smiled and gestured toward the door. Ethan walked out, and she followed suit, then shut the door behind her, leaving Morgan and me alone in his office.

Together.

I kept my gaze on the floor, trying to will myself invisible.

Without preface, Morgan spoke up. "How are things between you two?"

Given the blush on my cheeks, I was glad I'd turned back to face the window, but I ignored the undertone of his question. "I think we have a pretty good working relationship."

"That's not what I meant."

"No," I corrected, unwilling to answer deferentially when he couldn't manage a civil conversation with me, "that's not what you want to hear, but that answers your question."

"I heard you attacked him. Was that prompted by our conversation?"

"It was prompted by Celina's attacking me on the street." I didn't offer details, assuming Ethan had at least filled him in on his former Master's ill-advised return to Chicago.

There was silence for a moment, long enough that I glanced back at Morgan. There was regret in his expression.

"You knew," I guessed, turning back toward him. "You knew she was in town, and you didn't tell anyone." And then I remembered what I'd seen when Celina had attacked me. "She was wearing a new Navarre medal. She came by here," I said with sudden realization. "She came to the House, and you saw her. That's how she got the medal."

Morgan looked at the floor, his gaze shifting left and right as he prepared his allocution. "She built this House," he quietly said. "She is my Master, and she built my House. She asked for a medal to replace what was taken from her." When he lifted his gaze to mine, I could see the conflict in his eyes. He truly wanted to honor the vampire who'd given him immortality, to do right by her. But I wasn't sure harboring a criminal— Master or not—was the way to go about it.

And with thoughts like that, maybe I *was* ready to think about Red Guard membership. . . .

"Is she still in Chicago?"

"I don't know."

I played Ethan, arching an eyebrow back at Morgan.

"Honestly," he said, both hands raised, "I told her she couldn't stay here. I told her I wouldn't report her to the GP, but that she couldn't stay here." And then something interesting happened—there was a sudden glint in his eyes, a sign of Master-worthy strategy. "But I didn't promise not to tell you."

Nice of him to lay that burden on me, but there was nothing to do about it now. "Any thoughts on where she is?"

Morgan leaned back in his chair. "Nothing specific. But it's Celina—she loves fashion, elegance." He indicated the office around him. "Case in point, this place is practically a museum."

"An homage to her?"

He glanced up at me, humor in his eyes, and for a moment I saw the thing that had attracted me to Morgan in the first place. For all that Ethan complained about Morgan's being "too human," it was the humanity that sparked his precocious sense of humor and that fueled his compassion for his former Master, however undeserved.

"Something like that, yeah," he said. "So if she had decided to camp out in Chicago, you'd expect it to be nice. She wouldn't be sharing a fourplex. You'd have to look for her in Hyde Park, the Gold Coast, Streeterville. Somewhere with a doorman, an elevator, a view. A penthouse. A condo on the Lake. A golden age mansion. Something like that. But I don't think she'd stay here. Her face was all over the television, and there are just too many eyes on the ground."

I wasn't sure I bought the argument that she'd travel all the way back to the States to harass me, then take off for Europe again. But then again, Celina wasn't exactly operating by the same rules as the rest of us. "Then where do you think she is?"

Morgan blew out a breath. "Honestly? I'd put money on France. It's where she's from, and staying in Europe keeps the GP and the CPD off her back."

My doubts notwithstanding, he had a point. "Well, I appreciate the intel."

He shrugged. "What will you do now?"

"I'll tell Ethan." I wasn't sure what Ethan would want to do, although the fact that there was a chance, no matter how slim, that Celina was still in Chicago was probably something he'd want to pursue after the convocation. But today we had enough on our plate.

"Of course you will," Morgan said. And there was the downside of his humanity—that snarky, teenage petulance.

"You might remember that he's my Master. So all that deference you show Celina, I show to him."

Morgan sat up again, then swiveled in his chair to face the spread of papers on his desk. "And I'm sure your relationship is entirely professional, since you always take his side."

"I take Cadogan's side. That's the point of being Sentinel."

"Whatever," he said. "You attacked Ethan."

"I did."

"And yet, here you are." He looked me up and down, the gaze I'd once found undeniably attractive taking on an uncomfortably lascivious bent. "No punishment for the teacher's pet?"

"I was punished," I assured him, even if I could agree that being named House social chair, even for an introvert, was a light one. On the other hand, Celina was free after a murderous rampage. Maybe vampire punishment standards were just low.

"Mmm-hmm," he said.

"I get that you aren't happy, but can we just try to work together without the sniping?"

Morgan opened his mouth to retort, but before he got out words, the office door opened. Ethan walked in, tucking his cell phone into his pocket. "We have some things to take care of," he said, looking between us, "if we're done here?"

Morgan looked at me for a moment before finally turning to Ethan. "I appreciate your coming by."

"Perhaps we all need to remember that there are three Houses in Chicago," Ethan said, "and that those Houses are not enemies." With that, he turned to me and beckoned, and we made our exit.

CHAPTER ELEVEN

ALL IN THE FAMILY

The Breckenridge estate—and it was an estate—was located in the rolling Illinois countryside outside Chicago, so we had a drive to get through. Knowing we'd have plenty of time to debrief, I waited until we were in the car before I spilled the Celina beans.

"Morgan saw Celina before she came to Cadogan," I told him. "He gave her a new Navarre medal. She was wearing it when she attacked me."

"Sad to say, that doesn't entirely surprise me. Any other information?"

"Morgan doesn't think she's still in town. He's betting she's decamped to Europe. But if she is here, he thinks she'd probably be somewhere fancy."

"That would fit Celina's sense of self."

"As much as I hate to admit it, once ConPack's done, we probably need to start taking some active steps to, I don't know, minimize the damage she could cause?"

"There's only so much we can do in that regard, given the GP's protectiveness. They chose to release her, after all."

"I know. But if the GP isn't going to keep her from riling up the Houses and the Packs, that's precisely why we need to do some creative thinking."

"Perhaps," he said, then paused. "It occurs to me that it was a mistake to encourage you to date Morgan."

I bit back a smile. "Are you admitting you were wrong?"

"Only in a manner of speaking. There's a tension between you that we'd have been spared if you hadn't dated. You can hardly stand to be in the same room together."

My stomach twisted a bit at his conclusion, and I wondered whether the next sentence out of his mouth would be something along the lines of, *And speaking of ill-advised relationships* . . . But if he had concerns about us, he didn't raise them.

"Well, it's water under the bridge now," he said.

"You know, you once told me that he was too human. I didn't agree at the time, being recently human myself, but now I get it. He's smart, capable, funny—"

"Perhaps *you* should be dating."

"*Ha.* But he can be really juvenile. He's been a vampire for forty years. He should be past adolescence and midlife crisis."

"Sentinel, there are men who've been human for forty years who aren't past adolescence and midlife crisis."

I gave him the point there. It also occurred to me that I hadn't actually heard Ethan's phone ring. "Did you fake a phone call to leave me and Morgan alone?"

"I did not. Although I thought it would do you both good to clear the air."

"I see. Who called?"

"Catcher, unfortunately. The forensic unit tested Tony's bike. They found gunpowder on the tank, some on the seat."

"Hmm. That won't tie it to the drive-by with one hundred

percent certainty; it doesn't look good circumstantially. Have Tony or his Pack taken credit for the hit?"

"Not that I'm aware of," Ethan said. "I plan to ask Gabriel tonight."

Ethan switched on the radio, and we listened to a public station for the duration of the drive. The buildings and parking lots eventually gave way to trees and farmland and to the French château perched in the midst of the acres of Breckenridge land. Ethan pulled into the long driveway, flanked today by dozens of bikes arranged in two rows. They were an interesting contrast to the luxe mansion, with its chimneys, steep roof, and pale stone.

Ethan parked the car at the end of one of the rows of bikes. I hesitated, wondering if I should bring my katana along. I held up the scabbard, the question in my expression.

"Bring it," Ethan said, belting on his own sword. "If the hit at the bar was a shot at Gabriel, we can't be sure a member of the Pack wasn't involved."

"Fair enough," I said, and belted mine on, as well.

We walked the rest of the driveway to the front door. The last time we'd visited, a white-gloved attendant had helped us out of the car, and Mrs. Breckenridge—Nick's mom—had met us inside.

Today, our greeter was a little bit different.

She pulled the door open forcefully, then propped a hand on her hip. "I got it, Mrs. B," she called back, then looked at us expectantly. She was tallish and fit, and wore a snug T-shirt. Knee-high black boots covered her snug jeans to the knees, and her short nails were tidy and painted glossy black. A dozen earrings dotted each ear, and her wrists were tattooed with tribally inspired bracelets. She had delicately pretty features and Gabriel's same golden eyes, her hair a mass of sun-kissed curls that spilled around her shoulders.

Another Keene, I supposed.

She gave me a quick look, then shifted her gaze to Ethan. "Sullivan?"

Ethan bobbed his head. "And Merit."

"You're in the right place," she said. "Mrs. B said you'd already jumped the vampire invitation hoop, so she extended your invite for tonight for whatever." She stepped to the side, holding the door open to allow us entry. "Come on in."

Ethan stepped inside; I followed, catching a cloud of citrus-and-spice perfume as I walked past the girl.

"I didn't catch your name," Ethan said.

She held out a hand. "Fallon Keene."

"Ethan Sullivan," he said, shaking her hand.

She turned to me.

"Merit," I said, doing the same.

"I'll tell Gabe you're here," she said, then looked at us askew. "Vamps at a Pack party. It's definitely a new era." Her tone was open enough that I wasn't sure whether she approved or disapproved of that new era.

Ethan's answer wasn't nearly so equivocal. "Let's hope so. Let's hope so."

The house overflowed with people and happiness and earthy, peppery magic. Men and women ate and drank and chatted while children ran to and fro amongst them, joy in their expressions, toys in hand. The doors to the elegant ballroom were open, and a long buffet overflowing with food lined one wall. It felt more like a holiday gathering than a last (pre-convocation) supper.

"Merit!"

Before I could react, Jeff was in front of me, arms wrapped around me, his lips pressed to my cheek. "We're so glad you're here."

I smiled and hugged him back. I assumed his elation had something to do with his crush on me, at least until he reached out to Ethan and gave him the same bone-crushing embrace.

Ethan, helplessness on his face, looked to me. I winked back.

"This is huge, your being here," Jeff said, releasing Ethan and taking a step back. "Huge. We've never had vamps at a potluck before."

"This is quite a potluck," Ethan said, his gaze scanning the crowd.

"It's fabulous. You two should get something to eat. Did you meet Fallon?"

I nodded. "She met us at the door. She's Gabriel's sister?"

"His only sister. And second in line to the throne, so to speak," Jeff confirmed. "Most of the rest of them are here to-night." He pointed through the crowd at various lion-maned men, all of whom shared the Keene tawny hair. Adam glanced over and waved, dimples perked at the corners of his mouth. Two young boys, plastic cars in hand, suddenly ran between us, leaving *vroom* noises in their wake.

"It's a joyful occasion," Ethan observed.

"We're together," Jeff said. "A family, come together. That's a good reason for celebration, even if ConPack means we might leave you." He looked at me with concern in his eyes. "I wouldn't want to leave. I wouldn't want to abandon you."

"I know," I comforted, then squeezed his hand. "I wouldn't want you to leave."

His eyes went wide, and a crimson blush suddenly rode his cheeks.

"In a Platonic way, Jeff. A cherished-friend kind of way."

"Whew," he said, shoulders bobbing in relief. "I actually wanted to talk to you about that."

At the blush on his cheeks, I took a guess. "Jeff, is there someone else?"

He offered some equivocal ums and uhs, but when his gaze slipped back into the crowd—and followed the bobbing curly hair of Fallon Keene across the room—I had my answer.

"Does she know?"

He looked back at me, and that boyish blush had turned into something much more mature. "Of course she does. I have some pretty serious game, Merit."

I leaned in and pressed a kiss to his cheek. "I know you do, Jeff. Now, other than your romancing Fallon Keene, what's on the agenda for the evening?"

Jeff shrugged. "This is pretty much it. Reminiscing. Enjoying one another's company. Gabe will say a few words later. And food, of course." He winged up his eyebrows. "Have you seen the buffet?"

"Only across the room."

Jeff clucked his tongue at Ethan. "If you're going to do right by her, you'd better get the girl a plate."

With that, he disappeared into the crowd. Ethan and I stood there quietly for a moment. "I suppose he's my competition?"

"Then you would be correct." I slid him a glance. "Do you have a strategy to woo me better?"

He smiled slowly, wickedly. "I believe I've demonstrated my prowess at wooing you, Sentinel."

I humphed, but inwardly grinned, the repartee unexpected,

and that much more fun. Were we actually *together*? Was this really happening?

"Well, I suppose I could follow his advice. Are you hungry?"

"Surprisingly enough, not at the moment."

"Will miracles never cease?"

"Ha," I said, then scanned the mass of shifters. Parents carried children, plates were passed among family members, and lovers embraced. "This is not your typical Breckenridge party."

"My parents throw all kind of bashes," said a voice behind me.

We both glanced back. Nick Breckenridge—tall, dark, and handsome—stood behind us, hands in his pockets. He wore a dark button-up shirt, the sleeves rolled up, and dark jeans. His hair was Caesar-cut, his eyes blue. He had a Roman nose and heavy brow, and he was handsome in the manner of a Spartan soldier—stoically handsome.

At the moment, he was keeping a stoic hold on his emotions. We'd see how long that lasted. . . .

"Ponytailed Avenger?" I wondered aloud.

"Not my idea."

"I'm assuming the story wasn't, either?"

Nick bobbed his head. "The editor originally farmed it out to someone else. I convinced them the story would be a burden to write and took it off their hands. We don't need an enterprising reporter poking around the bar, wondering about the guys in the NAC jackets."

"It was awfully pro–Cadogan House. And pro-Sentinel."

"I may have rushed to judgment," Nick said. "I am capable of admitting when I'm wrong. But, more important, it keeps the focus on vamps—"

"And off shifters?" I finished.

He nodded.

"Understandable. I didn't know you were working for the paper."

"Just freelance for now." Nick looked between me and Ethan. "It's a big deal, your being here. Gabriel's vetting you."

"We've heard," Ethan said. "And we appreciate the opportunity."

They were silent for a moment, sizing each other up, I assumed, and debating whether to make peace or war.

"Speaking of Gabriel," I said, gesturing to the room, "is this a way of mending fences?"

"As you know, I was the prime mover behind some ripples he isn't thrilled about," Nick darkly agreed, "but I hope eventually I can regain his trust. This is a step in that direction. As for ConPack, I don't think the Pack will vote to stay."

"It's a distinct possibility they'll leave," Ethan said. "And if that's the vote that's made, we'll figure out a way to adapt."

I wondered if the Brecks would have to adapt, as well. From what I'd seen, they didn't seem like typical shifters—no Harleys and no leather. Instead, they were a family with strong ties to Chicago and stronger ties to their land.

"If they vote to leave," I asked him, "would you go? Pack up Michael and Fin and Jamie and your parents and head north?"

"I can't answer that."

I cocked my head at him. "Because it's a secret?"

"Because I don't know."

There was defeat—and guilt—in his voice. It was the guilt of a man who wanted to believe, but who hadn't quite decided whether to play follow the leader. Even considering the drama

Nick had created for vampires, my heart clenched in sympathy. Doubt was a debilitating, frightening thing.

Nick was spared further predictions by the splitting of the crowd. I could see the ripple of people moving in our direction, and then Berna stood before us, having elbowed her way through the shifters, an overflowing plate of food in hand. It brimmed with an assortment of meats and casseroles and vegetables, a steaming yeast roll parked on top like the cherry on a sundae.

The shifters around us had quieted and turned their gazes on the two women who stood, facing off: me, the tallish, slender vampire with the dark ponytail and gleaming red scabbard, and Berna, the shortish, roundish woman with bleached hair and gnarled fingers, her arms extended in offering.

She thrust the plate toward me. "You eat."

I started to object, but the venom in her eyes made me think better of it. "Thank you, Berna. That was very thoughtful of you to bring me a plate."

"Humph," she said, then pulled a fork from the chest pocket of her zip-up polyester shirt. She handed that over, too. I slid Ethan a glance and, at his nod—and to the amusement of the shifters who'd watched the exchange—dipped the fork into a heap of potato casserole, and took a bite.

My eyes closed as I savored tender potatoes, butter, paprika, and more cream than should probably be allowed in a single dish. "Oh, Berna. This is amazing."

"Mmm-hmm," she said, self-satisfaction in her voice. I opened my eyes to watch her turn on her heel and march away, the crowd swallowing her up again.

I speared another bite of casserole, then aimed the fork at Ethan. He regarded it for a moment, but, at my own threatening glance, leaned in.

Half a second later, his own eyes drifted shut as he enjoyed the bite.

"Told you," I said, then took back the fork.

"You have a gift."

"I know, right?" I absently said, but I was already gone, adrift on a sea of carbohydrates.

After a bit, Nick merged back into the crowd, and Ethan slipped away to make a call, leaving me in the midst of the Pack. That was when Adam made his approach. He was dressed casually—a thin, cotton button-up shirt over jeans, thick boots, and a long chain and Celtic pendant around his neck.

"You two seem to be quite the hit," he said. "Berna doesn't cook for many. I know she appreciates what you did for her."

"I'm just glad I was able to get there in time," I said, then nodded to the crowd around us. "It seems everyone's having a great time."

"We usually do. It's the kind of thing we do back home. Big reunions, barbecues, that kind of thing."

"I've heard Gabriel lives in Memphis. Is that where you live, as well?"

Adam smiled slyly, lips curving, his deep dimples pert. I guess you could have called his smile wolfish, as there was definitely something predatory about it. "I live wherever I want."

"Nomadic, or just afraid of commitment?"

This time he smiled with teeth. "You wanna try me out?"

I snorted. "I have enough problems managing the vampires in my life."

"How do you know shifters wouldn't be easier to manage?"

"It's not about how easy or hard they are to manage. It's

about keeping out people who require management. I prefer a drama-free existence."

"Probably shouldn't have become a vampire."

"Didn't exactly have a choice."

That stopped him. His smile dropped, replaced by an expression of slightly morbid curiosity. "Didn't have a choice? I thought vampires had to take oaths? Consent to the transformation or something?"

I looked away and moistened my lips nervously. Although the entire city knew I'd been made a vampire, the facts of my change—the fact that I hadn't exactly consented to it—were only known by a precious few. I'd made the offhand remark without thinking . . . but I wasn't sure I was prepared to tell this guy the truth, dimples or not.

"There were considerations other than the drama," I told him, hoping that would answer the question enough to keep him from asking any more. "It wasn't just about becoming a vampire." It was about staying alive. "That's true for a number of us."

When I looked at him again, there was something surprising in his eyes—respect.

"You're a fighter," he concluded. "A warrior, of a sort."

"I stand Sentinel for the House," I said. "A guard, in a manner of speaking."

"A knight amongst kings?"

I smiled. "Something like that. And how do you spend your waking hours, Mr. Keene? Other than wooing girls with those dimples?"

He looked down shyly, but I didn't buy it, especially not when he lifted his gaze again, grinning wickedly. "I'm a man of simple pleasures, Ms. Sentinel."

"And what are those?"

He shrugged negligently, then waved to a man who passed with plastic cups of juice on a tray. Family friendly, I assumed. Adam grabbed two, then handed one to me.

"Next time we have a drink, I'll make it fancier. What are my chances?"

I took a sip of warm apple juice. "Slim to none."

He chuckled good-naturedly. "Taken?"

"And not interested."

"*Ouch*," he said, drawing out the word, "you are a sassy one. I like that."

In spite of myself, I smiled. I wasn't tempted by his offer—and as a matter of fact I *was* taken, it seemed—but that didn't make it any less flattering. Adam Keene was a lethal combination of good looks, charm, and an undercurrent of wickedness.

"I'm also a curious one," I admitted. "And in the few minutes we've been in here, you've avoided every personal question I've asked you."

He held up his free hand. "Sorry, sorry. I don't mean to be evasive. You're a vampire; I'm a shifter. And while I dig that *Romeo and Juliet* vibe, we tend to be a little on the cautious side when it comes to answering to the fanged."

"I can understand that," I allowed with a nod. "But that doesn't make me any less curious."

"Stubborn, aren't you?"

I was hearing that a lot lately. "I am," I admitted. "Let's try again. What does a shifter like you enjoy doing in your free time?"

"Well," he said, looking down at the floor and blinking as he considered, "I grill. I do some lifting. I sling a pretty good guitar."

I lifted my eyebrows. "You sling a guitar? Like, you throw one?" I had an image of two men in a mixed martial arts cage, beating the crap out of each other with curvy acoustic guitars, wood and strings flying.

He chuckled. "Sling as in play. I mess around with a twelve-string. Nothing formal. Just something to relax, maybe out on the back deck with a beer, staring up at the stars."

"That sounds like a pretty nice way to spend an evening." I wondered where that deck was located. "Where are you from?" I asked again.

He paused, fiddling with the edge of his plastic cup, then looked up at me. "You were right about Memphis," he finally said. "We have a den on the East Side—outside the city, so the glare doesn't get in the way of the stars." He frowned. "It's weird to be here—great city, lots of stuff to see, and I like the water—but there're no stars."

"Not many," I agreed. "But I haven't really seen too many of them anywhere else, either. I've lived in New York and California."

"You seem to like concrete."

"It does seem that way. Although the idea of sitting out on a deck with a beer in hand sounds pretty good right now, too."

"That's exactly the point, isn't it?"

I cocked my head at him. "How do you mean?"

Adam gestured at the room. "This. All this. We could all be sitting out on a deck with a beer in hand. Instead of doing that, we're in some fancy house in Chicago, waiting to argue about our future." He shrugged. "I'll do what Gabe asks me to do, but I understand the urge to go home."

"Speaking of the drama, has there been any word from

Tony? Is he taking responsibility for the hit? Challenging Gabriel?"

Adam shook his head. "Not as far as I know. But that's a question for Gabriel."

"You know, I think we just had an actual conversation. That wasn't so bad, was it?"

He raised a hand to his neck. "My carotid appears to be intact, so, no, it wasn't so hard."

"We aren't all chomping at the bit to break open a vein, you know."

Well, unless you put me in a room with Ethan Sullivan.

CHAPTER TWELVE

PACK UP THE MOON

Until Gabriel stepped onto an ottoman in the middle of the Brecks' living room, it seemed, as Adam said, as though we were guests at a family reunion.

Until then.

Gabriel got the crowd's attention with a fierce whistle that nearly made my eardrums pop. That sound was followed by the cacophonous *clink*ing of a hundred silver forks on a hundred wineglasses that stopped only when he jumped atop the ottoman and lifted his hands in the air.

"Pack!" he screamed out, and the room erupted with the sound of a hundred voices—yells, hoots, whistles, screams, and howls. And along with the sounds erupted a sudden charge of magic. The air sizzled with the electric buzz of it, all at once life-affirming and frightening. After all, this was a predatory energy that wasn't mine.

I itched with the urge to move, and nearly jumped out of my skin until Ethan moved close enough to align the sides of our bodies. I wasn't sure if he was moving toward me or away from the Pack members around us, but there was something innately comforting about the feel of him at my side. It was calming, something familiar amidst sensations that my vampire sensibilities weren't too keen on.

Be still, he silently said, expressing not the words of a lover, but an order from Master to Novitiate vampire to calm myself. And as if he'd ordered it, my pulse began to slow.

Jeff, on his way to the front of the room, paused at our sides. "He's calling the Pack," he explained. "As far as I'm aware, you're the first vampires to witness it."

"In Chicago?" I queried.

"In history," he said, then moved forward.

"We are the Pack!" Gabriel announced, and the shifters began to move together, to cluster toward him. As the back of the room cleared, I saw Nick standing alone at the edge of the crowd, a position I assumed he'd adopted since he was still on the outs with Gabriel. And being on the outs with Gabriel, I guessed, was akin to being on the outs with the Pack.

The rest of them embraced, arms linked as they tightened into a rugbylike knot. But this time, the magic didn't leak outward. It condensed as they gathered together, only the boundary tangible from our spot at the edge of the crowd. They linked arms in rings around Gabriel, and then the howls began again. Some were constant, like a four-part harmony of animal sounds; others were random yips. The sounds rose together into a frantic crescendo, the knitted rows of shifters swaying in alternating bands as they sang.

Realization struck—these weren't just vocalizations; they were communications—reassurances amongst the Pack members that they were together, that their families were safe and that the Pack was secure.

It's beautiful, I told Ethan, and considered myself fortunate to be witness to something no vampires had seen before.

The calling continued for another ten or fifteen minutes, the shifters slowly disbanding—one ring at a time—until they were separate again.

Gabriel still stood on the ottoman, hands in the air, his fitted dark T-shirt drenched in sweat. Calling the Pack—maybe reigning in all that magic—must have been hard work.

"Welcome to Chicago," he said, smiling tiredly and getting another hoot from the audience. "Soon enough, we will convene. We will take our collective fate to the Packs, and we will decide whether to stay or go."

The crowd quieted.

"The time will come to make that decision," he said. "But that time is not tonight." He reached down, and when he rose again, held a pink-cheeked toddler in his arms. He pressed a kiss to the child's forehead.

"Our future is clouded. But we will persevere, whatever the outcome. The Pack is eternal, everlasting." He reached down and handed the child back to the outstretched arms of his mother, then rose to face the crowd again, hands fisted on his hips.

"Tonight, we welcome strangers into our midst. We call them vampires, but we know them as friends. They have cared for one of our own, and so we invite them here in friendship tonight."

Gabriel gestured toward us, and in response the Pack members turned to face me and Ethan. Some wore smiles. Others bore expressions of outright distrust and disdain. But even those men and women nodded, begrudging acceptance of the vampires in their midst, vampires who'd saved one of their own.

Thank God for Berna, I silently told Ethan.

Thank God you were quick enough to step forward, he replied.

"All of our lives are intertwined," Gabriel said. "Vampire or shifter, man or woman, our heartbeats echo the very pulse of the earth. And ours are not the only hearts connected." He looked at Ethan, then me. Someone handed him a cup, and Gabriel raised it to us. "We offer our friendship."

Ethan's eyes went instantaneously wide, but he shuttered the emotion and offered a humble bow to the shifters around us as they drank a toast.

"But we don't convene tonight," Gabriel said. "Tonight, we live and breathe and love and enjoy the company of our friends and family. Tonight," he said, winking at me, "we eat."

Another ten or fifteen minutes passed before Gabriel padded through the crowd to us, his expression a bevy of emotions. Even the magic around him seemed conflicted.

"Thank you for allowing us the opportunity to be here," Ethan told him. "It was quite a thing to witness."

Gabriel nodded. "You took a risk that not all would have taken."

"It was the least we could do," Ethan said.

Gabriel looked at me. "You went after her. You risked yourself to get her out of harm's way, to make her safe."

"I did what anyone would have done."

"You saved a *life*." The words were earnest, but there was still something sharp in his tone, something unhappy in his expression.

He seems pretty conflicted about that, I told Ethan.

"Are you . . . concerned about something?" Ethan asked.

He shook his head. "I will owe Merit a debt," he said. "I've repaid part of it—dealing with the Breckenridges and their unfounded animosity."

We already knew that part—Gabriel had confessed it when he'd visited Cadogan House. I had no idea what debt he was referring to, but it had something, I thought, to do with family. Whether his or mine, Pack or vampire, I didn't know.

And I figured there was no harm in asking. "What's the debt you'll owe?"

"I can't reveal that, Sentinel. The future is fluid. I can see the ripples, far into the water, but that doesn't mean the future is immutable, that events cannot be altered." Shifters were different from sorcerers on that point; sorcerers prophesized whenever they could, although the prophecies themselves were usually hard to understand.

"Can you give me a hint? You said something about family. Mine? Yours?"

Gabriel looked up and across the room. I followed his gaze to a woman who stood on the edge of it, friends or relations at her side. Her dark hair was loose around her face, her cheeks freshly pink, her hands supporting the swell of her belly. This was Tonya, his wife, and Connor, his child, a future member of the Keene clan and the North American Central Pack. A future Apex?

"I won't be giving away too much," he said, "to suggest that the safety of my family lies within your sphere of influence."

We were all silent for a moment, the weight of that pronouncement between us. I wasn't sure if I should be flattered that Gabriel deemed me capable of protecting his family—or worried that the responsibility lay on my shoulders.

"On the other hand, the Packs shouldn't carry the burden

of my debts to others." He swallowed thickly. "I can't make any guarantees about alliances. All I can say is that I won't shut down the idea entirely. That's all I can offer."

And with that simple suggestion—the idea that he might be willing to *consider* an alliance with vampires—Gabriel Keene made history.

"Before we go," I said, bringing us back around to current concerns, "have you heard about Tony's bike? About the forensic results?"

He nodded. "I know they found GSR."

"Have you heard anything from him?" Ethan asked.

"Not word one. Why?"

"We wondered if he'd take responsibility for the bar," Ethan said, "maybe try to take an overt stand against you or the convocation. If he was involved, and he's really trying to sway the balance of power, that'd be the logical way to go."

Gabriel furrowed his brow, then shook his head. "We haven't heard from him, and Tony's lieutenant hasn't heard from him, either. I assumed he'd gone underground to save his ass."

"That is a possibility," Ethan agreed.

Gabriel's gaze shifted as Fallon waved to him from the other side of the room. "I need to go. I'll see you tomorrow night."

Without another word, he turned and walked back to the bar, leaving Ethan and me staring after him.

Ethan didn't wait before getting to the good stuff. "He may not have offered a formal allegiance, but that is by far the closest we've come."

"We're a good team," I said with a cheeky smile.

He humphed, but there was a smile on his face.

"Now that I've gotten us into a Pack potluck and maybe dropped an alliance into your lap, I'm going to check out the buffet."

"You just ate."

I gave him a sardonic look. "I'm a vampire with a metabolism faster than a speeding bullet. Besides, that plate was all meat and sides. I didn't get dessert."

"Go," he said, shooing me with a hand. "Go find chocolate."

I smiled grandly, then took off for the giant buffet.

It was even more impressive up close than it had been from far away. The food was homemade, from steaming casseroles and roasted vegetables to pink-frosted and coconut-topped cakes. I aimed straight for the desserts, picking up a small plate and fork along the way to host my bounty.

Trouble came calling just as I put a homemade cookie on my plate.

"Vampire, huh?"

I looked over at the shifter who'd spoken. He was tall and broad shouldered, his thick dark hair pulled into a low ponytail and braid. Most of his face was covered by a thick beard.

"Yep," I politely said, offering him a smile. "Vampire."

He grunted, then leaned toward me, the smells of leather, cheap whiskey, and cigar smoke moving with him. "You think you're so hot, right? Little vampire?"

Gabriel's willingness to extend friendship to vampires was clearly not a unanimous emotion. But that friendship was on the line, so I kept my rising ire to myself and moved a couple of feet down the table.

"Just having some dessert," I said lightly. "Looks delicious."

He made a couple of warthogish snorts, as if shocked that I had the gall to ignore his attempt to rile me up. "I was talking to you," he finally said, his voice low and menacing.

"And I was politely ignoring you." I mustered up my bravery and slid him a warning glance. "I'm a guest in this house, and I plan on acting like one. Maybe you should, too."

That was the end of the discussion—because his next step was physical. He reached out and grabbed my arm, then jerked me forward, spewing curses at me as he moved. I jerked back to try to free my arm, dropping the plate in my hand. It hit the floor and shattered, crumbs and porcelain flying across the floor.

But before I could react, he was gone.

Because before I could react, Ethan had the man by the collar of his shirt and was pushing him back toward the wall.

"Keep your hands *off* her," he gritted out.

With a quick twist of his hands, the shifter threw Ethan's arms away, then gave him a powerful shove for good measure. "Who the fuck do you think you are?"

Ethan stumbled back a couple of feet, but leaned forward quickly enough again, apparently intent on making a second run at the guy. "You come anywhere near her again, and you'll answer to me, Pack be damned."

Shock giving way to political awareness, I reached out and grabbed his arm, then hauled him around so he and the shifter weren't facing each other down. "*Ethan*," I whispered fiercely. "Calm down."

Gabriel rushed toward us, Fallon and Adam behind him.

"What the fuck is going on in here?"

The ballroom went completely silent, all eyes on the vampires creating chaos in the midst of their party.

The shifter rolled his shoulders, as if tossing off the insult, then pointed at Ethan. "I was having a conversation with this *vampire*, and then this asshole pushed me. And now I'm going to push him back."

Thank God I was a vampire, as that added dose of strength was the only thing that allowed me to hold Ethan back. He made another drive, enough to carry me forward a couple of feet before I could stop him again.

Adam and Fallon jumped between the two of them, ready to intervene if he tried again.

Ethan, I mentally told him. *Stop it! Enough!*

"He grabbed her," Ethan said through clenched teeth, then shook off my arms. "I'm fine." He pushed his hands through his hair. "I'm fine, and you need to get your shifters under control."

Gabriel stared at Ethan, his expression fierce, his hands clenched into fists. Magic rose again, a suffocating cloud of it, as he decided our fate.

I cursed mentally, assuming this was the end of our shifter détente.

But just then, Tonya stepped behind him. One hand on her stomach, she reached out with the other to touch Gabriel's back. As if answering her caress, Gabriel glanced between me and Ethan. And after a moment, I watched understanding soften the fury in his face.

He'd figured out that Ethan had nearly taken a shot at one of his Pack members because that Pack member had nearly taken a shot at me.

After a moment of silence, Gabriel took a step toward Ethan, then leaned in as though offering advice to a colleague. "If you want this friendship to work, then you will keep yourself in line. I get your reasons," he said, pausing for emphasis, "but this kind of shit will not fly. Not with my Pack. Not with my people."

Ethan nodded, his gaze on the ground.

Gabriel's voice softened. "Are you going to be ready to work the convocation tomorrow?"

"Of course."

After a moment, he nodded. "Then I'm taking your word on that, and that's good enough for me." He stood straight again. "We're done here," he announced to the room. It's over. It's over, and everything's fine, so let's get back to dinner, shall we?" Then he took Tonya's hand and approached my aggressor, clasping a big hand on his shoulder. "Let's go have a drink and talk about manners."

As he moved into the crowd, the din of noise and conversation began to envelop us again.

"We should go," Ethan said.

I nodded and let him lead me out.

He was silent on the way to the car. That silence and the ensuing tension thickened the air in the car until we were well away from the Breckenridge property and on our way back to Hyde Park.

I'd seen his protectiveness twice now. His gestures had been powerful, but they also put uneasiness between us—as if the gestures were too powerful for a relationship as new and green as ours.

"My reaction was uncalled for," he finally said.

"You thought he was going to hurt me."

Ethan shook his head. "I've been critiquing Morgan. I've complained that he overreacts. That he allows his emotions to get in the way of the needs of his House."

My stomach twisted, and I had the sickening feeling that I knew where this conversation was going. "Ethan," I said, but he shook his head.

"If Morgan had pulled that stunt, I'd have taken him out. I'd have hauled him out of the room and reminded him of his obligations. Of his duties to his House and the rest of them. I'm frankly surprised Gabriel didn't take action of his own."

Gabriel hadn't, I thought, because with a touch, Tonya had reminded Gabriel of the reason Ethan had acted—*for me*.

"You stepped in to protect me. It's understandable."

"It's *unacceptable*," he countered.

That word stung like a punch, and I turned my face to the passenger side window so he couldn't see the tears that had begun to fill my eyes. However grand his gesture at the Breck house, Ethan was preparing his excuse.

"I could have mooted all of Gabriel's overtures, destroyed all the good rapport he's building between shifters and vampires, because of my reaction. Just like that," he added, snapping his fingers.

Then he went quiet for a moment.

"It's been a long time for me since I've cared for someone. Since I've allowed instinct to take over." His voice softened, as if he'd forgotten I was in the car. "I should have seen it coming. I should have considered the possibility that I'd react in such a way."

Was I supposed to appreciate the admission that he cared for me when he was drowning in regret about it?

"What if Gabriel did offer an alliance, friendship, because of what you'd done for Berna? If we continued our relationship, and our emotions became intertwined, entangled, and it came to the same end as yours and Morgan's—what then? All the bitterness? The bad feelings?"

What was I supposed to say? Was I supposed to argue with him? Remind him of the physical bliss? Reassure him that he wasn't Morgan, and that our relationship was different?

"If we form an allegiance with the Pack, we'll have made history. We'll have made an allegiance that's unique in history. And now my reaction has put that allegiance at risk. If that's how I'm going to react, then I'm not ready for this—maybe not capable of it. Not when it puts the safety and security of the House at risk." He was quiet for a moment. "There are *three hundred* Cadogan vampires, Merit."

And I'm one of those three hundred, I silently thought, and forced myself to ask the next question. "So what are you saying?"

"I'm saying I can't do this. Not now. Things are too fragile."

I waited to speak until I was sure my voice wouldn't waver. "I don't want to just pretend it didn't happen."

"I don't have the luxury of remembering. A girl isn't reason enough to throw away my House."

I swallowed the lump in my throat and, with tears drying on my cheeks, made my decision. I'd spurned Ethan's advances when he'd offered just sex. But I'd given in when he'd said he needed me.

In fact, he'd decided I was disposable.

I felt stupid—naïve. But I wouldn't let him see it, so I locked down my heart and found I could speak in that same cold voice he'd used. "You've changed your mind before. If you end it now and change your mind again, I won't come back. I'll stand Sentinel, but only as your employee. Not as your lover."

It took a moment for him to answer . . . and break my heart.

"Then that's the risk I take."

We rode home in silence broken only by Ethan's reminder that we were meeting with Luc before dawn to discuss the convocation. I managed not to reach across the center console and throttle him, but as soon as we were parked in the garage, I jumped out of the car and headed up the basement stairs and out the front door again.

There were hours yet until dawn, and I couldn't spend them in the House.

I was too embarrassed to stay there, too humiliated at having been so unceremoniously dumped for the possibility of Ethan's burgeoning friendship with Gabriel. He'd given me up because dating me risked his bond with the Pack.

A bond, ironically enough, that I'd helped create.

I got into my car and headed north across the river, hoping distance would help ease the hurt. At the very least I wouldn't have to cry within earshot of the Cadogan vampires.

I should have known better. I should have known he wasn't capable of adapting, that he would always pick strategy over love, that no matter the words he'd used, he was still the same cold bloodsucker.

I considered calling Noah and consenting to join the Red Guard right then and there, consenting to partner with Jonah to oversee the Masters, to judge them, to take action when they fell short of their potential. But that was a betrayal I still couldn't commit. Ethan had his reasons for deciding a relationship between us wouldn't work. Even if I didn't agree with them, I understood them.

None of that, unfortunately, diminished the embarrassment, the feeling that I'd offered and been found lacking, the feeling that being put aside was wholly my own doing.

And, most important, the feeling that in taking Ethan's

side, I'd stood against one of two people in the world who loved me unconditionally.

That regret sent me to Wicker Park, not even sure if she'd be there, but without a better idea. I parked outside her narrow brownstone and hopped up the stairs, then knocked on the door.

She opened it a second later. Her ice blue hair was getting longer and now reached her shoulders. She wore a simple skirt and short-sleeved shirt, her feet bare, her toes painted in a rainbow of colors, from indigo to red.

Her smile faded almost immediately. "Mer? What is it?"

Despite the speech I'd planned on the way over, a regret-filled "I'm sorry" was all I managed to get out. "I'm so, so sorry."

Mallory gave me an up-and-down appraisal before meeting my gaze again. "Oh, Merit. Tell me you didn't."

—•◦—◦◦◦◦—◦—

CHAPTER THIRTEEN

YOU'RE MY BEST FRIEND

Mallory knew me way too well. I gave her a pitiful smile.

She stepped aside and held open the door. Walking into the foyer, I was immediately comforted by the sounds and smells of home—lemon furniture polish, cinnamon and sugar, the slightly musty smell of an older home, the low murmur of the television.

"Couch," she directed. "Sit."

I did, taking a seat on the middle cushion.

Mallory grabbed a handful of tissues from a box on the side table, then sat beside me, handed them over, and pushed the hair from my face. "Tell me."

I did. I told her about the shifter bar, the pizza, the chocolate. I told her about the party, Gabriel's friendship, and the bully; about Ethan's reaction and the "risk" he was willing to take. By the end of it, I was in her arms, crying into her shoulder. Crying like a girl whose heart had been shattered into tiny, brittle pieces, even if it had been my fault for falling in the first place.

"I gave him the benefit of the doubt," I said, mopping at my face with a tissue. "At first, I thought, oh, he's just afraid. He just can't give more because he's not capable right now." I shook my head. "It's not because he isn't capable. It's because he wants something else."

That sickening feeling rolled through my stomach again, that horrible twist that only rejection could trigger.

Mallory sat back on the couch, hands in her lap, and sighed, long and hard. "In this case, Merit—and I don't want to make a martyr of him, because he is far beneath our consideration at the moment—it's probably a little of both. I've seen him with you. I've seen the way he looks at you. I know I'm hard on him."

Her voice softened. "I know I was hard on you. But there's more than just desire in his eyes when he looks at you. It's not just the physical stuff. There's something else—some kind of affection, maybe. Some kind of appreciation that's not just about hormones and pink parts. The problem is, he's a four-hundred-year-old vampire. He's *not* human, and he hasn't been in a long time. We don't even know if he thinks the same or wants the same things."

"Don't blame the vampire," I told her. "That doesn't get him off the hook."

"Oh, trust me," she said. "You give me ten minutes alone with Darth Sullivan, and he will feel my most excellent wrath." A tingle of magic lit the air and sent a prickle of foreboding down my spine. Powerful, was my sorceress friend.

"All I'm saying is, it sounds as if he doesn't think he has a choice. That's not an excuse, but it's an explanation."

I blew out a slow breath and knuckled tears from beneath my eyes. "It's not as if I don't know those things. I know he's not human, not really, even though he has these incredibly vulnerable moments that make my heart clench. You should have seen him when he jumped the shifter, Mallory. He went ballistic—shoved the guy against a wall."

"Just like I would have done. But with sorcerer juju instead of vampire juju."

I nodded. "But you wouldn't have regretted it. He did. Gabriel understood why he'd done it—I know he did. But that wasn't good enough. I mean, it's as if I'm being punished because Ethan's black nugget of a heart actually started beating again."

"It's definitely not fair, hon. And I wish I had some magic thing to say that would fix the whole scenario, but I don't."

"It's just—I know he's not perfect. He can be cold and controlling. But I've seen that passion, the affection that he's locked away. I've seen what he's capable of. He's just—he's also, I don't know—"

"He's Ethan."

I looked over at her and sniffed.

"He's Ethan. For some bizarre reason, he seems to be *your* Ethan. And for better or worse, you seem to be his Merit. That irritates me on a daily basis."

"I'm so stupid."

"Not stupid. Just a little too human for your own good."

I didn't mention that we'd both criticized Morgan for exactly the same thing. "Sometimes too human, sometimes not human enough. And either way, sometimes a stone-cold idiot."

"Now, that," Mallory said, "I can agree with."

"He's been in love, you know."

Mallory looked over at me. "In love? Ethan?"

I nodded and relayed the information Lindsey had once

passed along. "Her name was Lacey Sheridan. She was a guard for a couple of decades, I guess. Lindsey thinks he was in love with her, although they broke it off years ago when she started her own House."

"She's a Master?"

"One of twelve."

"Is it perfectly fitting that if you were the next Master in line, you'd be the thirteenth House?"

"Given my luck, pretty damned appropriate."

She rose off the couch, then walked toward the hallway. "Come on, genius. Let's get you something to eat."

I wrapped my hands around my stomach, which was just beginning to stop swimming. "I'm not hungry."

She glanced back and offered a flat stare.

"Well, not *that* hungry," I said, but followed her to the kitchen anyway. I had missed dessert, after all.

"Dear Lord," I said, stepping into the kitchen. What had once been a tiny cottage kitchen had become a—well, I wasn't sure what to call it. The potions classroom from Hogwarts, maybe?

I walked to the kitchen island and trailed my fingers over stacks of books, a deck of tarot cards, boxes of salt, glass jars of feathers, grapevines, corked bottles of oils, matches, and dried rose petals.

I plucked a card from the tarot deck—the ace of swords. Fitting, I thought, placing the card gingerly atop the rest of the deck. "What is all this stuff?"

"Homework," she grumbled.

"Oh, my God, it *is* Hogwarts."

She gave me a snarky look and began to clear off an area

on the island. "I'm playing catch-up with little witches who've been doing this stuff for years."

I pulled out a stool and sat down. "I thought you were training alone?"

"I am. But I'm not the first student my teacher's had. Before he was sent to the Siberia of sorcery—"

"Schaumburg?"

"Schaumburg," she confirmed. "Before that, he taught lots and lots of kids. Kids who were much younger than me when they got their magic. Turns out, hitting my magical stride at twenty-seven puts me pretty far behind the rest of the pack."

"But I bet you make up for it with sass and charm."

She narrowed her gaze. "I make up for it with being twice as powerful as anyone else."

"For serial?"

"Completely for serial."

I surveyed the spread on the table. "So why the homework? I distinctly remember a lecture by Catcher about how you guys don't have to use spells or potions or whatever"—I dropped my voice an octave and bobbed my shoulders in what I'm sure was an Oscar-worthy impression of Catcher Bell—"but could funnel the power directly through your bodies."

"Was that supposed to be Catcher?"

"Kinda. Yeah."

"Huh. Sounded more like John Goodman."

"I'm not an actress. I just play one on TV. Get to the point."

"This will shock you," Mallory said, pulling out a stool beside mine and plopping down, "but it turns out Catcher's a little pretentious about the magic thing."

I snorted. "I feel bad you're only just figuring that out."

"As if there's a way to miss it. Consider anything that comes out of his mouth about magic—except for the major Keys; he's got those right—to be a matter of opinion. He thinks the only legit way to do magic is to will things to happen. That's not true," she said, shoulders slumped as she surveyed the piles of materials. "Sorcerers are like craftsmen of magic."

"Craftsmen how?"

"Well, the four Keys are a little like painting. You've got folks who paint with oils, with acrylics, with watercolors. In the end, you still get art. You just used different tools to get there. You can use any of the four Keys to make magic." She held up a cork-stoppered glass jar of white powder to the light and spun it around like a connoisseur might twirl a glass of wine before taking a sip. Its pearlescent sparkle made it seem extraordinarily white; densely white.

"Ground unicorn horn?" I wondered.

"Glitter from that craft store on Division."

"Close enough," I said. I fingered the Cadogan medal at my neck, working up the nerve to get out the thing we hadn't talked about yet—the speech I hadn't yet made. "I've missed you."

She swallowed, but didn't look at me. "I've missed you, too."

"I wasn't there for you. Not like you were for me."

Mallory blew out a slow breath. "No, Merit, you weren't. But I was unfair about the Morgan thing. I didn't mean to push you; I just didn't want you to get hurt. And that thing I said—"

"About my daddy issues?" That one still stung.

"Completely uncalled for. I am so sorry."

I nodded, but the silence returned again, as if we hadn't quite worked through the wall of awkwardness between us.

"Turns out, I was *completely* right about the Ethan thing."

I rolled my eyes. "And so humble about it, too. Fine—yes, you were right. He was—*is*—dangerous, and I fell right into his trap."

She opened her mouth to speak, then snapped it shut again. She shook her head, as if unable to decide whether to voice the words in her head. When she did decide, the words flew out in a rush. "Okay, I'm so sorry, but I have to ask. How was it? I mean, seriously. Grade-A asshole or not, the man is gorgeous."

A corner of my mouth quirked up into a smile. "It was almost worth the emotional trauma."

"How almost?"

"Multiple times almost."

"Huh," she said. "That both figures—as pretty as he is—and irritates. You kinda hope a guy who pulls a stunt like he did this evening is seriously lacking in the nookie skills department. And your performance?"

"Mallory."

She made the sign of a cross over her chest. "I have a point, I swear."

I rolled my eyes, but grinned a little. "I was impressive."

"So impressive that the next time he sees you in that leather, he's going to rue walking out?"

I grinned at her. "Now I recall why I best-friended you."

"You have a faulty memory. I best-friended you."

We looked at each other for a minute, schoolgirl-silly grins on our faces.

We were back.

A few minutes and the replay of a few *Sex and the City*–worthy details later, Mallory was off her stool and headed for the fridge.

"I have cold pizza if you want some," she said, "but I'll warn you, it's a little . . . different."

I picked up a foot-long black feather and twirled it in my hand. "How different?"

"Catcher Bell different." She opened the fridge, pulled out a wide, flat pizza box, and shut the door again with a bump. I leaned up and used both hands to push containers out of the way, leaving a bare spot big enough for the pizza box. This one was from another Wicker Park joint, the kind that made artisanal pizza with goat cheese and organic herbs. It wasn't my favorite, but it definitely had its place in my repertoire. Hand-pulled crust, homemade sauce, coins of fresh mozzarella.

"How different could it be?" I asked.

And then she placed the box on the island and flipped it open.

I stared at it, tilted my head at it, trying to figure out what, exactly, he'd done to pizza. "Is that celery? And carrots?"

"And mashed potatoes."

It was like being dumped all over again, but this time by something I never imagined would hurt me. I looked up at Mallory, despair in my eyes, then pointed down at the pizza again. "Is that a pea? On *pizza*?"

"It's some kind of shepherd's pic thing. His mom was experimenting one day and made it, and it's the only good thing from his childhood or something, and he paid the restaurant a buttload of cash to make it."

My shoulders slumped, and my voice went petulant. "But . . . it's *pizza*."

"If it makes you feel better, they protested pretty well," Mallory said. "They tried to sell us a cream cheese and double bacon—"

"The official pizza of the Merit/Carmichael ticket," I put in.

"But Catcher can beg as well as the rest of them." Mal smiled knowingly. "Not that I know anything about that."

I groaned, but grinned. If Mallory was back to discussing doin' it with Catcher, our friendship was on the mend. Still—not anything I needed to know about. "That's disgusting. He was my trainer."

"So was Ethan," she pointed out. "And look how well *that* turned out. At least you've notched your bedpost with a Master vampire and you can finally move on." She got very still, then glanced at me. "You are moving on, right?"

Something in my stomach flipped over and clenched. It took a minute before I could answer. "Yeah. I told him it was his one chance. That if he left, the risk was on him." I shrugged. "He opted for the risk."

"His loss, Mer. His loss."

"Easy to say that, but I'd feel better if he slipped into a profound depression or something."

"I bet he's doing that right now. Probably flogging himself as we speak."

"There's no need to be dramatic. Just like there's no need to waste this—let's not call it pizza—carrot concoction."

And so I let her ply me with leftover shepherd's pie pizza. And when I'd finished, because she'd offered the thing she hadn't previously been willing to give me—understanding about Ethan—I gave her the thing I hadn't previously been willing to give her—time.

"Can I tell you about the magic now?" she'd sheepishly asked.

"Let her rip, tater chip," I told her, and gave her my full attention.

She sat cross-legged on her kitchen stool, hands in the air as she prepared to tell me the things I hadn't made time to hear before. She started with the basics.

"Okay," she began, "so you know about the four major Keys."

I nodded. "The divisions of magic. Weapons. Beings. Power. Texts." Catcher had taught me that lesson.

"Right. Well, as I was saying before, those are like your paints—your tools for making things happen."

I frowned, put an elbow on the island, and put my chin in my hand. "And what kind of things can you make happen, exactly?"

"The whole range," she said, "from Merlin to Marie Laveau. And you use one or more of the Keys to do it. Power— that's the First Key. It's the elemental force, the pure expression of will."

"The only legit way to perform magic in Catcher's eyes."

Mallory nodded. "And the irony is, he's a master of the Second Key."

"Weapons," I offered, and she nodded again.

"Right. But lots of things can be weapons." She spread her arms over her piles of materials. "All this stuff—potions, runes, fetishes. And not the sex kind," she added, as if anticipating that I'd make a snarky comment. Fair enough, 'cause I would have.

"None of it is inherently magical, but when you put them together in the right combinations, you create a catalyst for a magical reaction."

I frowned. "What about my sword?"

"Remember when Catcher pricked your palm? Tempered the blade with blood?"

I nodded. He'd done that in my grandfather's backyard on the evening of my twenty-eighth birthday. I'd had the ability to sense steel from that night on. "Yep," I said, rubbing my palm sympathetically.

"Your blade had potential. When you tempered the blade, you brought forth that potential, making it real. Now, the last two major Keys are obvious. Beings—creatures that are inherently magical. Sorcerers can do it. Vampires kind of 'shed' it. Shifters are all over it. And texts—books, spells, written names. Words that operate like the blood you shed on your blade."

"Catalysts for magic?"

"Exactly. That's why spells and incantations work. The words together, in the right order, with the right power behind them."

"So you've learned all this stuff," I said, sitting up again. "Can you actually use it?"

"Eh, maybe." She uncrossed her legs and turned back to the island, looked over the spread of stuff, then plucked a thin glass canister of what looked like birch bark from the array. "Can you grab something for me? There's a little black notebook on the coffee table in the living room. It has gold writing on the spine."

"Are you going to work some magical mojo?"

"If you get off your butt before I turn you into a toad, yes."

I hopped off my stool. "If you turn me into a toad, you'd have already worked your mojo."

"You're too smart for your own good," she called out, but I was already heading down the hallway. The house looked pretty much the same as it had the last time I'd visited a couple of weeks ago, although there was more evidence of a boy in residence—random receipts here and there; a pair of beat-up running shoes; a copy of *Men's Health* on the dining room table; a stack of audio equipment in one corner.

So as I trolled back into the living room, I was prepared to see guy stuff. Balled-up sweat socks, maybe, or a half-empty can of Pabst or a bottle of 312, or whatever Catcher drank.

I wasn't prepared for an empty room . . . that had been filled with furniture only a little while ago.

"Holy shit," I swore, hands on my hips as I surveyed the room. "*Mal*," I called out. "Come here! I think you were robbed!"

But how could they have moved out an entire roomful of furniture and knickknacks—and without our knowing it?

"Look up!"

"Seriously—come here! I'm not kidding!"

"Merit!" she yelled back. "Just flippin' look up."

I did.

My mouth dropped.

"Holy shit."

The room had gone completely *Poltergeist*. All of the furniture—from couch to end table to entertainment console and television—was on the ceiling. Everything was in its place, but everything was upside down. It was like standing beneath the looking glass—a mirror image of what had been here before. It was also as if gravity took a vacation. I saw the tiny black book Mallory wanted, but it was stuck to the top (bottom?) of the coffee table that was now perched a few feet above my head.

"I guess I could jump for it," I murmured with a small smile, then instinctively glanced back toward the door. She stood in the doorway, arms over her chest, one ankle crossed over the other, a supremely smug smile on her face.

"You know, you look just like Catcher when you stand like that."

Mallory, this girl who'd mooted gravity, stuck out her tongue at me.

"I guess you learned a few things."

She shrugged, then pushed off the door.

"How did you do it?" I asked, walking around, head tipped up as I moved across the room, to survey what she'd done.

"First Key," she said. "Power. There are energies in the universe that act on all of us. I moved the energies, spun the currents a little, and the universe shifted itself."

Well, I guess Ethan had been partly right. "So it's like the Force?"

"That's not a bad analogy, actually."

My best friend could cause the universe to shift. So much for my being a badass. "That is just . . . splendiferous."

She chuckled, but then screwed up her face. "The problem is, I'm not very good at getting it back down again."

"So what are you going to do? Leave it for Catcher?"

"Dear God, no. He's already fixed it three times this week. I'll just give it the old college try." She cleared her throat and lifted her arms, then glanced back at me. "You may want to get out of the way. It can get a little messy."

I took the warning to heart, then hightailed it to the threshold between the living room and the dining room, where I turned back around to watch.

Mallory closed her eyes, and her hair lifted as if she'd put a hand on a Tesla coil. I felt my own ponytail lift as energy swirled through the air, as strong as the currents and eddies in a river.

"It's just a matter," Mallory said, "of shifting the currents."

I looked up. The furniture began to vibrate, then bobble on its feet, the vibration of all those marching bits of furniture sending down a light shower of plaster.

"This is the hard part," she said.

"You can do it."

Like a marching band at halftime, the pieces began to march in little lines around the ceiling. I watched in awe as the love seat followed the couch, which followed a side table around in a circle and then, after a little bob, onto the side-wall. Gravity had no more effect there than it had on the ceiling, and the furniture began to move, *Fantasia*-like, down the walls and toward the baseboards.

"Tricky, tricky," she said as the furniture stepped down onto the floor again.

I glanced back at Mallory. Her outstretched arms, shaking with the effort, shone with sweat. I'd seen her like this before, one of the first times I'd seen her work her magic. We'd been at a rave sight at the time, and she'd offered up a prophecy. But it had taken a lot out of her, and she'd slept in the car on the way home.

This looked a lot like that—with much heavier consequences.

"Mal? Do you need some help?"

"I'll get it," she bit out, and the furniture continued its

dance, the floor now vibrating beneath us as it marched back into place.

"Uh-oh," she said.

"Uh-oh?" I repeated, then took a step backward. "I don't like the sound of 'uh-oh.'"

"I think I'm kicking up dust."

I managed to mutter a curse before she sneezed and the rest of the stuff on the ceiling crashed to the ground. Luckily, the electronics had already made their way down. But the rest of the stuff that I could see, after I'd waved a hand at the dust she'd kicked up, was in a shambles.

"Mal?"

"I'm okay," she said, then appeared through the fog of plaster and dust that had accumulated over the twenty years her aunt had lived in the brownstone. She stood by me and turned around, and we surveyed the damage. There was a snowfall of knickknacks on the ground—kittens and porcelain roses and other items purchased by Mal's aunt on one of her television shopping network sprees. The sofa had successfully finished the journey right-side-up, but the love seat stood precariously on its side. The bookcase was facedown, but the books were stacked in tidy piles beside it.

"Hey, the books look *nice*."

"Watch it, smartass."

I bit back a snicker that threatened to bubble up, and I had to press my lips together to keep from laughing.

"I'm still learning," she said.

"Even vampires need practice," I supportively added.

"No shit, since Celina batted you around like you were Tom to her Jerry."

I slid her a sideways—and none too friendly—glance.

"What?" she asked with a shrug. "So Celina likes to play with her food."

"At least Celina didn't destroy Cadogan House in the process."

"Oh, yeah? Check this." She stomped—literally, stomped—back to the kitchen, moved around the island, and pulled open the long drawer that held my chocolate stash.

She reached in and, her eyes still on me, moved a hand through my treasure trove until she pulled out a long paper-wrapped bar of gourmet dark chocolate. Grinning evilly at her bounty, she held it before her with both hands, then ripped a corner off the packaging.

"That's one of my favorites," I warned her.

"Oh, is it?" she asked, then used her teeth to snap off a giant corner of the bar.

"Mallory! That's just hateful."

"Sometimes, a woman needs to hate," was what I thought she said over a mouthful of seventy-three percent dark chocolate that I'd been able to find only at a tiny shop near U of C. On the other hand, I'd done without for this long. . . .

"Fine," I said, crossing my arms over my chest. If we were going to fight like adolescent sisters, might as well go the distance. "Eat it. Eat the whole thing while I'm standing here."

"Maybe I—," she broke off, raising the back of her free hand and chewing a mouthful of chocolate. "Maybe I will," she finally got out. As if acting on a dare, she arched an eyebrow, then snapped another bite—although a tiny one—off the end.

"Don't snap my chocolate at me."

"I'll snap whatever I want at you *whenever* I want. It's my house."

"It's my chocolate."

"Then you probably shouldn't have left it here," said a manly voice in the doorway. We both turned to look at the door. Catcher stood in the doorway, hands on his hips. "Does either one of you want to explain what the hell happened to my house?"

"We're making up," Mallory said, still trying to masticate the mouthful of chocolate.

"By destroying the living room and going into sugar shock?"

She shrugged and swallowed. "It seemed like a good idea at the time." As if suddenly realizing that the gruff boy she loved had come home, she smiled. Her face lit up with it. "Hey, baby."

He shook his head in amusement, then pushed off the door and went to her.

I rolled my eyes. "Can we keep it PG for the kids, please? Think of the children."

Catcher stopped when he reached her and clucked her chin between his thumb and fist. "Just for that, we're going to have a steamy make-out scene."

I rolled my eyes and looked away, but not before I caught sight of him dipping his head for a kiss. I gave them a few seconds before I began clearing my throat, the universal symbol of uncomfortable friends and roommates everywhere.

"So," Catcher said, moving around me to nab the last piece of casserole-style pizza from the box when they finally unlocked lips. "How are things in Cadogan House?"

"Merit and Ethan did it."

He paused midbite, then turned to stare at me.

My cheeks flamed red.

"If you're here instead of basking in the glow, I assume he did something incredibly stupid."

"That's my boy," Mallory said, then slapped him on the butt and headed for the fridge. She opened it, grabbed two cans of diet soda, handed one to me, then popped the top on the other one.

"What an idiot," Catcher said, and put the rest of the slice back in the box. He placed his hands on his hips, his expression mystified. "You know that I've known Sullivan a long time, right?"

When he looked at me, brows raised, I nodded. I didn't know how they knew each other, but I knew they went "way back," or so Catcher had said.

"This may not come as much consolation after the deed is done, so to speak, but he'll regret it, and probably sooner than later. But you got something out of it, at least."

At my lifted brows, he pointed at Mallory. "You two are talking again."

Mallory looked at me from across the island. "Funny, isn't it, that it took Darth Sullivan to bring us back together?"

"Well, he did have the honor of tearing us asunder in the first place."

She held out her hands and wiggled her fingers. "Come on over. Let's hug it out."

And so we did.

When Catcher got his appetite back, he worked on the last slice while Mallory and I rummaged through my chocolate collection. As an act of good faith, I donated most of it to the Carmichael-Bell house, but that didn't stop me from stuffing chocolate bars filled with almonds and dried cherries into my pockets before I left. I also nabbed a bag of chocolate-coated pecans and sat down to catch up with Mallory's beau. He didn't yet have any additional information about the investigation of the bar shooting, but I filled him in on the basic details of the Pack meeting at the Brecks'.

Eventually, I thought to check my watch. Dawn was approaching, and I still had to meet Ethan and Luc to discuss the convocation. "I need to head back to the House."

"Maybe Ethan's come to his senses since you've been gone," Mallory said. "Maybe he's pining outside your door."

We both contemplated that for a second before snorting simultaneously.

"And leprechauns might poop rainbows on your pillow," she said.

"What do I do, Mal? Do I argue with him? Tell him he's wrong and we can work this out? Ignore him? Scream? How am I supposed to work with him?"

"I think that's exactly his point, Mer. As for arguing, think about it this way: do you want to be with a man who has to be convinced to be with you?"

"Not when you put it like that."

She nodded, then patted my cheek. "You're ready. Go home."

I knew when to take an order.

CHAPTER FOURTEEN

HOUSE OF PAIN

I found Luc perched on the edge of the conference table that took up the middle of the Operations Room. Lindsey was at the computer station opposite Luc, where she could monitor feed from the security cameras in and around the House or research whatever supernatural drama was threatening to bubble over into Hyde Park.

They both looked up when I entered.

"How bad was it?" Luc asked. I guessed he and Ethan had talked about what had happened at the Brecks.

"It wasn't fabulous."

Lindsey swiveled around in her chair. "Is there anything else you want to talk about?" Her voice rang with quiet concern.

"Not especially."

"Ethan seemed weird," she said. "He didn't tell us anything about you and him, but he seemed really weird." I almost snarked back, but when I saw the worry in her expression, and heard the concern in her tone, I threw her a bone.

"I was dumped, and I'd like to think about something else

for a little while." I pointed at the spread of documents on the conference table. "What's all this?"

"I—he did what?"

I appreciated the shock and dismay in Lindsey's voice but shook my head. "Business, please."

"Your show, Sentinel," Luc said, then hopped off the table and turned to face it. "This is prep work for your convocation field trip—schematics of St. Bridget's Cathedral."

The door behind us opened, and Ethan walked in. He gave me a quick nod of acknowledgment before settling his gaze on the table.

I reminded myself that I'd managed a relatively professional relationship with Ethan for all but one of the nights we'd known each other. If he was going to reject me for fear of mixing the personal and the professional, I could play the all-business vampire, as well.

"Plans?" Ethan asked.

Luc nodded. "Ask and ye shall receive."

"Technically," Lindsey said, turning back to her monitor, "check your e-mail and ye shall receive them from the Apex of the North American Central."

"Details," Luc said. "They're here now."

Ethan walked around the conference table to stand next to Luc. I followed and took point at Luc's other side.

"Your analysis?" Ethan asked.

Luc put on his game face. "I had two main goals. One— identifying trouble spots. Areas that snipers could sneak into, parson's holes, that kind of thing. Two—identifying exits."

"And what did you find?" Ethan asked.

Luc began flipping through the blueprints. "There are two main parts to the church. First up, the original structure, built in the late nineteenth century. Old religious architecture in Chicago means architectural anomalies. This architect was apparently paranoid, so there are plenty of hidey-holes."

"Shifters," Ethan and I simultaneously guessed.

"Quite possibly," Luc said. "We've found two trapdoors in the main part of the building." He pointed them out on the plans—one in the sanctuary proper, just behind the pulpit, and one in the choir stalls behind the pulpit.

"What else?" Ethan asked.

Luc flipped over a couple of sheets of paper. "In the 1970s, they remodeled the building and added the classroom wing. And at that time, they added what looks to be a panic room." He pointed it out on the blueprints. "It's in the basement. Looks like it started out as a bomb shelter, but in the remodel they reinforced it with concrete and added some wiring. So those are your question marks."

Ethan nodded. "Exits?"

Luc flipped back to the schematic of the main floor of the church. "Front doors, obviously. There's also an exit inside the sanctuary on the right." He pointed it out, then traced his finger down the long, narrow sanctuary, and then through a doorway on the left to another set of rooms. "These are the offices and classrooms." He pointed out the exit at the end of that corridor. "Exit point is here, although there are windows in all the rooms in the event things go completely fubar."

I leaned toward Lindsey, who'd stood up to join us at the table, still wearing the slim, wireless headset that kept her in communication with the guard on ground patrol tonight (either Kelley or Juliet, since they were the only remaining guards) and the fairies outside the gate. "He seems to be having fun," I told her.

"He's in hog heaven," she whispered back. "Things have been peaceful for so long, he hasn't needed to do this kind of advance work. All of a sudden, we get a Sentinel, and shifters want vampires to come out and play."

"Yeah," I said dryly. "Clearly this whole convocation idea is focused on getting to know me better. It's the mixer you've always dreamed of."

"But hairier," she said. "Much hairier."

Ethan rubbed a hand across his jaw. "What else do we need to know?"

"That's about it for the architecture," Luc said. He pulled out a chair and sat down. Ethan and I did the same. Lindsey returned to her computer station.

"But if it's going to be you two against three hundred-odd shifters, we need to talk about contingencies. Worst-case scenarios."

Ethan crossed one leg over the other, settling in for a strategic conference. "Your thoughts?"

"Three scenarios come to mind. First, an attack from outside the conference, something akin to what you saw at the bar. Second, the shifters are pissed that you're there, and they attack you."

"Good times," Lindsey whispered. I nodded, my stomach knotting a bit. Hunkering down behind a bar to avoid bullets—or even a little arm-grabbing by a Pack bully—was one thing; facing off against portions of four Packs of shifters was something else entirely.

"Third, the shifters can't make a decision, they get pissed at one another, and things go magically wonky."

Ethan slid Luc a glance. "Wonky? That's your official conclusion?"

"Signed and sealed. I assume you get the larger point."

Ethan blew out a breath. "I get it. I'm not thrilled about it, but I get it. Well, what can we do to keep things calm?"

"How proactive can we be on that?" I asked.

Heads turned to face me. "What are you thinking, Sentinel?" Ethan asked.

"Vampires have the ability to glamour. I can't seem to do it"—I shifted my gaze to Ethan—"but I bet you can."

The room was quiet for a moment.

"You're thinking we glamour a church full of shifters to keep them calm? Anesthetized?"

"Could it be done?"

Luc hunched over the table, placed an elbow atop it, and put his chin in his hand. "It's theoretically possible, but we've never seen evidence shifters are especially susceptible to glamour. They're magical beings. I'd be afraid they'd sense it, feel it. And if they suspected we were attempting to manipulate them—"

"All hell would break loose," Ethan finished. "Interesting proposal, Sentinel, but let's stick to basic bluffing. We'll stand there with our swords and smile politely, and reach for the handles if things get nasty."

"Oh, and speaking of," Luc said, sitting up again and pushing back his chair. He walked over to his desk, where he picked up a small glossy white box. "End of the fiscal year is coming up, and we had a little bit of extra coin in our budget."

"Thank you for returning it to the House treasury," Ethan muttered, but I could see the gleam of boyish pleasure in his eyes as Luc flipped open the lid and pulled out two tiny earpieces.

"The tiniest buds on the market," Luc said, dropping the

earbuds into his hand and walking them back to us. He flipped his hand over and placed them on the table. "Receiver, microphone, wireless transmitter. There's one for each of you. We'll hear you through the receivers. If things do, in fact, go wonky, just give the word and we'll have a dozen guards outside the church."

"A dozen?" I asked, surprised. "We're down a guard, and even if you, Lindsey, Juliet, and Kelley were there, that leaves eight missing vamps and no one guarding the House."

"Since your field trip to Navarre," Luc began, "we've spoken with the Guard Captains at Navarre and Grey. They've loaned us vampires in the event of an emergency."

I sat straight up at the mention of Jonah, my would-be Red Guard partner. I guess he wasn't above offering a little help to the Cadogan Sentinel, even if he didn't think much of her abilities.

Ethan cocked his head at me. "Are you all right, Sentinel? You seem flushed."

"I'm fine," I covered, smiling weakly. "Just surprised about the interoffice cooperation."

Ethan shook his head. "We haven't cleared additional guards with Gabriel. I'm not sure they'd appreciate having nearly a dozen more vampires at their convocation."

Luc shrugged. "Can't be helped. I'm sure as shit not sending you in without the possibility of backup. Besides, if this thing goes bad enough to require us to send in a dozen more friendlies, I'm guessing Gabriel's not going to be too concerned."

Ethan nodded.

"We wouldn't have a lot of time to negotiate the details of a full contract, but I could also give the fairies a call to see if they'd be interested in posting some sentries or snipers around the church."

Frowning contemplatively, Ethan crossed his arms. "I think the cost of recruiting and negotiating with the fairies at this point would exceed the benefit, especially since there's no guarantee we'd need them."

"Whatever you think best, Liege," Luc said with a snicker.

"I have decided opinions in that area," Ethan said crisply, approbation in his voice. "And our safe word?"

"Wonderwall."

Lindsey turned around and cast Luc a sardonic look. "Your safe word is the name of an Oasis song?"

"Blondie, I am the arbiter of all things fashionable in this House. Why not music?"

Lindsey snorted, then turned back to her monitor and began clicking through computer screens. "Spoken by a man wearing cowboy boots. I mean, seriously. Who wears cowboy boots?"

Ethan and I both checked out his shoes. He was, indeed, wearing well-worn, alligator skin boots.

"Epitome of fashion," Luc said. "I watch the MTVs. I know what the kids are wearing."

"The kids are a century younger than you, hoss."

"Children," Ethan interjected, although the amusement was clear on his face, "let's stay on point. I have matters to attend to."

Lindsey, chastened, moved back to her monitor. I had the same urge to turn away, but no computer to turn to. I was used to their flirty banter, and usually I participated in it. But today it left me feeling hollow. It was too casual, and I was still trying to find my emotional footing. It helped a little that Ethan seemed equally discomforted; half of his questions had been one or two words, and he'd hardly spared a word about convocation prep. This was business, sure, but even Ethan had a sense of humor. Well, on occasion.

"Our plan in the event of these contingencies?" Ethan asked.

Luc stood up again, moved to the blueprints, and pulled out a map of Ukrainian Village. "If things do go wonky, get out of the building however you can," he said. "Then meet here." He tapped a point on the map about two blocks from the church, and we all leaned up to see.

"We're meeting at Joe's Chicken and Biscuits," Luc said. "As the name suggests, Joe's is one of the Windy City's finest purveyors of chicken and biscuits. That's your rendezvous point. Anything happens, get back there. We'll pick you up. I'd just ask that you grab a ten-piece for me and the missus here."

"If things go bad, do we fight back?"

Ethan looked at me.

"Some of the shifters were already suspicious of us," I said, leaving unspoken the probability that they'd be even more suspicious after tonight. "I don't want to make things worse."

Ethan frowned and rubbed his forehead. "The GP has a position statement on shifters."

"Do not fire until fired upon," Luc offered.

Ethan nodded matter-of-factly. "We do not strike with weapons unless we are threatened, or unless they are threatening to harm Gabriel."

We were all silent for a moment, maybe wondering whether I'd been sufficiently threatened to justify Ethan's reaction . . . or whether the GP was going to want a few words with our Master.

We all jumped a bit when Ethan's cell phone rang. He pulled it from his pocket, checked the screen, then pushed back his chair and rose. "You may respond if necessary, but we are there to offer our support, not to make enemies without provocation. There are likely alliances within the Packs just as there are outside them, and we don't want to run afoul of any lines there."

I'd been born to one of Chicago's wealthiest families. I was trained to play standoffish.

"I have an appointment," Ethan said, then slipped the phone back into his jacket. "You're dismissed. We'll assemble here two hours before midnight tomorrow."

"Liege," I respectfully said, and caught Lindsey's eye roll at my Grateful Condescension—the fancy vampire term for ass-kissing. When Ethan was out of the room, presumably on his way to some important meeting, and the door was shut behind him, she snorted.

"I can't believe you're playing polite after he bailed."

"I warned you earlier—no personal commentary."

"One or two questions? They're pretty specific. Biologically specific, that is."

"Luc, your employee is being petulant."

"Welcome to my world, Sentinel. Welcome to my world."

It being bare minutes before dawn, Lindsey and Luc shut down the House controls and officially handed the protection of the House to the mercenary fairies who guarded it while we slept. She offered to walk me upstairs for moral support; more likely, she wanted time to quiz me on Ethan's decision that we couldn't date.

"I only need a detail or two," she said as soon as we'd closed the Ops Room door behind us.

"There are no details to offer. We had a fling; he decided he couldn't afford to date me, so I'm now working on my I-Will-Survive vibe."

We took the stairs to the first floor, and had just turned the corner at the stairwell when we were blocked by an entourage of vampires—Margot, Katherine, and a female vamp with a shaved head and cocoa skin whom I didn't yet know. They literally stopped in front of us, a blockade to the rest of the first floor.

"*Chicas*," Lindsey said, propping her hands on her hips, "what's up?"

The girls shared a look, then glanced at me, then turned back to Lindsey.

"I hate to be the bearer of bad news," Margot said, "but we have a visitor."

Lindsey looked at me and frowned. "Right now? It's nearly dawn. And there wasn't anyone in the dailies." The dailies were our once-daily dossiers of news and events at the House, planned guests, and off-campus trips planned by Ethan or Malik. Today's had been dominated by the shifter party, so I shook my head.

Margot, who looked mighty uncomfortable, gnawed on the edge of her lip. "I'm not supposed to say anything."

Katherine bumped her with an elbow. "Spill it."

"It's just—he asked me a couple of hours ago to make a big sunset meal," Margot said. "Steak *au poivre*, soufflé, the whole bit. And I thought something was odd, because he hasn't asked for steak *au poivre* in years."

My first thought, given that the food was French and the arrival secret, was that Ethan had invited Celina over for a sit-down. Since she'd tried to have me killed, it made sense that he'd want to keep the meeting on the down-low.

"Then we heard he was bringing in a guest," said the new girl, "and that she's on her way from the airport."

"Oh, and this is Michelle," Lindsey absently whispered, gesturing toward the new girl. I offered Michelle a smile and a wave.

"If it matters at all," Katherine said, "if it makes any difference, he's being a huge asshole, and we were totally rooting for you." There was pity in her expression.

My stomach tightened with nerves.

"Alrighty, ladies," Lindsey said, holding up her hands. "Dawn is on its final approach, so someone start at the beginning. What in the sam hell is going on?"

The three girls glanced at one another again before Michelle, misery in her expression, looked back at Lindsey.

"It's the Ice Queen."

"Oh, *shit*," Lindsey murmured.

Margot nodded. "Lacey Sheridan's on her way to the House."

My heart nearly stopped.

That sickening feeling returned again, twisting my stomach and threatening to push back the pizza I'd eaten earlier. Not only had Ethan decided I wasn't worth the trouble—he'd already made arrangements to pick up the pieces of our stunted relationship with someone else.

I didn't know how not to take that personally.

"Good Lord," Lindsey muttered. "Hot or not, the boy has issues."

"I can't believe he'd ask her to come back here," Margot said. "Especially now."

Especially now that he'd slept with me, or broken up with me?

The pity in Margot's voice brought hot tears to the edges of my lashes, but I blinked them back and looked up at the plastered ceiling to keep them from tracing down my cheeks. In that moment of weakness, when I was focused only on not crying in front of these virtual strangers, some of the walls that kept back the noise and sound began to tumble. The whispers I could no longer filter out began to circle around me. I belatedly realized we weren't the only vampires clustered together in the foyer, waiting for something to happen.

Black-clad vampires stood in groups of three or four, some with heads together as they whispered, some with eyes on me, some with gazes out the front windows that flanked the front door.

"She's on her way to the House," someone said.

"What about Merit?" asked someone else.

I clenched my eyes shut. My name was being whispered around the room. There were ninety witnesses to the act and now to the request that Lacey get to Chicago *as soon as goddamned possible.*

I opened my eyes again. I could feel my skin beginning to heat as humiliation and defeat gave way to that much more satisfying emotion—anger. Grief twisted into fury, and I could understand exactly how Celina's dismissal by some English beau could pull an emotional trigger, turning sadness outward into a spray of bitter shrapnel. I'm sure she wasn't the only woman—or man—in history for whom rejection had become fuel, that fire in the belly that moved her to action—to violence, to war, to destruction.

The vampire ego was no less fragile than the human one.

It was comforting, that anger; the ability to direct the emotion toward Ethan, instead of seeing my rejection as my own failure. I closed my eyes as goose bumps lifted on my arms, my body sinking into the feeling as though into hot bathwater.

When the room went silent, I opened them again.

The girls had silenced their pity party, all heads turning as Ethan walked through the main hallway and past us toward the front door.

"She must be here," Margot muttered, and we turned to watch him move.

She, I realized, must have been the reason for the phone call he'd received when he left the Ops Room—the reason he'd dismissed us.

Ethan opened the door, then leaned forward to embrace a woman. "Lacey," he said, "thank you for coming on such short notice."

His voice was warm, the implication of his words clear—he'd asked her here.

She must have been the cool sherbet to my garlic sauce, the palate cleanser he needed after a night with me. I swallowed down a sudden bout of nausea.

When he released her and stepped clear, then began shaking hands with the remainder of her entourage, I got my first look.

She was tall and slender, her blond hair cut into a sharp bob that ended just below her chin. Her face was model perfect—straight, long nose, wide mouth, blue eyes that held an icy sheen. She was dressed in a pale blue pantsuit that hugged her lean body; on her right hand was a single ring that carried an oversized pearl.

She was beautiful, put together, elegant.

She was everything he'd want.

And she was here, in Chicago, from San Diego, because he'd asked her.

"The House looks lovely, Ethan. I like what you've done."

He turned back to her and smiled. But as he turned his head to look over the room, as he caught sight of the knots of vampires in the hallway, his smile faded. He surveyed us, body tensing, and finally met my eyes.

As we stared at each other, I wondered why he'd called her here, what succor he thought she could provide.

I wondered why dating me would have been a sacrifice, but inviting back a former lover was not.

I saw nothing in his eyes that would explain it, only a dose of shock that I'd caught him in the act. I don't know what I wanted to say to him, but I took a step forward, intent on telling him *something*.

"Whoa, whoa," Lindsey said, moving to stand in front of me. "Don't go storming over there. You don't want to be that girl."

I snorted, half the room's attention on me now. "What girl? The girl who got replaced within a matter of *hours*?" I fiercely whispered, then looked around the room. "They may not have known about the breakup, but the evidence is pretty clear. Is there anyone who doesn't think it now?"

Margot, Katherine, and Michelle all looked away.

"Mer," Lindsey said, putting her hands on my arms, "we're your friends, your fellow Novitiates. But Ethan's a Master, and so is Lacey. Embarrassing yourself in front of them would be a whole different level of humiliating."

She had a point.

Okay, I decided. I wouldn't confront him, but I also wouldn't hurt myself further by watching their interactions.

I turned around and, without another word, took the stairs to the second floor. I went to my room and locked the door behind me. I didn't cry—*wouldn't cry*. Not again.

I also wouldn't sleep.

It being minutes before dawn, I changed into pajamas and climbed into bed. It had been a long night, but I lay awake, one arm behind my pillow, staring at the ceiling. Dawn was coming, the pull of it enticing my eyes to close, my brain to shut off. But the human part of me kept replaying the moments we'd shared, few though they were, and wondering if there was something I could have done, should have said, to give us a chance.

I'd made myself vulnerable, and I was paying the price. But the real insult was that the entire House now knew—or would soon enough—about my being summarily dumped and replaced.

Admittedly, I'd given him a chance. But that didn't mean I had to keep making bad decisions. I blew out a breath and swore off dating vampires.

It was at that moment, ironically, that my would-be RG partner decided to give me a call. Assuming he was getting in touch because he'd heard from Luc about ConPack, I plucked up my phone and flipped it open. "Merit."

"It's Jonah," he said. "Are you ready for this thing tomorrow night?" I appreciated the concern in his voice, but I wasn't sure if it was directed at me on a personal level, or because I was potentially an RG asset.

"We've met the Pack leaders, spent some time with the NAC, and seen schematics of the building. We have a communications plan, and you guys are backup." I shrugged. "That's as prepared as we can be." I skipped the details of the interaction that would have embarrassed Ethan; no point in both of us feeling miserable.

Jonah offered a vague sound of agreement. "If I'm asked later, we never had this conversation. But I'm wondering if this is a time to request RG backup? To have guards on standby?"

I couldn't get the words out fast enough. "This is definitely *not* that time. I appreciate the offer of support, but there are plenty of shifters out there who hate us." I'd seen that in action, firsthand. "Sending in special ops and black helicopters isn't going to help. It will only fuel the fire. Trust me—we're in better stead than we might have been if we hadn't been at the bar, but we're not 'in' by any means."

He was quiet for a moment. "And if the shit goes down?"

"Then Luc will call you in. You're a Red Guard, which means at that point you'd have the authority to make decisions on their behalf. But you can't move early on this one. They think we're too political. Untrustworthy. If we show up with extra vampires in tow—and without a crisis to justify it—we've proved their point. Let's go in assuming there'll be trouble that we can handle. And if things escalate into your jurisdiction, you can make the call."

Another moment of consideration. "We'll stand by for now. Good luck."

I hoped we wouldn't need it.

CHAPTER FIFTEEN

GOTV (GET OUT THE VAMPIRE)

Even as the sun descended again, I lay in bed for a good fifteen minutes. Have you ever noticed that however uncomfortable you might have been when you first went to bed—the room too hot or too cold; the pillows not quite right; the mattress lumpy; the sheets scratchy—by the time you should get up, your bed has transformed itself into the Platonic ideal of beds? The room is cool, the bed is soft, and the pillow may as well have been God's Own Headrest. The transformation inevitably happens, of course, when you're obligated to get up and out, when nothing sounds better than hunkering down in a pile of cool cotton—especially when facing your recent fling and his former lover is the other option.

But even Sentinels have to act like grown-ups, so I sat up and threw off the covers.

It had been a good week since I'd gone for a run. Since I had a couple of hours before we'd meet to go to the convocation, I pulled on a running bra, tank, and running shorts so I could kick out three miles through Hyde Park. Training with

Ethan or the guards was a workout, certainly, but not the kind that loosened up your bones and mind, cleared away everything but the pounding of the pavement, the rhythm of your breathing, and a good old-fashioned sweat.

But first, I needed some fuel for the gas tank. I wasn't ready to face down the rest of the vampires in the House, or risk the possibility of a Sheridan-Sullivan meeting. So I opted to avoid whatever drama might be awaiting me downstairs and scavenge breakfast on the second floor. I headed down the hallway and through a swinging door into the tiny rectangular kitchen. Granite-topped maple cabinets lined both long sides of the room, and a refrigerator and other appliances were built into the cabinets in the same maple wood. The countertops held baskets of napkins and the like and smaller appliances. The refrigerator was covered in magnets and take-out menus from Chinese, Greek, and pizza places in Hyde Park. That was the advantage of living near U of C—the undergrads kept food delivery in business at all hours, and that was good for the rest of us.

I went for the refrigerator and pulled it open. It wasn't unlike something you might have seen in an office building—a lot of leftover takeout, yogurt containers, and half-eaten desserts with initials marked on the top. It was all the detritus of prior vampires' meals and dates, labeled to keep other fangs away.

But there were also House-supplied goodies, including lots and lots of blood in pourable pint bags and smaller drink boxes. I took a second to appraise my need and decided it was time to stock up. I grabbed two drink boxes, shook and poked in the attached straw, sipped . . . and grimaced. Biting Ethan had been like drinking a rare vintage—rich, complex, intoxicating. Drinking from a plastic box now tasted exactly like that—flat, plasticky, sterile. It tasted dead, somehow, as if the blood had lost the infusion of energy you got from drinking from the tap, so to speak.

But since that particular supply had been cut off, I knocked it back, then did the same to the second box. This wasn't the time to let personal preference stand in the way of biological need, especially in light of the physical and emotional challenges I could be facing in a couple of hours.

I tossed the empty boxes in the trash and out of curiosity opened a couple of the upper cabinets. They were stocked with healthy snacks—bags of granola, nuts, high-protein cereals, natural popcorn.

"Blech," I muttered, then closed the cabinet doors again and headed through the swinging kitchen door. When they stocked the cabinets with Twinkies, I'd be back. I made a note to talk to Helen, the House's den mother, about that.

Breakfast in the bag, I headed outside. It was a warm and muggy June night. Not terribly late, but the streets were still quiet. I thought avoiding the paparazzi altogether risked making them a little too interested in vampire activities, so I headed down the street to the right and toward the group at the corner. I smiled and waved, flashbulbs snapping and popping as I moved nearer.

"Hey," one called out, "it's the Ponytailed Avenger!"

"Good evening, gentlemen."

"Any comment on the bar shooting, Merit?"

I smiled thoughtfully at the reporter, a youngish kid in jeans and a T-shirt, a laminated press badge around his neck. "Only that I hope the perpetrators are caught."

"Any comment on the stakings in Alabama?" he asked.

My blood ran cold. "What stakings?"

The man beside him—older, pudgier, with a mass of frizzy white hair and similar mustache—gestured with his small, reporter-style notebook. "Four vamps were taken out at a, well, they're calling it a 'nest' of vampires. Apparently part of some kind of underground, anti-fang movement."

Gabriel's concern about rumblings, then, had clearly been real. Maybe it was only an isolated incident. Maybe it was a horrible, but random, act of violence that didn't signal the turning of the tide for the rest of us.

But maybe it wasn't.

"I hadn't heard," I said quietly, "but my thoughts and prayers go out to their friends and families. That kind of violence, the kind that grows from prejudice, is indefensible."

The reporters were quiet for a moment as they scribbled down my comments. "I should get going. Thanks for the update, gentlemen."

They called out my name, trying to get in additional questions before I trotted off into the night, but I'd done my duty. I needed the run, the chance to clear my head, before heading back into Cadogan House and the drama that undoubtedly awaited me there—political or otherwise.

The first mile was uncomfortable; doable, especially as a vampire, but painful in the way first miles often were. But I eventually found a rhythm, my breathing and footfalls aligned, and made a circle around the neighborhood. I skirted U of C, the wound of no longer being enrolled in my would-have-been alma mater still a bit too raw.

A breeze had stirred up by the time I made it back around to Cadogan House, and I nodded at the guards as I reentered the grounds, trying to slow my breathing, hands on my hips. I had to run faster as a vampire to get my heart rate up, and I wasn't really sure how much good it did, but I felt better for having done it. It felt good to escape the confines of Cadogan House for a little while, to focus only on my speed and rhythm and kick.

Figuring cleanliness was next on my to-do list, I went back to my room to grab a shower.

I made it as far as my door.

There was a smallish bulletin board on every dormlike room in Cadogan House. A flyer was tacked to mine—a thick bit of cardstock bearing an announcement in fancy script letters:

Greet the Master!

*Join us Saturday at 10:00 p.m.
to welcome Lacey Sheridan,
Master of Sheridan House.*

Cocktails and Music.

Casual Attire.

Rolling my eyes, I pulled the invitation off the door, then stepped back to glance down the hall. The same black-and-white flyer was posted on every door I could see—a GOTV effort that had nothing to do with voting or democracy. I wondered if this had been his idea—a chance to show the Novitiates of Cadogan House whose team he was on?

Maybe more important, how mandatory was something like this? Was I required to make an appearance? Toast Lacey Sheridan? Bring a gift?

I crushed the card in my hand, then opened my door and stepped inside, but before I could close it again, I heard footsteps in the hallway. There were rarely vampires moving through this part of the building, so I nosily peeked through the crack . . . and got an eyeful.

Ethan and Lacey were walking side by side down the corridor. Ethan wore jeans and a snug, long-sleeved T-shirt in a pale smoky green. His hair was pulled back, the Cadogan medal at his neck. The ensemble was casual enough that I assumed he'd be wearing it to the convocation.

Lacey wore a gray tweed dress with a modern, folded neckline and a pair of patterned black stilettos. Every strand of blond hair was in place, and her makeup was as perfect as that of any airbrushed cover model.

"It should worry you," Lacey was saying.

"Meaning?" Ethan asked.

"Sentinel or otherwise, she's common, Ethan. A common soldier. And I have to say, I really don't get all the fuss."

My lips parted. Did she just call me *common*?

"I'm not sure that 'common' is a word I'd equate with Merit, Lacey. I don't deny she's a soldier, but I don't think 'common' gives her due credit."

"Still—brawn doesn't make a Master."

"Well, either she'll Test one day, or she won't."

Lacey chuckled. "You mean, either you'll nominate her or you won't."

Lacey was the only other Master vampire Ethan had nominated in his nearly four hundred years as vampire. He hadn't even taken Testing. Masters like Ethan and Morgan, who'd risen to the ranks when their own Masters were killed, were allowed to skip the exam.

She sounded irritatingly confident that Ethan wouldn't nominate me.

"Admittedly, she's young," Ethan said. "She has a lot of

learning to do before she's ready—a lot of immortality to get through before she's ready. And only time will bear it out. But I believe she'll prove capable."

He chose that moment to glance up—and meet my eyes through the crack in the door. I made a split-second decision and pushed the door open as if I'd been on my way out.

Ethan lifted his eyebrows in surprise. "Mer—Sentinel?"

Lacey stepped behind him.

I played innocent. "Oh, hello. I was just on my way out."

They both looked over my sweaty workout ensemble, and I felt like the heroine in a John Hughes movie, all awkwardness and deer-in-the-headlights eyes.

"Out?" he repeated.

Think! I silently demanded, and when genius struck, I nodded, reached behind me, and pulled up my right foot, imitating a stretch. "I just got in a run, so I was heading to the stairs to do some stretches."

Ethan's brow furrowed, worry suddenly in his eyes. Did he care if I'd heard? Would it bother him if she had hurt me?

"Are you going to introduce us?" Lacey asked.

For a split second, just enough for him to glimpse but not so long that she caught it, I tilted my head at him, letting him see the snarky question in my eyes: *Yes, Ethan. Are you going to introduce us?*

"Lacey Sheridan," she said, not letting Ethan make the choice. She didn't extend a hand, but just stood there smugly, as if the mere mention of her name was supposed to knock me back a couple of pegs.

"Merit. Sentinel," I added, in case she needed the reminder that I was the one in Ethan's House now. I bit back a smile at the twitch in her jaw.

"I was a guard, as well," she said, her gaze scanning my body as she sized me up, an opponent preparing to do battle. Were we battling for Ethan? For some kind of in-House superiority? Whatever the reason, I wasn't going to play the game. I'd already gone all-in, and I'd lost my entire stack of chips in the bargain.

"That's what I've heard," I politely said. "I'm friends with Lindsey. You two were guards together, I understand, before you took Testing."

"Yes, I know Lindsey. She's a solid guard. Particularly good at ferreting out motivations." She offered Lindsey's evaluation as if, rather than discussing a friend or colleague, she'd been asked for a professional reference.

I shifted my gaze back to Ethan. "I assume you heard about Alabama?"

His expression clouded. "I did. Gabriel's rumblings?"

I nodded. "That was my guess."

He blew out a breath, then nodded. "It is what it is. I'd like to leave for the church within the hour."

"Liege," I said again, obedience in my voice.

He didn't growl, exactly, but the acquiescence clearly irritated him. I smiled as I walked away.

I was showered and dressed—jeans, boots, and a tank top beneath my leather jacket—and on my way downstairs to Ethan's office when my phone rang. I pulled it from my pocket and checked the screen. It was Mallory.

"Yo," I answered.

"I know you're heading out, but I'm about to pull up in front of Cadogan House. Catcher wants to talk to Ethan, and I have something for you."

"Something tasty?"

"Do you only love me for my choice cooking?"

"Well, no, but I'll admit it's one of the reasons."

"As long as the reasons are many and varied. Get your butt down here."

Knowing when to take an order, I closed and repocketed the phone, then completed my trip to the front door. The foyer was Master vampire free, so I headed outside with a pleasant lack of drama.

Mal stood at the front gate in stovepipe jeans and a long tank, hands at her hips. She looked to be interrogating the guard. I hopped down the steps, then took the sidewalk to the gate. Catcher stepped beside her just as I approached, probably having just parked the car, a mix of amusement and defeat in his expression.

"And I'd heard you folks were really great at the Third Key," she was saying. "Do you have any advice for me?"

The mercenary fairy at the gate stared down at her with maliciousness in his eyes. "'You folks'?"

Mallory grinned. "Sorry, it's just, your traditions are so interesting. So natural. So woodsy. Would you be willing to sit down with me and maybe you could share—"

"Okay," Catcher interrupted, putting his hands on her shoulders and turning her toward the House. "That's enough of that. My apologies," he offered to the guard, then guided Mallory up the sidewalk.

"Making new friends?" I asked her.

"They're a really fascinating people."

"I bet *they* like being called by their names."

Mallory slid Catcher a flat stare. "Do you know his name?" He looked at me. I shrugged. "I just work here."

"Species-ism among supernaturals really is the last bastion

of acceptable prejudice in this country," Mal said, then seemed to realize I was dressed in leather and holding my sword. "You look ready to chase down some shifters."

"Let's hope it doesn't come to that. You're not in Schaumburg tonight?"

She shook her head. "I have practicum again tonight, which means I'm supposed to be at home making potions and whatnot."

"Good luck with that."

"Good luck with your shifters. And that's why I'm here." She stuck her fingers into the snug pocket at her hip and fished around. "Hold out your hand."

I arched a skeptical eyebrow, but did as I was directed. Mallory fished something out, then deposited it into my palm.

It was an antique bracelet—a gold link chain, dark from wear, that bore a circular locket. I held it up. The image of a bird was engraved in the top.

"It's an apotrope," she proudly said.

"It's a what?"

"Apotrope. It's a charm for luck, to ward off bad juju." She leaned forward and pointed at the inscription. "That's a raven. It's a symbol of protection. I found the bracelet in a shop in the Scandinavian District."

I frowned at her, puzzled. "Chicago has a Scandinavian District?"

"Nope," Catcher said. "But the store was next-door to a restaurant that sold pickled herring. She decided that was the Scandinavian District."

"First you're moving furniture; then you're moving neighborhoods."

"I'm an up-and-comer," she said. "Anywho, I worked a little Second Key action of my own, and there you go."

"Well, that was very thoughtful, even without the gratuitous urban planning. Thanks, Mal."

She shrugged. "I wanted to give you a tincture of wolfsbane, but party pooper over here said no."

"Wolfsbane?" I asked, looking between them.

"It's poisonous to shifters," Catcher said, mid–eye roll.

I nodded in understanding. "Yeah, might be bad form to wear wolf poison to a shifter convocation."

"I only would have put a little in there," Mallory said. "Not enough to give anyone a stomachache, much less actually kill somebody. And no one has to know about it."

"Still better to stick with the raven. Thank you for bringing it." I held out my right wrist so that she could clasp on the bracelet, but I glanced up when Catcher made a low whistle of warning.

"Company," he said, and since his gaze was on the door, I guessed who that might be.

"Ooh, she's pretty," Mal whispered, looking up once she'd secured the bracelet. "Who is she?"

"That would be Lacey Sheridan."

Mallory blinked at me. "Lacey Sheridan? The vampire Ethan—"

I interrupted her with a nod.

"Were you going to let me know that his former girlfriend was in town?"

"I figured you'd already had a good dose of Merit humiliation for the week."

She patted my arm. "Don't be silly. Vampire humiliation is like a fine wine. It should be shared between friends."

I stuck out my tongue, but Catcher shook his hand. "Here they come," he warned. "Put on your happy face."

I plastered on a fake smile and turned to greet them. His katana in one hand, he used the other to gesture toward Lacey.

"Mallory Carmichael and Catcher Bell," he said. "Catcher, I believe you and Lacey met when she was in the House."

"Yep." That was all Catcher said. He didn't bother extending a hand.

"It's nice to see you again, Catcher."

He barely acknowledged the greeting, and my heart warmed. Catcher was gruff, sure, but that usually didn't involve outright snubbing people, at least in my experience. I may have given him and Mallory a lot of crap about their naked shenanigans, but he knew which team he was on.

"Mallory is Merit's former roommate," Ethan told Lacey, "and a newly identified sorceress. She's currently training with an Order representative in Schaumburg."

Lacey cocked her head. "I thought the Order didn't have representatives in the Chicago area."

Mallory put a hand on Catcher's arm before he could growl at Lacey, but you could see the urge to step forward in his expression. Catcher had been kicked out of the Order under circumstances that weren't altogether clear to me, but the lack of an Order office in Chicago had something to do with it.

"That's a long story," Mallory said, "and it's nice to meet you." She glanced at Ethan. "Are you going to take care of my girl tonight?"

"I always take care of my vampires."

Mallory smiled sweetly. "All evidence to the contrary."

Catcher put a hand on Mallory's shoulder and looked gravely at Ethan. "We actually came by here for a reason other than skewering you, and it's not good news. A body was found in a warehouse about eight blocks from the bar. It was Tony."

Ethan blew out a slow breath. "I'm bothered by that on a number of levels, not the least of which is the fact that he was our prime suspect."

"He still could have been behind the hit," I pointed out. "But someone else might not have been happy about that—or wanted to keep him quiet."

Catcher nodded. "At the very least, there's more than one person involved in whatever shifter mess is going on."

"Does Gabriel know?" Ethan asked.

Catcher nodded. "Jeff made the call a little earlier."

"This is not the kind of information I like having two hours before the convocation."

"No," Catcher agreed, "it's not. And it's probably not the last of your problems tonight."

"I'd expect trouble," Lacey said, apparently joining the conversation. "It's highly unlikely the first attack was random, and since the perpetrators haven't managed to forestall the meeting, I'd predict that a second strike is imminent."

"We've arranged backup," Ethan said, but his gaze was on the lawn, his expression blank, as if he were contemplating unpleasant things. "Guards from Grey and Navarre. We'll have communications open."

"Best you can do," Catcher said.

We stood there for a moment, all of us probably wondering what the night had in store.

"I'm going to get Lacey settled in so she can work in my office while we're away," Ethan said, glancing at me. "Meet me at the first-floor stairs in five."

"Liege," I said, dipping my head with perfectly Graceful Condescension.

His upper lip curled in dissatisfaction, but after a wave to Mallory and Catcher and some awkward goodbyes between Lacey and Mallory, he escorted Lacey back down the sidewalk.

"Liege?" Catcher repeated. "I bet I could count on one hand how many times I've heard you say that."

"I'm opting for acquiescent," I said, my gaze still on the Masters.

Catcher grinned a bit evilly. "I bet that's pissing him off."

I gave him a grin. "I think he hates it. Which makes it all the more enjoyable."

"And since he's wanted Merit the Acquiescent since the day you stepped foot in Cadogan House," Mallory pointed out, "it's not even immature. You're just giving him what he asked for."

"Precisely," I agreed with a nod, although I didn't entirely agree—it was fun, sure, and appropriate in its way, but still immature.

"You know," Mallory said, her head tilted as she watched them walk, "she's all blond and fusty . . . like an attorney or something. And that's not a compliment."

"Bloodsuckers either way," Catcher muttered.

I patted his arm. "You know, that was very sweet, what you did. Being snarky to Little Miss Sunshine."

"Don't get too excited. It's not that I'm on your side," Catcher said, then nodded toward Mallory. "But I'd be sleeping on the couch for a week if I didn't take *her* side."

"And my side is your side," Mallory concluded, then held out her hands. "We need to run. I need to start cooking. You be good tonight, okay?"

I stepped forward and embraced her, then stepped back again. "I'll be as good as possible, and I'd ask the same thing of you two." I gave them my best motherly stare.

Catcher snorted. "If we're not playing naked Twister, we're wasting our waking hours."

"Yep," Mallory said as she tugged him down the sidewalk, "that's the love of my life. He's a romantic at heart."

True to his word, Ethan met me in the lobby five minutes later, sans the Master of Sheridan House. But he was followed by Luc and Malik. Luc was in jeans and a white T-shirt. Malik—tall, dark skinned, and green eyed—wore black suit pants, square-toed black shoes, and a crisp, white, button-up shirt, the top button of his shirt open to reveal his Cadogan medal. Malik, the only married vampire in my acquaintance, was also one of the most handsome—shaved head, wide, clear eyes, sharp cheekbones. But he had the most solemn countenance of any vampire I'd met.

"I believe we're ready," Ethan said, glancing between them. "Malik, the House is left in your care and trusting. Luc, check in with our ground team. God willing, the need of them won't prove necessary. But just in case . . ."

"It's done," Luc said. "We liaised earlier, and we're all in contact. Grey and Navarre are on standby. You both have your earpieces?"

Like obedient students, we pulled out our earpieces, which we'd both stashed in our pockets, and showed them to Luc.

"Good children," he said with a chuckle. "You don't need to put them in until you're on-site. You might want to do that in a private moment, and not with shifters breathing down your necks, lest they think we're even more conniving than they already believe we are. When you get 'em in, we'll be on the other end."

"Do you want me to try Darius again?"

We all turned to Malik. Darius was the head of the Greenwich Presidium, the Western European council.

Ethan shook his head. "Not now. We've tried to reach him once, and he didn't get back to us. At this point, it's better to ask for forgiveness later than permission now."

"You think he might say no?" I asked. Ethan slid me a glance.

"I think the GP is unpredictable in its current form. We tell them we're liaising with shifters—that we're offering strategic support to hundreds of shifters—and we push the GP panic button."

"We invite a shitstorm," Luc translated.

I nodded my understanding. Ethan blew out a breath. "If you're all comfortable with your respective stations, we'll head out."

"Good luck," Luc said, then gave me a pat on the shoulder. "Kick ass, Sentinel."

"I'm really hoping it doesn't come to that."

"That makes two of us," Ethan said. He and Malik whispered something together—the act was probably one of the rituals related to Ethan's leaving the House in Malik's care—then took the stairs to the basement.

CHAPTER SIXTEEN

THE BIG BAD WOLVES

We drove to Ukrainian Village in silence. When we arrived, Ethan pulled the Mercedes into a slot on the street. We were early for ConPack, but it was still late on a Friday night for the rest of the neighborhood, which was quiet and mostly empty of traffic. We got out of the car, buckled on our katanas, and walked toward St. Bridget's, which was well lit by streetlights and spotlights in the landscaping.

I stopped for a moment to gaze up at the cathedral.

"Cathedral" was definitely an appropriate moniker. St. Bridget's was a gorgeous building, with peach-colored stone and a handful of towers topped by turquoise domes that looked like ski hats. A giant stained-glass window was set into the front of the building, its three rectangular panels showing a pastoral scene of trees and butterflies, a fawn reclining peacefully in the middle.

The church was an architectural jewel in the midst of the working-class neighborhood, like a lost remnant from an ancient fairy tale—a page that history forgot to turn, transported from the deep woods of Eastern Europe to the west side of Chicago.

It was, however, very much like the neighborhood around it in one respect—it was very, very quiet. It's not that I expected picketers and protests, but from what we'd seen before, shifters weren't the type to go gently into that good night.

"I maintain it's weird they're meeting at a church," I said.

"It is unusual," Ethan said beside me, "but it wasn't our call to make."

We stood there in silence for a moment, long enough that I glanced over at him. I found his gaze on me.

"What?" I asked.

He gave me a flat look.

"We're here on business."

"I want the air to be clear."

"The air is as clear as it's going to get. We made a mistake. We've both since remedied it, so let's move on, shall we?"

"A mistake." He actually had the gall to sound surprised at my answer, but I didn't buy it. He hadn't used the word "mistake" in his post-Breckenridge guilt party, but that was pretty much what he'd said.

"A mistake," I repeated. "Can we get to work?"

"Merit—," he began, regret in his voice, but I held up a hand. His guilt wasn't going to make me feel any better.

"Let's get to work."

We took the stairs to the slate of doors that spanned the front of the church. I assumed this was where people gathered after services, maybe shaking hands with the clergy, maybe making plans for dinner or lunch.

The doors were unlocked and opened into a small receiving room, the walls of which bore signs directing parishioners toward children's care rooms and morning coffees.

We pushed through a second set of doors, and I gaped at the sight before us, walking inside past Ethan to take in the full view. The church's exterior was impressive, but that was nothing compared to the interior. The sanctuary was like a treasure chest, with floors of gleaming stone, walls of stained glass, gold-framed icons, gilded alcoves and frescoes. Gleaming columns and ornate brass latticework marked the church aisles.

Robin, Jason, Gabriel, and Adam stood at the front of the sanctuary, but it was Berna who first got our attention.

"You will eat," she said, stepping in front of us, a disposable aluminum pan in her outstretched arms. The pan was covered with foil, but it steamed with heat, and I could smell what was inside: meat, cabbage, spices—Eastern European deliciousness.

"You take," she said, and shoved the pan, still hot, into my arms.

"I appreciate the sentiment, but you didn't have to keep feeding me."

She clucked her tongue. "Too thin," she said, then reached out two knobby fingers and pinched my arm. *Hard.*

"*Ow.*"

"No meat," she said, disapproval in her voice. "No meat on bones, you don't find man." Then she cast an appraising glance at Ethan, one bottle-blond eyebrow raised. "You are . . . *man.*"

Not that I disagreed, but she was making the wrong match.

"Thank you, Berna," I said, hoping to draw her attention back to me and distract her from her love connecting.

Slowly, as if guessing my game, she glanced back at me,

then gave me an up-and-down appraisal that was none too flattering. After clucking her tongue again, she walked around us and disappeared into the lobby.

I glanced over at Ethan and proffered the cabbage rolls. "Should I just put this in your car while we're here?"

He blanched, apparently not crazy about the idea that his Mercedes would smell like the back room of a Ukrainian pub.

"Good evening, vampires." I turned to find Adam grinning at the pan in my hands. He was dressed simply—plaid button-up over gray T-shirt, and jeans over heavy black boots—but that didn't diminish the wolfish appeal.

"Good evening." I held out the pan. "She keeps pushing food at me."

"That's Berna. It's her way of showing affection."

Not for my physique, apparently. That notwithstanding, I still had a steaming pan to deal with. "Is there somewhere I could put this for a few hours?"

"You think holding a pan of cabbage rolls will interrupt your vampire mojo?"

"It will make it a little harder to swing my sword."

"Well, we wouldn't want that," he said coyly. "I'll take you to the kitchen and you can drop it off there. Also gives you a chance to see a little more of the church."

"Thanks."

I'll wait here, Ethan silently said. *I'd like to talk to Gabriel about Tony.*

Good luck, I offered back, wondering whether the fight at the Brecks' was truly water under the bridge or whether Gabe was going to hold it against us. On the other hand, he hadn't changed his mind about our providing security, so he must have been comfortable enough.

Keep your guard up.

Liege, I dutifully answered back.

I followed Adam down the aisle on the left side of the church, offering Gabriel and Jason a wave as I passed. He moved through a door and into the side wing Luc had showed us earlier. It was obvious we'd moved from the original architecture to the 1970s renovation. Where the chapel was luxurious, the side wing was straight-lined and kind of sterile. Function had won out over form here, from the industrially carpeted floors to the cinder block walls.

But as we passed the nursery rooms, it became clear that the parishioners were less concerned about what the church looked like than what went on there. I stopped at an open door and glanced inside. Drawings and educational posters decorated the walls. Toddler-sized tables and chairs dotted the room, and worn stuffed animals and wooden blocks were stacked neatly on a windowsill.

"They're a tight community," Adam said beside me.

"I can tell."

When we'd both looked our fill, Adam continued down the hallway, then turned into an industrial-style kitchen clearly meant for preparing meals for a big, hungry congregation. He held open the door of the refrigerator while I slid the pan onto a shelf. That done, he closed the door again, then leaned against one of the stainless-steel islands in the middle of the room.

I spied a bulletin board on the facing wall and walked over for a better look. A sign-up sheet for an after-church luncheon was posted beside a flyer for a canned food drive. Get a little; give a little, I thought.

And speaking of getting a little, I decided to take the op-

238 ♦ CHLOE NEILL

portunity to learn a little more about Adam and his crew. I
started with the geography.

"So, I was just curious—why Ukrainian Village? What's
your connection to this neighborhood?"

"Shifters?"

I nodded.

"We have roots in Eastern Europe. Our families are tight-
knit. You put the two together, you get Ukrainian Village."

"Huh," I said. "That's interesting."

He arched his eyebrows at me. "Is it interesting, or are you
just making nice to do your part for a vampire-shifter alliance?"

He spoke the words with sarcasm, but there was a thread
of something more in his voice. Irritation? Anger? Disgust? I
wasn't sure if that was animosity toward vampires or toward
politics generally. Both were shifter-esque emotions.

Not wanting to fight it out, I mimicked that negligent shrug
he'd given earlier. "Just making friendly conversation. Nothing wrong with that, is there?"

A twinkle in his eye, he answered back, "No, ma'am, there
most definitely is not."

We chatted a little longer, just enough for me to feel him
more. I'd anticipated getting some of the "youngest brother of
a Pack leader" vibe, and while he was quite the smartass, he
seemed earnestly concerned about the Pack.

"I'm nervous about tonight," he admitted as we took the
hallway back to the main chapel. "It's not that I think Gabe
couldn't handle whatever popped up, but I'd prefer we keep
things as violence free as possible."

"Any thoughts on a culprit for the bar shooting?"

He shook his head, his expression tightening. He was holding back.

"I heard Tony . . ." I wasn't sure how to finish the sentence, so I didn't.

"His death changes things," Adam said, "but I don't know if that means he was behind the attack."

"We had the same thought."

Adam frowned. "It's just that a planned assassination isn't a very Pack thing to do. Crime of passion, sure, but not assassination. It's a little, maybe, *vampire*?"

I arched a suspicious eyebrow. Anti-vampire prejudice wasn't really the vibe I wanted right now. I was much too outnumbered. And speaking of prejudice, I asked, "Has Gabriel said anything about the incident at the Brecks'?"

Adam chuckled mirthlessly. "The incident with Ethan?"

I nodded.

"Well, he wasn't thrilled about the disruption, but I think he was more amused by the whole thing."

I crossed my arms over my chest. "Amused?"

Adam shrugged. "They've known each other for a while. Gabe knows Sullivan to be cold, calm, calculated. And that was definitely not cold, calm, or calculated. Gabe figures Sullivan has it pretty bad for you."

"You'd be surprised," I said dryly. The vibration of my cell phone saved me from further elaboration. I pulled it out of my pocket and glanced at the screen. It was a text message, but not from Luc or Malik or the Cadogan guards. It was from Nick—and it wasn't good.

"TIP SAYS CONTRACT ON TOP DOG; HIT IMMINENT," the message read. It was signed "NB."

I stopped in the middle of the hallway, my heart suddenly pounding. We'd been right—whoever the culprit, the violence wasn't limited to the attack on the bar.

Someone meant to take out Gabriel, with or without Tony.

I glanced up at the door to the chapel in front of me. I needed to tell Ethan and Gabriel, but first I wanted facts. If Nick had information—a source, a time, anything—I wanted to hear it from his lips before I took it to the men who'd doubt its veracity the most. The vampire and shifter who were already suspicious of Nick.

I glanced up at Adam, who'd stopped a few feet away, his head cocked as he looked at me. "Everything okay?"

I hitched a thumb back toward one of the nursery rooms. "Okay if I use a room for a couple of minutes? I need to make a quick phone call."

"Something up?"

I faked nonchalance. No sense sounding the alarms until I had proof in hand. "Not really, but it's time sensitive."

It took a few seconds, but he finally nodded. "Help yourself. You can meet us back in the chapel when you're done."

I smiled brightly. "Thanks, Adam. And thanks for the chat."

"You're very welcome, Kitten. Anytime you want more than chatting, Gabriel knows how to reach me."

For now, the key was reaching Nick.

Turns out, reaching Nick wasn't that difficult. Once I was in one of the nursery rooms with the door shut, I simply dialed back the number that sent the text message, and he answered on the first ring.

"Breckenridge."

"Nick? It's Merit."

"That was fast."

"Seemed important, what with the death threat and all. What did you hear?"

"Someone called the paper's tip line and asked for me specifically."

I frowned. "So they knew enough not to spill the details about shifters to the switchboard guy?"

"That was my first thought, too. He must have been a shifter, but I couldn't tell who. You know those voice manipulators that kidnappers use in the movies to change the pitch of their voices? This guy had one."

"What did he say?"

"The message was short and simple." I heard the shuffling of paper, as if Nick were flipping through a notebook. "He said the shots at the bar weren't an accident. He said someone issued a contract on Gabriel, and the second attempt is supposed to take place tonight."

"In a church full of shifters? Not exactly a quiet way to take someone out."

"Yeah, a tip for the uninitiated—at some point, it'll be chaos in there. I don't think a gunshot, even a hit at close range, would be that hard to accomplish."

Well, that information would have been useful before today. "Anything else?"

"That was it, except for one more thing," he said, then paused. Building drama, I thought, like any good writer.

"He said to find the culprit, we had to check the top of the Packs."

"You heard they found Tony?"

"Yeah. But that doesn't mean he wasn't involved. He had the opportunity—it was his bike they found. And he may have had motive, too."

"Such as?"

"Installing someone else in Gabriel's seat. Maybe attempting a consolidation of the Packs. It wouldn't be the first time. Or maybe the simplest possibility—scaring everybody back to Aurora."

"Something else is weird, you know."

"What?"

"The tip," I said. "Think about it—someone learned Gabriel was in trouble, and they have the forethought to call you, but they use a device to disguise their voice?"

"Maybe they were afraid of being caught."

"By calling an anonymous tip line?"

"If you have the information, you're probably close enough to the crime to be part of it."

"Or maybe they knew you'd recognize their voice."

We both considered that quietly for a moment. "I think it would be better if you didn't tell them the tip came from me," he finally said.

I knew why he wanted to remain anonymous—the Brecks were still on the outs with the Pack. They were trying to get back in, certainly, but learning that Nick was the information source about a hit was only going to make Gabe more suspicious. On the other hand, "I'm a vampire, Nick. If someone has information like that, why are they going to tell me?"

"Because you're the Ponytailed Avenger."

"I'm hardly capable of avenging anyone. And as you pointed out, I'm a *vampire*. It's not like my helping Berna brought everyone into the vampire camp." I blew out a breath. "I'll tell Gabe it was anonymous. But if Ethan asks, I'm not going to lie to him."

Nick was quiet for a moment. "Deal," he finally said.

"Are you coming tonight?"

"We aren't. We've given proxies to other members of the Pack—it's a symbolic thing, another way to make reparations."

"Well, then I suppose I'll see you later. Or I won't," I allowed, in case the vote necessitated a shifter retreat.

"Good luck," he said solemnly, and the line went dead.

Information in hand, I trotted back to the chapel to find Ethan. There were more shifters in the pews now, and a few milling about with sound equipment and clipboards. Like the American Pack leaders, they were all men, except for Fallon Keene, who stood at the front of the chapel in a snug, long-sleeved black shirt, a short, pleated black skirt, and knee-high military-style boots, her suspicious gaze on the congregation.

I found Ethan in the back of the room with Gabriel, the two of them alone in a corner, standing side by side, their gazes on the crowd. They both looked up as my boot heels clacked against the stone floors.

Sentinel? Ethan silently asked.

I didn't answer; this one needed to be spilled to both of them.

I decided it was best to stick as close to the truth as possible. "I got a call," I said when I reached them. "There was no caller ID, and the caller used one of those voice-disguising deals." I looked at Gabriel. "He said there was a contract hit on you, and it was supposed to go down tonight."

He closed his eyes for a moment. "It's not that I'm surprised, but that's damned inconvenient timing. Violence begets violence, and I don't want more trouble because someone thinks they can best the Apex. I don't want that spilling out and affecting the vote. The Pack needs to be here. The decision needs to be made—and made by them."

Ethan frowned, that familiar line of worry between his eyes. "What, precisely, did the caller say?"

"Just what I said—that there's a hit on Gabriel, and that the hit's going down tonight. Imminent," I added. "I think he said 'imminent.'"

"I can't—*won't* cancel ConPack. The Packs are coming here tonight with shit on their minds. We can't just dismiss that—just send all that pent-up energy back into the universe with no outlet. That would be a very bad idea for the Packs and the city."

Given the earnestness of his voice, and the electric buzz that was beginning to stir in the chapel as the audience began to grow, I took him at his word. We didn't need a few hundred frustrated shifters running around Chicago.

"We understand your position," Ethan said, "and we commend your devotion to your people. But the continuity of the convention isn't the only issue. They take you out, and they disrupt the balance of power. No—completely alter the balance of power. Those implications are equally bad." If Ethan was being that frank, I guessed he and Gabriel had worked through any lingering tension.

"What do you propose?" Gabriel said.

"Given our limited amount of time, as many precautions as we can take," Ethan said. "Not to be morbid, but if they try a hit, any thoughts on likely scenarios?"

"The debate can get rowdy. It's not impossible they'd try to take advantage of that chaos, make a move in the middle of it."

"Then we'll stick by you when the convocation begins. We know you're strong, but you aren't immortal. As Merit has demonstrated, we can take hits you can't."

"I'm not sure insulting me is the way to go here," Gabriel muttered.

"You know what I meant," Ethan said. "Who in the sanctuary do you trust?"

Gabriel scanned the crowd for a moment. "Fallon. I trust Fallon."

"Even though she's next in line for the Pack behind you?"

Ever so slowly, Gabriel turned his head toward me, his gaze suddenly menacing. "Are you accusing Fallon of something, Sentinel?" Magic—astringent and sharp—electrified the air.

I kept my eyes on Gabriel, my expression neutral, as if I were staring down an attacking dog. "I'm accusing no one. I am, however, playing devil's advocate for the purpose of ensuring your safety. Tonight that's my job."

It took a few seconds for the magic to dissipate, but he finally nodded.

Ethan put a hand at my back. "We're going to take a walk around the church, get a sense for whether anything is out of the ordinary. We'll talk to Fallon on the way out. Stay within her line of sight while we're gone."

"Is he always this bossy, Sentinel?"

"You have no idea."

"Be that as it may," Ethan said, "do us a solid and keep yourself alive for the time being." At Gabriel's nod, we walked toward Fallon's corner.

"Sometimes," Ethan whispered as we moved, "the work of protecting others is in convincing them they need protection in the first place."

CHAPTER SEVENTEEN

POLITICAL ANIMALS

Fallon didn't look in our direction as we approached, but from the set of her shoulders and scanning gaze, I had no doubt she knew exactly where we were. We stayed at her side, ensuring she had a clear view across the sanctuary.

"We're going to take a walk around," Ethan told her. "Gabriel suggested he trusted you to keep an eye on him in the meantime."

Fallon slid him a glance. "My brother said that?"

"He did."

"Huh," she said, her face suddenly brightening with pleasure. "That makes for a nice change. Feel free to take a walk around. I have things in hand here."

From the altered currents of magic around her body—a signal she wore weapons (plural) of honed steel—I bet she did.

Ethan nodded at her, then moved toward the sanctuary door. But Fallon wasn't done with us.

"You're friends with Jeff, right?"

I stopped and glanced back at her. "He's a good friend, yeah."

She nibbled the edge of her lip. "Is he—does he—what's his status? You know, girlfriendwise."

I had to work to bite back a smile. "Single. You should take a stab at him."

She lifted her nose and looked back at the crowd. "Lots going on tonight."

"That is true," I said, then looked over at the doorway to the side wing of the church where Ethan stood, waiting for me. "But having a partner in a crisis can be a big help. Anyway, we'll be back in a few minutes."

"Noted."

We exchanged a nod, and I joined my own partner again.

As we moved into the side wing, the air pressure changed. I belatedly realized magic was fully buzzing in the chapel. Much like the frog in the soup pot, I hadn't even noticed until we'd stepped away. I told Ethan about the buildup as we moved down the hallway.

"Is it just magic," he asked, "or is it steel, as well?"

I frowned. "I'm not sure I could separate it out. Probably both?"

"Probably," he agreed, then pointed toward the doors that led off from the main hallway. "What are these?"

"Classrooms. Nurseries."

"Unlikely spots for the making of assassination plans."

"You'd think. If someone's going to make an attempt against Gabe, they've probably done the planning somewhere else." I pointed toward the last door. "The one on the end is the kitchen."

He stopped, turned in a half circle, and perused the hallway, his gaze tripping over the handouts, children's art, and religious posters. "Anything of interest there?"

"Does my pan of cabbage rolls count?"

He made a sarcastic sound. "Only for you, Sentinel. And now that we're out of Gabriel's hearing, is there anything you'd like to tell me about your anonymous phone call?"

"Are you suggesting I didn't tell you the whole truth?"

He gave me a flat look.

"It wouldn't be incorrect to assume the caller has a journalistic bent." Ethan opened his mouth to respond, but before he could form words, the exit door at the end of the hallway crashed open. Ethan and I both whipped around, hands on our swords. Two tall men in black suits, shades over their eyes, walked inside.

One of the men carried a package wrapped in brown paper, the sides wrapped in black electrical tape.

My heart thudded. I'd only seen packages like that on television cop shows—right before they exploded into shrapnel. Vampires didn't care for shrapnel, especially not the wooden variety.

Steady now, Sentinel, Ethan silently said to me, as if sensing my sudden fear. And since I was undoubtedly throwing magic into the air, he probably could.

"Can we help you, gentlemen?" Ethan asked.

Both men arched eyebrows over their glasses, but kept moving forward. Despite the thudding of my heart, I moved to stand beside Ethan, a barricade of vampires. A song from *Les Misérables* began, however inappropriately, to echo through my head.

"We have a delivery," said the man who wasn't holding the package. He reached into his suit pocket, but Ethan had his sword up and out before the man could pull out whatever he was reaching for.

I unsnapped the thumb guard on my handle.

"Whoa," said the man with the package, his Chicagoland accent heavy enough that it bled through the single word. "We're only here to make a drop-off, right?" He extended the package in his hands.

"You hold that," Ethan told him, then looked back at the man whose jugular was currently inches from the tip of his sword. "And you," he said to the other one, "pull that hand back very, very slowly."

The man swallowed, but did as he was told. And when his hand was clear of his jacket, he offered up a black leather wallet. "Just getting the ID, pal."

"Open it," Ethan said.

He flipped it open, then held it out for Ethan to see, then me.

"I got an import/export business," he said. "I'm just a businessman."

"And what's in the package?"

The two men exchanged a glance. "It's a gift for, uh, the head honcho, if you get my meanin'." He winged up his eyebrows, as if willing Ethan to understand.

"For *your* head honcho?" Ethan asked.

The men nodded with relief. Apparently, they were members of the North American Central (and good at hiding that fact), and they were relieved not to have to admit it aloud. Maybe living in hiding wasn't as easy as Tony had made it out to be. . . .

"And what's in the box?" Ethan asked.

The man with the package leaned forward, moistening his

lips nervously. "It's a rather fine vintage, if you get me? A vintage of the red variety? It's a gift from a family that's prominent here in Chicago, to the family of Mr. Keene."

"Ahhh," said Ethan aloud, then switched to silent mode. *What's in the box?*

I leaned down a little and frowned at it, clearing my mind to block out the extraneous noise and magic. But the box was a blank slate—no metal, no magic—so I switched to a simpler sense and took a sniff. There it was.

"It's booze," I said, standing straight again. "Good stuff, too, as far as I can tell."

The man without the package rolled his shoulders and adjusted his tie. "Of course it's good. Who do you think we are? Bit players?"

Ethan smiled politely, put his left hand at his scabbard, and carefully resheathed his sword. Then he stepped aside. "Enjoy the convocation, gentlemen."

We turned to watch them proceed down the hallway.

"I believe those gentlemen are connected, Sentinel."

"They're related?"

"Connected to something a little more, shall we say, *organized*?"

It took a moment for the implication to sink in—Ethan thought they were mobsters. "And you let them walk into the chapel?"

"And with alcohol to boot. They're Pack members with bounty in hand. We can't stop every Pack member who tries to walk into the church with booze." He snickered. "The chapel would be empty."

I chuckled in spite of myself.

He bobbed his head toward the kitchen door again. "That was the kitchen?"

"Yep."

"I'm going to get something to drink."

I followed him inside and waited by the door while he inspected the fridge. He pulled out a bottle of water, unscrewed the top, and took a long drink. When he was done, he tossed the empty bottle and cap in a recycling bin, then nodded toward the door again.

I was about to push it open when I froze. The exterior door at the end of the hall had been opened again, and I could hear voices moving toward us down the hallway.

And this time, a metallic buzz accompanied them.

It could have been something simple—shifters who carried weapons as part of their normal course of business. But this just felt . . . wrong.

Silently, I held up a hand to stop Ethan, then pointed at the door, then my ear, then held up two fingers. He nodded, moved forward, and put his ear to the door.

"You think you can take him out?" asked one of them.

"Damned right. The faster we get it done, the faster the money's in hand, so I'm definitely gonna take a goddamned chance at it," whispered another. There was venomous anger in his voice.

"Huh. I just don't know if we can make this work tonight. Not like he wants us to. There's a lot of goddamned bodies gonna be in that room in a few minutes."

Ethan arched his brows at me. I nodded.

The footsteps moved closer.

Weapons, I silently told him. *Guns or knives, I don't know. But they're heavily armed.*

Then let's move, he replied.

Ignoring the nervous flutter in my chest, I went first, pushing through the kitchen door. The two men—both in jeans, boots, and leather jackets—jumped as we appeared, hands moving toward their waists. I assumed they were reaching for guns.

"Gentlemen," I said, flipping the thumb guard on my katana and lifting it from its scabbard just enough to reveal the gleam of steel. "What's happening?"

They looked at each other, then at me. "We have business here, vampire."

"Yeah, I get that. The problem is, I'm getting the sense your kind of business won't be good for the rest of us."

The one on the left—shorter, balding at the edges—took a half step forward. He flipped back the side of his leather jacket, revealing a handgun stuck into the waistband of his 1980s-style jeans.

At the sight of the gun, I dug my fingers into the handle of my katana to keep my hand from shaking. I'd already been shot twice this week; I wasn't eager for more.

"Honey, why don't you and your boyfriend here take your little knives and go for a nice long walk, all right? This ain't your concern."

"Problem is, hoss," I said, unsheathing my sword and enjoying the widening of their eyes, "it *is* our concern. It sounds like you have some kind of issue with the leader of the Pack, so to speak, and he's a friend of mine."

The taller one—younger, cuter, but just as egotistical—elbowed his friend. "I'll take this one."

Get behind me, I told Ethan, as the younger guy took a step forward. He reached inside his leather jacket and pulled a matte black handgun from an interior pocket.

"You're cute," he said, "so I'm gonna give you one more chance." He waggled the gun in our direction. "Take a goddamned hike, and we'll go about our business and everyone's happy. Right?"

I had no doubt he'd pull the trigger. He was the type—brave to the point of stupid; narcissistic in a completely self-defeating way. And although he knew we were vampires, he clearly had no understanding of what that really meant—that a bullet, though it might hurt like a son of a bitch, would be pretty ineffective in taking me down.

I rolled my eyes and rotated my wrist to turn the sword, then pulled out a threat that Celina had once used against me. "I'll have you down before you can snap off a shot."

"*Bitch*," he said.

It was the last thing he said.

He lifted the gun, then raised his other hand to support it. But I was already moving. I rotated my body, bringing my leg around in a sweeping high kick that knocked the gun from his hands. It hit the floor and slid behind me, and I felt the air shift as Ethan reached for it. I completed the rotation, then shifted the weight of my sword and thrust the handle into his chest as hard as I could. In what seemed like slow motion, he *umph*ed and fell backward, hands clawing at his breastbone.

By the time he hit the ground, I'd righted my katana and held it before me, then glanced over at his shorter friend. "What about you, bud? You wanna try me, too?"

Eyes wide and panicked—the air thick with fearful magic—he took a few shaky steps before turning for the exit. But help had arrived—two blondish Keene brothers stood before the door, arms crossed and knowing gazes on the traitors in their midst. They must have sensed the trouble—or Fallon had sent them out here to keep an eye on me and Ethan. Bright girl.

"Excellent timing," I said, keeping an eye on the man on

the floor until they could reach him. Both taller and brawnier than the interlopers, they had them in hand in a matter of seconds.

"We do what we can," said the Keene brother on the left, a grip on the collar of the man I'd knocked down. "It occurs to me we haven't met. I'm Christopher."

"Ben," said the other one, who had the neck of the older man beneath his arm. The man struggled in the awkward position, but Ben didn't bat an eyelash.

I grinned back. "Lovely to meet you both," I said, then glanced back at Ethan. He stared at me, his eyes pools of quicksilver.

I guessed I'd managed to impress him.

"Not bad for a 'common soldier,' hmm?" I quietly asked, then reshcathed my katana and headed back toward the chapel. I could feel his gaze on my back as I walked away, so I decided to play it up. I paused at the sanctuary door, then looked back over my shoulder and smiled vampishly through hooded eyes. "Coming?"

Without waiting, I walked inside.

Now that, my friends, is what we vampires call a good exit.

—•—◄◦►◦►—•—

CHAPTER EIGHTEEN

LET'S GIVE 'EM SOMETHING TO TALK ABOUT

The chapel was nearly full when we returned, the room abuzz with enough magic and weaponry to give me a caffeine-esque buzz. Gabriel stood behind the podium, chatting with Adam and two other unfamiliar shifters. As we walked toward him, I noticed our would-be company men sitting in a pew, the box across the lap of the man who'd carried it in, both chatting politely with the shifters beside them.

"We need a minute," Ethan told him, and Gabriel excused the others.

"I heard there was commotion in the hallway?"

Ethan nodded. "We may have found the men who took the contract. We overheard them talking about the money and the hit. And they were well armed."

Gabriel's brows lifted. "The guys sent to kill me talked about the hit in the church?"

"Not the brightest bulbs," I put in.

Christopher and Ben approached Adam, then leaned in to

whisper something to him. Adam nodded, then signaled to Gabriel.

"They've been taken care of," Gabriel said flatly. His tone raised the hair at the back of my neck, and I reminded myself never to cross him. "Can we proceed?"

"There's a chance that whoever put out the contract will try again," Ethan warned him. "That we dealt with these two doesn't mean we eliminated the risk."

Gabriel reached out and gave him a manly arm pat. "The show must go on."

With no fanfare, and no introduction, Gabriel stepped to the lectern. Ethan and I took positions on his right. At his immediate left stood Robin and Jason. Adam and Fallon stood point on the far left. I found Jeff in the crowd, sitting on the end of the second pew, arms crossed over his chest, his expression grave.

Gabriel began to speak, his voice booming through the church's speaker system, the sound bouncing across the stone walls.

And weirder still, he recited a poem. It was Yeats, I think, if my nearly completed PhD in English lit was working correctly.

"'I have heard the pigeons of the seven woods/make their faint thunder,'" he said. "'And the garden bees/hum in the lime-tree flowers; and put away/the unavailing outcries and the old bitterness/that empty the heart.'"

I couldn't help it; my jaw dropped. A room full of three hundred shifters in varying degrees of denim and leather, carrying all manner of weaponry, was now staring rapt at the leader of the North American Central Pack of shifters as he read them a poem about nature. They nodded their agreement, heads bobbing like faithful parishioners in church, which, I suppose, they were.

"'I have forgot awhile/Tara uprooted, and new commonness/upon the throne and crying about the streets/and hanging its paper flowers from post to post./Because it is alone of all things happy./*I am contented*—'"

Gabe paused, lifted his gaze, and lifted his hands to the crowd around him. They shouted their affirmations, some standing, some with hands raised, eyes closed rapturously as they celebrated the world and pronounced their contentment. Goose bumps rose on my arms, and not just because the magic in the room had reached electric levels.

"'For I know that quiet/wanders laughing and eating her wild heart/among pigeons and bees, while that Great Archer, who but awaits his hour to shoot, still hangs/a cloudy quiver—'"

"'*Over Pairc-na-lee!*'" finished the entire group of them together, and then they burst into raucous applause.

Without waiting for the thunder to quiet again, Gabriel dropped the bomb.

"Tony Marino, leader of the Great Northwestern Pack, is dead."

The chapel went immediately silent.

"We convene today with four Packs, but three alphas. When we are done, the Great Northwestern will begin the task of choosing another to speak for the communal voice, for the Great Family. But today, we must focus on the business at hand."

A tall, thin, rough-looking man stood up from his seat in the middle of the room and punched a finger in Gabe's direction. "*Fuck that*," he said. "Our Apex, our father, is dead, and you tell us this *now*? This is bullshit."

More shifters popped out of their seats, their voices join-ing the clamor. You could see the pain in their faces, the shock of their loss. But that was nothing compared to their irritation at the leader of the North American Central.

Adam, Jason, and the others tensed, moving a half step for-ward as if preparing for inevitable violence. I raised my right hand to the handle of my katana, the easier to free it should the need arise.

"And you've brought goddamned *vampires* to a convoca-tion!" accused one man with a military-style crew cut. "This is our meeting, our gathering. A gathering of Pack, of kith and kin. They *contaminate* it."

Gabriel crossed his arms over his chest, waiting as they hurled insults and anger in his direction. He looked unfazed by the allegations, but I was close enough to feel the angry magic that rose from his body in a greasy wave.

On the other hand, I understood now why he'd insisted on going forward with the convocation. There was a lot of emotion in the room, and the city was undoubtedly better served by al-lowing the shifters to hurl it in Gabriel's direction—instead of outside at the rest of Chicago.

Gabe had broad shoulders; I had no doubt he could handle the barrage.

After a few minutes, he held up his hands. And when that didn't work, he bellowed—in words and magic—across the room.

"*Silence.*"

To a man, the chapel quieted. And when Gabriel spoke again, there was no mistaking why he was Apex, or what the repercussions would be for not heeding his word.

"You are here because the Packs have called a convocation.

If you wish to have issues decided without your input, you needn't be here. All or any of you can stand up and walk out of this room with impunity." He leaned over the lectern. "But whether you stay or leave, you will goddamned follow the dictates of the Packs. That is our way. That is the only way. And that is not up for debate."

The collective energy in the room diminished, as if the shifters in the chapel had tucked their tails between their legs.

"You're right," he continued. "There are vampires in our midst, and that's a change in Pack protocol. We aren't like them, and maybe we'll never heal the wounds between our people. But rest assured, war is coming whether we like it or not. And you're right—there are vampires who care little for the Packs, just as there are Pack members who are willing to assassinate their alphas. But I have *seen* things."

You could have heard a pin drop in the room at that revelation. The Pack members must have trusted in whatever prophecy Gabriel was about to make.

"I have seen that future," he said. "I have seen the future of my child." He beat a fist against his chest. "My *son*. I have seen the face of those who will keep him safe when times become the hardest for all of us."

He dropped his gaze, and when he raised it again, knowledge in his eyes, he turned his head . . . and he looked at me.

There was pleading in his eyes.

My lips parted.

"Vampires will keep him safe," he said, and we stared at each other, and I saw the racing events of his future—and mine—in his eyes. No story lines, no dates, but I saw enough, including the eyes of his child, and another set of green eyes,

eyes that looked nothing—and everything—like Ethan's. I had no way of knowing how powerful, how accurate, a shifter's visions were . . . but it packed a punch.

Tears stinging my eyes, Gabriel looked away again.

I dropped my gaze to the floor, trying to take in what he'd said, trying to keep my breath from becoming so shallow that I passed out in the church.

Merit? Ethan silently asked, but I shook my head. This needed processing before it needed debate. Before I'd be ready for discussing it . . . if I ever would be ready to discuss it.

The crowd had quieted again, the weight of the information Gabriel had shared enough to make them contemplative, to make them seriously consider the things he was going to ask them.

"You will face death," he told them. "Tony's death, and possibly others', if we stay. But we will face death if we go, as well. The world is a harsh place. We know that. We live by its code—a different code from vampires or humankind—but our code, just the same. That's the decision you must make tonight."

He held up his hands. "Let the discussion begin."

"Discussion" was a nice word for what commenced. As soon as Gabriel opened the floor to debate, most of the shifters who'd already bellowed at Gabriel flipped off the crowd and walked out. That prompted the remaining two hundred shifters to stand and yell at the deserters.

Chaos, indeed.

Gabriel rolled his eyes, but saluted the walk-outs.

"Let them go," he said into the microphone. "They aren't obliged to stay. None of you are required to stay. But whether you walk our or you stay and participate, *you will abide by the decision made here.*" It was clear by the tone of his voice and the menace in his eyes that he wasn't making a request. He was issuing an order, reminding the Packs of their obligations. Those who chose to ignore those obligations did so at their own risk.

The remaining shifters chastened, the debate over their future began in earnest. A microphone had been placed in the middle of the church's center aisle for the shifters' use. I wasn't crazy about the location—it gave anyone who stepped up to the mic a direct shot at Gabriel—but there wasn't much help for it.

But that didn't mean I couldn't be proactive. Without asking for Ethan's permission—I'd seen the fear in his eyes after I'd helped Berna beside the bar—I left my post at his side and walked to the front of the church, then stood directly in front of the podium.

Bullets—and shifters—who wanted a shot at Gabriel would have to go through me first.

Good thought, Ethan silently complimented, *but a heads-up would have been nice.*

Better to ask forgiveness than permission, I reminded him.

Although the shifters were a rainbow of shape, size, and skin tone, the views they espoused at the microphone fell into two categories. Half were pissed at the thought of having to leave their homes and businesses for Aurora. They mostly yelled at us, screamed at Gabriel, made rude gestures.

The other half wanted nothing to do with vampires or vampire politics, and they were convinced the threat to their well-being as a society was vampire in origin.

They also mostly yelled at us, screamed at Gabriel, and made rude gestures.

After long minutes of vitriolic monologues, the final speaker reached the microphone.

He was tall and burly, a giant black leather vest over his barrel chest. He wore a bandanna on his head, and his long beard had been bundled into consecutive bands. After waiting patiently for his turn to speak, he stepped up to the mic, then gestured toward Gabriel.

"You know me, sir. I ain't one with words or talk. You know I work hard, follow the rules, do right by my family."

I couldn't see Gabriel's face, but given the soft earnestness in this big man's voice, I imagined he nodded in understanding.

"I don't see the future, so I don't know about war. I tend to stick to my kind, and I don't know much about vampires or the like. I don't know what's coming down the road, what kind of things we'll see when the dust kicks up, or when it settles again. Frankly, I don't know exactly why we're here, or why we think we need to run." He swallowed thickly. "But I've lived among humans for many, many moons. I've been in human wars and fought beside 'em when I thought it necessary. They've stood up to protect me and mine.

"I also heard talk these vamps did right by us. And here they are again, and they step up to protect you like they're willing to take any danger comin' your way." He half shrugged modestly. "Politics and such ain't my thing, but I know what's right. They step forward, but we don't?" He shook his head. "I don't mean disrespect to you or your kin, but that ain't right. It just ain't."

He nodded at me, this man in the leather vest, then turned and walked humbly back to his pew in the middle of the church. He slid inside, then sat down, blinking as he waited for whatever came next.

My heart ached with emotion. I couldn't very well leave my post, but I watched him until he made eye contact, then offered a nod. He nodded back, two would-be foes acknowledging the virtue of the other.

Life as a vampire wasn't always what I expected it to be.

"As is our way," Gabriel said into the silence of the chapel, "in the pews before you are two chits. One black, one white. Black, we return home to the sanctity of the Seven Woods. White, we stay. We risk the fight—whatever fight that might be. Place your vote in the box as it's passed. If you have a proxy, you may cast those votes, as well. Cast your ballots according to your conscience," he said.

Jason stepped down from the platform, a wooden box in his hands. He carried it to the back of the chapel, then handed it to the last man in the last row.

It took eighteen minutes for the vote to be cast—eighteen nerve-wracking minutes, during which most every shifter in the room gave me alternatingly curious and grave looks. I had to work not to shuffle uncomfortably under the weight of their collective stares.

When the box had traversed the chapel, Jason hauled it back to the front of the room, and then the counting began. A long board, not unlike the marker for a cribbage game, was placed on the table where the box had rested. As each marble-shaped chit was pulled from the box, it was placed upon the holder.

Black, then white, then black, then three whites, then six blacks, and so on. Although my new friend had spoken eloquently, the shifters hadn't been completely convinced. Whatever the vote, it wouldn't be unanimous.

After a few minutes of counting, Gabriel stepped down off

the platform, then beside me, moving closer to the crowd. He was symbolically rejoining them, committing to abide by their decision, whatever it might be.

Gabriel held up a closed fist. "The final chit. The deciding chit." He opened his palm. The marble was white.

They were staying.

For a full five seconds, there was silence.

And then chaos broke out.

We'd been right, unfortunately. Although the men in the hallway might have had it in for Gabriel, they weren't the only ones who did. And they hadn't cared about the vote—they'd planned to affect the balance of power afterward.

The room erupted in sound as shifters began to rush the stage, ripping guns and knives from their leather as they moved. I was closest to Gabriel, so I unsheathed my sword and jumped in front of him until Ethan and Adam appeared to whisk him away and behind the podium.

Gabriel protected, Fallon, Jason, and Robin jumped down to the chapel floor. Fallon pulled dual daggers from her boots and joined me at the front. Jason and Robin tapped Jeff, then moved to the sides of the chapel to rein in the attack from the sides.

They weren't the only ones who'd jumped to Gabe's defense; however the shifters might have felt about the vote, the chits had been cast, and the decision had been made. The rest of them would abide by the decision. They would stay and fight.

And they would not abide traitors in their midst.

Send Christopher and Ben to the exit doors, I silently told Ethan. *If this thing spills outside, someone will call the cops. We don't need that right now.*

Fallon and I shared a nod, then prepared to wield our steel.

The first wave was all bravado. A man in a leather jacket came at me with a murderous grin and a revolver.

"Oh, that's almost too easy," I said with a smile, and before he could snark back, I wrapped my fingers around his trigger hand and twisted upward, keeping the handgun pointed at the ceiling and out of harm's way. I used the torque to bend his elbow, and he fell to his knees as tendon, sinew, and bone stretched to the breaking point.

When he muttered a few very unclassy epithets, I decided he'd be happier unconscious. I slipped the gun from his hand, and a low kick to the side of his head put him out of commission.

I glanced down at the raven bracelet on my wrist. It might not do much about animosity toward vamps, but it was great with the ass kicking.

The next shifter in line opted for a knife, and he was quicker than his now-sleeping friend. He used little thrusts and stabs that would have nailed me if I were a slower vampire. But I was fast, and I could dodge them, and he wasn't the most creative of fighters. Unfortunately for him, he used the same little thrusts and stabs over and over again. Disarming him was a cinch, and I put him out with a knee to the chest that knocked the wind right out of him.

I glanced over and found Fallon eyeing me with amusement. "I like you," she said, her own pile of bloodied shifters at her feet. "You're very tidy."

I grinned back. "I do hate a mess."

While we had a second, I glanced around to take in the rest of the action. There were Keenes posted at the back and side chapel doors to keep the melee contained. Jason and

Robin stood in the wings, fighting back their own bands of angry shifters. Robin's lack of sight clearly didn't impact his ability to kick ass. About one-third of the congregation was still seated; the other two-thirds were fighting one another in whatever snug space they could find.

"Quite a conference," I muttered, then positioned my body for round two.

The second wave of attackers had seen us best the first wave, so their faces weren't nearly as confident. But they bore the grim, determined expressions of believers—they didn't care if they won or not; this fight was about *principle*. They were also smarter fighters; they'd waited to see the infantry move, and they knew how we fought.

At least I got to use my sword for this round.

The first shifter was a woman, a petite thing with permed hair and curvy, Gothic daggers in her hands. She was nimble with her steel and good at defending my slashes. But she didn't strike out; her moves were all defensive. That meant—at least I assumed—that she'd tire out before I did.

But there was no sense in delaying the inevitable.

When she nicked me on the forearm, I put the final plan in motion. I slashed forward, rearranging our positions so that she stood a few feet in front of the first pew, her back to the seat. A sideways kick to her torso threw her back against the bench. She hit the pew and slumped, hitting the ground, still upright, head forward as if in midnap.

"Behind you!" Fallon yelled. I dropped down and heard the *whoosh* of a kick fly over my head. I rolled and kicked both legs out toward the shifter behind me. I wasn't close enough for a full-contact shot, so he stumbled backward before regaining his balance and coming at me again.

Fallon, finished with her cluster of traitors, used one hand to tuck long curls behind her ear, then delicately stuck out a booted foot. The man tripped and went sprawling, arms pinwheeling as he hit the ground. Fallon nudged him on his back, then put a boot on his neck until he passed out from lack of oxygen. Hands on her hips, she glanced up at me.

"I appreciate the help," I told her.

"Anytime. You're good."

"So are you," I said, with a smile, thinking Jeff definitely had his hands full.

The sanctuary was a mess. A couple of pews were broken. Candles were overturned, spilling wax onto the floor, and there were bullet holes in the marble columns. The violent shifters had been hauled into mostly unconscious piles, ready for their punishments.

I wiped down my katana with the edge of my tank, then slid it back into its scabbard. It deserved a better cleaning, but that would have to wait until we were safe at home again.

I scanned the crowd and found Jeff and Fallon in a corner. They chatted, their bodies close, their body language speaking of mutual concern . . . and mutual interest. Jeff looked up and over.

"You okay?" I mouthed.

He gave me a thumbs-up before turning back to Fallon. I'd all but lost him, I thought with a grin. But who better to keep Jeff busy—and smiling—than the gorgeous, dagger-wielding heir to the North American Central Pack?

Jeff secure, I moved back to the podium to check in with the bodyguards.

Ethan, Adam, and Gabriel sat in the choir stalls. Ethan met my gaze and nodded—an employer satisfied with the effort of his employee.

Unfortunately, this time it was Gabriel who'd taken a hit—a shot in his left bicep. Adam attended to it, wrapping what looked like an altar cloth around the wound to staunch the bleeding. Gabriel glanced up at me. "So," he said, a hint of a smile at his lips, "I guess we're staying."

"That's what I hear," I said, then adopted a schoolteacher tone. "I'm really going to need to see some better behavior out of your children."

He smiled grandly. "I do enjoy your smartassery, Kitten."

I nodded at the compliment, then looked to Ethan. "You okay?"

"Quite. You and Fallon made a good team."

"Don't give them ideas," Gabriel muttered, then slid Adam a narrowed gaze. "Could you possibly make that tighter?"

Adam gave him a grunty smile as he tied off the make-do bandage. "I was taught by a certain big brother not to half-ass things."

"Yeah, and look how well that turned out for me," Gabriel said ruefully, surveying the sanctuary. "We've half destroyed a church. Although the damage still isn't as bad as the ninety-two ConPack."

"Or ninety-four," Adam added with a wicked smile. He rubbed a hand across his stomach. "Ninety-four was a wild ride."

Gabriel gave a gravelly chuckle, then knocked knuckles with his brother. "True, true."

"What'll happen to the fighters?" I asked.

Gabriel stood, cradling his arm. "We'll have a little discussion about Pack behavior and what it means to abide by Pack rules."

"They try to take you out, and they just get a discussion?" I wondered aloud.

Gabriel gave me a sardonic look. "I don't mean 'discussion' literally."

"Will you punish them the same?" Ethan asked. "I mean, those who set up the hit and those who actually tried to take you out?"

Gabe muttered something I didn't catch. Given his tone, I assumed it was unflattering about vampires. "We don't just line them up and start shooting, Sullivan. There are degrees of culpability, just like in the human world. As for convocation, the decision's been made. Irrespective of the contract or the hit, they voted the way they voted, and the Packs will stay." He glanced over at Ethan. "The things we discussed—about friendship?—my people are too wired for that right now. Maybe in the future, maybe never, but certainly not right now."

Ethan did a good job of maintaining his composure in the face of Gabriel's rejection, but I knew he was cursing inside. He'd practically bet the House—or at least his Sentinel—on the possibility of an alliance between Cadogan and the Pack.

"Understood," Ethan said, "but the contract wasn't fulfilled. You're still alive. That means there's still a possibility someone will take a shot."

Gabriel shook his head. "Pack leadership passes through the family. So if something happens to me, Fallon becomes Apex, then Eli, and so on down to Ben and Adam. The only reason to try to take me out would have been to influence the

vote. But the die's been cast, so there's no chance of that now."
He shrugged. "By my math, I'm off the hook."

I wasn't sure if I bought Gabriel's theory, especially since
the violence had erupted *after* the vote was counted, but I
understood the urge to move on and clear the vampires out
of his belfry. Besides, we couldn't guard him twenty-four
hours a day. We barely had staff enough to cover our own
House.

Gabe held out his uninjured hand to Ethan. "Thank you
again for your help. Your Sentinel does good work."

They shook hands. "That she does," Ethan said.

"Might be time to think about that raise."

"Don't push your luck, Sentinel."

A girl had to try.

I'd stripped off my leather jacket when we returned to the
Mercedes, the June heat providing more than enough insula-
tion. But it took a few minutes of driving before I noticed the
tiny nubbin in the pocket.

"Oh, damn," I muttered.

Ethan looked over in alarm. "What?"

I reached into the jacket pocket, then pulled out the ear-
piece Luc had given me. "I totally forgot to use this."

An eyebrow quirked up, Ethan reached inside his own
jeans pocket and pulled out his earbud. I guess I hadn't been
the only forgetful vampire.

He offered me a secret smile. "Let's not tell Luc about
this, perhaps."

"You know what else?"

"What's that, Sentinel?"

"I also forgot my cabbage rolls."

He rolled his eyes, but he was grinning when he did it.

"You'll have to live without them, because you couldn't pay me enough to go back to that church."

"Too much shifter tonight?"

"By a large degree, Sentinel. And the irony is, we've convinced them to stay."

"Well, that's kind of a victory, isn't it?"

"Given our other options, I suppose so. You did good today, and I mean that sincerely. You showed a lot of bravery, and you executed well. Your work honors Cadogan House."

Ethan's tone was solemn, earnest. I'd heard his Master vampire tone of appreciation; this was different. More like affection than professional approbation. And since he was the one who'd pushed me away—something he'd undertaken at his own risk—I opted to ignore the undercurrent. Being rejected and trying to stay professional—pushing down my feelings to stay focused on the task at hand—was hard enough on its own. I couldn't bear his remorse, too, and it wasn't fair for him to try to use me to make himself feel better.

So I kept the mood light. "Least I could do."

He shifted in his seat as if preparing a monologue. I thought quickly, then made my move. I turned on the radio, found a station playing a song I had to sing along with, then rolled down my window. I leaned an elbow on the door and turned my face to the wind, letting the city and the sound roll over me.

The rest of the ride was quiet.

Maybe he got the hint.

CHAPTER NINETEEN

GIRLS' NIGHT OUT

When we arrived back at the House, Ethan gave me the final hours of darkness off, then headed to the Ops Room to update Luc.

I immediately headed to my room and into the shower to scrub off the residue of magic, then pulled on a T-shirt and yoga pants and made my way to the second-floor kitchen. The convocation had been draining—physically and emotionally. I finished off two pints of blood from the fridge's stash before I felt balanced again.

When I was satiated—and after I'd texted Mallory to let her know Ethan and I had come through the convocation unscathed—I decided to check in on Linds. It would have been just as easy to lock myself in my room with a book, but I was House social chair. No harm in making good on that promise.

I could hear her room before I could see it, as noise spilled out into the hallway from Lindsey's open door. I peeked inside and found Margot, Lindsey, and Michelle preparing for what looked like a late evening on the town.

"Hey!" Lindsey said, waving from her spot in front of the

mirror. "We were just about to come get you. Since you managed to kick some ass at the convocation"—the room broke into applause—"we've decided we're sweeping you off to Temple Bar!"

"We want you to know we support you," Margot said with a nod and a grin, raising a glass of red wine. "Especially since you've been very . . . um . . ."

"Ill-used?" Michelle offered.

Margot smiled slyly. "Thanks, 'Chelle. Ill-used."

"It's Cadogan-only night at Temple," Lindsey said, "which means no humans and no Navarre vamps in attendance. So we're gonna spend our final hours before dawn having a couple of drinks, unwinding, and generally having fun, no Masters allowed. And this isn't an optional trip," she added, when I opened my mouth to beg off.

"It's been a long day."

"Which is exactly why you need this," Lindsey said.

"Is there any chance I'm getting out of it?"

"Not even slightly."

"Then I guess I'm in."

Lindsey winked but then frowned as she took in my loungewear. "First things first, the wardrobe." She turned back to the other vampires and twirled a finger in the air. "Saddle up, then meet us in the lobby in twenty. The cabs should be there by then."

When she'd cleared them all out, we walked back down to my room.

"So," she said when she was finally perched in front of my open closet door, "this is the first time you've gone out with us since Commendation. It's also the first time you've gone out since you were, you know . . ."

"Dumped? Thrown back? Replaced?"

"Is there a polite way to say it?"

"Not really. What's your point?"

"My point is, the best revenge is a life well lived or whatever. That means you need to look completely, insanely fabulous, and you need to have a fantastic time." She pulled a pale blue sleeveless shirt with a drapey neckline from a hanger, then grabbed a pair of straight-legged black pants. The outfit assembled, she turned back to me. "The place will be full of Cadogan vamps, and you know word travels. That means it's time to teach him a lesson."

I grimaced. I didn't want to play the "teaching Ethan a lesson" game, especially since I was working on swearing him off, but I knew when I'd been beat.

I held out a hand, then opened and closed my fingers. "Gimme," I said, then took the bundle and headed for the bathroom.

Ten minutes later, I emerged ponytailed and lipsticked, my beeper clipped at my waist. Lindsey had demanded I wear my hair up. Combined with the drapey neckline, she'd explained, it was the vampire way of announcing that you were single . . . and that your carotid was available. I wasn't much interested in looking for love, but I figured arguing the point would just take too long.

We headed downstairs where the rest of our entourage waited in equally trendy, neck-baring attire. Like a woman on a mission, Lindsey gave a hand signal, and we all dutifully filed outside. A line of black and white cabs was parked outside the House, ready to ferry us to Temple Bar. The official Cadogan House watering hole was situated in my favorite neighborhood, Wrigleyville, just blocks from Wrigley Field.

Paparazzi snapped pictures as we crammed into the cabs, and their comrades in arms were waiting outside the bar when we arrived fifteen gloriously traffic-free minutes later. (There were obvious advantages to doing most of your driving while most of the population was asleep.)

We were ushered into the bar, a PRIVATE PARTY sign on the door warning humans and others that they wouldn't make the grade tonight.

Membership, I supposed, did have its privileges.

Even as late in the night as it was, the bar was still hopping, the two bartenders—Sean and Colin—passing out drinks while classic rock played on the stereo system. Lindsey led us through the crowd of vamps to a table marked RESERVED.

Unlike Cadogan House, Temple Bar lacked fine antiques and carefully chosen paintings. But it did have new and vintage Cubs gear of every shape and size—vintage jackets, pennants, bobble-head dolls. As you might imagine, I felt right at home.

We'd only just pulled out chairs and taken our seats when Sean popped up on the other side of the table. Like Colin, Sean was tall and lean, and he had short, ruddy hair framing an oval face and bright blue eyes. Sean was handsome in a kind of earnest, old-fashioned way, as if he might have stepped out of the photograph of a World War II battalion.

On the other hand, he was a vampire, and immortal. He very well might have been a member of a World War II battalion.

Sean crossed his arms and looked us over with amusement. "And what brings Cadogan's finest to our little neck of the woods tonight?"

Everyone pointed at me. My cheeks heated.

"Ahhh," he said, then glanced over at me. "So our Sentinel has finally escaped the confines?"

"She has," Lindsey said, wrapping an arm around my shoulders. "She's done her duty with the shifters, and now she's working on a little oblivion. What would you recommend?"

"Hmm," he said, looking me over. "Girly or manly?"

I blinked at him. "I'm sorry?"

He moved around to my side of the table, then crouched down on one knee, one hand on the back of my chair.

"Women who drink socially tend to fall into two categories," he said with the confidence of a sociologist or purveyor of spirits, the jobs probably having a lot in common. "Women who drink girly: women who stick to colorful things in martini glasses, white wine, frozen drinks; and women who drink manly: women who aren't afraid to sip at a good Irish whiskey, or a bit of stiff Scotch. Which type of woman are you, Sentinel o' mine?"

I smiled back at him from beneath my bangs. "Why don't you decide?"

He winked. "I do like a girl with moxie."

Well, he was definitely going to like me.

Sean apparently deemed me worthy of a manly drink. He brought back a chubby glass half filled with ice and golden liquid. "You can handle this," he advised in a whisper, then moved on to put drinks in front of everyone else.

Cautiously, I lifted the glass and took a sniff. I'd never been much of a drinker, and this smelled only slightly more palatable than diesel fuel. But I liked the idea of being the girl who ordered a Scotch on the rocks—assuming that was what this was. There was something kick-ass about it, like being the girl who drove a Wrangler, the girl who wore her boyfriend's jeans, the girl who played flag football with the guys on a cool fall day . . . and won.

I lifted the glass and took a cautious sip . . . then spent the next few seconds coughing.

Margot, laughing beside me, patted me on the back. "How's that drink, Sentinel?"

I shook my head, a fist at my mouth as I tried to catch my breath. "Rocket fuel," I wheezed out.

"Did you let him choose your drink?"

I nodded.

"Yep, that's your mistake. Never let Sean or Colin choose the drink, Merit. They have a sadistic side. But they do the same thing to everyone, if that makes you feel better. She lifted her glass. "Welcome to the club."

"Speaking of the club," I asked her, motioning to the partygoers around us, "where did all these people come from? There must be a hundred vampires in here."

"Remember, there are still three hundred and something vamps affiliated with Cadogan, even if they don't live in the House. For some strange reason, those couple hundred have no desire to play vampire sorority girls and hang out with the rest of us."

Given the week I'd had so far, I didn't think there was much mystery as to why.

We spent the next hour chatting, me holding the drink in my hands as if it were providing necessary warmth, and taking a sip only when my throat had cooled down sufficiently from each previous drink. The vampires around me regaled me with stories of life in Cadogan House—from the time the fire alarm sounded during the 2007 Commendation, to the 1979 boycott of Blood4You, to the breaching of the gate by a fusty Hyde Park resident who was convinced the House was the site of secret occult rituals.

Suddenly, Margot put down her drink, pushed back her chair, then stood up on it. When she was standing, she motioned to the bar. Sean grinned back, and rang a brass bell that hung from a short post behind the bar.

The entire room erupted into raucous applause.

"What's going on?" I murmured to Lindsey, but she lifted a hand.

"Just keep listening. You'll get it."

"Cadogan vampires," Sean yelled, as every vampire in the bar quieted again. "It is now time to partake of a proud Temple Bar tradition. Not that the tradition is proud, but Temple Bar certainly is."

"Long live Temple Bar!" shouted the vampires in unison.

Sean offered a kingly bow, then gestured toward Margot.

There was hooting in the crowd, then the squeak of wood on wood as chairs were turned to face her. She raised her hands.

"Ladies and vampires," she shouted, "it's time for a round of drinks honoring the various and sundry personality tics of the Master with the mostest—Ethan Sullivan!"

I couldn't stop the grin that spread across my face.

"Tonight, we welcome into the sacred covenant . . . our Sentinel!" She lifted her glass to me, as every other vampire in the room did the same. Cheeks flushed, I raised my still mostly full glass to the rest of them, bobbing my head in acknowledgment.

Margot looked at me, glass still raised, and winked. "And may Lacey Sheridan, God bless her soul, choke on it."

The room burst into applause. My cheeks ached from the

smile on my face. Lindsey leaned over and pressed a kiss to my cheek.

"I *so* told you that you needed this."

"I very definitely needed this," I agreed.

"Everyone have fun," Margot said. "Everyone drink within reason. And afterward, everyone make use of Chicago's greatest attraction—public transportation!"

With the help of the vampire beside her, Margot stepped down and took her seat again. Everyone at our table set down their glasses and moved their chairs in a bit closer together.

"All right," I said, shyness gone. "So what exactly are we doing here?"

"Well, Sentinel," Margot said, "may I call you Sentinel?"

I grinned, and nodded.

She nodded back. "I don't think we're giving anything away by saying that our dear Master and liege, Ethan Sullivan, is a little bit—"

"Particular," Lindsey finished. "He's very, very particular."

"Yeah," I said dryly, "I had a sense."

"He's also a creature of routine," Margot explained. "Of personality tics and habits. Quirks, you might say, that can grate on the nerves."

"Like the tag in the back of a really scratchy sweater," Lindsey suggested.

Margot winked at her. "Every so often, we gather together. We take a little time—a little *cathartic* time—to vent about those quirks that drive us crazy."

Elbows on the table, I leaned forward. "So, which of the quirks are we talking about?"

"First item on the list—the raising of the eyebrow." To demonstrate, she arched a carefully sculpted black brow of her own, then peered around at each of us.

"Drink!" Lindsey yelled, and we all took a sip.

"I hate it when he does that," Michelle said, gesturing with her drink. "And he does it *constantly*."

"It's like the world's most irritating nervous twitch," I agreed.

"Nervous my ass," Margo said. "He thinks it's intimidating. It's the gesture of the Master vampire speaking to a lowly Novitiate." Her voice had deepened into an obnoxiously crisp imitation of the perfectly condescending Master vampire tone. Maybe she had a little Master in her, as well.

"So what's number two?" I asked.

"I got this one," Lindsey said. "Number two—when Ethan refers to you not by your name, but by your title." She dipped her chin and looked at me through hooded eyes. "Sentinel," she growled out.

I snorted. "I always thought you looked familiar."

"Drink!" Margot yelled, and we raised our glasses again.

The next hour and a half continued in pretty much the same fashion—Ethan, maybe not surprisingly, had a lot of tics and quirks. That meant a lot of drinks. And if anyone came up with a quirk not catalogued before, we had to take a double round.

Since I'd made virtually no headway with my "manly" drink, Sean took pity on me and brought over a plastic cup of ice water. That I wasn't drinking alcohol didn't make fun at the expense of the most pretentious of vampires any less enjoyable.

We drank for every mention of Amit Patel, for every speech Ethan gave about duty, for each mention of alliances, for each time he answered a knock at his office door by saying, simply, "Come." We drank for each time he jiggled his watch, each time he straightened his cuff links, each time he shuffled papers when you reported to him in his office.

Ethan had quirks enough that half the table had switched to soda or water by the time we were through. Ethan had quirks enough that I had to excuse myself from the table. And that was why I was on the way back to the table from the back of the bar when I saw them—photos that had been tacked to the wall, decades of pictures of vampires together, all taken at Temple Bar.

"Cool," I murmured, my gaze scanning the gathering of pictures. There were Afros and disco wear, 1980s hairstyles and shoulder pads . . . and a picture that was half tucked into a corner of the display.

With my fingertips, I turned the photograph on its thumbtack pivot to get a better view. The white Polaroid border framed a beautiful boy with cut cheekbones and a fall of blond hair across his face. At his side was a blond girl, her arm tucked in his, a martini glass in her hands.

He looked at her . . . with adoration in his eyes.

My stomach knotted.

It was Ethan and Lacey, a picture taken some years ago, given the outfits in the photograph, but a picture of them just the same—a boy and girl, happy together, love in their eyes.

I slid the picture back into its place, partially hiding it from view. But there was no unringing the bell. He'd definitely had feelings for her.

And after he'd slept with me, he'd called her back.

I leaned against the wall and closed my eyes. I couldn't begrudge him love. I couldn't. Not if that was what they had together. But goddamn, did I rue being in the middle of it, being the trigger for his reminiscence of that emotion.

Sometimes, knowledge did no one any good. I stood in the hallway for a few seconds, until I was ready to face the vampires again. When I finally returned to the table, I paused at my chair and touched Lindsey's shoulder.

She looked up, her smile fading as her gaze tracked my face. "Are you okay?"

I nodded. "I'm fine." I hitched a thumb toward the front door. "I'm going to take a little breather."

"You sure you're okay?"

I gave her my best smile. "I'm fine, really. I just want to get some air." That was the truth. My shifter-magic-induced headache wasn't helped by the spilt magic of a hundred vampires.

She looked at me for a moment, apparently debating whether I was telling the truth. "You need company?"

"I'm fine. I'll be back in a few minutes."

"Okay. But if you meet any cute humans out there who need any blood work, you let me know."

"You'll be the first vampire I call."

I wove through the bar to the front door, then accepted a hand stamp from a cute, smiling, curly-haired vamp at the door.

Once prepped for reentry, I walked down the sidewalk, my gaze on the restaurants, bars, and eclectic shops that filled this part of Wrigleyville. I figured I might as well scope out interesting places to visit the next time I made the trip.

I'd just passed a dusty used bookstore—now at the top of my to-visit list—when I heard footsteps *scratch* on the sidewalk behind me. I instinctively put a hand at my waist, at the place my sword would usually be belted, before realizing I'd left it at the House.

"You wouldn't need it even if you did have it," said a low voice behind me.

CHAPTER TWENTY

WHAT'S IN A NAME?

I froze, then glanced back over my shoulder.

Jonah stood in a puddle of streetlight, auburn hair kind of curving softly around his face. He wore a snug, dark button-up shirt with jeans, and brown boots on his feet.

"Merit," he said.

I lifted my eyebrows. "Jonah."

"I was in the neighborhood."

"Grey House isn't far from here, right?"

"It's down Addison," he said, then bobbed his head to the left. "A little farther west. It's a converted warehouse."

"And you decided to take a walk and see what was happening at the Cadogan House bar?"

Jonah looked away for a moment before meeting my gaze again. "It may not be entirely coincidental that I'm here."

I waited for elaboration. When none came, I prodded. "And exactly how noncoincidental is it?"

He took a step toward me, hands in his pockets. He was close enough, and tall enough, that I had to look up to see his face.

"If you join us," he said quietly, "you'll be my partner. My asset. My companion. The one I follow into battle, the one who takes up arms to protect me. I don't take that responsibility lightly."

"Are you guarding me, or making sure I meet your standards?"

"Fair enough," he admitted. "A little of both, probably." He nodded toward an alley between the buildings, then walked toward it. I followed. The moon was high enough to light the alley, although the view was hardly worth the light: bricks, graffiti, empty wooden packing crates, and the steel skeletons of rusty fire escapes.

"You've made a name for yourself," Jonah said, turning to face me again, arms crossed over his shirt. The angel and devil on his arms stared back at me, both with empty eyes, as if neither was pleased with the side they'd chosen. "With a profile that high, humans may get a little too curious about the newest vamp celeb. And curiosity might be the nicest of their emotions."

"I didn't ask for the press," I pointed out. "The story was a kind of favor."

"I hear you managed to hold your own at the shifter convocation."

I assumed Luc had given the other Guard Captains a debriefing, so I nodded my agreement.

"And there are rumors Gabriel Keene likes you."

That one I wouldn't confirm. Reviewing the basics of our security plan at the convocation was one thing—Luc had already talked to Jonah about that. But the things I'd heard from Gabriel were among Ethan, me, and the Pack.

Besides, if I was going to sell out Ethan, I wasn't going to do it without being a full-fledged guard member. If I was going to incite his rage, I was at least going to get a membership card out of it.

"Gabriel's a friendly guy," I finally said.

"Playing it close to the chest?"

"I'm not a Red Guard."

"*Yet.*" Jonah's tone was pretentious. I'd had plenty of pretentious today, so I half turned to leave, hitching a thumb over my shoulder.

"Unless you have something interesting to say, I'm going back to join my friends."

"You may not join," he said, surprise in his voice. "You might actually say no."

I let my silence stand in for an answer.

"I'm told no one's ever said no."

I turned around again and smiled lightly. "Then maybe I'll start a new tradition of thinking for myself, instead of doing something just because everyone else has done it."

"That's obnoxious."

"I've had an obnoxious night. Look," I said, crossing my arms, "I don't mean to be rude, but it's been a long night, and a longer week. I'm not crazy about being stalked because someone I might work with in the future wanted to find out if I was as incompetent as he imagined."

He didn't protest. Wasn't that flattering?

"Maybe you should look into requesting another partner," I said. "You don't know me, and I don't know you. With all due respect, I'd rather have a partner who waits to judge me until after we've had three or four conversations."

"And I'd rather have a partner who takes her job seriously."

I nearly snarled at him. "Buddy, if you knew anything about me, you'd know just how seriously I take my job."

We stood silently for a minute, the unspoken question hanging in the air—was I going to be his partner?

"What are you going to do?" he finally asked.

"I don't know," I answered quietly after a moment.

I looked up at the lights of the city and thought about Ethan. I thought about what we'd done, what he'd wanted, what he could and couldn't offer me.

I figured I had two options.

One, I could give Ethan the metaphorical finger and join the Red Guard. I'd be setting up a quick Cadogan House exit, either when humans decided they'd had enough of Cadogan vampires (or Celina decided it for them), or when Ethan found out and ripped the Cadogan medal from my neck.

Two, I could give Jonah the metaphorical finger by telling Noah, "No, thanks." I'd be committing to Cadogan House; committing to Ethan.

Wasn't that ironic?

I wasn't really feeling either option. Both felt like ploys in a supernatural game, and I wasn't sure I was holding the right pieces. I certainly wasn't crazy about picking one or the other based on which vampire I wanted to piss off more, especially given what was at stake—my life, my friends, the shape of my immortality.

"I'll call Noah when I've made a decision," I finally told him, then turned and headed back toward the bar.

For obvious reasons, I kept the conversation with Jonah to myself. I faked a smile back at Temple Bar, then faked a yawn so that I could extricate myself from the crowd and head back to the House. Lindsey decided to stay, so I took a cab home, ready to spend the little rest of my evening in the thrall of the books. Say what you had to about Ethan, but the boy filled a library very, very well.

Okay—arguably, that wasn't the only thing he filled out well, but let's stay on track.

The library was a two-story space that occupied a chunk of the second floor toward the front of the House. The room itself was two stories tall and ringed by a balcony full of books, the balcony ringed by a red wrought-iron railing. A spiral stair-case in the same iron led up to it. Three giant windows filled the room with light, and tidy rows of library tables filled the middle.

Long story slightly shorter, it was lush—a booklover's dream.

When I reached the second floor, I slipped inside the library's double doors, then glanced around, hands on my hips. I didn't have a research assignment per se, but I also didn't think I had the knowledge I needed to live and work hand in hand with shifters.

Historical animosity or not, there had to be material on shifters in here. Unfortunately, as big and well organized as the library was, it was still old-school about one thing: it had a card catalog—and not just any card catalog, but three massive oak cabinets with slender drawers, each containing thousands of alphabetized cards.

I went to the *S* row, pulled out the appropriate drawer, then set it onto a slide-out shelf. There were lots of entries for books on shifters, from the *Encyclopaedia Tractus*—the "preeminent guide to shifter territories across the world"—to *A Life in Fur: One Man's Journey*.

I scribbled down the call numbers of a handful of nonfiction titles (minus the biographies and memoirs), then slid the drawer back into place. I bumped a hip against the slide-out shelf to fit it back into its slot, then scanned the slips of paper I'd collected to figure out what parts of the library the books might be in . . . and ran face-first into a brown-haired twentysomething who scowled up at me with obvious irritation.

"Oh, God, I'm sorry. I didn't mean—"

"Surely you didn't think you were the only Novitiate who used this room. Surely you didn't think the books just organized themselves?"

I blinked at the man—shortish, cute, bedeviled expression—who'd just cut me off midapology. "I—um—no? Of course not?" Stuttering or not, I was actually being honest. The first time I'd seen the library, I'd assumed it had to have a librarian to keep things organized. I'd thought it weird, actually, that I hadn't seen him or her before. I guessed this was him.

The librarian seemed to relax a little at the answer, then ran a hand through his hair, which made it stand up on end. He wore jeans and a black polo shirt—another vampire apparently exempt from Cadogan's all-black dress code.

"Of course not," he repeated. "That would be incredibly naïve." He motioned at the books behind him. "There are tens of thousands of titles in this library, you know, not to mention that we're an official *Canon* depository." He lifted his eyebrows, as if waiting for my response—my *awed* response.

"Yeah," I said, "that's—*wow*. Tens of thousands of titles? And an official *Canon* depository? Also very wow."

He crossed his arms over his chest, his expression all skepticism. "Are you just saying that or are you really impressed?"

I scrunched up my face. "How would you like me to answer that?"

One corner of his mouth quirked up. "Cute and you don't kiss ass. I can appreciate that. You're the new Sentinel? The researcher."

"Former researcher," I said, holding out a hand. "And you are?"

"The librarian," he said, apparently not interested in offering a name. He also didn't take my hand. Instead, he waggled his fingers and bobbed his head at the papers in my hand. "Gimme your notes and we'll find what you need."

I did as I was told, then followed as he turned and headed toward the social sciences section. Funny, I thought, that most libraries probably stocked books about shape-shifters and were-creatures in the myths and fantasy section. But here, in the confines of this vampire-owned library, they were real. That meant the books were more akin to anthropology (or maybe zoology?) than mythology.

We walked to the back-right corner of the room, the librarian's gaze on my notes as we moved. He didn't bother to read the signs on the ends of the shelves, apparently having memorized the locations of the volumes.

"Vampires are talking," he began as he turned into a narrow aisle between shelves. I followed him, books of every shape and size, new and old, paper- and leather-bound, stretching above us.

"Talking about what?"

"The convocation." He stopped in the middle of the aisle and turned to face one of the shelves, then glanced back at me. "Word is, they voted not to leave for Aurora, and then attacked you."

Stories of the convocation had traveled; truth, unfortunately, hadn't. "They voted to stay and support us, not to run away," I clarified. "The attack was against one of the Pack leaders. They didn't attack me. I just helped defend."

"Still," he said, "doesn't that just show what they're like? Fickle? And meeting to discuss their future in Chicago. Who'd have thought the day would come?" When he began to run a fingertip across the books' spines, I assumed the comment was rhetorical. But I still had a question.

"Why are they called 'Pretenders'?" I asked. I'd heard Peter Spencer use the term against shifters, as well. I knew it wasn't flattering, but I wasn't sure of its origin.

The librarian pulled a long, slim, brown leather book from the shelves, then handed it over. It was actually a portfolio that held sketches of shifters in animal form. The usual suspects were there: wolves, big cats, birds of prey. There were also a few more unusual options, including seals. Maybe that was the origin of the silkie myth.

"Shifters pose as humans," he said. "They *pretend* to be humans. They mingle among them, even if they aren't really humans."

I had to admit, the argument confused me. "But we aren't humans, either, right?"

"We are what we are. Predators. Humans, plus a little genetic restructuring. We don't change forms to disguise ourselves." He took a step back, then gestured at his body with his hands. "This is me. This is us," he said, frustration in his voice, then turned back to the shelves from which he started plucking volumes. "Whenever humans have tried to take out supernaturals, the shifters have *still* pretended they were humans."

I managed not to argue that vampires had been hiding in plain sight for centuries, pretending to be humans in order to avoid staking. Frankly, I didn't think he'd appreciate the comparison. This was the kind of prejudice that didn't bend to logic.

"Is that what they did in the Second Clearing?" I wondered aloud as the librarian began stacking books in my arms. "Pretended to be humans and ignored that vampires were being killed?"

"I think that's enough, don't you?" he asked darkly.

I guess that explained the prejudice. I knew the wound caused by the shifters' failure to help vampires during the Second Clearing—to put themselves on the line to save vampires—was a deep one. And not just deep, but still jagged and unhealed, even more than a century later. I'd seen the animosity from the shifters' side; they'd shown it clearly enough. Their urge to retreat sounded as if it was based on fear of what would come, so I still wasn't sure why so many shifters seemed so bitter about the past.

But even as enlightened as Ethan imagined his vampires to be, the anger, the bitterness, were just as present in our camp, as well. . . . Even in this archive of learning and knowledge, it lingered.

He finally stopped pulling books from the shelves, then glanced back at me. "That should be all you need," he said. "These will give you the basics."

I nodded, working to keep my smile neutral, then watched as he walked around me and back into the main aisle.

"I know what you think," he said when he reached it, glancing back, hands on his hips. His expression had turned stern, concern evident in the tightness around his eyes. "That I'm just ignorant, or that I'm pissed about something that happened a hundred years ago." His eyes suddenly flashed silver, and the hair at my neck stood on end as magic spread through our corner of the library, leaking as his emotions rose.

"We are *immortal*, Sentinel. These were not harms done to our ancestors, to our forebears. They were harms done to *us*. Our families. Our lovers. Our children. Ourselves."

With that, he walked away.

A foot-high stack of books in my arms, I blinked after him for a moment, thinking not just about the anger in his voice, the pain over acts that had happened, but the fear, the worry that without vigilance, such things could happen again.

And I thought of the passion I'd heard in Gabriel's voice, his desire to protect his Pack members. I thought of the anger I'd once heard in Nick's voice, his desire to keep his family safe.

I matched all that disdain and contention together . . . and I still wondered who was the bigger threat.

CHAPTER TWENTY-ONE

JUST DANCE

The next night dawned cool and clear. I pulled open my anti-sun shutter and cracked my window. A welcome breeze was blowing through the city, clearing out a little of yesterday's humidity. I was scheduled to train with Ethan again, so I got up and headed over to the kitchen, grabbed some orange juice, blood, and a bacon-topped donut shellacked in maple frosting. Yes, you heard that correctly. Bacon. And maple. In a *donut*.

Sure, I wasn't thrilled about training again. I'd seen a lot of Ethan over the week, and I wouldn't have minded an evening to myself, without political drama or relationship conflict, without swordplay or side kicks. But what could I do? Because I'd sworn my oaths, camping out in my room, donut in hand, wasn't an option. So, after I'd scarfed down breakfast, I slipped into flip-flops and pulled on a track jacket, then headed down the hallway.

I was about to take the stairs to the basement when I saw her. She stood on the landing between the first and second floors in a black suit, her arms crossed and one eyebrow arched.

She was a Master made in her own Master's image.

I took the steps but stopped a riser or two above the landing, my eyebrows arched. "Waiting for me?"

"You and Ethan have a unique relationship," Lacey said.

"We have a relationship?"

"I don't play games, Merit."

All evidence to the contrary, but I forced myself to be polite. "Respectfully, ma'am, I don't, either. May I help you with something?"

"I don't give up easily. He and I are perfect for each other."

I almost snarked out a response, but held back. If she truly believed that, more power to her. Besides—he'd invited her here, so maybe he believed it, too.

"You know what?" I asked instead, moving past her. "Good luck with that."

She followed me down to the first floor. Ethan, timing as impeccable as always, picked that moment to begin the climb upstairs toward us, his suit jacket discarded, body hugged by lean, dark trousers, a white button-down, and black tie. He must have been on his way up to change.

His eyes widened at the sight of us together, as if he wasn't quite prepared for the meeting of old and slightly less old lovers—his own fault, since he'd thrown us together under one roof.

"How was your call?" Lacey asked. "And how are things in London?"

It was easy to read between the lines on that one—*Dear Sentinel: Your boss made a phone call to the GP he didn't tell you about. Guess you aren't in the loop about everything! Love, his most bestest protégé.*

Her second time at bat, she'd swung for the fence. I had to stifle down a growl.

"Not as helpful as I'd have liked, but so goes the GP," Ethan said. When he glanced at me, the line of worry had appeared between his eyes. "I'll meet you in the Sparring Room momentarily."

I nodded. "Liege."

He walked past me. "Lacey, with me, please," he said, and she obediently followed.

I glanced behind me and watched her trail after him like a puppy on a string as they took the stairs to the third floor.

Something struck me as she followed him. Ethan was, and always would be, her Master. And although I'd heard her disagree with him, raising concerns about my being a "common soldier," there was something acquiescent even in her *posture*. She moved as if she were his property, as if there were nothing she wanted more than to be at his side. Even though she had her own House, she wanted back in Cadogan.

Lindsey had told me that Lacey was a Very Strong Strat. So maybe part of the adoration was political. Maybe, like him, she was worried about alliances, wanted to ensure her link to the fourth-oldest House in the country.

Or maybe it was something simpler. Maybe she just wanted *him*.

Whatever the future had in store for me and Ethan (or me and *not* Ethan, as the case may have been), I made a vow then and there not to become one of those vampires. I vowed to stay my own person, to remember who I was, to think rationally about alliances and the people I might have allied with.

If only I'd remembered those things a few nights ago . . . or when Mallory had needed me. But what was done was done.

A girl could only move forward.

I was limbering up by practicing kicks when Ethan and Lacey made their appearances. He entered the Sparring Room from the main door; Lacey took her spot on the balcony, this time amongst a mass of vampires. The balcony was nearly full, from Lindsey and Luc—who must have been taking a break from their guarding duties—to Margot and Michelle and some of the other vampires I'd had drinks with. They waved at me, a fan club for a once-reticent vampire.

But I'd passed through reticence . . . and I'd become one of them, at least in part largely because I was a Novitiate who'd been wronged by a Master. Or Two, if you counted Lacey. Or Four, if you counted the former and current Masters of Navarre.

However regrettable (and however embarrassing), those wrongs had created a kind of bond between me and the other vampires of Cadogan House—a chance for me to get to know them without my rank between us.

Silver lining? Maybe. Or maybe the world just worked in mysterious ways.

Ethan walked toward me, his posture businesslike, his expression just shy of grim. "Prepare to fight," he said.

I guess we were skipping the complicated teaching protocols . . . and the greetings.

"Liege," I said, and angled my body toward his, knees soft, elbows bent, prepared to strike or defend.

He must have had aggression of his own to work out, as he immediately struck out with a punch-kick-punch combination that had me hurrying to defend myself. But I parried his punches and the kick, and then tried a shot myself—a crescent kick that he nevertheless fended off.

We bounced around the mat for a bit, offering up testing jabs, but not yet committing to an actual punch. The crowd began to murmur and call out for action.

I tried a side kick, which he easily blocked.

"You're hardly trying," he said, but he didn't stop moving. He bobbed around me before executing a perfect front kick that caught me in the right collarbone. I think he pulled the kick; it was still bone jarring, but the full force of it would have cracked the bone in half.

I rubbed the sore spot, anger beginning to boil my blood. Ethan kept bobbing and weaving; I kept trying to hit him. This, he seemed to think, was exactly the problem—that I was *trying* to do it, instead of actually doing it. Here we were again, and he was running out of ways to motivate me with fear and anger.

"I want you to use the skills you've learned," he said. "How to rely upon your senses, your instincts."

I ducked to avoid a strike. "I'm trying, Sullivan."

"Try *harder.*"

Why did people always think demanding we try *harder* was going to help? I was trying as hard as I could. My inability to best him wasn't for lack of effort on my part.

"Maybe you're just better than I am."

He stopped cold, then moved so close to me that the bottom of his white *gi* pants brushed my legs. "You are Sentinel of this House. It's not an issue of 'better than.'"

His expression softened, and he looked at me with those deep green eyes, and instead of baiting me, he *encouraged* me.

"I have seen you move, Merit. I have seen you perform the Katas with grace and speed, and I have seen you battle men twice your size. Your skill is not the problem. You *can do* this."

I nodded and blew out a breath, and I tried not to look up at the balcony to check the reactions of the vampires who were watching me. I didn't want to see mine or Ethan's frustration echoed on their faces.

Was that the problem? That I had an audience? It shouldn't have mattered. After all, I'd been a dancer; it wasn't as if I hadn't performed in front of a crowd before. And then I thought about the first time I'd challenged Ethan, and how proud he'd been of my skills as a newbie vamp. And I thought about what had been different then.

Suddenly . . . *insight*.

In that first fight, I'd *danced*.

I looked at Ethan again. "Can I get some music?"

He frowned. "Music?"

"Please."

"Any preferences?"

I let a smile slowly curl my lips. "Something I can dance to."

He nodded at someone behind me. After a moment, Rage Against the Machine began to echo through the Sparring Room.

I took a moment, closing my eyes and letting the pounding of "Guerilla Radio" loosen my limbs. I let my body adjust to its rhythm, and when the tension was gone and the world seemed to slow on its axis, I opened my eyes and I looked at him—not as his lover, or the vampire he'd made, or his Novitiate, but as a soldier in my own right.

"Ready?" he asked.

I nodded.

"Begin," he said, and as if it were the simplest thing in the world, I attacked.

I didn't think about it, didn't analyze it, didn't wonder how he might parry or defend. Instead, with the roaring bass line echoing through my chest, I struck out. I started with a high butterfly kick, and before he could defend, using the momentum I'd gained from the kick, I swept a high roundhouse at his face.

He grunted and dropped down with his usual speed, then struck out with a roundhouse kick. But I'd seen that kick before. I dodged the move, flipping backward and landing with my body bladed, ready for the next round. "You'll have to be faster than that, Sullivan."

The crowd came to its feet.

We both hopped out of our kicks, balancing on the balls of our feet as we waited for our next openings.

"That's better," he said.

I winked at him. "Then you're gonna love this one."

"Not if I move first," he said, then aimed a sidekick at my torso, but I spun around, one hand on the floor as I turned, then aimed a back kick at his head.

I missed his head . . . but caught him on the shoulder. His inertia brought him down to his knees, but he hopped up quickly enough.

The vampires in the balcony cheered appreciatively.

Hands on my hips, I gave him an appraising glance. "That's better."

He snorted with delight.

Ethan kicked again, and this time, I thought I'd try something a little different. I jumped backward into an exaggerated scissor-legged flip that took me ten feet in the air and out of the range of his kicks.

I landed again, and then the sparring really got started. We moved and torqued our bodies as if gravity made no difference at all, as if we were partners in a pas de deux.

"Good," he called out, but there was a brilliant gleam in his eyes.

That was when I used my best weapon. I looked at him and faked a side kick. "I am but a common soldier," I said.

He froze, his expression falling. And in that moment of discombobulation, I swiveled and offered up another butterfly kick.

This time, I caught him square in the chest.

He flew backward, then hit the ground with a thud.

The room went silent... and then burst into raucous applause.

Chest heaving, sweat dripping from the exertion, I walked over and stared down at him, not entirely sure about the protocol. What do you do when you've finally beaten your teacher at his own game?

I decided to enjoy it. I let my mouth curl into a grin and arched an eyebrow at him. "Why, Sullivan, I think I just kicked your ass."

His eyes were wide, emerald, and decidedly shocked. But even there on the ground he smiled up at me with pride and a kind of boyish pleasure.

When I'd stepped over his body, I offered him a hand. He took it, and I pulled him to his feet.

"Always remember," he whispered to me, "that you are an *un*common soldier, whatever they say. And you are quite a thing to behold."

I nodded, took the compliment, and glanced up at the crowd on the balcony. Lindsey and Katherine stood at the front, bodies pressed against the rail, both clapping along with the crowd. I grabbed the hems of an invisible skirt and curtsied, then held a hand in Ethan's direction. He chuckled but made a gallant bow.

"I believe we've had enough fun for today," he called up. "Back to work, vampires." There was grousing, but they headed for the exits, chatting with animation about what they'd seen.

That was when it hit me. My inability to best him, the sparring wall I'd had to work through, was mental, emotional. It was about letting go of all my human preconceptions about fighting, about movement. It was about, as Catcher had once told me, understanding my vampire body's strange new relationship with gravity. It was about remembering, as Ethan had said, what free dance was like—forgetting about whether the moves were perfect, whether they looked good, or whether they were "right," and remembering what it felt like to be truly *in* your body, to feel limbs move, hips sway, skin heat, heart pound, breath speed.

I saw the covetous silvering of his eyes, and I knew that he'd realized the same thing I had.

Lacey Sheridan wasn't going to be the only Master vampire Ethan had made.

And speaking of the last girl who'd gotten training from Ethan, I glanced up and oh so slowly shifted my gaze to the one who came before me. Lacey stared back at me, some new emotion in her eyes. It wasn't friendship, certainly; Lacey and I would never be friends, not with Ethan between us. But there was something akin to respect in her expression. It was the recognition that she'd met an enemy on the battlefield and found her equal to the challenge.

The old me wouldn't have wanted the confrontation.

But the new me liked the odds, even if I wasn't entirely sure the prize would be worth the fight.

I nodded, acknowledging the battle—the challenge. She arched an eyebrow—no doubt an imitation of Ethan, perfected after twenty years of service in his House—then nodded back.

Ethan leaned toward me. "Get dressed and changed," he whispered. "I'd like you to at least put in an appearance at her reception."

I managed not to growl at him. Instead, I offered Lacey a polite smile, then trotted up the stairs to shower and climb back into my Cadogan black.

CHAPTER TWENTY-TWO

KNOCK HIM (UN)DEAD

I didn't expect trouble during the cocktail reception, but my run-in with Jonah taught me a valuable lesson about heading out without any weaponry. I'd been lucky that the vampire stalking me outside the bar hadn't been out to get me—but that certainly wasn't true for everyone.

So as I climbed into my Cadogan black, I slipped a dagger into one of my boots. My hair went up, my Cadogan medal went around my neck, and my beeper was clipped on. I was as ready as I could be—at least physically.

Sure. I'd oblige him. I'd clean up and walk downstairs, and I'd put in an appearance at a party held in honor of his former flame. But I wasn't going to do that without backup, at least in spirit. So I grabbed my phone from the bookshelf, took a seat on the edge of my bed, and dialed up Mallory.

The first thing I heard was the clanking of pots and pans, and a bevy of faraway curses before she managed to right the phone.

"Oh, God, stop—stop—crap—*crap*—Merit? Are you there?"

"Mal? Are you okay?"

"I'm—seriously—*stop* it. *Right now*."

The din immediately quieted.

"What's going on over there?"

"Science experiments. I have to learn how to work with a cat; they're familiars, you know—and she's into everything. She's been here, like, four hours, and she thinks she owns my—*Seriously, bad kitty! Stop that!*—she thinks she owns my house. She's destroying my kitchen. So, what's up with you? I saw your text about some drama at the convocation?"

"Violence broke out, but Gabriel's alive, and that's the most important thing."

"I totally knew that apotrope would work—like a *charm*!" she exclaimed, snorting through the phone.

I rolled my eyes. "You did good, and I appreciate it. But I need a moment of best-friend butt-kissing."

"What's he got you doing now?"

Ah, she knew me so well. "He's hosting a cocktail party for Lacey Sheridan. He told me I had to put in an appearance."

"You know, I really dislike him in so many ways."

"That had occurred to me as well."

"Well, let's do the checklist—do you look fabulous?"

"I'm wearing my suit."

"Good enough. Are you going to follow him around at the party or kiss her ass?"

"No plans for either."

"Are you going to be your normally brilliant and funny self, reminding him by your very vivaciousness and joie de vivre how foolish he's being?"

And that was why I loved this girl. "I can certainly give it my best."

"That's all I can ask—Oh, God, *bad* kitty. Merit, I have to go. She's got my matches again. I'll talk to you later, okay?"

"Good night, Mallory."

"Good night, Merit. Knock him undead."

Like I told her, I'd give it my best.

Things were quiet when I emerged downstairs. I walked through the first-floor hallway to the back patio. Ethan's door was open, his office dark, as were the other administrative offices I passed. I was halfway there—nearly to the kitchen—when I heard it.

Music.

Through the windows at the back of the House, I could see the glow of a fire in the backyard and the mass of vampires gathered around it.

As quietly as I could, I opened the glass-and-iron back door, and stepped outside. Black-clad vampires stood in rings, surrounding the haunting strain of music. There was a single voice, a woman, accompanied by a violin. Her voice was clear and sad, the violin raspy, weeping. It sounded like a dirge, a low, sweet song of loss or love, the kind I'd run across in my own medieval studies.

The vampires' attention was rapt—the crowd silent, gazes on the musicians in the middle, whom I still couldn't see. They said music soothed the savage beast; I was a believer.

I saw Luc's tousled curls in front of me. When I reached him, he looked over and smiled before turning back to the musicians. I could finally see them—Katherine and a male vampire I didn't know. He played the lonely fiddle; the clear but melancholy voice was hers.

"It's a Civil War song," Luc whispered. "Ethan asked them, Thomas and Katherine, to do a song tonight."

This must be Katherine's brother, I realized. "It's beautiful," I told him.

They sat beside each other on a low, concrete bench, Katherine in a simple dress and sandals, Thomas in black pants and a button-down shirt. His eyes were closed, the violin tucked beneath his chin, his shoulders swaying as the song flowed from his strings.

Katherine's eyes were open, but her gaze was unfocused, as if she watched invisible memories play out before her as she traveled the verses of the song.

"She was changed in 1864," Luc whispered. "She and Thomas both. Her Master changed them after Katherine lost her husband, Caleb, to the war. They'd only been married for a week."

The song sounded autobiographical. Katherine sang for a young soldier's safe return, lamented the sound of gunfire across a valley, and lamented the soldier's death.

She mourned the death of her true love.

I'm not sure what made me look up, what made me search the crowd for Ethan, but I did. I saw Lacey first. Her expression was blank, emotionless. If she was touched by the song, by the lyrics, she didn't show it.

He stood beside her, arms crossed. His gaze . . . on me.

We looked at each other over the vampires, over the music, his eyes catching the glow of the garden lights, centuries of history in his gaze.

Centuries that had made him cold.

And then his voice echoed through my head. *Merit.*

He silently called my name, even as he stood beside her.

Liege? I answered back.

His eyes glinted. *Don't call me that.*

There is nothing else for me to call you. You are my employer. That is the deal we've struck.

There was something helpless in his eyes now, but I wasn't going to fall for it again. I turned my gaze to the fire. It licked toward the sky, forked tongues of flame creating glowing shadows on the tinder. The tangy wood smoke rose, the fragrance almost intoxicating, hinting at a wildness that vampires in the middle of downtown Chicago, forbidden from the sun, couldn't otherwise touch. I stared at the fire until the song was over, then clapped along with the others as Katherine and Thomas shared a soft, sad smile.

"Where did you head off to last night?" Luc asked as Katherine sipped from a cup and Thomas resituated his violin. I assumed he wasn't asking where I'd been—but where Lindsey had been.

"Temple Bar. Lindsey thought it would be a good idea to get me out of the House."

"And how are you holding up?"

"If you meant with respect to the shifters, pretty good. If you meant personally, he invited his ex-girlfriend back to town. You can probably guess how I feel about that."

Katherine and Thomas started again, this time a perkier song with an Irish cant. Luc and I stood together in silence, watching Katherine sing in a lilting Irish brogue, Thomas beside her, his fingers flying across the fiddle.

"I really do think he cares about you, you know."

"He has a strange way of showing it."

"He's a vampire. That makes him strange."

I glanced over at Luc. Even in the midst of supernatural

drama, he usually had a quirky grin on his face. But this time, his expression was weary, and I wasn't sure if we were still talking about Ethan . . . or Lindsey. Had something similar happened between them? If so, I could sympathize. It was hard to bear the burden of someone else's regret—and the contrition that apparently followed it.

"Are you and Lindsey okay?"

His expression hardened. "Lindsey and I . . . aren't. But that's status quo."

"Would you like to talk about it?"

The question was pretty girly, but the look I got back—eyes narrowed, stare flat—was all boy.

"No, Sentinel, I do not want to talk about it."

"Fair enough. Maybe," I suggested, "if this is the product of immortality, we have to ask if the sacrifice is worth it."

"It does make one wonder," Luc said.

Love was very definitely a bitch.

Katherine and Thomas finished singing to raucous applause, the clapping eventually giving way to the soft sounds of cello music.

Luc sighed. "I'm going to mingle. You gonna be okay here?"

"Right as rain," I told him. "Feel free."

I watched him disappear into the vampires. It probably wasn't a coincidence that I also saw Lindsey milling about in another part of the crowd.

"Katherine and Thomas are quite talented."

I glanced behind me. Ethan stood there, expression blank, hands in his pockets. "They're quite talented," he said again.

I looked back at the crowd, wondering where his companion had gone. I found her on the other side of the formal garden, chatting with Malik. For the moment, the risk of drama diminished. "Yes, they are."

"Gabriel called," he said. "He confirmed that shifters who attacked were trying to make good on the hit and collect the payment."

"Who ordered the hit?"

"They weren't told, and they apparently didn't ask."

"That's not exactly comforting. Is Gabe still sure the drama's over?"

Ethan nodded. "He is all but convinced. That said, he is remarkably short-sighted for a man with gifts of prophecy."

Or just not as neurotic as the fanged among him. "And the ultimate culprit?" I wondered.

"Who's to say? Tony may have been involved, but we still don't know whether he was the puppet master or just a puppet. And since we've been excused by Gabriel, that's how it will remain."

We stood in silence for another moment.

"You're quiet this evening," he said.

I pasted on a pleasant smile. "It's been a long week. I'm just trying to relax." And I was trying to avoid more drama.

He was quiet for two or three minutes, during which the two of us stood there together, black-clad vampires moving around us. "I can tell something's bothering—"

We had sex and you bailed, I silently thought, *and now your contrition is driving me crazy*. "I was just enjoying the music."

"I'm sorry."

I clenched my eyes shut, emotion washing over me. I didn't want to do this again. I certainly didn't want his apologies. They only made me feel pitied. "Please stop saying that."

"I wish—"

"Your indecision isn't making this easier."

"And you think it's easy for me?"

"Hey, kids," said a familiar voice in front of us. Lindsey approached, Lacey at her side, the traitor.

"Lovely party," Lindsey told Ethan, then looked at me. "And how are you faring this evening?"

"I'm good. And you?"

"Eh," she said with a shrug. "I'm not as popular as our dear Sentinel, of course." She put an arm around my shoulders. "We took her to Temple Bar last night, and she was a hit."

Ah, so that was the game—showing me off in front of Lacey.

Ethan looked at me, his expression chill. I guessed he wasn't impressed by my sudden popularity. "Meet me in my office in five minutes."

It took me a moment to adjust to the topic change, but I glanced between him and Lacey. "There's no need for you to leave the party. We can talk later."

Before I could finish, that eyebrow was arched. "That was not a request."

Without waiting for an answer, he walked away, a hand at Lacey's back to guide her along.

Lindsey frowned. "What was that about?"

"I have no clue. Why do you think he wants me to meet him in his office?"

"Well, he's either just figured out that you might win homecoming queen and he totally wanted that spot, or he wants to get down on one knee and apologize profusely for being an ass."

We looked at each other. She grinned. "So, since that second part is damned unlikely, are you interested in the home-coming queen bit?"

"Will there be a tiara?"

"What's a homecoming queen without one?" Then she put her hands on my arms. "Do me one favor—whatever he says about your relationship or your training or Lacey, don't play bashful. Don't play humble. You've been busting your ass this week, and you've been making him look good. You've earned that bravado. Promise?"

I promised.

I waited for fifteen minutes—fifteen minutes during which I forced myself to scan the books and trophies on his shelves, and tried to avoid wondering what—or who—had kept him.

I was leaning back against the conference table in his office when he walked in. He didn't look up, but shut the doors behind him and moved to his desk. He shuffled papers for a moment before bracing his hands on the edges of the desktop.

"We'll need to find a new physical challenge for you in order to ensure that your training is sufficient to allow you to progress."

Okay, maybe he really did want to talk about training. "Okay."

"This is also a good time for us to keep communications open with Gabriel. If the Packs aren't leaving, that means they're here. We should think about rules of engagement in case any more of them aren't happy with that decision."

"That seems appropriate."

He finally looked at me, his eyes clouded. "Enough of the

game, Merit. Enough with 'Yes, Liege' and 'No, Liege.' Quit rubber-stamping everything I say. You were more valuable when you were arguing with me."

For once, I hadn't been playing at acquiescence; I really did think it was appropriate. But his tone begged a response, and I was finally fed up with his back-and-forth.

"I was more 'valuable'? I'm not an antique. Nor am I a toy or a weapon for you to manipulate."

"I'm not playing with you, Sentinel."

I lifted my eyebrows. I was only Sentinel when he was pissed. "And I'm not playing with you, Sullivan."

We glared at each other for a moment, the room thick with unspoken words—the conversations we'd been avoiding.

"Watch it."

"No," I said, and his eyes widened. Ethan Sullivan, I imagined, wasn't used to his employees disobeying him.

"The only thing you ever want from me," I told him, "is for me to be something I'm not. If I argue, you complain I'm not being obedient. If I'm polite, you complain I'm rubber-stamping what you say. I can't keep playing this game with you, this constant back-and-forth."

"You know it's not that simple."

"It is that simple, Ethan. Take me as I am or let me go."

He shook his head. "I can't have you."

"Yes, you could have. You did. And then you changed your mind." I thought of Lacey, of the photograph I'd seen, of his having had a relationship with her despite his strategic considerations. Maybe that was what bothered me the most—what made me different? What did I lack? Why her, but not me?

"Was I not tempting enough?" I asked him. "Not classy enough?"

I didn't expect him to answer, but he did. And that was almost worse. "There's nothing wrong with you."

He'd stood up and slipped his hands into his pockets. I met his gaze and saw the green fire in his eyes. "You're perfect—beautiful, intelligent, intractable in a kind of . . . attractive way. Headstrong, but a good strategist. An amazing fighter."

"But that's not enough?"

"It's too much. You think I haven't thought about what it might be like to return to my rooms at the end of the night and find you there—to find you in my bed, to have your body and your laugh and your mind? To look across a room and know that you were mine—that *I'd* claimed you. *Me*."

He drummed a finger against his chest. "*Me*. Ethan Sullivan. Not the head of Cadogan House, not the four-hundred-year-old vampire, not the child of Balthasar or the Novitiate of Peter Cadogan. *Me*. Just me. Just you and me." He moistened his lips and shook his head. "I don't have that luxury, Merit. I am the Master of this House. The Master of hundreds of vampires I've sworn to protect."

"I'm one of your vampires," I reminded him.

He sighed and rubbed a hand across his forehead. "You are my greatest strength. You are my biggest weakness."

"You called Lacey here. She's not a weakness?"

He seemed startled. "Lacey?"

"You two had—*have*—a relationship, right?"

His expression softened. "Merit, Lacey is here for an evaluation. We've been—in my limited free time—reviewing the financial status of her House. This trip was scheduled six months ago. I didn't invite her here for a relationship."

"Everyone thought—"

He gave me a sardonic look. "You should know better than to regard the rumors that swirl around this House as fact."

I looked down, sufficiently reprimanded and silently thankful. But that didn't change the bigger issue. "I told you that you had one chance, and you decided we were better off as colleagues. I can't play the game of wondering—each and every day— where we stand. I'm your employee, your subordinate, and it's time we acted like it. So I'm asking you not to bring it up again—not to bring us up again. Not to remind me with a word or a glance how conflicted you are."

"I can't help that I'm conflicted."

"And I can't help you with *being* conflicted. You made your choice, Ethan, and we can't keep having this conversation over and over and over again. Do we or don't we? Do we or don't we? How are we supposed to work together like that?"

He asked the better question. "How are we *not* supposed to work together?"

We stood there quietly for a moment. "If that's all you wanted," I said, "I'm going back outside." I walked toward the door, but he finally stopped me in a word.

"Caroline."

I squeezed my eyes shut and clenched my hands into fists. I was eager to resist him, but he was my Master, and he'd called my name, and that alone was enough to halt my march to the door.

"Unfair," I told him. "Unfair and too late."

"Maybe if I had more time."

"Ethan, I don't think there's enough time in the world."

"What did I tell you about the Breckenridges, Merit?"

"Never burn bridges," I recited back to him, and turned around, knowing where he was going. "Before you accuse me of that, Ethan, recall that you're the one who walked away. I'm only complying with your request. We'll forget it happened, we'll work together, and we will do everything in our power to protect the House, and that will be the extent of it."

I stopped before walking into the hallway, unable to take that final step without glancing back at him. When I looked back, there was an ache in his expression. But I'd given him my best shot, and I wasn't up for sympathizing with a man who refused to reach for what he wanted.

"If that's all?" I asked.

He finally dropped his gaze. "Good night, Sentinel."

I nodded and left.

I walked through the first floor of the House, and I didn't stop at the front door. I took the sidewalk to the gate and nodded to the guards, then scanned the street to the left and right, checking the road for paparazzi. They were obediently clustered at their designated cordon at the corner to the right.

An easy call—I headed left.

I crossed my arms over my chest, head down as I walked. I knew Ethan would do this. It was the way he operated—one step forward, two steps back. Rinse and repeat. He'd make a move toward intimacy, then pull back. Then he would regret pulling back, and the cycle would start again. It's not that he didn't want me; he'd made that clear. But each time he let himself be human, the strategy chunk of his brain powered on and he retreated back to coldness. He had his reasons, and I could respect him enough not to imagine they didn't matter. But that didn't mean I agreed with him or that I thought his reasons—his excuses—were good ones.

I frowned at the sidewalk, feet moving beneath me, even

though I'd hardly paid attention to the motion. We were going to have to work together; that much was clear. I had to adapt. I'd adapted to being a vampire, and I was going to have to adapt to Ethan.

I looked up as a limo pulled up to the street.

It was long. Black. Curvy. Sleek. Undoubtedly expensive.

The back passenger side window rolled down. Adam Keene looked back at me from the backseat, boredom in his expression.

"Adam?"

"Gabe wants to meet with you at the bar."

I blinked, confused. "Gabe? He wants to meet with me?"

Adam rolled his eyes sympathetically. "You know how he is. Give me what I want, when I want it. Which usually means immediately. Probably not unlike a Master vampire?"

"Why me? Why not Ethan?"

Adam made a little snort, then looked down at the phone in his hand. "Mine is not to question why . . . ," he muttered, then flipped the phone's screen toward me.

"GET KITTEN," read a text message from Gabriel. Okay, so the request was legit. But that didn't mean getting into a limo with Adam was the right move.

I hesitated, glancing back at the gate, light from the House spilling onto the sidewalk. If I went, I figured I'd get a lecture from Ethan about leaving the House to talk to Gabe without permission . . . and without his oversight.

On the other hand, if I didn't go, I probably had a lecture in store about not being a team player and jumping when an Apex asked me to jump. And then I'd still have to hightail it to the bar, and not in the back of a swank limousine.

Besides, I had my dagger and my beeper. Ethan could find me if he needed to.

"Move over," I growled, then opened the door and climbed inside, pulling the door shut behind me. "Start me off with a Shirley Temple," I told him, nodding toward the bar on one side of the limo, "and we'll see how far we get."

The limo stopped in front of Little Red. The street was empty of bikes, and the plywood was still over the window. The CLOSED sign still hung from the door.

The driver got out and opened the back door, his face flat and emotionless. I threw out a "Thanks," then glanced back when Adam made no move to exit. He stayed in his seat, thumbs clicking at the keys on his phone. When he realized I'd paused, he looked up at me and grinned.

"It's not me he wanted to see," he said, dimples at the corner of his mouth. "I'll have Mr. Brown here circle the block a couple of times and give you two a minute, then join you when I'm done." He held up the phone in explanation. "I need to finish this."

"Your pitch," I said, then maneuvered out the door.

"Hey, Kitten," he said before I closed the door behind me. I glanced back.

"Have fun in there."

The window lifted again and the limousine pulled back onto the street, then took the first right around the block. I walked toward the door.

CHAPTER TWENTY-THREE

PACK OF LIES

I gave the room a three hundred sixty–degree perusal. The bar was empty of patrons, and Berna was nowhere in sight. But people or not, the air was thick with magic. It also smelled of fresh blood and bruises, my palate tingling at the possibility of an early lunch. But this wasn't blood to be sipped; it was blood already spilled.

Hank Williams crooned softly through the jukebox, warbling out a haunting song about whip-poor-wills and loneliness. The jukebox suddenly hiccuped, and the song skipped, stopped, then picked up again.

I walked to the bar, where the scent of blood was stronger, and gingerly touched my fingertips to a spot on the wood. I pulled back fingers, wet with blood.

"Oh, this is not good," I murmured, wiping my hands on my pants and scanning the room for signs of the struggle that put it there.

A low moan suddenly echoed from the back room. It was a sound of pain, maybe with some despair thrown in. The hair on my neck stood on end.

Blood on the bar and moaning in the back room—something was very, very wrong. I glanced back at the door, wishing I'd asked Adam to stay and escort me back into the bar.

What the hell had happened while he'd been on the way to pick me up?

And so much for Gabriel's theory that ConPack put an end to shifter drama.

I let out a curse and thought about my options. Option one: I could wait for Adam to return, but that left me in the bar, with God only knew what on the other side of the door.

Option two: I could make a move of my own. That, of course, risked injury and Ethan's wrath, but someone was injured in there. I couldn't very well just stand by and wait for them to die.

I lifted the hem of my pants, pulled the dagger from my boot, and adjusted it in my palm until the grip was perfect. I stood beside the bar for a few more seconds until I'd gathered up the courage to take a step. When I was ready, I blew out a breath and crept, weapon in hand, toward the door. When I reached the red leather, I put my hand on the door and pushed.

The room was black, light spilling around me as I stood in the doorway, one hand still on the leather. The smell of blood was strongest in here, along with something else . . . a tingle of emotion, of fear. Pack magic.

As my eyes adjusted to the darkness, a shape emerged—a man on the floor, propped against the wall, face bloodied and bruised, one knee up, the other leg extended. His T-shirt was torn, his jeans shredded at the knees.

Even though the tingle had felt familiar, it took my brain a moment to realize what I was seeing.

Whom I was seeing.

It was *Nick*.

"Oh, my God." I ran to him, ignoring the pain as my knees hit the tile floor. I dropped the dagger and began scoping out cuts and bruises. "Are you okay?"

He groaned in response.

"What happened to you?" I asked. And, more important, *how*? Nick was a shifter. He may not have been an Apex, but I'd felt the wake of his magic, knew he had power of his own. Who had the power to hurt Nick?

"Gabriel," Nick muttered, then coughed hoarsely. "It was Gabriel."

I blinked back confusion. "Gabriel?"

"He thinks I—," Nick began, but before he could finish, my dagger skittered to the other end of the room. Shocked, I froze, one hand at Nick's temple, my heart suddenly pounding in my chest, as I watched it spin in the far corner.

"Too late," Nick muttered.

Swallowing down a thick rise of fear, I glanced beside me at the booted foot that had kicked my dagger into the corner, and the shape-shifter it belonged to. Golden eyes glowed.

Gabriel.

My heart began to thud. Improved sparring skills or not, I felt as puny and weak as ever, huddled on the ground before a man who was piqued enough to make the air prickly with his magic.

"It was me," he confirmed.

He'd done this? To Nick? One of his own Pack members? I tried to play catch-up but couldn't make sense of it. What could Nick have done that would prompt Gabriel to this kind of violence?

Without words, Gabriel walked to the door and flipped on

the overhead fixture with a loud *click*, flooding the room with light. I blinked back white spots, then stood up and looked him over. His knuckles were raw, and a bruise bloomed over his right cheekbone. Nick had gotten in a hit, then, but had ultimately been bested by the alpha in the room.

And here I was in a room with him, my colleagues miles away, my dagger on the other side of the room. It was time to use the only weapon I had left—a good, old-fashioned vampire bluff.

I adopted the haughtiest tone I could muster. "What did you do to him?"

Gabriel arched an eyebrow, as if surprised I'd challenge his authority, his right to deal with a member of his Pack as he saw fit. After a moment of staring at me, he turned and slid a chair out from the table, then sat down. His posture was negligent—slouchy, legs sprawled, one elbow propped on the table. I wasn't sure if he was really that unconcerned that a vampire had just walked into . . . well, *something*, or if it was some kind of ploy.

"You lied to me, Merit."

"Excuse me?"

Gabriel crossed his legs at the ankles, then traced a circle on the tabletop with a fingertip. My skin began to itch with the pins-and-needles effect of his magic. I fought to hold back my fangs and the silvering of my eyes even as my genetics screamed out, *Run, or prepare to fight. Now.*

"You told me you learned about the contract on my life because you'd received an anonymous phone call." He looked up at me, the color in his irises swirling with obvious fury. "That was a lie."

I met his penetrating gaze with a neutral expression.

Gabriel bobbed his head toward Nick. "In fact, I've learned Mr. Breckenridge here was your not-so-anonymous source. A man with whom you've had a lengthy personal relationship."

I frowned at Gabriel. Nick had given me the information because he'd gotten an anonymous phone call. And, yes, I'd had a personal relationship with Nick . . . but in *high school.*

Confused, I glanced at Nick, who shook his head. "He thinks I did it. Thinks I planned it—the hits. The attempts on his life."

"You did have the knowledge," Gabriel said dryly.

Nick barked out a strangled laugh. "With all due respect, *Apex,* I'm a goddamned reporter. I get tips. It's my job."

"He was trying to help you," I added. "He told me so I could pass along the warning, so you'd know there was a risk of a hit at the conference. That's why we told you. That's why we were prepared when the chaos started."

"I'm now regretting that I called the convocation, that I didn't just pull the shifters back to Aurora. One shifter—a leader—is dead, and there's now a division between the rest of them. Do you have any idea how frustrated that makes me? When I trusted you?"

Given the angry magic in the air—and the sulfurous smell of it—I had a pretty good sense of it.

"Nick didn't do this. He couldn't have done this. You know he does everything possible to protect you, to protect the Pack. Do you recall a few weeks ago when he tried to bring down our House because he had just a *suspicion* that we might harm shifters? And you have no right to question my or Ethan's motivations after what we've done this week."

"We know what you call us," Gabriel said. "Pretenders."

I lifted my eyebrows. "I don't call you that. Ethan doesn't

call you that. And even if there are vampires who use that term, we certainly don't have a monopoly on prejudice. There are plenty of shifters with some grade-A hatred of vampires." Nick used to be one of those shifters. And here I was protecting him.

"You lied to me. I do not take kindly to treachery, Merit. I do not take kindly to being set up. Why should I let you escape that with impunity?"

Screw this, I thought, and darted for the dagger. Gabe let me get it; he didn't lift toe one from the floor as I came back and stood in front of Nicholas, weapon in hand.

I moved around, keeping my body and blade between Gabriel and Nick. It's not that I had a lot of lost love for Nick, but Gabriel was higher up on my shit list at this point. I was going to have to figure out what was going on, but I was damned sure going to do it with steel in my hand.

"Don't come any closer," I warned him, my dagger tipped out toward his chest. "I don't want to have to hurt you."

He grinned at me, wolfishly. "I'm amused you think you could hurt me, Merit. You've fought some shifters, sure. But they weren't alphas." As if to prove his point, he stood up and threw out a hand. I think he meant to casually disarm me, to push the dagger from my hand, but he underestimated my speed.

I slashed at him and made contact, a crimson line appearing across his forearm. His eyes instantaneously widened, and he looked down, surprised that I'd done it, but still not intimidated.

I, on the other hand, was feeling pretty damned intimidated.

"As you'll no doubt recall, I got shot yesterday. This is only a scratch. I'll just have Berna bring in a Band-Aid. *Berna*," he called out, his head half tilted back toward the door.

There was no answer.

"She's not out there," I told him. "The bar's empty."

"The bar's not empty," he said. "They're still working out there. *Berna*," Gabriel yelled again, but his call was met with silence.

He looked back at me, bewilderment in his expression.

The pieces fell together. "Adam," I whispered.

Gabriel's voice wavered. "What about Adam?"

"He picked me up at the House in a limousine and drove me here. He said you wanted to talk to me. He showed me a text message you sent. He dropped me off and said he was going to circle the block to give us a few minutes to talk."

"I didn't send a text message."

"I get that now. I think he set us up." I looked at Gabriel. "Did he tell you that Nick and I set you up?"

There was a flash of alarm in Gabriel's golden eyes, at least until he closed them again, his expression haggard. "He said you two were working together to create problems for me in Chicago." He glanced at Nick. "He said he had proof you were going to use your family's money to put yourself in charge of the Pack."

Nicholas scoffed and looked away. "I would never. *Never.*"

"He is my *brother*," Gabriel added quietly, frustration in his voice, as if willing Nick to understand why he'd trusted Adam, even if the story was a little too soap-operatic to be entirely believable.

"I assume he was trying to get you pissed at me and Nick," I said. "Maybe so you'd incapacitate us or just take us out altogether. And then what?"

"And then he tries to take me out while you're here—"

"And they'll think I did it," I finished for him. "Adam will take me out and claim he caught me in the act of killing you. And that's the first shot in the war between shifters and vampires." I softened my voice. "Gabriel, if you didn't call me here, why else would he have arranged for me to come?"

While Gabriel considered my question, I considered the fortuity that had put me outside the House. What if I hadn't been there? Would he have come into the House looking for Ethan? Would Ethan have been drawn into the trap?

"Did he tell you Ethan was in on it?" I asked.

Gabriel nodded. And then, as if the weight of his brother's betrayal had suddenly hit him, his eyelids fell shut. "Dear God," he said, shaking his head, as he puzzled it out. "You're right—why else would he have arranged for you to come?"

"Could he have been behind all of it?" I asked. "Tony's death? The attack on the bar? The convocation? The hit? I mean, he's your brother."

"I would assume that's the motivation. He's family. He's in line for the position of alpha—but last in line. He must want the position, and I'm the current obstacle to that plan. Not the only obstacle, since Fallon and the rest of them fall in line before Adam, but a current obstacle." He swore out a string of insults that reddened my ears and made Nick whimper from his spot on the floor.

"He killed an Apex, for Christ's sake." Gabriel crossed himself, two fingertips moving from head to heart, then across his chest, as if protecting himself from the karmic backlash that Adam's mortal wound would have incited . . . or perhaps apologizing to the universe for it.

"He's good," I said quietly. "He never directly implicated

Tony, but he pointed us in the right direction so that we implicated him ourselves."

"Which made the idea that much more believable."

I nodded, then glanced around. If Adam was still circling the block, waiting for Gabriel to take me out, we were going to need a plan, and *fast*. "Is there another way out of here?"

He shook his head. "There's a fire exit, but it's through the door on the other end of the bar."

I blew out a breath, squeezing and resqueezing the dagger's handle. We'd been set up, and some really, really bad shit was about to go down in this bar in Ukrainian Village.

Better yet, no one knew I was here, and I didn't have a phone on me. Adam had a phone, the little shit, but a fat lot of good that was going to do me now.

I tried to slow the hammering of my heart and hold back the silvering of my eyes. I did not want to be stuck in the back of a bar with no exit. I felt like the stupid heroine in a horror movie, willingly walking into the lion's den without phone or sword, now stuck in a family squabble between an Apex and his Cain-like brother.

Backup, I figured, was my only bet. I could call Luc or Ethan—or even Jonah—and report that Adam was trying to take us out. "Do you have a phone?"

"Behind the bar," Gabe said.

As we glanced at the red leather door that led back into the bar, preparing to make our move, the bell over the front door rang.

"He's back," Gabriel said.

My effort to hold them back notwithstanding, my fangs descended and my eyes silvered. The blood began to rush through my veins as my body prepared for the fight.

"Sire?" Nick called out. "Please?"

Gabriel moved to Nick, put a hand behind his head, and pressed his lips to Nick's forehead. He whispered something I couldn't hear, but the words were low and earnestly spoken. Then Gabriel glanced back at me, as if my presence affected whatever answer he was going to give to Nick's plea. "Shift," he said, "and do it quickly. I don't know how much time we'll have."

Nick closed his eyes in relief and began the slow process of standing.

"No vampire sees this and lives," Gabriel said, his voice gravelly. "I allow it now because one of my own put you in this position. But you saw none of it."

I nodded. Even if I hadn't taken his words to heart, the expression in his eyes signaled clearly enough that he was trusting me with something momentous—the right to watch a shape-shifter work his personal magic.

"Sir," I said, recognizing his authority. When Gabriel nodded and turned back for the door, the first line of defense against Adam's coming attack, I risked a glance at Nick. He'd stripped off his T-shirt, revealing a fuzzy—but bruised—chest, and was pulling off his jeans. Not expecting the show—weren't shifters supposed to rip through their clothes?—I turned away again, but not before Nick had caught me inadvertently peeking.

"It's not entirely necessary to strip down," I heard him say as fabric fell to the floor, "but these are my favorite jeans."

I bobbed my head in understanding but kept my eyes averted.

"If you want to see it," Nick quietly offered, "you'd better look now."

The only vampire alive to see a man shift into . . . something? No way was I going to miss that.

I glanced back, catching the Full Monty of a very naked and well-honed journalist. He had athletic feet, long, lean calves, and firm thighs. His shoulders were strong, his arms muscular, but he was also bumped and bruised, cut and bitten. He'd clearly taken a beating at Gabriel's hands.

Nick nodded, and then it began . . . and my mouth gaped open in shock. It wasn't what I'd expected.

I'd seen *Underworld* and the rest of the movies that detailed the transformation from human to wolf. I'd assumed the change was a physical one—a gory shifting of muscle and bone, an exchange of paws and fur for human skin and feet.

But there was nothing anatomical about this. I raised a hand to shield my eyes as light flashed around Nick's body, a cloud of shifting colors as the magic—thick enough to take tangible form—swirled around him.

I'd always thought, as was the common vampire understanding, that shifters were like us—superpredators who'd come into existence as the result of a genetic mutation that altered the form of their bodies. That was not what this was, this gentle light and haze of color.

Shifters were predators only secondarily.

First, and foremost, they were magic—clean, pure, inherent magic.

Not like us.

Gabriel turned to face me, his amber eyes alight with predatory arrogance. But the emotion softened.

I shook my head.

"I've seen that look before, Merit. It's neither as good nor as bad as you think."

I looked back at Nick, who was still wrapped in the fog of it, invisible through the mist that cocooned him. And then the mist changed shape, from the tall, lean form of a man, to something low, something horizontal.

And when he padded toward me through that mist, low and feline, a sleek, black cat—cougar? jaguar? puma?—in the middle of a bar in Chicago, my heart nearly stopped. He was tall—his head high enough to reach my elbow, his coat so sleek and black he gleamed like velvet beneath the overhead light, his paws heavy, big enough to take a chunk out of a vampire, should he feel the urge. There was no mistaking his power. There was also no mistaking his health. Where Nick had been beaten and bruised, the cat was healthy. Maybe that was why he'd asked to shift, so that he could heal himself and lose the bumps and bruises.

And maybe that was why he'd had to ask—because Gabriel had prevented his recuperation.

They might have imagined themselves to be casual, relaxed, less strategic and anxiety-ridden than vampires . . . but there was assuredly a hierarchy in the shifter food chain. And hierarchy mattered.

Nicholas padded toward me and nuzzled his face at my thigh.

"Now who's 'Kitten'?" I murmured, and although the low, grumbly sound he made was decidedly feline, it was still sarcastic.

"All right, children. Let's get ready for showtime. Breckenridge, take care of Merit." He lifted his gaze to me. "You'll be a soldier, a warrior, someday, when you're ready. That's the legacy of you and yours. You nicked me, even without your steel. But he is my brother. This is my fight, my family's fight, so I'm asking you to defer."

"You don't want my help?"

Gabe barked out a laugh. "I'm Apex, and he's kin. This is the natural order of things, the way our world operates. There's nothing you can do but get hurt, and get Sullivan pissed at me. In the event I survive this, I sure would like to avoid that."

My heart stuttered, but I was smart enough to take his advice, at least until honor required me to intervene. I looked around the room and decided on a table that sat in one corner, the stack of cards from the poker game atop it. I crawled beneath it—a vampire hiding from a fight. Sure, it was a little humiliating, but I, too, was hoping to walk out alive.

Nick followed me, then turned and arranged his haunches on the floor, putting himself between me and the door—a few hundred pounds of now-feline shifter between me and whatever hell was about to break loose.

Gabriel began the methodical process of stripping off his own clothes, the muscles of his body taut beneath them. When he was done and stood naked before the door, he crossed his arms, and we waited.

When Adam finally pushed open the door to the back room, there was shock in his expression.

I decided not to take it as a compliment that he was surprised I was still alive.

"What—happened in here?" he asked haltingly. He was scrambling, I imagined, to analyze the situation, to figure out whether there was a way to salvage the script he'd developed or whether he needed to write a new ending.

"I'm still alive," Gabriel pointed out. "Nick is also still alive, as is Merit. Everybody wave."

I skipped the wave, but offered up a lip-curling snarl, which

I directed at the boy who'd led me right into a trap—a trap he'd created.

"So just give me the basic refresher," Gabriel said. "The point was, what, to take out Tony, frame him for the attack on the bar, and have me assassinated? And when that didn't work, you decide to take me out yourself, take out Merit, frame her for my murder, and assume control of the Pack?" He crossed his arms over his chest. "And when that's all said and done, what? You take on the Houses and lead the Packs into genocidal glory?"

Adam's features hardened, his lips pulling into a thin line. And then his eyes darkened, and he stepped onto his soap box. "And what have you done for us? We have *meetings*, while vampires are treated like celebrities. They control the spin. We're part of this world—one with this world, like nothing else in existence—but we act like children running behind their mothers' skirts!"

I had to admit, that speech wasn't exactly hard to come by these days. Although the shifters at the convocation hadn't made it, Celina and her cronies had. It was the same argument made by vampires who wanted power in the human world. I'd heard Celina say it, and two weeks ago I'd heard Peter Spencer make the same argument.

"The Pack acts like the *Pack*," Gabriel countered. "We do not exist to control the fates of humans or vampires. We control our fate, and that's enough."

"Not when we could do more."

Being supernatural was clearly no immunity against the weaknesses of the ego.

"Leading this Pack is not about power," Gabriel earnestly said, as if we'd been thinking the same thing. "It's not about ego or wearing the mantle of leadership."

"I think Dad would have disagreed."

A pulse of chilling magic filled the air; I guessed Gabriel hadn't been thrilled about Adam's bringing their father into it.

"Dad is no longer here. I speak for the Pack now."

Adam rolled his eyes. "You hardly speak at all, and that's exactly my point, *brother*. We both know why I'm here. Let's get it over with. I have things to do."

The pressure in the room suddenly changed, as if the force of the magic they both brought to bear had altered the atmosphere, and that difference was enough to make my ears ache. And then they shifted.

The light was brighter than it had been when Nick transformed, maybe because Gabriel was an Apex, and Adam shared some of those genetics. Nick let out a low growl and bumped back closer to me, until his back haunch hit my knees. I'm not sure if the move was made to protect me, or because he was as nervous as I was. Too curious to resist, I reached out a hand and stroked his flank, which felt like thick velvet stretched over taut muscle. He flinched at the contact, but settled into it soon enough.

The mist rose again, surrounding Adam and Gabe, and then sank as they shifted, Adam's clothing apparently evaporating with the force of the magic.

They were enormous, and our intel had been correct. They were wolves, both of them, and huge. They were easily bigger than Nick, and both had thick, steel gray fur and pale green eyes. Their bodies were almost barrel-like, their muzzles pointy, their ears flat against their heads as they prepared to battle.

Adam was a little smaller than Gabriel, maybe because he was younger. He also had a white mark on his left shoulder, which was otherwise the only way to tell them apart as they moved.

And move they did. They made their first strike simultaneously, both of them standing on back legs to swipe at each other with their front paws. Their jaws were bared, lips pulled back to reveal thick white teeth. They jumped for a moment before hitting all four legs again, Adam in a lower position—maybe a recognition of his submissiveness to Gabriel—before apparently deciding that the time had passed for that submissiveness. With a high, keening cry, he pounced, teeth and claws at Gabriel's shoulders.

Gabriel scrambled to recover, but not before blood was seeping from a wound at his shoulder. He let out a high-pitched cry that made me clamp my hands over my ears, before the whine turned to a canine-bearing growl. He rolled, taking Adam with him, then kicked Adam with enough force to propel him across the room.

And as if the sights and sounds weren't enough, each time they lunged, they sent a pulse of magic into the air that made it hard to suck in oxygen. My senses, already on edge, were nearly overwhelmed. This wasn't just two wolves play-fighting to assert their dominance. This was a battle of magical forces—powerful magical forces—for control over the Pack and its members . . . and the future of shifters. Gabriel represented the status quo; Adam represented a much, much different future.

Adam stood up again, shook off the force of the impact, and, with tail high, hackles raised, and ears flat, attacked. He tried to best Gabriel again, blood-tipped teeth snapping at the larger wolf's muzzle, but Gabriel wouldn't give in. He scrambled to loose Adam from his hold, then made his own move for dominance, pinning Adam to the ground and snapping at Adam's snout. Adam yipped in pain, the sound more like that of a puppy than an oversized wolf, but Gabriel didn't yield.

Adam scrambled beneath him, trying to reverse their positions, but Gabe rotated as Adam moved, canines bared and emitting throaty growls to keep the dominant position. Like grappling cage fighters, they continued that way for a while, chairs sliding as they tousled across the floor of the back room and the linoleum beginning to bear the bloody marks of their fight. Adam wouldn't give up, but neither would Gabriel give ground. I wondered if Gabe had fought this fight before, and how many times he'd had to battle to keep his hold on the Apex position, or to keep order in the Pack.

Adam made one final attempt at the crown, running to the far side of the room as if to regroup, then bounding toward Gabriel with the strength he had left. There couldn't have been much left in him. They'd been grappling for ten or fifteen minutes, and Adam bore the brunt of the fighting. His once-thick, flat gray coat was now matted and bare in places, blood seeping from wounds on his face, neck, and front legs. But he came at Gabriel again, two-inch-long canines nipping at Gabe's snout as Adam tried to push him to the floor. Gabriel yipped at the contact but managed to maneuver his legs enough to get them beneath Adam's torso and push him again. This time, Adam squarely hit the thick wooden leg of a side table on the other side of the room. The vase of plastic flowers above it toppled, and the wood cracked as the table leg splintered with the impact.

Adam, still on his side, tail now tucked submissively between his legs, whimpered. He was alive, but he'd lost his quest for the Pack.

I wondered what fate awaited him.

Nick paced forward a few feet, and with another burst of flashbulb-worthy magic, shifted back into human form. Gabriel did the same, scratches and punctures still evident on his face and arms. I climbed out from under the table, ever the brave vampire, and dusted off my pants.

The room was quiet while they dressed again, slipping into jeans and T-shirts, then socks and shoes. Gabriel's gestures were simple and efficient, and I wondered if the act of redressing was a kind of meditation for him, a process of readjusting to the human world and to his human form, after time spent in the body of the wolf.

When Nick was dressed, he moved back to me. "You all right?" he asked, scanning my face. I nodded, then shifted my gaze to Gabriel.

"The shifting didn't heal him?" I whispered.

"Only wounds taken on as a human can be healed by shifting. Wounds taken on as a shifter are costlier. He'll heal eventually, but there's no quick fix."

Gabriel, now dressed, offered Nick and me nods of acknowledgment, then moved toward his now-prone brother. He crouched down on one knee and stared into Adam's eyes. Adam, still on his side, whimpered again.

"Change," Gabriel commanded.

I had just a moment to raise my hand against the sudden light. When I blinked again, Adam lay on the floor, naked and curled, his body a mess of cuts and bruises.

"You are a disappointment to me, to the family, to the Pack," Gabriel said.

Magic rose again in the room, but not the energetic buzz from before. This magic was old, heavy, and oppressive. Although it had nothing to do with me, my lungs burned with the effort of pushing in and out the air made heavy with the weight, and consequence, of Gabriel's disappointment. There was no missing it.

"You don't choose to be Apex," he told Adam. "The Pack chooses you. Being Apex isn't about power or wealth or status. It's about family and commitment. Lessons that I have, apparently, failed to teach you."

There was melancholy in his voice as he took on part of the burden of Adam's actions.

"Being Apex isn't about taking charge. It's sure as hell not about endangering family. And if you'd taken me out? What then? Fallon is next in line, not you. And I know she has strength and sense enough to hold the Pack. You're at the bottom of the ladder of succession, my boy, and while I might have wondered if you could prove yourself stronger than the rest of them, this proves to me that you will never be fit."

Gabriel rose again, then stared absently across the room, a decision seeming to weigh on his mind. After a minute of silence, he sighed. "You are responsible for the death of a Pack leader. I will not—cannot, given the vows I made to our father—take you out, despite the pain and embarrassment you have caused." Gabriel shook his head, resignation in his eyes. "And maybe you'll be lucky. Maybe the members of the Great Northwestern won't, either. But it will be their decision to make."

"Gabriel—," Adam hoarsely pled, but Gabriel shook him off.

"You will present yourself to the members of the Great Northwestern, and they will decide your fate. And if you're unwilling to go of your own accord, I'll ship you in a crate, if that's what it takes to get you there."

Adam's fate apparently decided, Gabriel blew out a breath that seemed to push the weight of the world off his shoulders, then glanced at me. "It seems I owe you another goddamned apology for bringing you into another Pack dispute. I don't care for owing apologies. I'll have someone call Sullivan so he's briefed when you get back. I'm guessing if he doesn't get that debriefing, you'll be spending the next two hours in his office, replaying events."

I nodded. "That's pretty much how it seems to work."

"And when he does ask you for your version of events, how much are you going to tell him?"

I gave the question some serious consideration. There was no way I was going to lie to Ethan. But omission? Maybe. Especially if I explained to him why I was omitting certain details.

"I'll tell him only the things he needs to know," I answered honestly. Gabriel seemed satisfied by that.

"Good enough. Although he's going to shit about this, about your being involved in something this goddamned stupid and dangerous."

"I'm an asset," I said remorsefully. "If he gets pissed, it's because you've endangered his weapon."

"Merit, if you really believe that, I have been giving you way too much credit."

His expression was serious enough to put surprise in mine. "Then he has an odd way of showing it."

"Babe, he's a vampire."

Why did everyone keep saying that?

I'd been about to ask for a ride home when my beeper sounded. Curious, I unclipped it and glanced down.

It read "CADGN. BREACH. ATTACK. 911."

I stared at the message; it took a moment to wrap my brain around the content. And then what should have been obvious from the first dawned: there'd been a breach, an attack, on Cadogan House.

"Oh, God," I said, my mind suddenly racing. Then I looked at Adam. "What did you do?"

"Merit?" Gabriel asked, but I put up a hand and kept my gaze on his brother.

"Adam, what did you do?"

He looked back over his shoulder, meanness in his eyes. "It's too late. The plan was in place. I already sent them to attack."

My heart nearly stopped. Even Gabriel paled. "You sent who?"

"Shifters. Some humans. Those who wanted to take down the vamps a few notches."

"Oh, God," I said. "There's a party going on. They're outside the House." *Unprotected.* "I've got to get back."

"Okay, okay," Gabriel said. "Nick, keep an eye on Adam. And call the Pack."

"And my grandfather!" I put in.

"Get as many to Hyde Park as you can. I've got my bike. We'll get you back, and we'll stop this."

God willing, we still could.

CHAPTER TWENTY-FOUR

BRINGING DOWN THE HOUSE

It was a good thing it wasn't yet close to dawn, since my way home was open air. I took a moment to use the bar phone and put in a quick phone call of my own while Gabriel prepped his bike. By the time I made my way outside, he sat on an Indian motorcycle, a low and long line of gleaming chrome, black studded leather, and silver enamel.

I pulled the extra helmet from the back of the bike, then swung a leg over.

"You ever ridden before?"

"Not in a while," I said.

Gabriel snorted, then revved up the engine. "Then I suggest you hold on tight."

I pulled on the helmet, climbed on, and wrapped my hands around his waist.

"Not quite that tight, Kitten. We're only going to Hyde Park."

"Sorry. Sorry."

The bike thundered, a hollow, rumbly sound. But even over the din of it, I thought I heard him mutter, "*Vampires.*"

Ten terrifying minutes later—on a trip that should have taken twenty—we made it back to Hyde Park. Gabriel drove as if the fires of hell were on his tail. From the column of smoke we could see rising from the neighborhood even blocks away, I worried they were.

The street was riotous—trucks and bikes were parked in the middle, probably to keep out the cops, who were nowhere to be seen. But the paparazzi were plentiful, snapping pictures of the vehicles and the shifters that emerged from them.

And, more important, from the smoke that billowed from the first floor of the House. My chest felt hollow. I was the Sentinel. This was *my House*. And I had been tricked into leaving it unsecured—leaving the vampires inside unsecured.

God, please let him be safe, I prayed, whipping my dagger from its sheath and jumping off before Gabriel had time to come to a full stop. He called after me, but I was already running, dagger in hand.

I made it only steps before a shifter came at me, bearing a katana that had probably been pilfered from one of our vampires. My vampish ire rising quickly and fiercely, I dropped to one knee, fangs descended, and forced the attacker to vault over me. As he stumbled through the air, I stuck an elbow upward into his chest and yanked the katana from his loosened grip.

I stood up again and rolled the katana in my hand, its weight comforting even if it wasn't my own. I turned on the man, who'd rolled to a stop, but in the most inconvenient location—at the boots of the Apex predator of the North American Central Pack.

"I got this one, Kitten," Gabe said, his narrow-eyed gaze on the shifter before him.

I hoped the man had sense enough to stay down.

With a nod of acknowledgment, I set off at a run, katana before me, sirens finally ringing out behind me. It was the fire department, I hoped, if I was still going to have a place to bed down before sunrise.

As I slashed at two more attacking shifters, I tried to quiet my mind enough to connect to Ethan. But although I called his name twice, then three times, I couldn't find him.

He wouldn't answer me back.

I made my way through marauders to the House's front gate, and found Luc there with two fairies, the three of them battling back the crowd of shifters who were trying to push through. Given the smoke, some must have made it, or else they'd snuck over the wall on other parts of the grounds.

"Luc!" I called out, giving an attacker a foot to the chin and watching him crumple.

Luc glanced around. "Sentinel, thank God. Some of them are humans, but I think the rest are shifters. They attacked the House!"

I had to yell out over the din of sirens and clanging steel. "It was Adam! He had a plan—we'll talk about it later. Is everyone okay?"

"I don't know. We left Lacey at the back of the House with Lindsey. Ethan, Juliet, Kelley, and Malik are inside."

"Merit!" I glanced behind me. Catcher, Jeff, and my grand-father, his gait a little slower, moved toward us amongst the dark-clad cops who were finally beginning to emerge from cars and wrangle the perpetrators together.

That raised a good question: how in God's name were we going to explain this to the cops? I guessed that was my grandfather's department.

"Just worry about your duties," my grandfather said, as if anticipating the question. "Nick called and explained. We'll get this calmed down out here. You do what you need to do to keep your people safe."

I nodded, then pointed a finger at Jeff. "You ready to fight?"

He grinned wildly. "Damned skippy."

"Then let's do this."

We moved inside the gate, my borrowed katana in hand and a shifter at my side. They swarmed us as we entered—half of them bearing the electric sizzle of agitated shifters, but none of them in animal form.

"Why haven't they shifted?" I asked him, raising the katana and preparing to strike.

"Paparazzi," he said, which made sense. Jeff bounced on his heels, fists curled. It was an odd-looking position for the lanky computer programmer, but I knew Jeff could take care of himself.

And unlike the convocation, where we fought on different sides of the room, this time I got to watch. While I fought off the perps on the right, Jeff took the left.

And he *brought it*.

It was like watching a monk do battle—complete calm in his expression and his eyes, but every move perfect, every move precise. He was a fantastic fighter, his strikes and kicks on target and his blocks perfectly timed to defend against the blows of his attackers. At one point, he caught my stunned gaze and offered back a cheeky grin.

"Sorry, babe. I'm taken."

I rolled my eyes and swung my katana, and together we fought back the army of people and shifters hell-bent on destroying our House.

I'd taken down four attackers when I finally heard his answering call in my head.

Merit?

I said a silent thank-you to the universe. *Ethan, where are you?*

First floor. My office. Get here if you can. If not, find Malik and keep him safe.

My stomach sank. Malik was basically Ethan's vice president, the vampire charged with taking over the House if anything happened to Ethan. Had Ethan given up? Was he already trying to establish a line of succession?

I let out a curse that should have blistered Jeff's ears.

Stay where you are, I told him. *I'm on my way.*

Merit—

I am the Sentinel of this House, Ethan. It's my call.

That was met with silence.

"Jeff, Ethan's in trouble. I need to get inside. Can you find Malik and make sure he's okay?"

"Hands are full, Merit," he said, using a strike to the chest to push someone back. "Can you wait until we've secured the front yard?"

I glanced around, wondering how much longer that would take—and smiled.

I'd made the call, and the cavalry had arrived.

Six of them strode into the gate in black and red leather jackets, Noah at the front, five other vampires behind. Together, they looked like avenging angels, katanas bared, expressions fierce, ready to fight for vampirekind. Jonah wasn't among them, and I assumed he'd skipped the fight so he could maintain his anonymity as a member of the Red Guard.

Some of the tension left my shoulders at the sight of them. Noah signaled that they'd take the outside perimeter. When I nodded my agreement, he began to bark orders to the rest of his crew. They broke formation and dispersed into the crowd.

"Merit—to your left!"

At Jeff's warning, I immediately threw up my katana to block the attack. The perp's blow was deflected, and Jeff's punch to the guy's kidneys brought him down.

"Fun, fun," he said, smiling down at his fallen prey.

"Yep," I said, leaning forward to kiss him on the cheek. "You and Fallon are gonna get along just fine."

With that, I mounted the stairs and headed into the House.

Gray smoke was now spilling down from the second floor, vampires evacuating as firemen ran down the hallway, hoses in hand.

One of them paused on his way up the stairs and lifted his hood. "Ma'am, you need to evacuate!"

"Vampire!" I yelled out. "I'm immortal."

He winked at me. "Grey House," he said, then flipped down his hood and proceeded up the stairs with his comrades.

"Carry on, my friend," I said, then hustled down the hallway to Ethan's office.

His suit coat was discarded, spots of blood and smears of

smoke a sharp contrast against the white of his shirt. He stood at the back of the room, the office's velvet curtains now shredded and smoking behind him, a fan of four shifters in front of him.

But even the direness of the situation couldn't trump my relief at seeing him hearty and hale.

Need some help, Sullivan?

He scanned my body, looking for injuries. A look of relief crossed his face. *Thank God*, he said.

I offered him a smile before turning my attention to the shifters. "Aren't you kids a little outnumbered?" I asked. When they turned to look at me, Ethan took advantage of their distraction, sending two of them to the ground with lethal slashes. I edged around the other two, putting myself between them and Ethan.

Unfortunately, the perpetrators picked that moment to call out to four or five of their friends, who appeared at the door with weapons—guns and what looked like pieces of Cadogan House furniture—in hand.

They realized they had us cornered, and began to work their flanks, encircling us so that we stood in of the middle of them.

Back to back, I told him, and he nodded, then turned so we stood with our backs together, our swords horizontal in front of us, surrounded by foes.

And then we fought.

Whatever miracle of vampire genetics I might have been was nothing compared to the miracle of our fighting . . . *together*. We both swung out, the magic and power surrounding us seeming to actually increase as we fought, bullets flying as we battled back the interlopers who'd threatened our home.

The Master of Cadogan House and its Sentinel, their steel honed, tempered, and raised against a common foe.

We made quick work of the first couple of attackers, but then they started getting creative, moving around to make it more difficult for Ethan and me to coordinate our movements, even when we could give each other silent directions.

On the other hand, that also forced us to get a little more creative. Eventually, we were fighting side by side, Ethan slicing out with his katana to keep an attacker off balance, and me kicking him into submission. Ethan would spin into a high kick, and I'd use a low throw to force him to the ground when he tried to dodge Ethan's attack.

Eventually, the room was cleared, and we stood there together, chests heaving, a spray of shifters and humans on the floor in front of us. We weren't entirely undamaged—I'd taken a bruising shot to my right thigh, and Ethan had slices across his belly where he'd been caught with the edge of a bar of steel broken from someone's office chair.

But we were alive.

We glanced over at each other. I was just about to speak, but before I could get out words, his hand was at the back of my head, his mouth pressing against mine. The intensely possessive kiss left me gasping for breath, but even as he pulled back, his fingers stayed knotted in the back of my hair.

"Christ, Merit, I thought you were dead. You left after we talked, and no one could find you. And when they attacked and you didn't show—where the hell were you?"

"I was at the bar," I said. "I'll give you the details later. Long story short, this is all Adam's doing. He set it all up, had a plan to kill Gabriel and frame the House."

Ethan smiled wickedly. "And you figured it out before Adam could take you both out, but he'd already started the attack."

"Well, I *am* the Cadogan Sentinel."

"Indeed you are," he said, then kissed me with brutal force again. "This isn't over," he growled, and then he was gone, ready for battle again.

I wasn't going to waste the time arguing with him, but as soon as his back was turned, I raised my fingertips to my mouth, the feel of his lips still there.

I could feel it coming. The sun wasn't far from making its way above the horizon, and it had begun to pull at my shoulders. Fortunately, the combined strength of the Chicago Police Department, the Chicago Fire Department, the Ombud's office, half the North American Central Pack, the vampires of Cadogan House, and the Red Guard had finally managed to stop the attack.

Ethan seemed to take the Red Guard's participation in stride. He didn't bat an eyelash when he saw them, but he also didn't have any reason to tie their presence to me.

That meant if I decided to join them, I could still keep my secret under wraps.

But positives aside, the House wasn't without its casualties. Seven shifters and humans had been killed in the attack. We lost three vampires. I didn't know any of them to speak of, although two lived on the second floor not far from my room. Two were lost to wooden stakes; their ashen remains now mingled with the destruction in the House.

The third, however, had met a more gruesome end. She'd

been the victim of an old-fashioned torture. A crazed human attacker—one of the deceased—weakened her with an ill-placed stake and removed her heart.

In honor of her sacrifice, her body had been placed in the garden behind the House, to be given to the sun when it finally breached the sky.

As for Cadogan itself, the marauders had worked to bring down the House around us. While the sturdy stone construction had thwarted the worst of the damage, the furnishings and woodwork on the first and second floors had been damaged, some of the rooms rendered uninhabitable. Helen and Malik had been working the phones, making arrangements with Grey, Navarre, and the other Cadogan vamps in Chicago to find temporary homes for vamps whose rooms had been torched or were too wet and smoky to stay in. My room, in a back corridor of the second floor, had fortunately been spared.

As Ombudsman, my grandfather had jurisdiction over the city's response to the chaos. He helped sort out the good shifters from the bad, explaining the politics to any CPD cop he could corral long enough. He managed to keep them from arresting every shifter and vampire in sight; given the destruction and chaos, I called that a victory.

Unfortunately, he hadn't been able to keep the paparazzi from snapping pictures. They didn't venture into Cadogan House, but they hadn't needed to—one of Adam's shifters had been so grievously wounded in human form that he'd shifted in the middle of the front lawn to heal himself.

I might have been the first vampire to witness the shifting of a Pack member, but I hadn't been the last . . . and the paparazzi wouldn't be the last, either. They'd reportedly snapped pictures of the biker turned coyote—and the biker turning into a coyote. Having seen the transformation myself, I doubted the final photographs would show much more than lights and colors.

Regardless, it was obvious to the reporters that *something* supernatural had happened, something they hadn't seen before, and that set off a journalistic feeding frenzy. That's why my grandfather, at Gabriel's request, had cordoned the reporters into an area in front of the House. He stood behind a makeshift podium, Gabriel at his side, a bevy of uniformed cops surrounding them.

Waiting.

Gabriel raised his hands, and the crowd of reporters quieted just as the shifters had the night before.

"I have something to say," he announced, then used the back of his hand to push a trail of blood from his eyes.

He paused, the weight of the looming confession in his eyes. I knew what he was going to say, but I also knew what it would cost him—emotionally and politically.

"You'll soon see pictures that tell quite a tale. That prove that vampires are not the only supernatural beings in the world. We are shape-shifters," he said, "beings who can take animal or human form."

Ethan stood beside me, and at the mention of the magic word, slid his fingers into mine. I squeezed back.

The area erupted into a cacophony of camera flashes and questions. Gabriel ignored them, holding up a hand again so that he could continue speaking.

"We are shifters, and some of my number are responsible for this attack on Cadogan House—an attack on a band of citizens who have done nothing but assist and protect us. This attack was unjustified. We have already submitted the organizer of this attack into the custody of the Chicago Police Department. As he has violated the trust between our peoples, you may deal with him as you deem fit."

He paused, letting the weight of that statement sink in.

And when he was ready, he looked into the crowd and found Ethan and me. "And may God have mercy on us all."

A few minutes before dawn, I found Ethan in his office, poking through rubble. The ruined curtains had already been replaced by shabbier models, the switch necessary to block the coming sunlight.

He glanced up when I walked in, then scanned my face and body. "You're all right?"

I nodded. "As much as anyone can be. I'm sorry about the Novitiates you lost today."

Ethan nodded, then righted a chair that had been flipped onto its side. "It's not unforeseen that we would face violence. But that doesn't make the violent act any less shocking." He put one hand on his hip, then rubbed his temple with the fingers of his free hand. "I spoke with your grandfather about the events at the bar. Nick filled him in."

I waited for the inevitable lecture about leaving campus, or engaging in shifter-vampire dialogue without permission, or putting the House at risk.

"Well," he philosophically said, "Adam isn't the first narcissist to have put us in a bind. Has everyone been resettled?"

It took me a moment to realize I hadn't been chastised. "Scott and Morgan sent buses to pick up everyone. There's about a dozen vampires at each House. The rest of them are tucked in and accounted for. The front wing of the second floor needs airing out, but the fairies have agreed to keep guard so workmen can get started at dawn."

He nodded officially, but didn't meet my eyes. It was clear he had more to say, but he hadn't quite gotten around to it.

"Is there anything else?" I asked, giving him the chance to voice his thoughts.

Ethan opened his mouth, but then snapped it shut again. "We can talk tomorrow. Find a spot to rest. Get some sleep."

I nodded. "Good night, Sullivan."

"Good night, Sentinel."

My evenings were beginning to have the same endings, it seemed.

THE BEST OFFENSE ISN'T A GOOD DEFENSE— IT'S A GOOD OFFENSE

When I woke the next evening, my assorted cuts and scrapes were gone.

But the House, I knew, would still wear scars.

I got up and showered, scrubbing off soot and dried blood I'd been too exhausted to clean at dawn. Expecting to help rehab and reorganize the House, I dressed down—jeans, T-shirt, and Pumas; my hair in a ponytail; the ever-present Cadogan medal around my neck.

In case I suddenly forgot whom my allegiances were to.

But there was no chance of that. Whatever our personal issues, Ethan and I had proven we worked well together. We even *fought* well together. I'd had enough jobs—and glimpses of my father butting heads with his staff—that I knew what a rarity that was. Our personal issues notwithstanding, we were good colleagues. And just as he had chosen not to risk the professional by dabbling in the personal, I had my own sacrifice to make.

I couldn't leave my House without a Sentinel in the middle of a war.

So I found Noah's phone number and dialed. He answered after two rings.

"Beck."

"It's Merit."

"Sentinel," he said, his voice gravelly, "how are things at the House?"

"We're pulling things back together."

"I'm glad to hear it. It's going to take time, but I'm glad to hear it."

"I can't thank you enough for what you did last night. For showing up, for sacrificing your anonymity. For helping us fight."

"The time comes when we all have to sacrifice."

He was almost too right. "About your offer—I'm declining."

There was silence for a moment. "I'll be honest—I'm surprised to hear that."

"My loyalty is to the House," I explained. I'd chosen, as my grandmother once taught me, to dance with the one who brought me.

"Things can always change," Noah said. "But we may not have a slot if you wait."

"I understand the risk," I assured him. "And thank you for making the offer, even if I have to say no."

"Well, it would have been interesting. Good luck with the renovations."

"Good evening, Noah." I hung up the phone, then squeezed it in my hand. "Well," I murmured, "I suppose that's that."

There was a knock at the door. I assumed it was Lindsey, coming to gather me up for breakfast and rehab work, so I opened it without hesitation.

It was Ethan. He was back in jeans, paired again with a

T-shirt and dark boots. I guessed our Master was ready for work, as well. "How are you feeling?"

"Well healed," I told him. "You?"

"So far so good."

"Excellent."

"Mmm-hmm."

We stood there for a moment, the pink elephant dancing around us as we studiously worked to avoid her.

Ethan held out his hand. In his palm was a glossy blue box with a silver "C" engraved in the top. Brow furrowed, I took it from him.

"What's this?"

"An apology, of sorts."

I made a moue, but slipped the lid from the top . . . and then my breath left me.

Inside the box sat a baseball, its well-worn white leather marked by the signatures of every Cubs player from the team. It was just like the one I'd had—just like the one I'd told him about the night we made love.

I blinked down at the box, trying to take in the gravity of the gift. "What—where did you get this?"

Ethan slid his hands into his pockets. "I have my sources."

"You shouldn't have—"

He stopped me with his hand at my jaw, thumb against my chin. "Sometimes, people must adapt. Immortality doesn't make the things we love less important; it means we must learn to treasure them. Protect them."

I swallowed hard and made myself lift my gaze to him, fear and joy and more fear bursting in my chest.

"It is an apology," he said, "for not believing in you . . . or in us. Yesterday, I thought I'd lost you, and then we *fought* together," he said. "I pushed you away for fear of what our relationship would do, could do, to this House. And then we protected this House together. That is the true measure of what we could do."

He paused, then tapped a finger against the box. "This is a wish," he said quietly, "that even after four hundred years of existence, a man can be strong enough to accept the gifts he's given."

"Ethan—," I began, but he shook his head.

"I'm prepared to wait for a positive response."

"That's going to take a while."

Ethan lifted a single eyebrow, a grin lifting one corner of his mouth. "Sentinel, I am immortal."

He turned on his heel and began down the hall, then called back, "And we'll need to chat about your running off campus and into the arms of shifters without so much as a telephone call."

Sometimes, he was so predictable.

ACKNOWLEDGMENTS

Thanks, as always, to my family and friends. Special thanks to Jessica, my diligent editor; Lucienne, my fabulous agent; and the various folks who take time to read and comment, including Sandi, Heather, and Sara (the new queen of continuity!).

This one is dedicated to my fabulous readers—Go Team Eel!

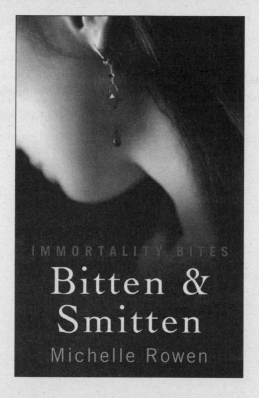

I was born and raised in the South, but now make my home in the Midwest, just close enough to Cadogan House to keep an eye on the vampires. When not transcribing Merit's adventures, I bake, watch entirely too much television, root for my favourite college football team (Go Big Red!), play with my dog, Baxter, and spend time with a pretty great – and very handsome – guy (who I'm pretty sure isn't a vampire).

Learn more about Chloe Neill and her novels at: www.chloeneill.com